D0500145

GARDEN
OF
SINS

ALSO AVAILABLE BY LAURA JOH ROWLAND

Victorian Mysteries

Portrait of Peril
The Woman in the Veil
The Hangman's Secret
A Mortal Likeness
The Ripper's Shadow

Sano Ichiro series
The Iris Fan
The Shogun's Daughter
The Incense Game
The Ronin's Mistress
The Cloud Pavillion
The Fire Kimono
The Snow Empress
Red Chrysanthemum
The Assassin's Touch
The Perfumed Sleeve
The Dragon Kong's Palace
The Pillow Book of Lady Wisteria
Black Lotus
The Samurai's Wife
The Concubine's Tattoo
The Way of the Traitor
Bundori
Shinju

Charlotte Brontë novels
Bedlam
The Secret Adventures of Charlotte Brontë

GARDEN OF SINS

A VICTORIAN MYSTERY

Laura Joh Rowland

CROOKED
LANE

NEW YORK

This is a work of fiction. All of the names, characters, organizations, places and events portrayed in this novel are either products of the author's imagination or are used fictitiously. Any resemblance to real or actual events, locales, or persons, living or dead, is entirely coincidental.

Copyright © 2022 by Laura Joh Rowland

All rights reserved.

Published in the United States by Crooked Lane Books, an imprint of The Quick Brown Fox & Company LLC.

Crooked Lane Books and its logo are trademarks of The Quick Brown Fox & Company LLC.

Library of Congress Catalog-in-Publication data available upon request.

ISBN (hardcover): 978-1-64385-794-7
ISBN (ebook): 978-1-64385-795-4

Cover design by Melanie Sun

Printed in the United States.

www.crookedlanebooks.com

Crooked Lane Books
34 West 27th St., 10th Floor
New York, NY 10001

First Edition: January 2022

10 9 8 7 6 5 4 3 2 1

GARDEN
OF
SINS

London, November 1890

CHAPTER 1

"Benjamin Bain Murder Trial Begins Tomorrow"

The headline blares at me from the newspaper on my lap as I ride in the underground train that speeds through the tunnels beneath London. I hold the paper up to the light and brush soot off the printed words and pictures.

My husband, Thomas Barrett, seated beside me, says, "You shouldn't read that, Sarah." He raises his voice over the racket of the train's iron wheels. "It'll only make you feel worse."

"I know." But I can't resist. The largest picture is an illustration of a girl lying on a kitchen floor, arms flung wide, her skirts hiked up to her knees, her face swollen, and an expression of terror in her protuberant eyes. She's the artist's rendition of fourteen-year-old Ellen Casey, raped and strangled to death in 1866. In the doorway stands the shadowy figure of her killer. His back turned toward his victim, his face invisible, he's intended to portray Benjamin Bain.

My father.

My father, the person I loved most in the world for the first decade of my life, until he disappeared; whom I believed was dead for the next twenty-two years, until I discovered that he was alive and wanted for Ellen Casey's murder. I found him after a harrowing search, and now, only four months after our joyous reunion, the law threatens to tear us apart.

"The jury will read articles like this and believe he's guilty," I say, angry at the press for sensationalizing the story every day since my father was arrested three weeks ago. The paper I'm reading is the *Daily World*, at which I'm employed as a crime scene photographer and reporter, though I'm currently on a leave of absence. I'd hoped the fact that I work there and that I've risked my life in the line of duty numerous times would gain me the favor of no coverage of the trial in its pages. But the *Daily World* is a commercial enterprise that can't ignore the biggest crime story of the season.

The article summarizes the basic elements of the story. In 1866, my father was a professional photographer who operated a studio out of his home. He took pictures of Ellen Casey the day she went missing, and he was the last person known to see her alive. The next day her dead body was found at a road construction site. Soon after being questioned by the police, my father disappeared—a fact constantly trumpeted as proof of his guilt. No other suspects were ever identified, but there's far more to the story than the press and the public know.

"How is he supposed to get a fair trial?" I ask.

"Not everyone believes everything that's in the newspapers," Barrett assures me. "And the jury will be instructed to disregard what they've read or heard, and to make up their own minds based on the evidence presented in court."

He's a detective sergeant with the Metropolitan Police, and he's testified in court many times. I've never attended a trial, but I know my father is at a huge disadvantage.

"So many trials end up with guilty verdicts, and there's no evidence that he's innocent." Furthermore, I know there are other damning circumstances aplenty.

"The defense doesn't need to prove he's innocent. The prosecution needs to prove he's guilty. That's how the legal system works."

"I wish that when I see him today, I could bring him the news that I found a witness who'll testify that he's not the sort of man who would violate and kill a young girl."

My father, in prison awaiting his trial, gave me a list of twenty people he remembered from the old days, to ask if they would serve as his character witnesses. Half of them are dead. This morning Barrett and I looked up a man named Theodore Aldrich, an old friend from Clerkenwell, where my family had lived. We'd located Mr. Aldrich, a retired mechanic, at his daughter's home in Hammersmith, but he'd said he was sorry; he couldn't vouch for

Benjamin Bain's good character. Other former friends, neighbors, and acquaintances also don't want to get involved. One man said, "I hope the bastard hangs." Another had physically threatened me; hence, Barrett's insistence on accompanying me this time.

Barrett clasps my hand. "Don't give up hope. I bet your father will be acquitted, and you'll be sorry you wasted time worrying."

I'm thankful for his moral support and his loyalty. Not all policemen would stand by wives whose kin are charged with heinous crimes. I smile at him. He's darkly handsome in a tough fashion, his keen gray eyes crystal clear. My heartbeat quickens, my usual response to him. Even though we've been lovers for more than a year, and married a month, I still can't believe that he's my husband. The circumstances under which we met were so inauspicious, and I daresay we've faced more serious troubles than most couples. Every day I thank heaven for my good luck; every day I fear it won't last.

"Besides, you've solved lots of problems that seemed impossible," Barrett says.

As a crime investigator for the *Daily World*, a private detective on my own, and an ordinary citizen, I've solved five major cases. One was Jack the Ripper. Barrett and I are among the few people who know his identity. It's a secret that I hold close, that haunts my life.

I unfold the newspaper. Below the article about the upcoming trial are two photographs. One shows police constables surrounding my father. The caption reads *Benjamin Bain taken to Newgate Prison after his arrest*. My father is in handcuffs, his heavy figure slumped, his head ducked so that only his disheveled white hair is visible. The caption below the other reads *Daughters believe him innocent*. The photo shows myself and my half-sister, Sally Albert, waiting in line to visit our father in jail. With our ash-blonde hair, angular features, and deep-set eyes, we look alike even though I'm thirty-three, she's ten years younger, and we were born to different mothers. But her face is softer and prettier, her hair pinned in a loose knot and adorned with a flower-trimmed hat. My expression is angry under my coronet of braids. While Sally cringes from the camera, I'm raising my hand to strike the photographer.

I glance around the train and see people reading the *Daily World*. One is a gentleman seated across the aisle between his two sons, who are perhaps nine and ten years old. They exchange punches across him. He ignores them and his wife, who holds a wailing baby. He glances up and meets my gaze, and I quickly look away, glad that I've taken to wearing a hat with a veil that partially conceals my face. Because of my exploits, I was notorious even before the publicity about my father's arrest and trial started, and unwanted attention has grown to a distressing degree.

"Look on the bright side," Barrett says. "Juries don't like sending a man to the gallows unless the evidence against him is solid— which it isn't in your father's case."

I'm sitting on evidence that I hope will never come to light. Barrett doesn't know about it, and the jury may never hear it, but it's festering in my mind, corroding my own belief that my father isn't a rapist and murderer.

The train slows as it approaches St. Paul's station, which is near Newgate Prison. I gather up my pocketbook and satchel, as I'll be departing alone while Barrett continues on to Whitechapel. Our home is there, as is his station of the Metropolitan Police. This will be my last time with my father before the trial starts at ten AM tomorrow, our last chance to prepare for the ordeal.

A sudden loud, squealing, grinding noise startles me. Outside the windows, sparks fly up, as if from fireworks ignited under the wheels. The train swerves, and amid violent jolting, veers sideways. It screeches to a halt in a series of loud crashes. Our carriage tips, and I feel collisions in front and in back of us. Barrett and I cry out as we hurtle forward into the empty seat opposite ours. Other passengers land in the aisles. The sound of glass shattering accompanies screams of terror.

The lights go out. Darkness engulfs us.

"Sarah!" Barrett cries. "Are you all right?"

My knees and elbows hurt where they struck the seat, but my hat cushioned my head. I'm shaken up but uninjured. "Yes. Are you?"

"Yes. What just happened?"

"I don't know—maybe the train hit something on the track."

Other passengers groan and exclaim, "Help!" and "Oh God." They call one another's names. Children cry. Flames leap outside the broken windows. Smoke billows up and invades the carriage, which is tilted at a precarious angle, as if the crash threw the whole world out of kilter.

"Fire!" a woman screams. "We're going to burn alive!"

"We have to get out of here." Barrett clambers to the door, on the upward-tilted side. He pounds and yanks at it until it opens, then helps the other passengers exit. I hold the baby while the father boosts his wife and other children out. After I hand the baby up to him, Barrett and I climb out of the carriage. The train is derailed, off the track; our carriage is smashed between the ones in front and those behind. Now that my initial fright has passed, I wish I had my camera; the *Daily World* will need pictures. My heart beats fast with exhilaration. Past experience has taught me that there's no thrill like surviving a brush with death, and although I fear danger, I'm also attracted to it, a quirk of my personality. Crawling from the wrecked train as though from a premature grave, I feel keenly, vibrantly alive.

In the cavernous tunnel, the high, arched ceiling is barely visible in the steam from the engine's boiler and the smoke from flames under the train. Sparks from the wheels must have set fire to the debris on the tracks. I breath hot, acrid air. Screams echo. The train resembles a gigantic, twisted, dead serpent. Carriages tangle around pillars and lie toppled on their sides. Passengers crawling out windows and doors sob and moan. Barrett hurries me toward the front of the train, where faint light emanates from the station.

"No, we have to rescue people," I say.

Whistles shrill and bright beams of lanterns in the distance cut through the smoke. Barrett says, "The police are here. You don't need to stay. I'll come back to help after I take you home."

His main concern is my safety, just one reason why I love him. But I survived while other passengers are injured and helpless; I can't abandon them. Coughing, eyes stinging and watering from the smoke, I hurry back to the adjacent carriage. Barrett follows me. The front is smashed, jammed against a barrier that separates the tracks. It's empty. The next cars are broken apart from the rest of the train. Some twenty feet down the tunnel, they stand upright, skewed across the tracks. People run and stagger away from them. Barrett and I enter the first carriage. Blood spatters broken glass on the floor. In the aisle, a woman dressed in dark clothes lies on her back. Her lace-up boots show under her disarranged skirts. My heart lurches.

"Ma'am?" I receive no answer. Barrett and I crouch near her. "Can you hear me?" I touch her cheek. Her soft skin is warm, but she doesn't respond.

Barrett lifts her gloved hand and clasps her wrist, seeking a pulse. His shoulders sag, and he bows his head. We're silent for a moment, distressed because we couldn't save her, grieved by what must be only one of many lives lost to the crash.

A lantern beam shines through the door. Squinting in the bright glare, I see the dark silhouette of the police constable who holds the lantern, his tall helmet atop his head. He says, "Hey, are you all right?"

"My wife and I are fine," Barrett says, "but this poor woman was killed."

The constable crosses himself. "That's a pity. Now come out of there before you suffocate."

Barrett and I don't move. We're staring at the woman, illuminated in the smoky lantern light. Above the collar of her brown wool coat, a thin, dark red line circles her throat.

"That's a ligature mark." Barrett touches her chin, turns her face upright. Framed by a brown felt hat and curls of rust-colored hair, her face is bloated, her wide brown eyes bulging, the whites laced with red veins. Her pink tongue protrudes between her teeth.

We look at each other, aghast. "The crash didn't kill her," I say. "She was strangled."

"Aww, Jesus," the constable says. "As if there wasn't enough trouble already."

I experience a familiar sensation of pity, horror, and nausea. Viewing dead bodies is a hazard of my profession; I've lost count of how many I've seen. The smoke is filling my lungs, making me wheeze, addling my thoughts.

"The murderer took advantage of the wreck and the confusion," Barrett says.

"There's no time to jabber about it. Nothing we can do for the poor lady," the constable says. "Come on—let's go."

"Officer, this is a crime scene," Barrett says. "We need to examine it."

"Yeah? Who says?"

Barrett is wearing ordinary clothes instead of his police uniform; it's his day off. He removes his badge from his pocket and shows it to the constable. "Detective Sergeant Barrett, Metropolitan Police, Whitechapel Division."

"You're out of your jurisdiction."

"Go rescue other people," Barrett says. "Leave your lantern."

His authoritative manner brooks no refusal. The constable reluctantly sets his lantern on the floor. Departing, he calls over his shoulder, "Make it quick, or you'll be two more casualties."

I miss my friends Mick O'Reilly and Lord Hugh Staunton, who work for the *Daily World* with me. We usually investigate crimes together, but Hugh is on leave because of an injury, and Mick is covering other crimes for the paper. Barrett and I cough and blink our streaming eyes as we study the scene. The carriage is littered with newspapers, umbrellas, and a tin of biscuits abandoned by fleeing passengers.

"I don't see a string or cord or anything that could have been used as the murder weapon," Barrett says.

I notice a brown leather handbag lying open under the seat near the woman. "This must be hers." Inside, I find only a crumpled handkerchief and a white business card. My eyes are so bleary, I can't read the print. I tuck the card in my own handbag. "Maybe the killer was a thief who stole her valuables."

"He's probably long gone by now." Barrett glances under the seat where I found the handbag. "What's this?" He pulls out a leather case with a strap, opens the clasps, and removes a box made of dark, polished wood, about four by five by eight inches. A metal key juts from the top. Barrett twists the key, and when nothing seems to happen, he pries at the edges of the box.

My breath catches, and as I cough, I exclaim, "No, don't!"

"Why not?"

"It's a camera." I point at the lens set in a circular hole on one end. "Opening it will ruin the photographs, if there are any inside."

"It's different from yours. I've never seen any like it."

"It's a new type, manufactured by the Kodak company in America. It uses a roll of film instead of a glass negative plate. The key is for winding the film. They don't sell Kodaks in England yet."

"It must be hers." Barrett glances at the woman, then around the carriage. "Nothing else of any value was left behind."

I shake my head to clear my smoke-dazed mind. "I wish I had my camera, so I could photograph the crime scene."

"Maybe the photographs in hers will give us some clues."

Through the windows, we see constables herding passengers down the tunnel. The smoke is thicker, noxious with the smell of hot metal and burnt grease. A male voice shouts through a megaphone, "Everyone, please proceed to the station at once!"

Barrett takes the camera and case as we reluctantly abandon the dead woman. I silently promise her that I will find her killer. Barrett reads the number on the carriage: "Three-oh-nine." Heading down the tunnel, he assists a man limping with an injured leg. I lend my arm to a woman whose face is a mess of cuts and blood. Other able-bodied people help scores of the crippled and maimed while conductors carry the bodies of the unconscious or dead. Firemen pump water from tanks onto the flames under the train. Vapor sizzles. The engine is crushed against a pillar, the tilted boiler still belching smoke and steam. The scene when we reach St. Paul's station resembles the carnage after a battle. Dozens of the injured lie on benches or on the floor, smeared with soot and blood, their groans piteous. Unscathed passengers stumble up the stairs to the street while ambulance crews and more police rush down to supply first aid and rescue those still trapped in the wreckage.

I halt amid the chaos, suddenly overwhelmed by our close call, by the knowledge that Barrett and I would have died but for the grace of God. The exhilaration of surviving the crash drains away, and I shiver violently, as though plunged into ice water.

"Sarah?" Barrett grasps my shoulders, peering into my face. His face is blackened with soot, somber with concern. "Are you all right?"

I nod. My mind scrambles to restore some semblance of my normal life. I take the dead woman's camera case from Barrett and say, "I don't know how to develop Kodak film, but I think I know someone who does."

"Forget about that for now. I'm taking you home."

I want nothing more than to crawl into bed with him and let sleep banish the horror of the disaster. Then I remember my appointment. "I have to go to Newgate Prison and see my father."

"I'll go with you." Barrett leads me around people lying on the floor, toward the stairs.

"No." I've kept my husband and my father apart, never introduced them to each other. I've told them I want to wait until the trial is over and my father is a free man. It's true, but I've another reason that's best kept to myself. Now I grasp at an excuse to go to Newgate alone. "You should look for people who were in the carriage with the murder victim. Maybe they saw the killer. If you wait, they'll be scattered all over the city."

Barrett frowns, torn between wanting to take care of me and to find witnesses before the killer's trail is cold.

"Go. I'll be fine," I reassure him.

"If you're sure . . ."

"Yes." All of a sudden, I remember our wedding and our promise to have and to hold each other until death do us part. Death almost parted us much sooner than we imagined. I pull him to me and press my mouth against his.

Usually, I avoid displays of intimacy in public, but at this moment I don't care who sees. If ever there was a time for a kiss, it's now. Barrett wraps his arms tight around me, his lips firm on mine. He tastes like smoke and the fever of excitement. The desire that flares between us reminds us that we're alive, together, and in love.

I have to tear myself away from him, and I hurry off without looking back.

CHAPTER 2

In the street above the station, I weave through mobs of people who heard the crash and are coming to see what happened. They flock around passengers giving breathless accounts of the crash, reporters interviewing survivors, and photographers taking pictures of men loading the injured into ambulance wagons. Smoke rising through grilles in the pavement marries the ever-present smoke from factories and the thick fog that descends on London in autumn and doesn't lift until spring. Above the buildings, the great dome of St. Paul's Cathedral is a mere shadow. I breathe deeply as I walk, but the cold, damp, murky air that reeks of chemicals and sewers does little to cleanse my lungs. Newgate Prison gradually materializes as though converting the mist into the solid, formidable granite edifice that occupies an entire block and houses hundreds of inmates. I make my way to the middle of the block, where the prison's administrative offices inhabit a four-story building flanked by gatehouses. I brace myself as I approach the wardens stationed by the ironclad door.

I don't need to tell them my name or who I'm here to see; they know me from my previous visits. They regard me with bold, insolent contempt, and they don't open the door for me. As I open it myself, a gob of chewed tobacco lands at my feet. The daughter of Benjamin Bain, the alleged pervert, rapist, and murderer, is fair game for discourtesy. Rude laughter follows me into the building, and I resist the urge to run back and kick the wardens. My prim, sedate facade conceals a temper that's made me a match for numerous bigger, stronger adversaries but has also gotten me in trouble.

Inside the hall, the police constable at the desk searches my pocketbook, satchel, and the Kodak camera case for weapons and other contraband. Fortunately, he doesn't try to open the camera. A warden searches my person, and I submit to his rough groping because if I don't, he won't let me see my father. He escorts me into the dungeon, along dank stone corridors lit by flames that sputter from gas jets on the walls, and up dingy staircases. We pass other wardens who deliberately bump into me while muttering lewd comments. I'm glad I didn't let Barrett accompany me; I don't want him to risk his life or career by doing battle in my defense, as he has when strangers on the street shouted, "Murderer's daughter," and obscenities at me. One confrontation led to blows, and my tormentor ended up facedown in the gutter. Barrett was in uniform at the time, and the man lodged a complaint at the police station.

My escort stops in a narrow passage, outside one of a few closed doors that each have a small, barred window set at eye level. These are the separate confinement cells. My father lives here because the other inmates don't take kindly to anyone who they think has raped and murdered a child. My escort unlocks and opens the door. After I enter, he locks it behind me, and the three people inside the small room stand up.

My gaze immediately focuses on Benjamin Bain, my father. A stocky man of sixty-eight, dressed in the prison uniform of baggy dark gray jacket, vest, and trousers, his hair and beard white, he looks humble and ordinary. But he's the man who taught me photography, whose love for me when I was a child sustained me through my often troubled, lonely adult life. His absence shaped my character; searching for him later consumed much of my energy, and since I found him this summer, his trouble with the law has dictated many of my actions. No matter how much I love the people with whom I've built a satisfying life, my father is an immovable center of gravity in my universe.

"You were supposed to be here at noon," my sister, Sally, says, her usually sweet countenance dark with disapproval.

"I'm sorry." Although I have a good excuse, I feel bad about my tardiness. Sally isn't just my only blood kin besides my father; she's also my best female friend. Her kind, generous nature enabled

us to have a close relationship despite the fact that we have different mothers and, until recently, each of us didn't know the other
existed. And I know that my being more than an hour late isn't the
cause of Sally's anger or the offense for which I'm apologizing. Our
real bone of contention is that Sally completely believes our father is
innocent, and she knows I'm far less certain. My uncertainty about
him is at odds with my loyalty to both my father and my sister.

"Never mind." Our father hastens to make peace. "Sarah is
here now, and that's what counts." He looks puzzled because he
doesn't understand the tension between his daughters. We haven't
explained because it would hurt him to know that one of us thinks
he could be guilty.

Unmollified, Sally gestures to our father's solicitor. "Mr.
Owusu has been waiting."

"It is no problem." John Owusu's deep voice has the faint,
musical inflection of his native Gold Coast. He's over six feet tall,
slender but muscular, with a proud posture. His black skin con-
trasts with the starched white shirt under his gray pinstriped suit.
His age could be anywhere between thirty and fifty. His shaving
lotion smells of lime and mint, in contrast to the stale, urine-
scented prison air. At first, I'd felt uncomfortable with him. I've
seen many black people around town, but those were sailors, servants, or laborers, and I'm not acquainted with any except a man
who delivers coal to my house and a woman at the neighborhood
laundry. I didn't know there were black solicitors until Sir Gerald
Mariner, my employer, provided my father's legal representation.

Sir Gerald is the owner of a banking empire as well as the
Daily World and other newspapers. I told him that I'd approached
nine solicitors, and all turned me down; none wanted to defend a
case they thought they were sure to lose because Benjamin Bain
already had been convicted in the court of public opinion. Sir
Gerald then engaged Mr. Owusu, paying his retainer. He didn't
tell Sally, our father, or me that Mr. Owusu is black. When we
met Mr. Owusu, he must have noticed our surprise, but he's been
unfailingly kind, and if he resents being saddled with a losing case,
he's never shown it. When I asked how Sir Gerald came to hire
him, he said he'd done legal work for Sir Gerald in the past, then

added with sly good humor, "In case you're worried, Sir Gerald didn't get where he is by hiring people who are incompetent." Sally and I knew that about Sir Gerald—she works for him too, as a reporter—and we had to laugh.

Now, Mr. Owusu says, "I'm sure Mrs. Barrett had a good reason for her tardiness." He smiles encouragingly at me.

"There was a train wreck. Barrett and I were in it." My voice trembles at the memory.

"Oh no!" Sally clutches her throat, her concern and love for me overriding her anger.

"Were you hurt?" my father says anxiously.

When I assure them that Barrett and I are both fine, my father sighs with relief and says, "Thank God."

Sally turns cool again. "I wish I could cover the accident for the *Daily World*. It'll be the front-page story."

"How terrible for you," Mr. Owusu says sympathetically. "Please, sit down." He indicates the chair from which he'd risen.

I collapse into the battered wooden chair, which is bolted to the floor and the only one in the cell. My father and Sally sit on the narrow iron cot, and Mr. Owusu stands by the barred window that overlooks the prison yard. There, male inmates trudge about, taking exercise. I don't mention the murder on the train. If Sally were to learn that I was late because I'd stayed at the wreck to investigate a crime, she would think I'd deliberately put it ahead of our father because I think he's guilty.

My mind shies away from the idea that she could be right.

"We'd best get down to business," Mr. Owusu says. "Are you all ready for tomorrow?"

"I brought your new clothes to wear in court, Father." Sally opens her valise, removes the black jacket, waistcoat, and trousers, white shirt, and blue-and-black-striped tie.

"Thank you." He gives her a fond smile. Sally doesn't mention that I paid for the clothes. She thinks I did it to salve my guilty conscience. "They should make a good impression on the jury."

"I'm glad your bruises are almost gone," Sally says.

My father touches the fading greenish blotches on his cheeks. The police had beaten him when they arrested him, and the other inmates had taken their turn before he was moved to separate confinement. I'm furious despite my doubts about him. According to the law, he's innocent until proven guilty and should be treated as such. I'm terrified that the wardens who detest him might kill him before the trial is finished and the verdict rendered.

"Have you had any luck recruiting character witnesses to testify on Mr. Bain's behalf?" Mr. Owusu asks me.

"The last person on the list refused," I say. "I'm sorry."

"Ah, well, that's no more than we expected," my father says, sad but resigned.

Sally frowns as if she thinks I didn't try hard enough. I squelch my impulse to retort that she could have done no better.

"Let us review our story one last time." Mr. Owusu addresses my father. "You said that after you photographed Ellen Casey, she went home, and you never saw her again. Do you want to stick with that story?"

"Yes. It's the truth. I didn't kill her. She was alive when she left my house, and I don't know what happened to her afterward."

Mr. Owusu looks suspicious of the unnecessary denials. "Are you sure there is nothing else you can tell me?" His query includes Sally and me.

We all nod. It's dangerous to withhold information from a man tasked with saving my father's life, but I can't tell him the secrets I'm concealing. One is a photograph that my father took of Ellen Casey. I came across it while looking for proof that he didn't kill her. The photograph shows Ellen posed in a seductive manner. She was fully clothed, but anyone who saw it now would think it damning evidence that my father had a carnal interest in Ellen and indeed had raped her. My father doesn't know I've seen it, and Sally doesn't know it exists. I hope it never comes to light.

Another secret is his own account of the events following Ellen's death. He said Ellen had died in our family home and that he hid her body in a trunk in the cellar, then late that night dumped the body in the ruins of a burned house. But the body was found at a road construction site. My father seems unaware of the discrepancy, and Sally forbade me to ask him about it; she doesn't want him to think we have any less than complete faith in his veracity and innocence. The information wouldn't help with his defense, for if it came out in court that he'd disposed of the body, no matter where it had ended up, the jury would conclude that he killed Ellen.

I can hide the evidence from other people, but the idea that my father actually committed the sinful crimes for which he's accused is an undeniable thorn in the loyalty I've harbored toward him since my childhood.

"I am duty-bound to inform you that you have not given Sir William much to go on," Mr. Owusu says.

Sir William Hall-Clarke is the barrister that Sir Gerald hired for my father. Custom requires the defendant in a trial to have two lawyers—a barrister and a solicitor. The solicitor finds evidence and witnesses, writes briefs, and does other preparatory work. The barrister represents the defendant in court, and it's his job to convince the jury that his client is innocent. My father, Sally, and I haven't met Sir William. The legal system is designed so that the barrister can concentrate on the trial rather than the footwork, and be objective while fighting for his client, undistracted by the complications of personal relationships. Although Sir Gerald assured me that Sir William is among the best defense barristers in London, I'm nervous about putting my father's life in the hands of a man I don't know. And it's as if we're sending Sir William into a joust without a horse and lance.

"If there is the slightest thing more you can think of that could help our case, now is your last chance to speak," Mr. Owusu says.

My father, Sally, and I shake our heads. I hide my thoughts behind an expression of regret while I meet Mr. Owusu's gaze, but my father looks at the floor, and Sally steals a wary glance at me.

Mr. Owusu's manner sharpens as he smells secrecy in our air. "What is it?"

My father casts a pleading look at me. "Sarah, no."

Despite my reluctance to ride roughshod over his wishes, I see no choice but to say, "Father, I must tell him." Sally squirms, caught in the middle of our conflict.

"Tell me what?" Mr. Owusu demands.

"You promised not to," my father protests.

Sympathetic but stern, Mr. Owusu says, "Mr. Bain, this is a matter of life and death."

"There's evidence that someone else killed Ellen Casey," I blurt.

My father buries his head in his hands. Sally pats his shoulder while Mr. Owusu's face takes on the expression of a man who thought he'd seen and heard everything but is nonetheless shocked. He doesn't waste time asking why we didn't tell him sooner, or scolding us.

"Who is it?" he says.

"My mother. Mary Bain. She died in 1875." Despite my eagerness to exonerate my father, I have to force the words out of my mouth. My feelings about my mother are mixed and complicated. By my father's account, she let him take the blame for her crime, and she told me he was dead although she knew he wasn't. For that I hate my mother. But when I was a child, I loved her, and a vestige of childish loyalty battles with my hatred. Because my father was always my favorite parent, I also feel a shameful guilt toward my mother, no matter that her behavior made her hard to love. From inquiries into her family history, I know she had her reasons for her coldness, neglectfulness, and harshness toward me. That doesn't make me hate her less or relieve my guilt as I prepare to reveal the vile secrets of the woman who brought me into the world.

"Very well," Mr. Owusu says. "Tell me what really happened."

"My father went downstairs to the darkroom to develop his photographs of Ellen," I say. "He left her in the kitchen with my mother. A while later, he heard Ellen screaming. By the time he got there, she was dead. My mother had strangled her." This is a near-verbatim recital of the story my father had told Sally and me.

My father covers his eyes, as if to blot out the vision of that terrible moment. His hands slide down to cover his mouth, as though he wishes he could take back the story.

The look that Mr. Owusu bends on him combines reproach and hope. "If this is true, it changes our prospects."

"It's true," Sally says with an apologetic glance at our father.

I keep silent. My inquiries produced independent evidence that supports my father's story, enough that I'm willing to let the jury decide whether to believe it. And the vengeful part of me would like my mother held accountable for the crime, albeit posthumously.

"I can't let it come out in court!" my father exclaims.

Mr. Owusu looks mystified. "Why not? It could pave the way to your acquittal."

Sally clutches our father's arm. "Listen to Mr. Owusu. He's right." Her unfriendly glance at me says that even if my revelation saves our father, that doesn't mean all is well between us. She feels guilty about siding with me against him, and she's angry at me for putting our family at odds.

"I can't do that to Mary," my father says.

"It can't hurt her," I remind him. "She's dead."

"She was my wife. I loved her. I still do. I don't want her reputation ruined." It's what he'd said when I previously suggested that he should incriminate her to clear his own name.

"Never mind her reputation!" Hatred of my mother temporarily eclipses my doubts about my father. "After everything she's done, she doesn't deserve your protection."

Sally nods. My father shakes his head and repeats, "She was my wife."

I wonder if I'm capable of taking my marriage vows as seriously as he takes his. Would I protect Barrett if he'd committed a crime for which I stood accused? Would he protect me if the circumstances were reversed? I don't know whether to be in awe of my father for his faithfulness or suspicious of his motives.

Mr. Owusu speaks in a gentle but firm voice. "An alternative suspect would strengthen your defense, Mr. Bain. The jury will want someone punished for the crime, and if you are innocent, it should not be you." This is the first hint that he too has doubts about my father's innocence.

Defiance straightens my father's posture. "I won't have mud thrown on Mary. If the jury thinks I'm guilty, then so be it."

I uneasily wonder if he hopes to be convicted because he's a guilty man with a guilty conscience.

"All right, we won't throw mud on Mary," says Sally. "Lucas Zehnpfennig is just as good an alternative suspect." She's obviously relieved to point out another scapegoat.

Mr. Owusu stares at us as if we've pulled a second rabbit out of a hat. "Who is Lucas Zehnpfennig?"

"He was Mary's son, my illegitimate half-brother." I ignore my father's shushing gestures. "Mary had him before she met my father." I'd discovered Lucas's existence while investigating my mother's past.

"He raped Ellen," Sally blushes at speaking the ugly word. "Mary killed Ellen to stop her screaming. Lucas is just as guilty as Mary was."

That, too, is according to my father, but I also have other evidence that Lucas was a pervert who violated other young girls.

"Sally, please," my father moans.

"This is promising." Mr. Owusu's eyes shine with elation at this new hope of an acquittal. "Where might Lucas be now?"

"He died in 1880," I say.

"What a pity," Mr. Owusu says. "The jurors might take issue with blaming the crimes on a dead man who can't speak for himself. However, mentioning Lucas could still raise enough doubt to convince them to acquit you, Mr. Bain."

"No." My father is breathing hard, frantic. "I won't let you smear Lucas."

"He's nothing to you." Frustrated and bewildered, Sally says, "Why do you care so much about protecting him?"

"Mary was ashamed that she'd born a child out of wedlock. She didn't want anyone to know Lucas was her son. I won't air her dirty laundry in court."

I suspect that's not his only reason. I think he harbors guilt about Lucas. He once told me that after Ellen's murder, he and my mother struck a bargain: He would help her and Lucas cover up their crimes if Lucas agreed to run away to America with him. My father thought he could keep an eye on Lucas and protect other girls—including me—from Lucas.

He was wrong.

He also promised my mother that he would look after Lucas too. He broke his promise in a most terrible fashion. That's something else I can't tell Mr. Owusu or Sally.

"It's Lucas's fault that you're in this predicament," Sally says. "If he'd left Ellen alone, we wouldn't be here now." She jumps up, stands in front of our father, and flings out her arms. "You won't give him over to the law, even to save your own life?"

He sits as though made of stone. "Not even to save my own life."

"Mr. Bain, I admire your integrity," Mr. Owusu says, his tolerance giving way to exasperation. "However, I must warn you: If you are convicted, you may change your mind about standing on your principles. By then it will be too late."

"So be it," my father repeats.

Here he sits in his prison cell, bruised and downtrodden, his uniform like a badge of honor earned by his willingness to take the blame for his wife and Lucas's crimes. My own exasperation blends with my doubts about my father and my love for him. When I was a child, he was always gentle, kind, and patient with me while teaching me photography, showing me how to see and capture the beauty and the secrets of the visual world. His love made up for my mother's coldness toward me and strengthened me enough that I could survive on my own. Should that not count for more than the possibility that he's guilty?

Sally has a right to be angry at me for my disloyalty to him. I'm angry at myself. If he's convicted and sentenced to death, I won't be glad that the jury validated my suspicions.

Mr. Owusu says to Sally and me, "Your father is my client. I cannot go against his wishes."

I once saw the gallows during an investigation that brought me to Newgate. I envision my father on the wooden platform in the shed, a noose around his neck, a hood over his head, and the hangman pulling the lever that opens the trapdoor under his feet. I can't bear to imagine my life afterward, with the memory of his love for me, and mine for him, tainted by horror.

"Is there anything you can do?" I ask Mr. Owusu.

"What happens during the trial is up to Sir William. He will poke as many holes in the prosecution's case as he can. Aside from that . . ."

Sally and I lean toward him, hungry for any crumb of encouragement.

"We can pray," Mr. Owusu says.

CHAPTER 3

Outside the door of Newgate, Sally pauses and gulps the foggy air as if to purge the prison miasma from her lungs. Taking her arm, I say, "Let's get a cup of tea somewhere."

She withdraws from my touch. "I can't. I'm busy."

I know she doesn't have to work. Sir Gerald gave us both paid leaves of absence so that we could prepare for the trial and attend court. She's estranged from her mother, and she lost contact with old friends after she started working for the *Daily World*. I picture her brooding alone in her room at the lodging house where she lives.

"Come to dinner at my house tonight," I say.

"Thank you, but no." Sally walks past the people waiting in line at the visitors' entrance to Newgate.

I hurry after her. "Sally, please. I'm sorry," I apologize for the hundredth time. Being at odds with her during this time of crisis is awful. I'd thought my sister was sweet, uncomplicated, and docile, and I'm astonished to discover that she can be so obstinate. She's more like me than I'd thought.

"I'll see you tomorrow." Sally hurries away.

As I watch her slim figure disappear into the fog, I try not to imagine life without both my father and Sally. My husband and my friends, although infinitely dear to me, couldn't compensate for the loss of my only, beloved blood kin.

Time weighs heavily on my hands, and I can think of but one way to spend it. I sling the strap of the Kodak camera case over my shoulder and hail a cab because the train wreck must have disrupted underground service throughout London. A half-hour's ride takes me to Islington in the northern part of the city, to Holloway Road near the graveyard outside St. Mary Magdalene Church. On the busy thoroughfare, I enter a shop whose sign reads "Henderson Photography." Inside the display room, cameras for sale stand on tripods, lenses and other accessories fill glass cases, and racks hold jars of chemicals and boxes of negative plates and photographic print paper.

Mr. Henderson, the proprietor, catches sight of me and says, "We have the latest issue of the *London Photographic Almanac*." He points to shelves that contain copies of virtually every photography journal and book published in English. He's tall and stooped, with gold-rimmed spectacles, a balding head shaped like an egg, and a smile that shows gaps between large teeth. Photography seems to be his sole topic of conversation, and he treats his customers as nothing but ears to listen to his monologues. But his shop sells rare items, and his knowledge about photography is vast.

His sister, seated behind the cash register, is an older, female version of him with more hair. "Good afternoon, Mrs. Barrett. What can we do for you today?" She transacts the sales, keeps the books, and compensates for her brother's lack of social niceties.

After greeting her, I remove the camera from its case and set it on the counter. Mr. Henderson gasps with delight. "A Kodak! One doesn't often run across them in England. In America, they cost twenty-five dollars, including the case and a roll of film. They're so popular that the factory produces nine hundred feet of film every day."

"I need to have the film inside developed," I say. "Can you do it?"

Mr. Henderson doesn't ask me where I obtained the camera or why I need the pictures. "Of course." He picks up the Kodak and hurries through a door at the back of the shop.

Loath to let crime scene evidence out of my sight, I follow him. He runs a sideline business in repairing cameras and inventing gadgets, and his workshop is littered with tools, parts, and sketches.

"With a Kodak, anyone can be a photographer," he says. "All you do is point it and push the button." I join him in his darkroom, where he sets the Kodak on the worktop and turns its key. "This is how you wind the film." He pours chemicals into trays. "One usually doesn't need a darkroom to develop it. Some of us have figured out how to do it ourselves, but the standard practice is to mail your camera to the factory. They develop the film and mail the prints and the negatives to you, as well as your camera reloaded with blank film. That's a hundred exposures for ten dollars. The Kodak is going to put a lot of professional photographers out of business."

On that cheerful note, Mr. Henderson closes the door. In the pitch-black darkness, I stand against the wall as he bustles around and makes tinkering noises. If he were any other man, I might hesitate to be alone like this with him, but I think it safe to assume that his work is his only interest.

"First I take the back off the camera. Then I remove the assembly," Mr. Henderson chatters. "I remove the roll of film and pop it in the developer." The ticking of a timer accompanies swishing noises. Soon, the bell on the timer rings. "Now for the stop bath." More ticking, more swishing, another ring, and Mr. Henderson lights the safe lamp.

In the red glow, I see the disassembled Kodak. The back panel is attached to a contraption with rollers that held the film. The long, thin film lies coiled in clear liquid in a tray. On one end are five circles, each about two and a half inches in diameter with blackened areas. The rest of the film is transparent.

"Only five exposures were taken." Mr. Henderson uses scissors to cut them off the roll, then rinses them in fixer and water. "A waste of the other ninety-five."

The woman on the train apparently didn't have time to take the other photographs before she was murdered. I'm glad the camera contained photographs and Mr. Henderson seems to have developed them successfully. I hope they contain clues to the identity of the murderer.

Mr. Henderson fits the wet strip of negatives into a gadget equipped with a wind-up fan that blows air on them. When they're dry, I ask him to print them in triplicate. He enlarges and prints them using conventional equipment, then develops the prints and clips them to the string above the sink. He lights the lamps, and I eagerly examine the circular images.

All five appear to be candid shots rather than posed portraits, the subjects turned slightly away from the camera as if unaware that they were being photographed. The first shows a closeup of a man with bold eyes in a strong, handsome face. Clean-shaven, with thick dark hair that falls over his brow, he looks to be in his late twenties. His lips are parted; his image had been captured while he was speaking. It's cropped at his shoulders so that all I can see of the rest of him is a white ruff, as though he's costumed for a Shakespearean drama.

The man in the second photograph is a few years younger and shown full figure, standing outdoors amid trees. His body is slender and willowy in his smartly tailored dark coat and trousers. He has a thin, sensitive face with a fringe of mustache, a narrow nose, and a pouting mouth. A derby conceals his hair and shades hooded eyes that give him a furtive expression.

The subject of the other photographs, a woman, is the most striking. Her face is a long rectangle, her huge dark eyes deep-set beneath arched brows. A hump curves her long nose. Her lips are full and sensuous. Her long neck rises from the fur collar of a tent-like cape that hides her figure. A fur hat crowns dark hair drawn smoothly back from her forehead and twisted in a thick chignon. In the first of her three photographs, taken at middle distance, she opens an ornate white gate. In the second, she walks down a long avenue lined with trees and overhung with glass lamps suspended from iron arches. She glances over her shoulder, as if to see if anyone is following her. In the final shot, her tiny silhouette stands outside a building that resembles a fantasy of an Arabian Nights palace. Four tall, thin, striped towers ringed with balconies decorate the facade. My heart jumps with excitement.

"The photographer didn't use a tripod," Mr. Henderson says. "The horizon isn't level." He points to the picture of the building, which is tilted. "But these are remarkably clear, considering that the Kodak doesn't have a focus adjuster."

I barely hear him. The people in the photographs are all strangers to me, but that building is familiar. If only I could remember where I've seen it before.

CHAPTER 4

O n Commercial Street in Whitechapel, I climb out of a cab that's stuck in heavier traffic than usual for six o'clock in the evening. Newsboys hawking papers shout, "Underground train service stopped due to the wreck at St. Paul's station—read all about it!" My trip from Islington took two hours, and to walk the last half mile will be faster. Cabs, carriages, and wagons block intersections; policemen frantically wave and blow their whistles. It's as if London has been thrown back to the old days before train travel, but there are thousands more people than there were then, all trying to go somewhere. The fog resounds with curses and complaints as I join mobs of people making their way home on foot. We struggle through the thicker crush outside the grocer's, butcher's, and bakery shops. Whitechapel is notorious as the hunting ground of Jack the Ripper, but if he were abroad tonight, he would find inadequate privacy to commit murder.

I hear Barrett call my name, and turn to see his head bobbing amid the crowd. I'm exhausted and tense, but I'm so happy to see him that a smile blooms on my face. The train wreck and the murder made me painfully aware that our time on earth may be of short duration, and every time we face death together and survive, I wonder if our luck will run out. Barrett's smile says he's equally glad to see me. He holds my hand tight as we forge through the crowd. An aftereffect of my father's disappearance was my lifelong fear that any man I dared to love would leave me. I'm so glad my husband is the one who won't.

When I ask him if he made any progress with the murder investigation, he says, "None at all." His eyes are bloodshot, his cheeks gray with soot. "I must have talked to hundreds of passengers, but they couldn't remember which carriage they'd been in or who'd been in it with them. Nobody recognized my description of the victim."

I'm disappointed but not surprised. "A train wreck would erase everything else from one's memory."

Barrett's somber expression deepens. "The death toll was at fifteen people when I left the station. Dozens were taken to the hospital with serious injuries."

I silently thank God that we weren't among the casualties. I'm about to tell Barrett about the Kodak photographs, when a female voice behind us trills, "Oh, Thomas."

We turn to see Jane Lambert. Tall and slender, dressed in a royal blue coat and hat that flatter her blonde hair and fair complexion, Jane is the woman to whom Barrett was unofficially engaged when he and I met. Her bright smile casts a cold, dark shadow over me. Although I'm the one Barrett married, I'm insecure about Jane. One reason is that we're both the physical type he likes, but she's prettier—and she knows it. I can tell from the satisfaction in her eyes as she looks me up and down. Grimy and disheveled from the train wreck, I feel plainer than ever.

"Hullo, Jane," Barrett says.

She seems unfazed by his strained manner. "Fancy meeting you here."

"We do live in Whitechapel." I'm annoyed because now that she's given me the once-over, she's ignoring me. "In fact, we're almost home. It was nice to see you again." I tug Barrett's hand.

Jane moves closer, backing him and me into the alley that separates our building from the Angel public house. In the narrow passage, the three of us are alone for the moment.

Barrett clears his throat. "So. What brings you here, Jane?"

"I was buying shoelaces," she says, holding up a small paper bag.

"They don't sell shoelaces in Bethnal Green?" I say.

Bethnal Green is her own part of town, two miles away. Jane smiles sweetly at my hint that her errand was a mere excuse and pretends she hasn't "accidentally" run into us three other times in as many weeks. "I saw your mother at her whist party last night, Tommy." Her use of the nickname grates on my nerves. I prefer calling my husband by his surname.

"That's nice." Barrett detaches his hand from mine, takes off his hat, and rumples his dark hair, his habit when nervous.

Jane lives with her parents, down the block from Barrett's parents. Jane and Barrett grew up together. They were also physically intimate over an extended period that includes the time while he was courting me. As if that weren't enough to make me insecure, their families are old, close friends. Jane's father is a police officer in the same division where Barrett's father served until his retirement, and Jane is like a daughter to my in-laws while I'm still on shaky footing with them. Furthermore, Jane is a schoolteacher, a profession more socially acceptable than mine. I can't help thinking that Barrett would be better off with a wife whose job would cause him less trouble than mine has. I'm sure Jane thinks she should be that wife.

"Isn't this where you live?" she asks, glancing up at our building.

Barrett nods. "I moved in with Sarah and her friends."

"That sounds interesting." Jane's wide, blue-flecked hazel eyes shine with curiosity about our home.

I can tell she wants to be invited in, and Barrett's shrug says the decision is up to me. He knows I don't like Jane, and he doesn't want to invite her and make me mad, but he doesn't want to snub her. My temper heats up because my husband cares about his ex-fiancée's feelings. I say to Jane, "You must be in a hurry, so don't let us keep you. Good night."

I grab Barrett by the arm and drag him out of the alley. Glancing over my shoulder, I see Jane standing with her gloved fists clenched, her eyes shooting daggers at me. Barrett unlocks the door to our house, one in a row of eighteenth-century shop buildings with businesses on the ground floor and living quarters above. The gold letters on the display window proclaim "S. Barrett Photographer & Co."

"That was rude," Barrett says.

"It was ruder for Jane to come looking for you. Again."

"She just happened to be in the neighborhood."

"Do you really believe that?" I laugh. "All four times?" Men can be so dense.

"I've never known her to lie."

I flinch at the thought of how well he knows Jane. My conscience stings because we both know I've lied to him before, and it's a permanently sore spot in our relationship.

"She wants you back," I say.

Barrett opens the door and sighs with frustration. "Sarah." We've had this argument before, and he obviously he doesn't want to have it now. "She knows I'm married."

"Knowing you're married isn't the same thing as accepting it. I don't trust her."

"Well, I wish you would trust *me*," Barrett retorts.

Trust, or lack thereof, has been a thorn in our relationship. We have pasts about which we've been less than frank with each other. Even now, not all my cards are on the table, and I don't know that his are either.

"I'm not interested in Jane," Barrett says. "You're the one I love. All right?"

I decide to be satisfied with that. Since our marriage, I've had no cause to think he's been unfaithful to me. "All right."

Inside my studio, I feel my usual pride in the elegance of the crystal gas chandelier, the red Turkish carpet and the carved furniture, and the cameras on tripods. I adore my home, the first one where I've felt loved and secure since I was a child, since before my father disappeared. The other people who live here comprise my family, unconventional and unrelated to me by blood, but every bit as dear as if they were. When I touch a camera, dust smudges my glove. My assignments for the *Daily World* leave me little time for other work, and since my father's arrest, I've done no photography at all. How I miss it! The act of composing a shot is both soothing and stimulating, and when the finished print achieves the result I wanted, it's a satisfaction like no other. The absence of photography is a painful void in my heart, and I wonder if my life will ever be normal again.

The trial looms like a storm front blocking the path to the future.

Barrett follows me as I carry my pocketbook, satchel, and the Kodak camera upstairs. On the second floor, the kitchen is dimly lit and the parlor dark. Hearing gasps and scuffling noises, I call, "Is anyone home?"

A shriek of dismay answers me, and when Barrett lights the lamp, the couple seated close together on the divan spring apart. They're Mick O'Reilly—one of Barrett's and my three house-mates—and his friend Anjali Lodge.

"Hey, Sarah." Mick grins sheepishly, his cheeks as red as his hair.

Anjali hurriedly buttons the white blouse of her school uni-form. Her black hair hangs in long, tangled waves. Of mixed Indian and English blood, she has a creamy brown complexion that doesn't hide the blush that suffuses her pretty face.

"Hello, Mr. and Mrs. Barrett," she says in a small voice, too mortified to look at us.

I drop my things on the table and stare in consternation. I'm aware that boys of fifteen and girls of fourteen have sex, but Mick and Anjali have known each other for only a few weeks. I like Anjali; she's a pure ray of light cheering up a household that's seen too much darkness. The world can't be such a bad place when it contains her. I'm glad Mick has a girlfriend, but I'm afraid he'll get her in trouble.

"Does your father know you're here?" I ask Anjali.

"No. He's at work every night, doing experiments."

Her father, Dr. Everard Lodge, is a scientist whom Mick and I met during our last investigation. He's protective toward his only child, and he doesn't approve of Mick. I can't blame him. No conscientious father would want his young, innocent daughter involved with a former street urchin who has a history of petty crime and a job that often requires hunting murderers.

"Isn't anyone looking after you while your father is gone?" Barrett asks.

"My old nanny. But she drinks too much and falls asleep." Anjali confesses, "I sneaked out of the house."

"Where are Hugh and Fitzmorris?" Lord Hugh Staunton and his valet are our other two housemates, and I think they should have acted as chaperones for Mick and Anjali.

Mick points at the ceiling. I hurry upstairs. In one bedroom I see thin, gray-haired Fitzmorris asleep on his bed, fully clothed. Fitzmorris, officially Hugh's valet, is also unofficially our housekeeper, manager, cook, and accountant. His family has served the Stauntons for generations; he's devoted to Hugh, and lately his duties include round-the-clock nursing. I haven't the heart to wake him. I knock on Hugh's closed door, then barge in and draw my breath to say, "Do you know what Mick and Anjali have been doing while you've been hiding up here?"

The sight of Hugh shrivels the rebuke in my throat. He's lying abed, the quilts pulled up to his chin. The room is bitterly cold; the fire in the hearth has gone out.

"What is it, Sarah?" His voice is devoid of his usual spirit. He sounds as though he couldn't care less whether I've come to announce that I've won at the races or that England is at war.

My concern for him shunts the problem of Mick and Anjali to the back of my mind. As a result of our last investigation, Hugh almost bled to death from a deep, vicious cut to his right shoulder and arm. The doctors saved him, thank God, but his arm is crippled. Fitzmorris's care brought him through the worst of his ordeal, but on his bedside table are new bottles of the medicine he takes for the pain.

"How are you feeling?" I ask, hurrying to build up the fire.

"About the same." He's still among the handsomest men I've ever seen, but the bones of his face are too sharp, his blond hair matted under his nightcap. His sunken green eyes reflect the light from the fire, which doesn't penetrate the bleakness within his soul.

My sympathy doesn't dispel the impatience that's been growing in me lately. Since Hugh came home from the hospital last week, he has yet to leave his room. He only gets out of bed when Fitzmorris changes his sheets and bathes him; he refuses to wear anything but pajamas; and he has to be coaxed to eat. But his injury isn't the only thing that ails him. It coincided with the loss of the man he loved—Sir Gerald's son Tristan Mariner. I never trusted Tristan, and I think Hugh is better off without him. I also think Hugh's lethargy is endangering his recovery.

"The doctor said you should get up and move around," I say. "How about coming downstairs for dinner?"

"Maybe tomorrow."

"He also said that unless you exercise your muscles, they'll atrophy." I'm afraid he'll become permanently crippled. "Did you work with the physical therapist today?"

"I didn't feel up to it."

Guilt laps at my impatience. Hugh was injured in the act of saving Barrett's life. If not for Hugh, I would be a widow, my beloved husband gone forever. I vacillate between wanting to order him to help himself and knowing I've no right to ask him for anything.

"Barrett and I were in a train accident today," I say, hoping to pique his interest.

"Oh? You weren't hurt, I hope?" The response costs him a visibly wearying effort.

"We're fine. But we discovered a murder on the train."

In the past, a new case always spurred him to enthusiastic action. Now, as I tell him the details, he closes his eyes and says, "I'm a little tired."

I stand beside him, tearful with frustration and fear. He's my best friend, my comrade in adventure, a pillar upon whom the security of our family depends. He's risked his life to save mine more than once; he's buoyed my spirits during troubles that seemed insurmountable. It's as though a part of Hugh died when he was injured, and the thread that ties him to life is weakening day by day. He looks like a carved stone effigy on his own tomb. I want to fall to my knees by him and weep for the bright, exuberant man he once was. I would do anything for him, but I can't force him to regain the will to live.

I tiptoe from his room, quietly shut the door, and wipe my eyes as I trudge downstairs. In the kitchen, Mick and Barrett are seated at the table. Anjali, her hair neatly braided, is frying sausages and eggs. Her smile is anxious as she fills a plate for me, obviously trying to make amends for her wanton behavior. I drop into a chair, too tired, hungry, and worried about Hugh and the trial to take Anjali and Mick to task.

"Barrett says you found a body in a train wreck," Mick says, just as obviously hoping to divert my mind from the amorous scene I interrupted.

Mick is not only my stalwart friend; he's like a little brother and just young enough to be my son. I can't help feeling responsible for him and wanting to protect him, but he considers himself an adult and doesn't like to be babied or bossed. Now, in an apparently serious relationship with Anjali, he's growing away from the family that he, Hugh, Barrett, and I have made together. I suppose it's natural, but it's also sad.

We eat while Barrett and I describe the crime scene. Murder talk and dining aren't mutually exclusive activities in this house. I show my companions the photographs from the Kodak.

Barrett picks up the photograph of the slender, mustached man. "This chap looks familiar, but I can't place him." He examines the other man's photograph. "I've never seen him before."

"I don't know any of 'em," Mick says.

"Nor do I." Anjali points at the three pictures of the woman. "She looks sneaky."

Indeed, the woman has a furtive air as she opens the gate and walks down the avenue. I'm suddenly breathless because now I can place the Arabian building. I point at it and exclaim, "That's the fireworks temple in Cremorne Gardens!"

"Good work, Sarah," Barrett says.

I remember the first time I saw Cremorne Gardens, one summer day when I was seven or eight years old and my father took me there. We rode the three-penny steamer down the river to the pier in Chelsea. One shilling apiece gained us admission to a pleasure park that contained a circus, marionette theater, sideshows, a maze, and other attractions set in beautiful flower gardens. The highlight of the day was a medieval tournament. Knights in armor jousted as we sat in the stands amid thousands of cheering spectators. Flags fluttered and heralds blew trumpets; people costumed as kings, queens, and courtiers strolled about, and jesters entertained us between matches. Afterward, my father and I went up in a balloon that was tethered on the green. Then came supper at a refreshment bar while watching the orchestra and dancing at the pavilion. The day ended with fireworks launched from the towers of the fireworks temple. It was a rare, delightful treat.

"I thought Cremorne Gardens was closed," Barrett says.

"I did too," I say.

When I was twenty, alone in the world and struggling to establish my photography business, I went back to Cremorne. I thought to relive the happiness of that day with my father and take pictures I could sell. I found the buildings in disrepair, the flowerbeds overgrown. Rowdy, drunken men reveled with women who looked to be of ill repute. As I explored the grounds, a gang of toughs followed me. They tried to steal my camera and pocketbook, but a police constable came to my rescue. The gang fled, and the constable warned me that Cremorne wasn't safe for a lady by herself. I regretted going back; I should have left my memory of my father's treat unsullied by latter-day reality. Not long afterward, I heard that Cremorne had been closed down due to rampant crime and many complaints from its neighbors.

"If the photographs in the Kodak were taken recently, then at least part of Cremorne Gardens was left intact," I say.

"Seems like a good place to look for clues." Mick sounds excited about a new case.

"I'll help," Anjali says eagerly. "If I go there, maybe I'll have a vision of the murderer."

Anjali claims to have psychic powers. She and her father allege that when she touches people or objects, or goes to places, she can read them as if they're books and obtain information that she couldn't have known. Sometimes her visions predict future events. I'm a skeptic, and I take their claims with a big grain of salt, but events that transpired during my last investigation shook my belief that the supernatural is hogwash.

"Great idea!" Mick says.

I remember the terrible end to that investigation. "Absolutely not. It's too dangerous."

"How dangerous could it be, just looking around Cremorne Gardens?" Mick says.

"Looking around leads to other things." I glance up the stairs toward the room where Hugh lies wasting away from his injury.

"Right." Mick sounds chastened but unpersuaded, irked by my authority. He's at the age when people think they're invincible even when they've had as many brushes with death as Mick.

Disappointment clouds Anjali's face. She's seen murder, but the memory must have faded in the glow of young romance and the novel idea of herself and Mick as detective partners.

"There isn't going to be an investigation for us," Barrett says. "The murder happened outside the Metropolitan Police district. The case belongs to the City of London Police. And Sarah and Hugh are on leave from the *Daily World*."

"I could ask Sir Gerald to let me investigate the murder," Mick says, brightening.

"Don't." I can just imagine Mick and Anjali running around London completely unsupervised, getting into God knows what predicaments. "Anjali, it's time you went home." The girl shouldn't be here without her father's permission or knowledge.

Anjali casts a wistful glance at Mick, who says, "I'll get a cab and take you home."

I'll have to have a talk with them later. "On your way back, stop at the *Daily World* and give these to the night editor, in case he wants them for tomorrow's paper." I give Mick a set of the photographs from the Kodak and my notes about the crime, written during my trip home.

After Mick and Anjali leave, Barrett says, "I bet they'll take up where they left off and steam up the windows of the cab. How about we go to bed and steam up our window?" He pulls me onto his lap and kisses my neck.

We're passionate lovers, but it's as if I've traveled years past that moment in the train station when I craved intimacy with him as an affirmation of life. I'm still tense from our encounter with Jane, and my mind skitters between thoughts about the wreck and the murder, Hugh, Mick, and Anjali, and always returns to the trial.

"I don't think I can relax enough." I'm sorry that circumstances are disrupting the honeymoon phase of our marriage.

"I understand." Disappointed but sympathetic, Barrett lets me go.

I thank him with a smile. I love him because he really does understand and care about my feelings. He doesn't put his own desires first, as other husbands would.

"You'll have to give the evidence from the murder scene to the City of London police," I say. "Why don't we see if we can find some more clues for them?" I fetch my pocketbook and bring out the white card, which reads "Great Northern Hotel."

Surprise lifts Barrett's eyebrows. "You want to go there now?"

I feel a proprietary interest in the case and a duty to the woman whose body I discovered— and the photographs piqued my curiosity. I also crave a distraction from thoughts of the trial, and a little sleuthing will burn off my nervous energy so I can sleep tonight and be fresh for tomorrow.

"Yes, let's go. This is our last chance to investigate the murder."

★　★　★

The Great Northern Hotel is a crescent-shaped building six stories high, wedged between Victoria station and St. Pancras station. Built some thirty years ago, it's among the grand railway hotels, but not at its best when the cab lets Barrett and me out at the entrance. Its brick walls are grimy with soot, its heights obscured by clouds of smoke and steam from the stations. The noise of train whistles blowing, brakes screeching, and iron wheels rattling is so incessantly loud that I wonder how the guests can sleep, but the hotel is convenient for travelers.

The doorman opens the door for us, and Barrett removes his helmet as we enter the hotel. Before we left the house, he changed into his police uniform, which gains him access to places where ordinary citizens aren't allowed. The lobby smells of bleach, and a maid mopping the black-and-white checkerboard marble floor demonstrates the hotel's efforts to maintain cleanliness in a dirty location. Guests move in and out of lounges and restaurants. The grandeur is faded; the atmosphere pleasant but hardly luxurious. Still, I don't think the rooms come cheap. From my brief impression of the woman murdered on the train, she wasn't wealthy. How did she afford to stay here?

We approach the clerk at the front desk. Barrett identifies himself, introduces me as his wife, and says, "We're looking for information about a woman who may be registered as a guest."

"What is her name?" says the clerk, a bald man dressed in a formal black suit.

"That's what I'm trying to find out," Barrett says. "You may have heard about the train wreck near St. Paul's station. She was one of the fatalities."

"How tragic," the clerk murmurs.

"She was carrying a card from this hotel," Barrett says.

"We have ninety rooms and many female guests registered. Can you describe her?"

"She was about average size, with reddish-brown hair, dressed in a brown coat and hat."

The clerk ponders, then shakes his head. "It doesn't ring a bell. I'm sorry."

I think of the Kodak. "She may be American."

"Ah!" The clerk leafs through the register book, turns it around to face Barrett and me, and points to a line on a page dated three weeks ago.

Written in neat, plain cursive is the name "Miss Katherine Oliver" and an address in New York City.

"That could be her!" Excitement revives my flagging energy.

"We need to see her room," Barrett tells the clerk. "Can you let us in?"

Possessed of a spare key, Barrett and I go up to the second floor. We walk along a dark carpet, past closed doors, until we reach the one labeled 230. Barrett knocks. When nobody answers, he lets us into a room whose air is cold, still, and smells of perfumed soap. I light the lamps and we look around. The spacious room has dark, polished furniture set on a brown and gold floral carpet. The hearth contains unlit coals, and beige damask curtains match the counterpanes on the two beds.

"Maybe Katherine Oliver had company." I lift the counterpanes. Both beds are made up with clean, ironed sheets.

Barrett examines two battered leather suitcases on the rack. They have tags with her name and address written on them, and stickers from the White Star steamship line. "Katherine Oliver, what were you doing in London?" He sounds sad that she crossed the ocean perhaps only to die here. He opens the suitcases to reveal that they're empty.

I search the armoire. The few frocks, blouses, skirts, and shoes are clean and in good repair, but not new or very fashionable. The labels are from stores, presumably American, whose names I don't recognize. The personal articles in the bathroom and on the vanity appear inexpensive and well used. Her belongings confirm my sense that their owner had been of modest means that wouldn't cover international travel.

Barrett rummages in the desk drawer. "Here's a ship ticket with an open date for the return trip. She must not have known how long she would be staying in England."

Standing at the vanity, I notice a picture stuck in the mirror frame. I take down the oval photographic portrait of a girl perhaps eighteen years old. Wearing a frothy white dress, she has light, fluffy hair pulled back from her forehead and curled in ringlets down her shoulders. Her bare neckline displays a pearl necklace with a gem-encrusted starburst pendant. She's pretty despite heavy features, and a touch of sauciness in her eyes enlivens her unsmiling expression. On her cheek are three tiny gray spots arranged in a triangle. They seem to be defects in the print, which otherwise is of high quality.

"Who is that?" Barrett says.

I look at the back of the photograph. Only the name of the studio, "Andrews & Sons, New York," is printed there. "It doesn't say."

Barrett takes a small cardboard-covered notebook from the drawer. I look over his shoulder at a handwritten list of expenses for meals, train travel, and cab fare. In the drawer I find picture postcards of famous places around London and a guidebook with local attractions marked. St. Paul's Cathedral is one.

"She might have been on her way to visit St. Paul's when the train crashed." I pity the woman whose travels ended so disastrously.

Barrett reaches in the back of the drawer, pulls out a small, square brown leather folder and opens it. "Hey, what have we here?"

Inside the righthand flap gleams a shield-shaped badge. Etched into the silver metal are the words, "Pinkerton's National Detective Agency." On the opposite flap, a white card bears a photograph of Katherine Oliver, who is indeed the woman murdered on the train. In life she was attractive but not beautiful, her features sharp, her expression shrewd. Beside her photograph is an insignia—a drawing of an eye with "We Never Sleep" printed under it. Katherine's name and vital information are typed into the provided spaces: height, five feet two; weight, one hundred sixteen pounds; date of birth, July 20, 1864; hair, brown; eyes, brown; race, white; citizenship, United States of America. She'd signed her name in the neat cursive we saw in the hotel register, above the words, "This is to certify that Katherine Oliver, Special Detective, is employed by the New York City office of this agency, 154 Nassau St., New York, NY."

Barrett and I exclaim, "She was a detective!"

I feel a sense of kinship with her, and a cold, uneasy prickling on my skin. In her work, Katherine Oliver must have discovered things that people preferred to keep hidden, as have I in my work. Now she's been murdered at age twenty-six, eight years younger than I am.

"I didn't know Pinkerton employed women," Barrett says.

"I've heard of them, but I don't know anything about them."

"They're a big private inquiry firm. They solve train robberies and spy on union organizers at coal mines and break strikes in America. I don't know if they work on other kinds of cases in other countries."

"If she was here on a case, that would explain how she was able to afford this hotel and her ship fare. The client must be paying."

"It would also explain this list of expenses." Barrett taps the notebook. "She was keeping track of them so Pinkerton's could bill the client."

"But who is the client, and what case was she investigating?"

We're silent a moment. All we hear is the thunder of a train outside the hotel. If the spirit of Katherine Oliver lingers in the room, it offers no answers.

"I have a hunch that the case involves this girl." I hold up the photograph.

Barrett smiles. "Your hunches have been correct in the past." He gathers up the badge folder and other items from the desk, takes the photo from me, and adds it to the collection. "I'll turn this lot and the Kodak pictures over to the City of London Police tomorrow morning."

My sense of identification with Katherine makes the case personal to me, but alas, it's not mine to solve.

CHAPTER 5

On Thursday, I wake up at four in the morning. Lying beside Barrett, I picture my father in his prison cell, waiting for the trial that's six hours away. At five thirty comes the jangle of the bell on the front door. I hear a window open, a man's voice in the street call, "Twenty-two Goulston Street," then frantic activity downstairs. Mick must have been called to photograph a crime scene. Soon after the door slams behind him, Barrett gets up and prepares to go to work. All hope of slumber lost, I wash and dress, donning my most respectable dark gray woolen frock. My face in the mirror is pale and tense as I apply hair pomade to keep the strands from escaping my coronet of braids. My meticulous grooming is as much to give myself a mental suit of armor as to look decent in court.

Downstairs in the kitchen, Barrett fills the kettle while Fitzmorris builds up the fire in the stove. I fetch eggs, bread, and butter from the pantry.

"You needn't." Fitzmorris regards me with sympathy. We share most of the chores, but he knows today is the dreaded ordeal.

"If I don't keep busy, I'll just fret," I say.

When breakfast is ready, Fitzmorris carries a tray upstairs to Hugh. I drink coffee, but I can't eat; my stomach feels tied in knots. Barrett finishes his food, kisses me, and says, "Good luck," then goes to work. He had offered to attend the trial with me, to lend his moral support, but I refused. A murder trial where my father is the defendant is hardly my ideal venue for introducing them.

It's only seven o'clock. Sally, Mr. Owusu, and I agreed to meet at the courthouse at nine thirty to go over any last-minute issues before the trial. I busy myself cleaning up the kitchen. At eight, I'm in my coat and hat when the doorbell jangles again. I hurry downstairs, and when I open the door, the stranger outside tips his hat.

"Sir Gerald Mariner sent me to call on Lord Hugh Staunton. Are you Mrs. Barrett?"

Startled, I say, "Yes."

The man is of average height, very thin; his black tweed coat and dark trousers hang on him like clothes from a rack. Tousled, unfashionably long black hair frames a pale, narrow face with craggy cheekbones and a prominent nose. None of this adds up to classic good looks, but his smile and the intelligence in his deep-set black eyes render him attractive.

"Dr. Joshua Lewes." His voice is a clear tenor with a Welsh accent. He extends his hand for me to shake. His grip is strong and firm, but not painful. "Sir Gerald tells me that Lord Hugh is struggling to recover from an injury. He thought I might be able to help."

I'm surprised because Sir Gerald has already paid for Hugh's hospital bills as well as my father's lawyers. "Come in."

I lead Dr. Lewes upstairs. He seems the last resort, for nobody else has been able to bring Hugh out of his depression. We find Hugh sitting in bed while Fitzmorris shaves him. When I introduce Dr. Lewes and explain why he's here, Hugh gives him a wary look.

"Nice to meet you." A slight edge sharpens his apathetic tone. "But I already have plenty of doctors."

I'm disturbed to see Hugh immediately take against Joshua Lewes, but the man seems unfazed. "I'm not that sort of doctor. I'm a psychologist."

Hugh regards him with distaste. "You mean a head doctor? The kind that pries into people's thoughts and feelings?"

"I do help my patients explore their thoughts and feelings and resolve mental issues." Dr. Lewes smiles.

I like him for his pleasant manner in the face of resistance, but Hugh bends his knees and pushes himself up against the headboard, literally digging in his heels. "Mental issues? Oh, I get it—Sir Gerald thinks I'm crazy, and he sent you here to fix me." He bends an accusing gaze on me. "Sarah, what have you been telling Sir Gerald?"

This is the liveliest emotion I've seen Hugh display since before his injury. "Sir Gerald asked me when you're coming back to work. I had to tell him that you're not well enough yet."

"I'm not crazy." Hugh glares at the doctor. Smears of shaving soap on his cheeks detract from his dignity.

"One needn't be crazy to benefit from psychological treatment," Dr. Lewes says calmly. "The mind has great power, and counseling therapy can help people harness it and recover from physical ailments. We can talk about exactly what the therapy involves." He unbuttons his coat and points at the chair by Hugh's bed. "May I?"

"No. Don't make yourself comfortable. You aren't staying."

"Hugh!" I say, alarmed by his rudeness.

Fitzmorris says, "At least listen to what the doctor has to say." He's haggard from worry and the long days and nights of caring for Hugh. He loves Hugh as a younger brother and stood by him after Hugh was disowned by his family and ostracized by his friends because of his homosexuality. Of all the people in the world, Fitzmorris is the most terrified that Hugh will never be well. "Maybe he can help you."

"Psychology is nothing but new-fangled quackery," Hugh declares.

"Granted, psychology is a new science," Dr. Lewes says, "but it deals with the mind, a vast, uncharted territory that other disciplines lack the tools to probe."

Hugh recoils with an exaggerated shiver, as though the doctor had brandished an ice pick. "I'll thank you to keep your tools out of my mind."

Although I hate to coerce him, I desperately want him to accept help. "If you want to stay on Sir Gerald's payroll, you had better cooperate with Dr. Lewes."

"Sir Gerald's payroll be damned."

"Psychological treatment can also help patients regain their passion for life," Dr. Lewes says.

Hugh utters a humorless chuckle. "Passion for life as a cripple?" He pulls open his pajama top. Stitch marks crisscross the thick purple scar that runs from his shoulder at an angle down his arm. Even though the wound has healed, his muscles are wasted, his hand apparently useless. With a violent motion of his other hand, Hugh says to Dr. Lewes, "Get out!"

Fitzmorris pleads with Hugh, and I scold him, but Dr. Lewes says, "I'll go."

I follow him downstairs to the door. "I'm sorry."

"It's all right. Lord Hugh isn't the first person to have that sort of reaction to a psychologist." Dr. Lewes smiles, and the compassion in his black eyes says he understands how afraid I am for Hugh. "Sometimes it takes a while to win a patient's trust. Don't worry. As you probably know, Sir Gerald doesn't hire people who give up easily."

★   ★   ★

Train service is still shut down because of the wreck. In the streets, newsboys sell papers whose headlines explain that a broken rail had thrown the train off the track. I hurry through the morning crowds, trying to hail a cab. Every single one I see is occupied. Rain begins to fall, and I bump umbrellas with other folks as I run the two miles to Old Bailey. The massive stone courthouse is overshadowed by the even more massive bulk of Newgate Prison. Their proximity to each other allows prisoners a short walk to their trials and, if convicted and sentenced to death, a convenient last return trip to the jail, the gallows, and subsequent burial under the building.

I pray that my father never has to make that last trip.

Outside a wall topped with a high, iron fence, a long queue of people waits. I cut to the front, ignoring protests, and say to the constable at the gate, "I'm here for Benjamin Bain's trial."

"The courtroom's full. Everybody's waiting for seats to open up."

The trial has blown up into an even huger sensation than I feared. Lowering my voice so that people nearby won't hear, I say, "Benjamin Bain is my father."

As the constable waves me through the gate, someone exclaims, "That's the daughter!"

A crowd swamps me into the courtyard, beyond the semicircular brick wall that barricades the door to Old Bailey. Once inside the vast hall, reporters surround me, yelling questions. Photographers aim cameras at me, ignite flash lamps. White light explodes in my face. Half blind, I stumble into the courtroom that Mr. Owusu showed Sally and me last week, to familiarize us with it. A hubbub from the assembly greets my awkward entrance. All I see is a dark blur pocked with afterimages of the flash lamps. As my eyes adjust, the courtroom comes into clear view, a vast space with a ceiling some thirty feet high. At the front is the judge's bench—an elevated wooden throne behind a podium, overhung by a pediment and flanked by seats for court officials. Facing the bench, built against the opposite wall, and also elevated, is the dock—a wooden box with glass windows on the sides. Between the dock and the bench, perpendicular to them, are rows of long, narrow tables for the counsels. Leather-upholstered benches accommodate lawyers in white horsehair wigs. They and their clerks sit facing the jury box, which contains twelve solemn men dressed in business suits, seated in two tiers. Police constables stand around the room to keep order.

Sally calls my name, and I see her sitting in the bottom row of the stalls of the gallery that mounts the wall behind the counsels' tables. I hurry to the seat she saved for me. All the others are filled. Out of breath, I gasp air that smells of mildew, bleach, old varnish, damp wool, and the gas that hisses from the light fixtures. Sally cuts her eyes at the clock on the wall; it's five minutes to ten. She thinks my doubt about our father is why I'm late, and I've let them both down. I don't try to explain. Telling her about Dr. Lewes's unexpected visit would only justify her belief that I put something ahead of our father today of all days.

"Good morning, Mrs. Barrett." Mr. Owusu turns and speaks from the counsel table directly in front of me. He introduces me to the white-wigged, black-robed man seated beside him. "This is Sir William Hall-Clarke."

The barrister, in his late forties, has a pale, square face with a sharp jawline. His brows arch haughtily above cold blue eyes, and he looks down his long nose at me. "A pleasure to make your acquaintance, Mrs. Barrett." His voice is upper class, cultured, suave. I instinctively dislike him, but since he's on my father's side, I hope he's as good a lawyer as Sir Gerald's recommendation suggests.

The clerk at the front of the room shouts, "All rise."

Everyone stands as the judge, dignified in his long wig and black robe, walks into the courtroom. My father, escorted by a constable, enters the dock from a door at its rear. His new suit fits, and his white hair, beard, and mustache are neatly groomed; but with his head bowed as he faces the judge, he seems dressed for a funeral. Standing with his hands clasped in front of him as though they were shackled, he looks a far cry from an innocent man determined to have his day in court and clear his name. From a table below the dock, reporters equipped with notebooks and pencils watch him as if they're jackals and he's a dying deer. I behold him with love and grief so strong that they almost obliterate my doubts.

"Benjamin Bain, you are charged with the willful murder of Ellen Casey," the clerk says. "Do you plead guilty or not guilty?"

"Not guilty." Defeat suffuses my father's voice.

Mutters from the stalls indicate that the spectators don't believe him. Sally looks worried. I'm torn between pity for my father and vexation because he won't try to make a better showing.

At the table in front of Mr. Owusu and Sir William Hall-Clarke's, the prosecutor stands up. His name is George Ingleby. He's thirty years old—young for a barrister—and a rising star in the legal profession, according to the newspapers. Barristers can choose which sides of cases they want to argue for—the prosecution or the defense—and Mr. Ingleby opted to concentrate on prosecution because he wants to deliver criminals to justice, not help them escape it. He took this case because if he wins, the publicity will burnish his reputation. My father's conviction is a rung on this talented, ambitious man's ladder to success.

"Your Lordship, and Gentlemen of the Jury, the circumstances of this case are well known because of all the publicity." Mr. Ingleby's voice is strong enough to carry to the upper stalls. His accent is educated but not aristocratic; he's the son of a school headmaster. "I ask you, gentlemen, to put aside everything you have heard and every opinion you have formed and not allow it to affect your consideration of whether the defendant is guilty or innocent."

I don't see how that's possible. If the newspapers and the gossip have convinced the jurors that my father is a murderer, can anything change their minds?

Mr. Ingleby goes on to describe Ellen Casey and Benjamin Bain as if they're characters in a novel, saying that she went to my family home, my father took photographs of her, and nobody saw her afterward until her body turned up the next day. In lurid detail that elicits gasps from the spectators, he describes the strangulation bruises around Ellen's neck and the damage that the rape caused to her private regions. He paints Benjamin Bain as a monster and Ellen as innocent prey. The jury beholds my passive, dejected father with revulsion. Struggling to control my anger, I appraise Mr. Ingleby as best I can with his back toward me. He's short and plump, and the face in his newspaper photographs is moon-shaped and bland, but he exudes vigor and passion. He looks like a butterball, yet he's a ball of fire.

"I ask you to judge the evidence according to your common sense," Mr. Ingleby concludes. "If it proves that Benjamin Bain took the life of Ellen Casey, then you must find him guilty." He turns to the judge, affording me a view of his double chin and snub nose. "May it please your Lordship, I shall call my first witness."

"Proceed," Mr. Justice Archibald Webster says in a resonant voice at odds with his frail, stooped figure. He's in his sixties, and his wig frames a deeply lined face. Gold-rimmed spectacles perch on his nose. Mr. Owusu told me that he's fair but strict.

"Ordinarily, the investigating officer and the medical examiner would testify at this point," Mr. Ingleby says, "but the crime occurred twenty-four years ago, and unfortunately, those gentlemen are deceased. Therefore, I call Inspector Edmund Reid, the officer who took over the police investigation and subsequently arrested the defendant."

The very name causes my blood to boil. As the man approaches the witness box located in the corner between the jury and the bench, I tremble with anger and hatred. Inspector Reid has donned a new gray suit and had his fringe of iron-gray hair and fluffy mustache and beard trimmed for this occasion. His expression genial, he nods to judge, jury, and prosecutor.

The clerk hands him a Bible and says, "Do you swear by Almighty God to tell the truth, the whole truth, and nothing but the truth?"

"I do." Taking his seat in the box, Reid surveys the courtroom. His gaze, when it meets mine, turns cold as ice. Beneath the ice simmers a hatred that matches my own.

Reid and I have been enemies since we first clashed two years ago, during the Ripper's reign of terror. Reid believes I have secret knowledge about the murders and I'm the reason the police weren't able to catch the Ripper. He also believes I'm responsible for his ensuing troubles with his superiors. That he's right on those counts doesn't excuse his offenses against me. Reid has accused and arrested my friends and me for crimes we didn't commit; he's jeopardized Barrett's career and tried his best to destroy us all. Now he's bitter because I've come out on top in too many battles in our ongoing feud, and he's out to take revenge on me through my father.

"Inspector Reid, can you describe the events that led up to your arresting Benjamin Bain?" Mr. Ingleby sounds confident that his opening move will put him ahead in the game.

Reid's long look at me says, *"You could have prevented this trial if you'd confessed what you know about Jack the Ripper when I gave you the chance."* Reid doesn't know that my confession would have doomed my friends and me to death rather than save my father.

Turning to the jury, Reid says, "I periodically review open cases and endeavor to close them. When I read the file on Ellen Casey's murder, I discovered that Benjamin Bain was the prime suspect but had never been charged or arrested because he'd disappeared."

Jurors nod; Reid has impressed them as a conscientious policeman. I seethe with indignation because Benjamin Bain and the Ellen Casey murder came to his attention not while doing his duty to close old cases, but during an inquiry into my background.

"I mounted a search for Benjamin Bain," Reid says. "Murder

is murder, even if it happened twenty-four years ago. The victim deserves justice no matter how belated."

Hogwash! Reid went after my father to pressure me. Guilt permeates my anger. My father is in the dock because I ran afoul of Reid. Otherwise, a twenty-four-year-old murder case wouldn't have interested a police inspector who has many recent unsolved crimes on his books.

"I posted advertisements around town and in the newspapers, urging anyone with information regarding the whereabouts of Benjamin Bain to report it to the police. A man named Theodore Aldrich reported that he'd sighted Mr. Bain in Battersea. He and Mr. Bain had once been friends, and he was sure of his identification."

I didn't know how my father had been caught. I'm stunned because Theodore Aldrich is the man whom Barrett and I visited yesterday, who'd refused to serve as a character witness. My father looks mournful because his old friend turned against him.

"I asked the Battersea constables to watch for a man of Mr. Bain's description," Reid says. "They spotted him at the Gladstone Arms, a public house where he was renting a room. I hightailed it over there and nabbed him." Reid flashes a triumphant smile at me.

I glare, helpless to change the course of past events.

"And what did the defendant say when you arrested him?" Mr. Ingleby says.

"He said, 'So you've finally caught up with me.'"

Mr. Ingleby addresses the jury. "Now, gentlemen, does that sound like the reaction of an innocent man?" Jurors shake their heads. "Not at all. An innocent man would have said, 'I didn't do it. You've got the wrong person.'"

My father never told me the details of his arrest, and I have to admit that if this account is true, his words branded him as a criminal who'd tried and failed to escape justice.

"What happened next?" Mr. Ingleby asks.

"I took the defendant to the Clerkenwell Police Station jail and interrogated him."

"Did you ask him where he'd been for the past twenty-four years?"

"I did. He said he'd spent time in America. When he returned to England, he lived in various cities, including Brighton, his current place of residence."

"Was he known as Benjamin Bain during that time?"

"No. He used the names George Albert, John Clancy, and Howard Fenton, which was his most recent alias."

Mr. Ingleby asks the jury, "Do you think that an innocent man would have gone on the run for twenty-four years and hidden under different false names? I ask that you take the defendant's shady behavior into account before you render your verdict." He bows to the jury and judge, then says, "I have no further questions for this witness," and sits down.

He speaks as if he's made a giant step toward branding my father a guilty man, and I'm afraid he has. I twist my hands in my lap and pin my hopes on Sir William Hall-Clarke.

The barrister rises. He's some six inches taller than Mr. Ingleby, and his elegant confidence makes the prosecutor seem gauche. "Your Lordship and Gentlemen of the Jury, the murder of a young girl is tragically grievous, and the perpetrator deserves the severest punishment that the law allows. But the severity of the punishment requires that you be sure beyond a reasonable doubt that the defendant is indeed the perpetrator. Therefore, I ask that you consider that every story has two sides, and—"

The judge waves a hand, cutting him off. "The jury has already been given the proper instructions. Ask a question."

"Yes, Your Lordship."

My heart quails because Sir William has already earned the judge's rebuke, but he maintains his poise as he says to Reid, "The police report states that the victim went into the defendant's house and no one saw her come out. Is that accurate?"

Reid eyes Sir William as if they're facing each other across a dueling ground, pistols in hand. "Yes, sir."

"Those facts have already been presented," the judge says. "Move along, Sir William."

As I wonder if Sir William truly knows what he's doing, he says, "Did anyone see what happened inside the house while the victim was there?"

According to my father, Lucas and my mother not only witnessed the crimes but perpetrated them. If only my father would allow that story to be told!

Reid's smile barely conceals his annoyance. "Well, the defendant wouldn't have invited anyone to watch him commit murder, would he?"

"Just answer my question."

"No, sir."

"What do you mean?"

Mr. Ingleby rises. "Your Lordship, the defense is badgering the witness."

"I am fully capable of maintaining decorum in my courtroom," the judge says. "Sit down." Mr. Ingleby complies. "The witness will explain his meaning."

Reid speaks with exaggerated patience. "According to the report, nobody saw what happened."

"Thank you, Inspector Reid," Sir William says. "Would it be accurate to clarify that nobody actually witnessed Benjamin Bain violating or killing Ellen Casey?"

Reid grips the edges of the witness box, caught in the trap that Sir William set for him. "Yes, but—"

"Gentlemen of the jury, please note that there are no witnesses to vouch for the prosecution's claim that the defendant is responsible for the crimes," Sir William says. "The evidence is purely circumstantial."

I breathe easier, feeling a new respect for Sir William. I'm glad he's managed to nettle Reid and point up the weakness in the police's case. Now he says, "Inspector Reid, would it also be accurate to say that you have a history of disagreements and violent altercations with Mrs. Thomas Barrett, the defendant's daughter?"

Reid shifts in his seat. "I don't see how that's relevant."

"Is that a 'yes'?"

Mr. Ingleby starts to protest, but Sir William talks over him. "Inspector, isn't your feud with Mrs. Barrett the real reason why you took over the investigation into the Ellen Casey murder and hunted Mrs. Barrett's father down?"

Reid's jaw tightens, and he hesitates, as though reluctant to lie under oath.

"Let it be noted that the witness has a personal stake in convicting the defendant," Sir William says. "Thank you, Inspector Reid. No further questions."

"The witness is dismissed," the judge says.

Reid steps down from the witness box, his face dark with disgruntlement. I'm glad Sir William put my feud with Reid to good use, but as Reid stalks out of the courtroom, my triumph quickly fades because some jurors are watching him, shaking their heads in sympathy. When Sir William bows to the judge and takes his seat, I hear booing from gallery. I'm not sure he managed to poke a big enough hole in the prosecution's case.

Mr. Ingleby rises and calls his next witness: "Mrs. Patrick G. Logan."

I gasp as I recognize the woman who walks to the witness box. The same age as myself, she's buxom in her black coat and frock. A black hat with a little veil tops her upswept copper-colored hair. Her maiden name is Meg Casey, and she was my childhood best friend. The sight of her hurts me because I remember how close we once were. After my father disappeared and my mother and I left Clerkenwell, losing Meg was an additional blow. My mother and I moved away from Clerkenwell in 1866, and since then, I've seen Meg once—in 1889, when I went back to hunt for clues to my father's whereabouts. Our encounter was not pleasant. Now my body tenses as Meg prepares to stab me in the back.

After she's sworn in and taken her seat in the box, Mr. Ingleby asks her, "Mrs. Logan, can you tell us your relationship to Ellen Casey?"

Meg fidgets with her hands, the way she did at school when she had to recite a lesson. She speaks bravely in her faint Irish brogue: "Ellen was my older sister."

The audience behind me stirs, and I look up the gallery to a crowd of men and women nodding and smiling at Meg. They must be her relatives and friends. When I face forward, she stares at me, her expression hostile.

"Thank you, Mrs. Logan. I know it must be painful for you to relive the tragedy that has haunted your family all these years." Mr. Ingleby's voice oozes compassion. "But your testimony will help to obtain justice for your sister. Can you describe the events of the day Ellen went missing?"

"Ellen and I walked home from school. She said she was going to Mr. Bain's house." Meg glares at my father. "She said he wanted to take photographs of her."

I pray that Meg hasn't told Mr. Ingleby about the photograph she showed me the last time we met. It was the seductive photograph of Ellen, one of my reasons for my doubts about my father. Meg had discovered it among her late mother's possessions, and she still has it as, as far as I know. Her uncle, a police constable, had found it during a search of my family's house. I can imagine the effect on the jury should Mr. Ingleby produce that photograph as evidence.

"Did your parents know Ellen modeled for Mr. Bain?" Mr. Ingleby says.

"Yes. There was nothing secret about it. She did it any number of times. We didn't know what was going to happen." She wipes her eyes with her gloved hand. "We trusted Mr. Bain."

My father hangs his head lower, shamed by her tacit accusation that he'd betrayed the Casey family's trust.

"Did Ellen say she was going anywhere besides Mr. Bain's house?" Mr. Ingleby says.

"No. She said she would be home for supper. But that was the last time I saw her until her funeral." Meg turns to my father and says in a loud, trembling voice, "Ellen was a good, sweet, innocent girl. She didn't deserve to be violated and murdered by the likes of you!"

The Casey family cheers, whistles, and claps, and I see jurors nod as if they approve. My father cringes. The judge bangs his gavel and shouts, "Order!"

The hubbub quiets. Mr. Ingleby says to Sir William, "Your witness."

I exhale with relief. Meg told me that her family never showed the photograph to anyone else because they thought it would ruin

Ellen's posthumous reputation. She must be keeping it under wraps now for the same reason.

Sir William rises and speaks with gentle, apparently sincere compassion. "Mrs. Logan, please let me offer you my condolences for the loss of your sister."

"Thank you, sir." Her voice hoarse, Meg blinks away tears.

"I assure you that I want nothing more than the truth about what happened to Ellen, and anything you can tell me will be greatly appreciated."

"Yes, sir."

"Now, you testified that Ellen was a good girl."

"Yes, sir." Meg smiles as if he agrees with her opinion of her sister.

"But she modeled for a photographer, a man who was decades older than she, in his house," Sir William says in the same gentle manner. "Was that the behavior of a good girl?"

Disconcerted by the turn the conversation has taken, Meg frowns. "Why, I—"

"What happened during Ellen's previous photographic sessions with Benjamin Bain?"

"Nothing improper, I'm sure," Meg hastens to say.

"How can you be sure, Mrs. Logan?" Sir William's manner turns belligerent. "Were you there?"

"No, but—"

"So, Ellen could have flirted with Mr. Bain. She could have led him on, undressed in front of him, and enticed him with her feminine charms while you were none the wiser."

Meg exclaims in horror. "No!" I can't help feeling sorry for her. Although we're on opposite sides, a vestige of my childhood affection for her persists. Angry mutters erupt from her family.

"Maybe she wasn't such a good girl. Maybe she seduced Mr. Bain against his will. And you know, Mrs. Logan, that bad girls sometimes get what's coming to them."

I'm aghast. Sir William is implying that Ellen not only behaved improperly with my father, but she deserved to be killed! Sally covers her mouth with her hand while my father raises his head to stare in disbelief. The Casey family boos, hisses, and shouts at Sir William.

"How dare you insult our Ellen?"

"She was an angel. She didn't deserve to die!"

The judge pounds his gavel. "Order!"

The air fills with objects hurled by the Casey family. Sir William and the other lawyers duck under a barrage of rocks and crumpled newspapers. Meg looks both alarmed at her family's misbehavior and glad they're defending Ellen's honor. Policemen rush toward the gallery.

I grab Sally's hand, more afraid for her safety than mine. Even though I hate to desert our father, I say, "We have to get out of here."

Rooted to her seat, Sally swivels her head, watching the melee. A stone hits a window of the dock, breaking the glass. My father throws up his arms to shield his face from the flying shards. I stand up and shout at the Caseys, "Leave him alone!"

A rock hits my chest. At the moment, I don't care that their loved one has been murdered and they believe my father is responsible. These people are savages! Now they stampede down to the dock where my father cringes, a helpless target. While the constable with him makes no move to protect him, I hurry to his rescue. Crushed by the mob of Casey relatives and friends, I grab the legs of a man who's climbing into the dock.

"Stop!" I try to pull him down.

He kicks at me. The gavel hammers futilely as the judge shouts, "Court is adjourned until ten o'clock tomorrow." Mr. Owusu pulls me away from the mob, out the courtroom door. Breathless and agitated, I find myself in the hall with him, Sally, and Sir William.

"Are you all right?" Mr. Owusu asks me, his face grave with concern.

"No." I turn on Sir William. "It was wrong of you to smear Ellen Casey. And look what you've done!" I fling my hand toward the courtroom door. Officials, lawyers, and reporters run out while constables struggle to quell the riot inside.

"Sarah, calm down," Sally pleads.

I ignore her and demand of Sir William, "What are you trying to do?"

Undisturbed by the trouble he created, he favors me with his cold blue stare. "I am trying to win an acquittal by reducing the jury's sympathy for the victim. Your father didn't leave me much choice." He pivots on his heel and strides away.

I ask Mr. Owusu, "Did you know he was going to do it?" He nods, his expression somber. "And you didn't warn us!"

"I anticipated that you would disapprove. But it is a useful strategy. Make the victim seem unworthy of justice, and the jury will not be so eager to convict the defendant."

I'm startled to realize that the nice Mr. Owusu is of the same breed as Sir William—an ambitious, ruthless lawyer who wants to win, exactly the kind that Sir Gerald Mariner would hire. "Smearing Ellen could turn the jury harder against my father."

"Mr. Owusu and Sir William are doing the best they can," Sally says, ever the peacemaker despite her own obvious distress.

"Sarah!" Barrett, in police uniform, comes hurrying across the hall toward us.

I hadn't expected him, and alarm flashes through me. "What is it?" I think of Hugh and Mick; something must have happened to one or both.

"We've been summoned to Scotland Yard."

"What?" A summons to the headquarters of the City of London Police is the last thing I expected. "Why?"

"I don't know. But we have to go right now."

CHAPTER 6

"Who summoned us to Scotland Yard?" I ask Barrett.

"The police commissioner. Sir Edward Bradford. His office sent a telegram to the Whitechapel station. That's all I know."

We're aboard a Thames River Police launch that the commissioner sent for us. The meeting must be important. Barrett and I stand on the open deck, huddling under umbrellas in the cold, windswept rain while the miniature steamship chugs up the Thames. Fog drifts over the dirty gray water, veiling docks, jetties, and warehouses along the banks. Shouts ring out and horns blare as crews on barges try to avoid collisions. My mind drifts back to the moment at Old Bailey when Sally realized I was going off to attend to my own business and leaving her alone after the disastrous first day in court. She looked hurt and forlorn. I would rather she'd been angry.

I force my thoughts back to the present. A summons from the commissioner is unprecedented, ominous. "Do you think it's about the Ripper?" I say, lowering my voice so the policemen operating the launch won't hear.

"That was my first thought," Barrett says. The Waterloo Bridge casts a murky shadow over us as the launch passes beneath it. "But Commissioner Bradford can't possibly know. You and I haven't told anyone, and it's been almost two years. If someone were onto us, they would have taken action before now." Barrett sounds as if he wants to reassure himself as well as me.

"You're right." Still, maybe my father isn't the only one in danger of taking that short walk to the gallows at Newgate after receiving a death sentence at Old Bailey.

We pass Cleopatra's needle, the tall stone obelisk carved with hieroglyphics. Soon the launch pulls up to Westminster Pier, and we climb the steps to the Victoria Embankment. The trees along the waterfront promenade are devoid of leaves, the embankment almost deserted. We hurry through the rain toward Scotland Yard, a pair of adjacent new buildings that overlook the river. Their architecture boasts horizontal bands of red brick and white stone, and turrets with conical roofs. Big Ben, invisible in the fog, tolls twelve o'clock as Barrett and I approach the door of one building.

"Have you ever met Commissioner Bradford?" I ask.

"Once. When he was appointed this past summer, he visited each police station and spoke to all the men. He asked us what the problems were and what should be changed so that we can do our jobs better, and he took our answers seriously. He rotated the patrol beats so that the constables don't get bored on duty, and he put telegraph machines in all the stations. He's a right sort of man. By the way, I should tell you, he has only one arm."

"Thank you for the warning." Now I won't be taken by surprise and stare rudely.

"He served in the army in India. He lost his left arm when he was mauled by a tiger during a hunt."

"My goodness." Despite my apprehension, I'm interested to meet the man.

Inside the building, a constable leads us to an office on the top floor. There, behind the desk, a tall, dignified man with white hair and mustache stands up, the sleeve of his gray suit coat pinned to its side. Barrett and I stop in our tracks at the sight of the other man, who rises from a chair in front of the desk.

"Hello, Mr. and Mrs. Barrett." Sir Gerald Mariner, my employer, speaks with the Liverpool accent of his youth. He's robust, although in his sixties, his hair and beard streaked with gray but still mostly dark brown. The double-breasted waistcoat of his dark suit emphasizes his stout person, which radiates power and confidence. I know he's on friendly terms with people in high places, but Barrett and I didn't expect him to be here.

The commissioner greets us, introducing himself to me as "Edward Bradford." His voice is brusque, his manner without the airs that often accompany a title. His skin is leathery from exposure to the sun, and his hand, when he shakes mine, is warm, hard, and calloused. As he sizes me up, the twinkle in his eyes suggests kindliness as well as shrewd intelligence. I'm relieved because this meeting can't be about the Ripper; if it were, the commissioner wouldn't be this friendly.

"Good to see you again, Detective," he says as he shakes Barrett's hand. "Excellent work on the Charles Firth murder."

"Thank you, sir." Barrett is trying his best to keep his East End origins out of his accent, his habit when he feels uncertain.

Commissioner Bradford motions us to two chairs opposite Sir Gerald's. When we're all seated, I notice framed photographs and certificates on the walls. One photograph shows the commissioner in military uniform posing with turbaned Indian officials.

"What you hear in this room today is top secret," the commissioner says to Barrett and me. "You will disclose it to no one. Is that understood?"

"Yes, sir," we say, both of us mystified. Sir Gerald waits in silence, at ease. Presumably, he knows what's going on and has already been sworn to secrecy.

"This is about the murdered woman on the train," Commissioner Bradford says.

Barrett and I exchange surprised glances. Barrett says cautiously, "May I ask why the case is suddenly top secret?"

Sir Gerald explains. "I saw the photographs Mrs. Barrett sent to the *Daily World* last night." Whenever he's at the newspaper office—and he's there often, at all hours—he reviews the next issue before it goes to press. Now he opens a folder on the commissioner's desk, revealing the five circular Kodak prints, and taps the photograph of the slender, mustached young man. "That's Prince Albert Victor—the Queen's grandson, known as Prince Eddy."

"I see," Barrett says as he and I begin to understand the reason for this meeting.

It's an astonishing development—the first time for us that a member of the royal family has cropped up during an investigation. The case is more sensitive than we ever dreamed.

"I recognized Prince Eddy," Sir Gerald says. "Met him once at a banquet at the palace."

"I thought he looked familiar," Barrett says. "I must have seen his picture somewhere."

"Lucky thing I pulled your story before the paper went out," Sir Gerald says to me. "This involves the Crown. I couldn't throw it wide open to a scandal."

Ordinarily, an important person connected to a murder would be a sensation that Sir Gerald would capitalize on, to sell more papers and earn extra profit, but I understand that he prizes his relationship with the Crown. Not only does the success of his business empire depend in part on the Crown's favor, but the man who started his career as a cabin boy on a merchant ship must view the relationship as proof that he's risen to the highest echelon of society possible.

"To have a member of the royal family associated with a murder could damage the Crown's reputation at home and abroad." Commissioner Bradford fixes his shrewd gaze on Barrett and me. "Now do you understand the need for secrecy?"

We nod in agreement.

"Normally, the Home Office would handle this sort of case," the commissioner says. "But I need as few people as possible to know about Prince Eddy's connection to the murder. So, Detective Sergeant Barrett, I'm assigning the investigation to you."

Barrett sits straighter, proud to be thought worthy of such an important assignment. "I'll do my best, sir."

"Give this paperwork to your superior. It says you're on special leave from your regular duties." The commissioner hands Barrett an envelope, then says, "I understand that your wife is something of a detective." He probably learned that from Sir Gerald. "She can assist you."

I'm excited by the prospect of a challenging new case, glad of an opportunity to fulfill my promise to Katherine Oliver and bring her killer to justice, but my father's trial resumes tomorrow.

How will I have time to investigate the murder? But Barrett's police career may very well be riding on the outcome of the investigation, and this doesn't seem an assignment that I could refuse even if I wanted to.

"I would be honored to assist with the investigation," I say.

"Good," Commissioner Bradford says, and Sir Gerald nods in approval.

"There's a problem I should mention," Barrett says. "My wife and I aren't the only people who know about the murder."

"I'm aware that the constables at the scene viewed the body and removed it, and it's at the morgue for the postmortem examination," Commissioner Bradford says. "I'll issue orders that the case is top secret."

"My night editor at the *Daily World* is discreet," Sir Gerald says. "He won't talk, and I'll keep the story out of the paper."

"Mick O'Reilly and Lord Hugh Staunton know," I say.

"Ah, your partners in crime photography and investigation," the commissioner says. "They can help you with the case if need be."

Mick will jump at the chance; I wish Hugh would. Barrett glances at me, as if to say, *"Aren't you forgetting someone?"* I keep quiet about Anjali, wanting to shield the girl from business in which she should have no part. I'll swear her to secrecy and tell Mick not to let her anywhere near the investigation.

Sir Gerald stands. "If we're finished, I'll be getting back to work."

When he's gone, the commissioner says to Barrett and me, "You're to pursue this case on the quiet. Don't let anyone know you're investigating it, and don't attempt to apprehend the killer. When you identify him, tell me who he is, and I'll take it from there." In view of what we've heard already, these marching orders seem logical if not conventional. "Above all, do not approach Prince Eddy or let him know that he's under investigation."

"Yes, sir," Barrett says.

His tone is neutral, but I sense that he's as perturbed as I am. The commissioner is ordering us to stay away from a potential suspect, which could hinder our investigation. Furthermore, it occurs to me that the commissioner has taken the case into his own hands, without the knowledge or permission of the government and the Crown. Should something go wrong, where would that leave Barrett and me?

"I want daily briefings on your progress." Commissioner Bradford motions us toward the door. "It would be best if Prince Eddy is never implicated in the murder. Good luck, and report to me tomorrow night at six o'clock."

CHAPTER 7

"Was the commissioner instructing us to pin the murder on someone other than Prince Eddy?" I ask Barrett.

"Of course not. He was just commenting that it would be better if Prince Eddy isn't guilty." But Barrett sounds uncertain that the "right sort of man" wouldn't have an innocent person take the blame in order to avoid a scandal involving the royal family.

We're riding home in a cab; Barrett's police uniform enabled him to commandeer one of the scarce vehicles. "What if we discover that Prince Eddy is guilty?"

"We tell Commissioner Bradford. Then it's out of our hands."

"Do you think he'll let the murderer go free if it's Prince Eddy?"

Barrett's troubled expression is my answer. We stare out the window at the fog, as if trying to see the future. Is there a fork in our path, with one branch leading to the truth about the murder and justice for Katherine Oliver, and another, sanctioned by Commissioner Bradford, leading who knows where?

"We're getting ahead of ourselves," Barrett says. "We haven't determined that Prince Eddy is even a suspect."

"You're right." In an effort to put aside disturbing possibilities for now, I say, "Remember the studio portrait in Katherine Oliver's hotel room? I've a hunch that the woman in the photo is related to the case she was working on and to her murder."

"I'll send telegrams to New York," Barrett says. "I'll ask the police to go to the photography studio. Maybe someone there can identify her from a description. And I'll ask Pinkerton's about the case that Katherine was working on."

I can't help voicing another concern. "I think something's going on that Commissioner Bradford didn't tell us about."

So do I." Barrett's rueful look says he hoped he'd only imagined that the commissioner is withholding important facts.

I hesitate to put my other fear into words and make it more real. "I wonder whether we've been set up to take the blame if the case goes wrong."

"That did cross my mind. But the police force is like that—the troops on the battlefield take the fall for the generals in the fort. I would be surprised if this were different."

I recall the times when I've put my career and my life at risk for the sake of an investigation while Sir Gerald's wealth and power shielded him from bad consequences.

"At any rate, the job's ours," Barrett says, and we smile at each other, our relish for a juicy case undampened by the dubious circumstances. "I've been meaning to ask, what happened in court?"

After I tell him, Barrett says, "God, I'm sorry. I hope tomorrow goes better."

"The only good thing to come of it is, I have the rest of the day free. We can start investigating the case together."

"Let's go to Cremorne Gardens," Barrett says.

★ ★ ★

First, we head back to Whitechapel so that Barrett can send the telegrams from the police station. Then we stop at home, where we eat a quick lunch and Barrett changes his uniform for civilian clothes, the better to conduct a covert investigation. After a trip to Chelsea via omnibus, cab, and foot, it's two o'clock in the afternoon when we arrive at Cremorne Gardens.

The main entrance is located on King's Road, across from tenements that were built since my last visit. The fog cloaks grounds enclosed by an iron fence that's rusted through its white paint. I smell the fetid river nearby and pine-scented fumes from the turpentine factory on the opposite bank. The open twin doors of the gate feature decorative curlicues, vines, and flowers, its pillars crowned with ornate, unlit gas lamps.

"This is the same gate as in the Kodak photograph of the woman," I say.

Just inside the gates, three fashionably attired women stand at a pay box by a blue sign that bears words written in fancy gold letters:

CREMORNE GARDENS THEATER, MUSEUM,
AND OTHER ENTERTAINMENTS
OPEN 10:00 AM–6:00 PM
ADMISSION 3 SHILLINGS

The price has gone up, and I wonder what "Other Entertainments" consist of. The pay box is a little booth with a star-shaped lamp on top. The women, digging coins from their pocketbooks, step aside for Barrett and me. In the box sits a youth in a top hat, reading a newspaper. He smiles, showing crooked teeth framed by a sparse goatee, and says, "Welcome to Cremorne Gardens."

He extends his left hand. It's made of carved, unpainted wood. Barrett hesitates before he drops coins into the stiff wooden palm, and I think of Commissioner Bradford. Seeing two people missing body parts on the same day isn't rare in London; but for me, two connected with the same investigation is.

The youth takes a second look at me, holds up the paper, and points at a photograph. "Hey, ain't this you?"

There is my photograph, taken outside Newgate during a visit to my father. My face is clearly, unfortunately visible, and I'm wearing the same hat, coat, and hairstyle as now.

"You're Mrs. Sarah Barrett, the daughter of Benjamin Bain, the murderer!" the youth says. The women whisper and giggle behind their hands. "Everybody'll be amazed when I tell 'em we got a famous person here!" His sharp eyes light on Barrett. "And you must be her husband, the copper."

Barrett and I exchange rueful glances. On the first day of our top-secret investigation, our cloak of anonymity is torn. So much for covertly exploring Cremorne Gardens in search of suspects and clues, but I can use my notoriety to advantage.

"I'm a reporter for the *Daily World*," I say, pulling a notepad and pencil from my satchel. "I'm here to do a feature story about Cremorne Gardens."

"Blimey! Can you put me in the paper? I'm Rodney Smith."

"I certainly will." I jot down the name for the article I'll never write. "Is there someone who can show me around?"

"Go to the Little Theater and ask for Mr. Clarence Flynn. He's the manager."

Barrett and I start down the lane into the gardens, skirting a circular flowerbed of dead stalks overgrown with weeds. On either side of the lane, trees spread bare branches above leaf-strewn lawns where merrymakers once picnicked. We pass under two eroded stone arches and emerge into an open area. To our right, vines cover the ruins of buildings. To our left and ahead of us, more flowerbeds surround two circular fountains in which statues coated with moss rise from murky, stagnant water.

"When I was a child, this seemed the most beautiful place in the city." I grieve for those lost days and my father in prison. I point at a distant building. "There's the Little Theater."

The women we saw at the pay box follow us along cracked pavement toward the building where my father and I had watched a marionette show. The building's white walls are discolored with moss and soot. Across the front rise tall arches supported by thin, square columns and topped by an elaborate frieze. From the arches hang long gas lanterns. Above the frieze, statues missing their heads decorate the parapet. We mount the wide steps to the main floor entrance. When Barrett opens the door, applause resounds from beyond a lobby furnished with threadbare carpet and tarnished mirrors. A young man in evening dress greets us. I introduce us as Mrs. Barrett, reporter from the *Daily World*, and my husband, then ask to speak with Mr. Clarence Flynn.

"You'll have to wait until after the show."

We and the women enter the auditorium. The seats on the main level, enough for about three hundred people, are mostly filled. Gas lights around the stage illuminate an actor kneeling before a painted backdrop of a medieval castle. Barrett and I take seats in the last row. The actor, dark-haired and costumed

in a black tunic, gestures while his deep, resonant voice fills the
theater.

What do I fear? Myself? There's none else by.
Richard loves Richard; that is, I and I.

I recognize the lines from a class trip to the theater during my
school days. "Shakespeare's *Richard the Third*," I whisper to Barrett.
I was fascinated by the story of the villain who murders his broth-
ers, nephews, and wife, among others, in his scheme to become
King of England. This is the scene where his victims' ghosts haunt
Richard on the eve of the battle in which he dies.

"*Is there a murderer here?*" the actor intones. "*No. Yes, I am.*"

Then fly! What, from myself? Great reason why:
Lest I revenge. What, myself upon myself?
Alack, I love myself. Wherefore? For any good
That I myself have done unto myself?

"Can we take that as a confession?" Barrett whispers.

If only identifying Katherine Oliver's killer were so easy. Now
the actor staggers to his feet, and I clearly see the proportions of his
figure—his head and torso too large for his unusually short arms
and legs.

He is a dwarf.

He's eschewed the crutches and humpback that others use to
portray Richard; he's letting his own body serve the purpose. I
think him better than the other actor I saw. He averts his face,
clenches his small hands, and speaks in the deep voice that belies
his stature.

O, no! Alas, I rather hate myself
For hateful deeds committed by myself.

He raises his face, and the stage lights reveal familiar bold eyes
and strong, handsome features. I nudge Barrett. "He's the other
man in the Kodak photographs!"

The actor bows, the audience applauds enthusiastically, and the curtain closes, but the show isn't over; the other spectators remain seated, murmuring in eager anticipation. Soon the curtain opens on a backdrop that depicts a medieval banquet hall, a table spread with a feast. The same actor strides onto the stage, this time in a multicolored slashed doublet and purple hose. He smiles and says, "May I have a volunteer from the audience?"

The room erupts with squeals and giggles. Now I notice that the audience is comprised mostly of women, who all wave their hands and beg, "Pick me!"

To my surprise, the actor must be something of an idol, and these women are his fans. He points his finger at them, moving it left and right, building suspense. They plead louder and louder until his hand stops, and he says, "My lady," and beckons.

A stout, matronly older woman bustles toward him, cheered on by her friends. He lends her a hand as she climbs the steps to the stage, and she giggles with delight. He escorts her to center stage and stands on a box so that they're face to face. Taking her hand, he presses their palms together.

> If I profane with my unworthiest hand
> This holy shrine, the gentle sin is this:
> My lips, two blushing pilgrims, ready stand
> To smooth that rough touch with a tender kiss.

It's a scene from *Romeo and Juliet*, which I read in school but have never seen performed, and the actor is now the young, impetuous lover. The woman is so excited that she sputters the lines she apparently memorized for this occasion.

> Saints have hands that pilgrims' hands do touch,
> And palm to palm is holy palmers' kiss.

Gazing soulfully into her eyes, the actor says, "*O, then, dear saint, let lips do what hands do.*" He leans forward and gently, briefly, touches his mouth to hers.

The woman closes her eyes and moans. The audience sighs, I think with envy. Barrett and I gawp at each other, shocked by the audacity of the show. It seems one in a series that permits women to get up on stage in front of an audience and kiss a man they aren't married to, with whom they have no respectable acquaintance.

The actor raises his voice over the clamor: *"Thus from my lips, by yours, my sin is purged."*

"Then have my lips the sin that they have took!" the woman cries.

"Sin from thy lips? O trespass sweetly urged! Give me my sin again." He kisses her harder, longer, with a passion that seems imbued with genuine, lustful ardor.

Her knees buckle, and he puts his arm around her waist to prevent her falling. *Her* passion is obviously genuine, and I'm affected despite my knowledge that the show is a paid entertainment. I recall a time when I longed for a kiss from the man who's now the husband seated beside me. I'd have paid three shillings and taken it in public had there been no other option.

Stagehands rush over and help the swooning woman back to her seat. The actor jumps down from his box, smiles, and bows to a storm of applause and cheers. Women from the audience charge onto the stage, surrounding him, crying, "Mr. Flynn, can I have your autograph?"

Barrett and I exchange a glance, surprised anew that the actor is not only the man in the Kodak photograph but also the manager of Cremorne Gardens. We follow the crowd as Clarence Flynn signs autograph albums. The women, who look to be respectably middle class, range in age from twenties to fifties. Many are wearing wedding rings. Blushing and giggling, they fawn over Mr. Flynn. I wonder if their husbands know where they are, or if the authorities know about the shows, which I think must be illegal. Mr. Flynn has friendly words and a moment of undivided attention for each woman. His natural voice is still deep but more cheerful, with a slight accent I can't place.

"Katherine Oliver must have come to his show and taken his picture with her Kodak camera," Barrett says.

After the women finally depart, Flynn turns his attention on me. "Hello. I don't think I've seen you before." His dark hair has auburn lights; his eyes are a brilliant blue; and his mouth is rosy, shapely, and sensuous. This is an instance where the photograph didn't do justice to the man. "Is this your first time here?" After I reply that it is, he offers me his hand to shake. "Clarence Flynn. A pleasure to meet you, Miss . . .?"

"Sarah Barrett." Although he has to look up to me— he's little more than four feet tall, his head below my shoulders—I have the strange feeling that we're the same height. It's as if he's magically elongated himself to my size or reduced me to his. "Mrs.," I add.

Clarence Flynn smiles into my eyes and holds my hand in his small, warm, strong one for a moment. He smells of shaving lotion and his body's fresh masculine scent. My heart unexpectedly beats faster. It's not that I've never noticed other men since I fell in love with Barrett, but I've never felt the tug of physical attraction to anyone else until now. My cheeks warm as I begin to understand why so many women vie for a chance to kiss Clarence Flynn.

Barrett clears his throat. "I'm her husband."

The actor releases my hand and shakes Barrett's. "You're a lucky man." His smile blends sly mischief and wistful envy.

Although I've seen how talented at stagecraft he is, I can't help feeling flattered. Mr. Flynn gestures toward the notebook in my hand. "Would you like an autograph?"

"Yes, please." While he signs his name with a flourish, I'm embarrassed to place myself among his adoring fans. I tell him I'm a reporter from the *Daily World*. "May I interview you?"

"That would be wonderful!" If the idea of a reporter snooping around Cremorne Gardens disturbs Flynn, he doesn't let on. "We could use the publicity. Ask me whatever you like."

Barrett stands aside to let me carry on our ruse. We both want to know where Flynn was at the time of the train wreck, but because of the top-secret nature of our investigation, I can't ask him outright; nor can I ask him whether he knew Katherine Oliver.

"How did you become an actor?" I say.

"I was born to it," Flynn declares, then chuckles at his own grandiosity. "When I was a boy in Dorset, a traveling theater company set up a tent in the village square. That was where I saw my first play—*Macbeth*. I was so taken with it that when the company left, I ran away from home and followed them. I earned my keep by doing all sorts of work—stagehand, ticket seller, garbage collector, errand boy. They let me be an extra in their plays. I'll never forget my first time onstage, with the audience clapping and cheering."

The Little Theater in a deteriorated pleasure park seems a far cry from the brilliant career he must have dreamed of. "What brought you to Cremorne Gardens?"

"No legitimate theater was going to hire me for the roles I wanted. The dwarf is always the clown." Flynn speaks with a lack of self-pity that I can respect. "So, I joined Rosenfeld's Circus." That German circus is famous enough that I recognize the name. "It was glorious traveling around, performing in front of thousands of people, and it paid well. But it was all simple comedy skits between the main shows. My love is Shakespeare. I had friends at Rosenfeld's, and we wanted to be our own bosses. We came to England, scouted around, and happened onto Cremorne Gardens. We took it over, and"—Flynn spreads his arms and smiles proudly—"here we are."

I admire him for striking out on his own. I too had wanted to run my own establishment and pursue my artistic interests instead of working at a big photography studio.

"The place doesn't look like much," Flynn says, "but we're fixing it up gradually."

I remember my pride in my first humble studio. "Where do you live?" I want to know where else besides Cremorne Gardens I can find Flynn if necessary.

"My friends and I have rooms in the Cremorne House Hotel, on the premises."

As Barrett checks his pocket watch, I say to Flynn, "My readers would be interested to know about a typical day in your life as an actor and manager at Cremorne Gardens. Can you describe what you did yesterday, for example?"

"Certainly. I got up at six o'clock as usual and did my daily inspection, making sure everything was ready for opening. I had breakfast with my partners, and we discussed the day's schedule and the work that needed to be done and the new attractions we're planning. After we opened at ten, I roamed around, greeting customers, checking on exhibits, and supervising the staff. Then lunch. I don't do shows on Wednesdays, so I spent the rest of the day in my office, going over the account books."

I glance at Barrett, who nods to tell me that we've gotten as much information about Flynn's movements as we're likely to get without arousing suspicion. I ask Flynn, "Could I trouble you for introductions to your partners and staff? And a tour of Cremorne Gardens?"

"It would be my pleasure," Flynn says, "but it's near closing time, and you really should see the place and meet everyone when we're in full swing. Can you come back tomorrow?"

"Yes." But I don't know how it will be possible to squeeze in another trip to Cremorne Gardens, for I have to attend my father's trial, and I can't be in two places at once.

"Until tomorrow, then, Mrs. Barrett." Flynn clasps my hand and smiles into my eyes, as if we've arranged a tryst. My heart flutters.

CHAPTER 8

"Mr. Flynn doesn't want us hanging about after hours," Barrett says as we walk through the misty grounds toward the gate.

"I didn't get that impression," I say.

"He doesn't have an alibi for the murder. He could have slipped away from his account books without anyone noticing, hopped on the train, and strangled Katherine Oliver."

"What would be his reason?" When Barrett can't answer, I say, "If he was on the train, there should be witnesses. Did anyone you questioned yesterday say they'd seen a dwarf?"

"No, but then I didn't know to ask them." Barrett pauses. "You like him."

My cheeks flush. "No, I don't."

"Then why are you making excuses for him?"

"I'm not!" But I realize that I do like Clarence Flynn and don't want him to be the killer.

Barrett glances sideways at me. "It's bad to get fond of a suspect."

"He isn't a suspect yet."

"Yet."

Comprehension gives me a tingle of satisfaction. "I think you're jealous."

"I am not jealous. I just don't like to see my wife behaving like those silly women who made fools of themselves over that second-rate actor."

I think Flynn is far better than second-rate, but because I don't want to be caught defending him, I say, "Well, let's talk about Jane

Lambert. She's making a fool of herself over you. Why don't you call her silly? And how dare you question my faithfulness? *I'm* not the one with a former fiancée hovering around."

"Sarah." Barrett's tone warns me that we shouldn't have a marital tiff here and now. His gaze moves past me, and he points. "Look!"

I look even though I think he's just trying to distract me. Then I see the man standing by the fountain, holding a small box at waist level, gazing down at it. "That's a Kodak camera!"

"Two Kodaks associated with Cremorne Gardens can't be a coincidence," Barrett says.

The man takes a photograph and turns the key to wind the film. Tall and lanky, dressed in a tan mackintosh and brown derby, he carries an umbrella hooked over one arm and the strap of the Kodak's case over his shoulder. He has sharp features and straight hair the color of wet hay. He aims the camera again.

"I'm going to talk to him." Barrett starts toward the man.

I look in the direction the man is aiming the camera. Some twenty yards from us, a woman walks past a building I remember as the bowling saloon. I recognize her fur hat and her tent-like cape, which I'd thought was black but is actually dark purple. "That's the woman from the photograph!"

The man puts the Kodak into its case and strides toward the gate. The woman fades into the mist. I tell Barrett, "I'll follow her. You follow him." Before he can object to leaving me on my own, I hurry after the woman.

She walks quickly beneath iron arches mounted on pairs of trees that border an avenue, toward the far end of Cremorne Gardens. It's the avenue in the photograph. Her footsteps click on cracked pavement while I trail her at a distance. The lamps suspended from the arches are unlit, some of their glass shades broken. She's shorter than she looked in the photographs, where her slimness and straight posture made her seem tall. I hear boat horns and smell sewage as we near the river. To my right, above the treetops, I see the striped towers of the fireworks temple. The woman leads me into an open space around the bandstand, which resembles a cylindrical, two-tiered pagoda, its roofs striped blue and yellow.

There's no orchestra or dancers today, just a few visitors walking toward the exit. On the right stands the main theater, a grand neoclassical palace with Corinthian columns. The woman hurries past the large fountain outside the theater, to a lower, plainer, and dilapidated building whose weathered sign reads "Cremorne House Hotel."

The hotel forms one half of an "L" around the bandstand and dance pavilion. The other half is the adjoining supper rooms. The woman stops at the front door, and keys jingle as she unlocks it. She vanishes inside the hotel.

I run to catch up with her. I try the door; it's locked. Rapping on it, I call, "Hello?"

Nobody answers. But I've learned that she's not a mere visitor to Cremorne; she must live in the hotel with Clarence Flynn. If I come back, I can find her again. I head back down the avenue in search of Barrett. He's not where I left him. Reaching the pay box, I ask the youth inside, "Have you seen my husband?"

He points to the right down King's Road. I hurry out the gate, then past storefronts whose lighted windows glow through the mist. Carriages racket along the street, splashing water; an omnibus disgorges passengers. I don't see Barrett anywhere in the hurrying crowds. I forge ahead, peering down the darker, less populated side streets. From an alley between a public house and a tenement, I hear Barrett yell. There I see the figures of two men fighting, and their umbrellas and the Kodak camera fallen on the cobblestones.

I hurry to the men as they trade punches, and I hit Barrett's opponent with my umbrella, shouting, "Stop!" I hit him until I have him backed against the wall of the tenement.

"What the hell?" His accent is American.

"Why did you attack me?" Barrett demands.

"Why were you following me?" the man retorts.

"I wanted to talk to you."

"Then why didn't you say something instead of tailing me for eight blocks?"

"I wanted to see where you went," Barrett says.

The man regards Barrett with scorn. "*I* say you're a thief, and not a very clever one. Is she your partner in crime?"

Barrett takes his badge from his pocket and holds it up. "Detective Sergeant Thomas Barrett, Metropolitan Police. She's my wife. You can answer some questions, or I'm putting you under arrest."

"You're a cop?" Incredulity shows on the man's sharp features. Then he chuckles. "You could use a lesson in surveillance from a professional." He reaches in his pocket and pulls out a silver badge identical to the one we found in Katherine Oliver's hotel room. "Timothy Parnell, Pinkerton's National Detective Agency."

Barrett grins as a bit of the mystery clears up. "Maybe I needn't wait for a reply to my telegram. Mr. Parnell, are you acquainted with a Miss Katherine Oliver?"

Parnell's mouth drops. "How do you—why do you want to know?"

"I'll take that for 'yes,'" Barrett says. "What are you doing in London?"

Parnell narrows his eyes, as if considering how much information to divulge. "I'm chief of Pinkerton's branch office here. What's this about?"

"I'll make you a deal, Mr. Parnell. If you explain what Katherine Oliver was doing in London and why you were at Cremorne Gardens, I'll explain my interest in her and you."

Since Barrett can't tell of our investigation, I'm curious to see what he'll offer as his part of the bargain.

"I take it that your business is secret," Mr. Parnell says. "Otherwise, you wouldn't be lurking around in plain clothes. My business is secret too. If you and your wife agree to keep my information confidential, I'll do the same for yours, and we've got a deal."

The two cautiously shake hands, each as if the other might have a scorpion hidden in his palm. Barrett says, "I'll buy you a drink."

They retrieve their fallen possessions, and we go in the pub. When we're seated at a table, with pints of ale in hand, Mr. Parnell says, "Kate is here on a case. The client is a Mrs. Eugenie Chaffin, widow of a billionaire banker. Her only child, a daughter named Pauline, inherited a fortune. Ma wants Pauline to marry into the British aristocracy, so she sent Pauline to London."

I comprehend that Pauline Chaffin is a "dollar princess," a rich American girl who uses her fortune to buy the one thing she doesn't have—a title. Many British noblemen who've fallen on hard times are glad to marry American heiresses and live off their dowries.

"Trouble is," Mr. Parnell says, "Pauline's a little wild. She gets drunk at debutante parties and slums with gangsters. As soon as her ship docked in England, she gave her chaperone the slip and disappeared. Kate was sent to find her." He removes a photograph from his pocket. "This is Pauline."

The young blonde girl in the frothy white dress and starburst pendant is instantly recognizable. The photograph is a print from the same negative with the flecks on her cheek. I say to Barrett, "That's the same photograph we saw."

Mr. Parnell jumps on my words. "Saw it where?"

"In Kate's hotel room," Barrett says. We're beginning to think of her by her nickname.

"It's your turn to talk," Mr. Parnell says. "What were you doing in Kate's hotel room?"

Barrett voices the fact that's become evident to him and me. "You aren't aware of what happened to Kate, are you?"

"Happened? What do you mean?"

"You may have heard about the train wreck near St. Paul's station yesterday. Kate was a passenger on that train."

Shock blanches Parnell's face. "Are you telling me she's dead?"

Barrett's manner turns gentler, sympathetic. "Yes. I'm sorry. But it wasn't the wreck that killed her. She was strangled."

Parnell wipes his mouth with his hand. "Oh God." He sounds dismayed, but not grief-stricken; I think he respected Kate, but their relationship wasn't personal. "So that's why she didn't show up last night. We were supposed to have dinner at her hotel. I oversee the Pinkerton operatives working in England, and she briefed me every few days. She sent me a note, asking to meet. She said she'd discovered something important."

I'm excited to think that perhaps Kate's important discovery bears upon her murder. "Did she say what it was?"

"No." Parnell scrutinizes Barrett. "I get that you're investigating her murder. What put you onto me?"

Barrett points at the camera case whose strap is slung over Parnell's chair. "My wife and I were on the train, and we found Kate. She had a Kodak too."

"We Pinkertons like our new gadgets," Parnell says with a wry smile. "Were there any photos in her Kodak?" We hesitate, uncertain how much more to reveal. Parnell misinterprets our hesitation. "I'm sorry if you think it's crass of me to ask, but Kate wouldn't have wanted her last case to go unsolved. And Pauline Chaffin is still missing."

"My wife found someone to develop the photos. They were of Cremorne Gardens." Barrett doesn't mention the people in the pictures. "That's why we were there. Why were you?"

"At our last meeting, Kate said she had a lead on Pauline Chaffin. A porter at the dock saw Pauline get into a cab with a man—a musician from the ship's orchestra. Kate tracked the musician to a hotel. He and Pauline had stayed there for five days. Mrs. Chaffin doesn't want dirt like this to come out. If it became public that Pauline had been living with a man, her reputation would be ruined, and she would never make a good marriage. The hotel people didn't know where Pauline and the musician had gone, but they left a bag of dirty laundry. Kate looked through it and found a handbill in the pocket of a man's shirt. The handbill was from Cremorne Gardens."

I feel a new respect for Kate Oliver; her work had been professionally thorough.

"Kate told me she planned to go there, so after she didn't show up for our meeting, that's where I went looking for her. I was afraid something had happened to her." Parnell's shoulders slump. "I was right."

"Her murder may be connected to Cremorne Gardens," Barrett says. "Did you notice anything unusual while you were there?"

Parnell snorts. "The whole place is unusual. No trace of Pauline Chaffin, though. All I did was look around, because it was Kate's case, not mine. What did you see there?"

"Shakespeare performed by a dwarf," Barrett says.

Parnell laughs. "That sounds in keeping with the spirit of the place."

Barrett and I don't mention Clarence Flynn's weak alibi for the murder or the fact that I've a date for a guided tour tomorrow. "What's your next step?" Barrett asks Parnell.

Parnell's expression turns glum. "I'll have to cable Pinkerton's office in New York and break the news. By the way, where is Kate's body? I should make an official identification. And get a copy of the death certificate. And collect her belongings to send to her family."

"I can take you to the morgue and help you with the other business," Barrett says.

"Thanks. That's very kind of you."

They arrange to meet at the Pinkerton's office tomorrow morning. Our drinks finished, Barrett and I part ways with Parnell. We luckily find a cab, and we ride to Whitechapel, where Barrett tells the driver to let us out at 76 Leman Street, the H Division police station, so he can deliver the paperwork from Scotland Yard. Constables loiter by the drab brick building and the Brown Bear public house across the street. When Barrett and I approach the station, my muscles tense in preparation to run a gauntlet.

It's ironic that I married a policeman when the mere sight of a uniform still rouses my fear of the law, which originated when I was ten, the day two constables burst into my family's house and cornered my father, shouting threats at him. Now I know he was the prime suspect in Ellen Casey's murder, and they were trying to force him to confess. The memory is still sore, and I have reason to fear the law on my own account as well as my father's.

One of the constables outside the station, a hulk with a thick mustache, calls to Barrett: "Hey, guv. Where you been all day?" His tone balances on the edge of insolence.

Barrett gives the men a curt greeting. Many in the police force have turned against him of late, and I feel bad because it's partly my fault.

"Good evening, Mrs. Barrett." The constable moves to open the door for us. "How's your pa? Heard he had a little trouble in court today."

It seems the entire police force, with Barrett the lone exception, believes my father is guilty and welcomes any development that moves him closer to the gallows. Indeed, the newspaper stories indicate as much. How unfair that the police have made up their mind based on an old investigation that failed to uncover two additional suspects, namely Mary Bain and Lucas Zehnpfennig. Barrett touches my arm, warning me not to take the bait. I feel even worse because my husband must face this sort of hostility from his colleagues every day. His loyalty to me has compromised his loyalty to his police brethren.

Grinning, the constable pauses with his hand on the door just long enough for Barrett and me to wonder whether he's going to let us into the station or not. Then he opens the door, and he and his cronies follow us into the reception room. Inspector Reid is standing at the desk with the duty officer. A whip of anger cracks in my chest. When he sees me, his eyes flare; I think he's remembering Sir William Hall-Clarke attacking his testimony in court.

"It's about time you honored us with your presence, Detective Sergeant Barrett." His tone says how much he resents Barrett's promotion from constable. He suspects, rightly so, that Barrett is not only privy to my knowledge about the Ripper but played a part in the troubles Reid has experienced. "What took you so long at Scotland Yard?"

"This is from Commissioner Bradford." Barrett hands Reid the envelope. "It'll tell you everything you need to know."

Reid frowns as he opens the envelope and removes a letter. He reads aloud the handwritten text above the commissioner's signature and seal. "'As of this day, November twenty-seventh, Detective Sergeant Thomas Barrett is on special leave until such time as I order it canceled.'" He stares at Barrett. "What's the meaning of this?"

Barrett replies with a hint of spite. "I'm not at liberty to say."

Reid crumples the document in his fist, incensed because both his superior and his subordinate are keeping him in the dark. Then his eyes glint with dirty inspiration. "This must be about Benjamin Bain. Your wife knew where he was hiding. So did you, but instead of turning him in, you kept mum. That's aiding and abetting a fugitive." He ticks off points on his fingers, counting Barrett's sins. "You've helped her try to prove her father didn't kill

Ellen Casey. That's not only obstruction of justice—it's treason against your brother police!"

The constables mutter, "Yeah!" and "Hear, hear."

The accusations are so baseless that I laugh. I never told Barrett where my father was hiding; nor has Barrett ever been involved in my campaign to exonerate him. In fact, I've assiduously banned him from any actions that would compromise his duty to the police force.

"You are deluded," I tell Reid.

"Sarah." Barrett's hand on my arm warns me not to get in another spat with Reid while we're in Reid's territory, surrounded by his minions.

Ignoring me, Reid says to Barrett, "I think the commissioner reprimanded you. He doesn't want a traitor disgracing the badge, but he didn't sack you because your wife's newspaper would have raised a stink, so he put you on leave."

How unfortunate for Barrett that the murder of Katherine Oliver, with Prince Eddy a possible suspect, coincided with my father's trial. Barrett and I can't correct Reid's mistaken impression without violating Commissioner Bradford's order of secrecy.

A constable says to Reid, "Guv, you mean DS Barrett will draw full pay while he twiddles his thumbs, and the rest of us have to work?"

"That's the long and short of it," Reid says.

"It's not fair!"

"You oughta be ashamed of yourself," another constable tells Barrett.

I glare at Reid, whom I think has done the most to turn the police force against my husband. Reid smirks.

"Think what you will," Barrett says, his jaw tight with his effort to control his temper.

"I'll do more than think." The constable who just spoke shoves Barrett.

"Hey!" Barrett stumbles backward, anger overpowers him, and he shoves the man back.

The others set on Barrett, engulfing him in a storm of blows, curses, and shouts of, "Traitor!"

Furious, as I rush to join the melee, brandishing my umbrella, I call to Reid. "Look what you started!"

Reid responds with malicious glee. "*You* started it when you interfered with the Ripper investigation. Tell me what you know, and I'll call off the dogs."

"*You're* like a dog who won't let go of a bone!"

"All right, lads, that's enough." Reid knows from personal experience that I'm a savage fighter, and as much as he'd like to arrest me for disorderly conduct, he apparently doesn't want a full-scale battle in his station and a subsequent reprimand from his superiors. The constables release Barrett with a final shove out the door.

"If you ever get in deep shit on the job, don't expect help from us," one says.

As I follow Barrett, Reid calls, "Good luck in court tomorrow, Sarah."

CHAPTER 9

On Whitechapel High Street, Barrett stalks rapidly along, his expression so fierce that people step aside to let him pass. I hurry to keep up. I've rarely seen him so angry, and I hate that my family troubles are affecting his job. I feel all the more pressure to help him solve Kate Oliver's murder, for if he succeeds and Commissioner Bradford puts him back on regular duty, it might go some way toward mending the rift between him and the police brotherhood.

At home, Barrett pauses in the studio. "I need a minute. You can go up."

I leave him to cool his temper. What I find in the kitchen does nothing to improve mine. Anjali is there again, presumably without her father's permission or knowledge, eating supper with Mick and Fitzmorris.

"Don't scold," Mick says. "I'm takin' her home soon as we're done."

Hugh's loud, angry voice blares from above us. I tell Mick and Anjali, "Stay put. We need to talk."

Still in my coat and hat, I run upstairs to Hugh's room. Hugh is sitting in bed; Dr. Joshua Lewes occupies the chair, a notebook open on his lap. "How dare you?" Hugh demands of Dr. Lewes. His face is flushed pinker than I've seen since before his injury. "How dare you call me a coward?"

I raise my eyebrows at Dr. Lewes, alarmed to think that his treatments consist of insulting his patients. He bows to me in greeting, then says mildly to Hugh, "I didn't call you a coward."

"You said I'm malingering because I'm afraid to go back to investigating crimes."

"I only said I sensed a reluctance to resume your employment. I asked if it might be due to the often dangerous and violent nature of the work."

I had wondered this too. Hugh's injury isn't his first in the line of duty, and too many of our investigations include near brushes with death.

Hugh snorts. "That's the same damn thing as saying I'm afraid because I'm a coward. Is this what people pay you for? To mince words and insult them?"

Not eager to get in the middle of the argument, yet unwilling to let Hugh labor under an erroneous assumption to his own detriment, I murmur, "I don't think it's the same thing."

Hugh points at me. "You stay out of this."

"Perhaps you're the one who thinks you're a coward, and you're projecting your opinion onto me," Dr. Lewes says.

"I am not a coward," Hugh says with an icy glare. "If you knew half of what I've been through, you wouldn't think I am."

"I'm aware of some of your experiences. Why don't you tell me about the others?"

"I don't care to."

"Very well. Let's explore why you're not ready to go back to work."

Hugh rolls his eyes. "Here's the obvious answer." He points at his injured arm.

"Your physician says your wound is healed enough for you to resume light duty," Dr. Lewes says.

Hugh responds with a sardonic chuckle. "In my line of work, 'light duty' often leads to strenuous endeavors."

"Are you concerned that you might not be up to those endeavors?"

"Now you're questioning my professional competence!"

"Not at all. I'm asking whether you are questioning yourself."

"There you go again, mincing words. I've had enough of your prying into my business and manipulating me. Begone!"

"Very well." Dr. Lewes scribbles in his notebook.

"What the hell are you writing?" Hugh demands.

"A recommendation for you to go into a convalescent home. Here's the name and address." Dr. Lewes rises, tears the page from the notebook, and offers it to Hugh. "Perhaps the doctors there will be able to help you."

"A convalescent home? With old, doddering invalids?" In an explosive fury, Hugh swats the page out of Dr. Lewes's hand. "Go, or I'll—" He picks up the glass pitcher from his bedside table.

"I'm going." Dr. Lewes scrambles out the door.

Hugh hurls the pitcher after him. The pitcher hits the wall and breaks. Water splashes on the floor. Pity and love overpower my urge to scold Hugh as I clean up the mess.

"Lord, I'm sorry, Sarah," Hugh says. "That man rubs me the wrong way."

"Indeed." I think that Hugh should try to work with Dr. Lewes, but I don't say so, lest it set him off again. Instead, I say, "Do you remember that case I told you about yesterday?"

Hugh lies back on the pillows, exhausted by his fit of temper. "Something about a woman strangled on the train."

"There's been a new development." I tell him about the meeting with Commissioner Bradford and Sir Gerald.

"A top-secret investigation with the Queen's grandson a suspect? That's a first for us."

His voice sounds less apathetic than usual, but as I relate the progress that Barrett and I have made so far, he seems distracted, only half listening.

"You mustn't tell anyone about this," I say.

"I won't."

I'd like to include him in the investigation, but I can't ask him to take on a challenge for which he's not ready. I put the broken glass in the waste bin and go downstairs.

Barrett is alone in the kitchen, eating bacon, cheese toasted on bread, and tinned beans. He shrugs with a rueful smile. "All in a day's work," he says of the episode at the police station.

That he's naturally good-natured and doesn't stew about grudges or make everyone else suffer with him are among the reasons I love him. "Where are Mick and Anjali?"

He tilts his head toward the parlor. "I had to tell them about the new developments in the case, since they already knew the beginning of it. I swore them to secrecy."

I step into the parlor, bracing myself for the talk I need to have with them. They're seated on the divan, whispering excitedly. When they see me, they break off their conversation and arrange their faces in innocent expressions.

"We was just leavin'," Mick says.

He and Anjali run down the stairs before I can lecture them about the dangers of physical intimacy. I can't say I'm sorry, for despite my better judgment, I'm reluctant to interfere between them. I think their relationship means more to Mick than young romances mean to other boys his age. When he was little, his mother abandoned him, and his grandparents put him in an orphanage because they couldn't take care of him. He escaped the orphanage to live on the streets, which must have been a lonely, precarious existence, even though he speaks humorously of it. Now he has someone who satisfies his need for love in a way that other friends can't. Anjali would likely be better off without Mick, but I can't say the reverse would be true.

As I wonder what they were whispering about, I hear the front door open and Mick say, "Oh, hullo, Sally. Come on in. Sarah's upstairs."

I clasp my hand over my heart as Sally's footsteps ascend the stairs. This is the first time she's been here since before our father's arrest. Can there be a chance to mend our relationship?

Sally hesitantly enters the parlor, twisting her gloves in her hands. "Hello, Sarah. I hope you don't mind my dropping by without notice."

"Of course not." I want to embrace her and say how glad I am to see her, but she seems poised to flee, like a cat wary of strangers. "Let me take your coat. Have you eaten yet?"

"I'm not hungry. I don't need anything." She hands over her coat and hat.

I belatedly remove my own. "Well, I'm famished. Have a cup of tea with me while I eat."

In the kitchen, Barrett rises from the table and smiles. "It's good to see you, Sally. I'll let you and Sarah have a nice chat. Good night." He goes upstairs.

I fill two cups and plates despite Sally's protests, and we eat and drink like starved longshoremen. Then I wait anxiously for Sally to speak first. I'm afraid she's come to chastise me for abandoning her at court this morning.

Sally fidgets with her teacup. "Sarah, I can't bear to be at odds with you. I want us to be friends again."

"So do I." My voice is husky with emotion.

"But . . ."

But we can't be other than at odds as long as her belief in our father and my suspicion of him forms an ocean between us. "What are we going to do?"

"I've been thinking all day. I can try to be more objective and stop insisting that Father must be innocent just because I want him to be."

Eager to match Sally's readiness to change for the sake of our sisterly relationship, I say, "And I'll try to give Father more benefit of the doubt. I'll remember how good he was to me and other people when I was a child. I won't let the discrepancy about where Ellen's body was found weigh so heavily against what I know of his character."

Sally timidly moves her hand across the table toward me. I extend mine toward hers even while I remember our father's suggestive photograph of Ellen Casey. As our fingers touch, the doorbell rings.

"Who can that be?" I go downstairs and open the door to a woman who stands in the foggy drizzle outside. I'm startled to recognize Mrs. Genevieve Albert—Sally's mother, my father's second wife. She rarely darkens my door.

"Where's Sally?" Her terse, cold manner says this isn't a social call.

When I take her up to the kitchen, Sally gapes at her in surprise. "Mother, what are you doing here?"

"Looking for my daughter." Mrs. Albert is in her fifties, short and buxom under her black coat, the brunette hair under her feather-trimmed hat streaked with gray. She would still be pretty if her face weren't so careworn and grim. "Don't look at me as if I'm one of those criminals you write about for the newspaper."

"How did you know I was here?" Sally asks.

"Where else would you be when you're not at work or your lodgings?"

Mrs. Albert has hated me since the moment she laid eyes on me, and she disapproves of Sally's and my close relationship. Among other reasons, I'm an unpleasant reminder of the fact that her husband had a secret past that included a wife and daughter he'd abandoned when he went on the run to escape arrest for murder. When I invite her to sit and offer her tea, she refuses and glances around my kitchen with disdain. I love my home, but viewing it through Mrs. Albert's hostile eyes, I see the scarred worktop, the mismatched china and silverware from secondhand shops, and the old stove with caked-on grease that won't come off, no matter how hard I scrub. Even on the generous salary that Sir Gerald pays Mick and Hugh and me, plus Barrett's income, it would be difficult to afford a better house that's big enough for all of us and a photography studio.

Mrs. Albert gestures at the room and asks Sally, "Is this what you want?"

Another reason she hates me is that she thinks I'm a bad influence on Sally.

"I would like it better than living and working as a servant in someone else's house," Sally says.

"Don't you look down on me, girl," Mrs. Albert snaps. "My job put a roof over your head and food in your mouth."

"I'm not," Sally hurries to say. "I just want to be a writer, not a maid like I used to be."

"Being a maid is a perfectly respectable job. Unlike running around town, rubbing elbows with policemen and reporters and all manner of shady folks."

It's an argument they've been having since Sally quit her former employment and began working for the *Daily World*. Mrs. Albert glares at me; I recommended Sally for the job, and now that Sally lives independently, away from her mother's watchful eye, it's another sin added to my list.

"If you came here to argue, you can leave," Sally says. Before she met me, she never talked back to her mother.

Mrs. Albert makes a visible effort to subdue her ire. "Sally, I'm sorry—I got off on the wrong foot. I came here to"—she gathers a deep breath, as if for courage—"to beg you to stay away from your father's trial."

Sally exclaims in indignation. "But Father needs me for moral support. And if I stayed away, how would it look? The jury would think his own daughter thought he was guilty."

Mrs. Albert speaks with exasperated patience. "It's time for you to face the facts: He *is* guilty."

"You're wrong," Sally says defiantly.

I'm sad to see them estranged when they once were so close. After my father left them, it was the two of them against a world that's cruel to women without men to support and protect them. Together they made a stable if circumscribed life for themselves as domestic servants, but that life ended when Sally became a reporter and moved to her own lodgings. My father's return widened the rift between Sally and her mother. Mrs. Albert feels abandoned and betrayed while Sally feels disloyal and guilty.

Now Mrs. Albert says, "I know your father better than you do."

Scorn twists Sally's lips. "How can you? You haven't seen him in eleven years. You won't visit him in prison; you won't hear his side of the story."

"I don't need to." Equally obstinate, Mrs. Albert says, "Your father lied to me about his name and his past. He ran away and left us to fend for ourselves. Does that sound like an innocent man?"

"He was afraid of what you would think if you knew he was wanted by the law," Sally protests. "He had to run away to save himself from being arrested for a crime he didn't commit."

But I have to admit that his actions put him in as bad a light as Mrs. Albert thinks.

"Oh, stop making excuses for him!" Mrs. Albert says. "It's time to think of your reputation. You're ruining it by showing up at the jail and in court, telling the world you're standing by him because you think he's innocent. Cut your ties with him before it's too late."

"He is innocent!" Sally cries.

So much for keeping an open mind. Her mother is making her dig her heels deeper into her faith in our father.

"How will it be when he's hanged?" Mrs. Albert demands.

Sally gasps, stricken, as if her mother's words portend the outcome of the trial. "Don't you say that!"

Mrs. Albert triumphantly, bitterly drives her point home. "You'll be branded as a fool as well as a murderer's daughter. You'll lose your job. You'll be lucky if anyone will hire you even as a maid. And you'll never make a decent marriage."

Tears fill Sally's eyes. I know that along with her job and independence, Sally cherishes the hope of finding a husband who will be as good a match for her as Barrett is for me. But she speaks with fresh defiance. "I don't care what happens to me. I'm standing by Father whether you like it or not."

I'm fed up with her mother, even though I can't deny that her predictions could come true, and her advice to Sally is well meant. "Mrs. Albert, it's time you left."

"I'll see myself out." She aims a hate-filled glance at me and then one of love and pity at Sally. "Mark my words, girl—you'll wish you'd listened to me."

She thumps down the stairs and slams the door behind her. Sally wipes her eyes, and I leave to lock the door, giving her time to compose herself. When I return, her eyes are dry, sparking with anger.

"My mother is so prejudiced!" she bursts out. "She hates Father because he left her, and that's why she's eager to turn me against him."

I don't reply. It's occurred to me that perhaps Mrs. Albert knows something about Benjamin Bain that we don't. After all, she was married to him for more than ten years.

Sally notices my silence. "You think she's right, don't you?"

"No." I hear the lack of conviction in my own voice.

"You're on her side against Father and me!"

Just like that, Mrs. Albert's visit has revived our quarrel, ruined our attempt at rapprochement. In her haste to leave my house, Sally overturns her chair. "Wait," I beg her.

She's gone before I can think of what I could have said that would make any difference.

CHAPTER 10

That night, exhaustion makes me sleep so soundly that I don't hear Barrett get up, and when I awake at seven o'clock, he's already gone to work and left me a note saying he'll be home at five to take me to our meeting with Commissioner Bradford. Mick is nowhere in sight, probably out photographing a crime scene. While Fitzmorris and I eat breakfast, Hugh strolls into the kitchen. To our surprise, he's dressed in a gray suit, starched white shirt, and silk tie—clothes he hasn't worn since before his injury.

"What are you doing up?" I ask.

Hugh seats himself at the table. "Joining you for breakfast."

"Splendid!" All smiles, Fitzmorris hurries to serve Hugh coffee, eggs, and toast. "Are you going somewhere?"

The clothes are loose on Hugh because he's lost weight, but his hair is neatly groomed, and he smells of bay rum shaving lotion. "I thought I'd accompany you to court today, Sarah, and lend you some moral support."

I'm overjoyed by this sign of his return to life, but his handsome face is pale and drawn, and his hand trembles as he lifts his coffee cup. I suspect that he's trying to act normal, to prove he's as strong, competent, and brave as ever, and that he doesn't need a head doctor.

"Are you sure you feel up to it?" I ask.

"If I can sit around in bed, I can sit around in the courtroom." Hugh smiles at me.

"It will be crowded and noisy, and the traffic on the way will be terrible," Fitzmorris says. "On your first day out of bed, perhaps you should start with something less strenuous, like a walk around the block."

"You've been nagging me to get up," Hugh says with a touch of irritation. "Well, I'm up, so please let me choose how to occupy myself."

Reluctant to start an argument that might send Hugh back to bed, Fitzmorris and I watch him nibble half a slice of toast. He looks at the clock and says, "Ready, Sarah?"

"I'll hail a cab." Fitzmorris hurries downstairs.

In our hats and coats, equipped with umbrellas, Hugh and I wait outside the door until Fitzmorris comes running up the street, followed by a cab he was lucky to get during the morning rush and the disruption of train service. He whispers to me, "Take good care of him."

As we ride away in the cab, Hugh looks out the window with apparent enjoyment and waves to neighbors on the street. Hopeful that Dr. Lewes's treatment is working—at least it got Hugh out of the house—I tell myself that watching the trial can do him no harm. At Old Bailey, as we run the gauntlet of spectators, Hugh holds his wounded arm close to his side, but he remains calm even when reporters recognize him, call his name, and flash lamps explode in our faces. We're early enough that the courtroom isn't full, and two seats beside Sally are empty. Sally's strained expression says she feels as bad as I do about last night, but when she sees Hugh, she smiles.

"Hugh! It's so good to see you." She offers him her hand.

He kisses it. "Likewise."

When they first met, Sally was shy with Hugh; she'd had little to do with men, let alone men from the aristocracy. For his part, Hugh has been leery of strangers since he was caught in a police raid on a club for homosexual men, and he lives in constant fear of rejection by people who take offense at his nature. But his charm had put Sally at ease, and my sister's affection for him must in some small way compensate for the loss of his own family, including his own sister, who had disowned him after the widely publicized raid.

I let Hugh take the seat between Sally and me. He gestures toward the lawyers at the tables and says, "Which ones are on our side?"

Sally points out Sir William and Mr. Owusu, who are conversing in low voices. The courtroom fills, the clerk says, "All rise," and the judge takes the bench.

Hugh looks toward dock and whispers, "So that's your father. I hope to meet him someday under better circumstances."

My father looks worse after another night in prison, his eyes sunken and shadowed. Sally waves to him, but once again he doesn't look in our direction. Behind us, the Casey family hisses. I turn and see Meg Logan staring at me. She averts her gaze.

Mr. Ingleby calls his first witness. "Wilfred Johnson." The man who accepts the Bible from the clerk and swears to tell the truth is about seventy years old, leaning on a cane. A fringe of gray hair rims his scalp; his coat and trousers are shabby; and the hat in his hand, worn shapeless. As Mr. Johnson enters the witness box, Hugh asks me, "Do you know him?"

I shake my head. My father stares at Mr. Johnson as if he's seen a ghost.

Mr. Ingleby asks, "Mr. Johnson, can you please tell the court your relationship to the defendant?"

"We were friends in the old days." Mr. Johnson's voice is reedy but loud. "In Clerkenwell."

"Can you describe when and how you met the defendant?" Mr. Ingleby says.

"It was in early 1866. He came to the factory where I worked. He was organizing a demonstration on the Clerkenwell Green, and he invited us all to come and protest against our low wages and bad working conditions."

"What happened at the demonstration?"

"There were thousands of men marching, carrying signs and torches, and shouting, and thousands of people watching." Mr. Johnson's face glows with recollected excitement.

"Was there any violence?"

"Oh my, yes. The police tried to stop the march, and we fought them. There was a riot, and they beat some of us pretty bad. That's how I got hurt." Mr. Johnson points to his lame leg. "One of my friends took a club to his head and died."

I remember riots during the demonstrations, with the mobs, the screams, the flaming torches, and the sound of windows shattering. No wonder that when my mother told me that my father had been killed in a riot, I believed her.

"I see," Mr. Ingleby says. "And Benjamin Bain orchestrated the whole spectacle?"

"Yes."

Mr. Ingleby faces the jury. "Note that only months before Ellen Casey's murder, Benjamin Bain showed himself to be a trouble-maker with a taste for violence."

My father cringes from this ugly description. He ignores Mr. Johnson's apologetic glance, and he cowers under the jury's disapproving stares and applause from the Casey family. Sally looks woebegone, and Hugh says, "Whew, that's bad."

Sir William rises to cross-examine the witness. He begins in a friendly voice, "Mr. Johnson, do you know how many labor demonstrations have taken place in England throughout history?"

"A lot, I suppose."

"A lot," Sir William repeats. "Perhaps a hundred? Or several hundred? Thousands?"

"Perhaps." Mr. Johnson's voice grows reedier with confusion.

"And were they all organized by your friend Benjamin Bain?"

"They couldn't've been."

"Therefore, many other demonstrations must have been organized by many other men."

Cautiously, as if he suspects a trap, Mr. Johnson says, "Yes?"

Sir William addresses the jury. "Mr. Ingleby claims a connection between organizing labor demonstrations and the murder of a young girl. By his token, England should have seen rashes of murders of young girls by labor organizers across the kingdom throughout the centuries. But as we all know, there have been no such phenomena. Mr. Ingleby's claim is absurd. No further questions."

The Casey family grumbles, and Hugh whispers to me, "Your man is good." Sally's face brightens and Mr. Ingleby shakes his head as his witness limps out of the courtroom. I dare to hope that

Sir William has cleaned off the mud that the prosecution smeared on my father's character.

Mr. Ingleby rises and says, "I call Mrs. Florence Hodges."

It's my turn to stare as if I'm seeing a ghost. As the woman takes the witness stand, I whisper to Hugh and Sally, "That's my former neighbor from Clerkenwell."

Mrs. Hodges must be over eighty now. Time has shrunken her plump figure, and her toothless face is a caved-in mass of wrinkles, but her hairstyle of crimped white curls is the same, and her head nods involuntarily and continuously. I remember neighborhood children imitating her. She squints at the assembly. I don't think she sees me.

Mr. Ingleby speaks loudly; she must be deaf. "Mrs. Hodges, can you please tell us how you know the defendant?"

Mrs. Hodges squints at the prosecutor and replies in a quavering but clear voice. "I used to live across the street from him."

"Do you remember the twenty-second of April 1866?"

"Oh yes, sir. That was the day Ellen Casey went missing."

"And where were you that day?"

"I was sitting at my front window."

I recall seeing her there at all hours, watching everything that happened on our street.

"What did you see that afternoon?" Mr. Ingleby asks.

"I saw Ellen go into Mr. Bain's house," Mrs. Hodges says proudly. "I may be old, but my memory's clear as a bell."

"Did you see her come out again?"

"No, sir."

"Are you aware that when the police questioned Mr. Bain, he claimed Ellen left his house at approximately six o'clock that evening?"

"Yes, sir, but she couldn't have. I was at the window until half past eight. I'd have seen her. But I didn't."

"Gentlemen of the jury," Mr. Ingleby says, "you will recall that Ellen Casey was murdered sometime that night. The witness's testimony is evidence that it happened in the defendant's house, and she never left the house alive. Thank you, Mrs. Hodges. Your witness, Counsel."

Hugh whispers, "You could drive an omnibus through the hole in that story."

I clench my hands in my lap as Sir William rises and says, "Good morning, Mrs. Hodges. May I begin by asking you a personal question?"

"Yes, sir." Mrs. Hodges now seems ill at ease; her head bobs a little faster.

"Why are you squinting?" Sir William asks.

"My eyesight's not as good as it once was."

"How good was your eyesight in 1866?"

Mrs. Hodges laughs nervously. "Well, I've been nearsighted since I was a girl."

"Have you ever worn spectacles?"

"No, sir." Mrs. Hodges explains, "They make a woman look homely, don't they?"

"So, you were nearsighted and not wearing spectacles on April twenty-second, 1866," Sir William says. "Is it possible you missed seeing Ellen Casey come out of the defendant's house?"

Mrs. Hodges' head bobs harder. "No, sir. I would have seen her. It wasn't far from my house to Mr. Bain's front door."

Sir William pounces on her last words. "His *front* door. Could you see his back door from your window?"

"No, sir." Her whole body is shaking now.

"If Ellen Casey had left by the back door, the witness wouldn't have seen her," Sir William tells the jury, then addresses Mrs. Hodges. "What else did you see while you were spying on your neighbors that day?"

Mrs. Hodges purses her lips, obviously stung because what she thought of as a harmless pastime, he calls spying. "I—I don't remember."

"But surely, if your memory is as clear as a bell, you would remember."

"I remember about Ellen Casey because it was important." She makes a visible effort to firm up her quivering mouth.

"And you like being important, don't you, Mrs. Hodges?" Sir William's voice takes on a cold, contemptuous tone. "You like being the person who knows everyone else's business. And so, when the police came asking questions about Ellen Casey, it was natural for you to 'remember' that you saw her go inside Benjamin Bain's house and not come out."

"I did!" But Mrs. Hodges is obviously shaken, doubting her own veracity.

"One more question: Did you sit at the window from afternoon until half past eight with your attention riveted on Mr. Bain's house, without looking away or getting up for even a moment?"

Mrs. Hodges' head bobs like that of a woodpecker. "Well—"

"Thank you, Mrs. Hodges. You may step down."

Hugh whispers, "Bravo." Sally smiles. The Casey family mutters, disgruntled.

"Mr. Ingleby," the judge says, "I must say you have wasted the court's time with these two witnesses. If you want to secure a conviction, you should provide better evidence."

"Yes, Your Lordship." Chagrined, Mr. Ingleby sits down amid boos from the Casey family.

"That's a point for our side," Hugh says.

Thinking he's correct, cheered by his moral support, I relax a little. I glance at my father, whose expression seems less dejected.

A law clerk rushes into the courtroom, over to the prosecution's table, and whispers in Mr. Ingleby's ear. Mr. Ingleby starts; he whispers questions.

"Call your next witness," the judge says.

"Your Lordship, may I have a moment?" Mr. Ingleby says.

"No, you may not keep everyone waiting. If there is a problem, share it with the court."

"Your Lordship, new evidence in the case has just come to light." Mr. Ingleby is breathless with excitement. "The prosecution needs time to prepare it. I request a recess."

Sally, Hugh, and I look at each other in alarm. Mr. Owusu and Sir William put their heads together and whisper. The audience stirs, loudest among them the Casey family.

Sir William stands. "Your Lordship, Mr. Ingleby shouldn't be allowed to cook up new evidence in the middle of the trial just because things aren't going well for the prosecution."

The judge beckons Mr. Ingleby. "Approach."

Mr. Ingleby bustles over to the bench, the judge leans down, and Mr. Ingleby stands on tiptoe to whisper to him. How I wish I could read lips!

The judge listens, considers, then bangs his gavel. "Recess granted. Court is adjourned until tomorrow at ten o'clock."

The court clerk escorts the puzzled jury away. Reporters besiege Mr. Ingleby, who shakes his head, refusing to answer questions. The constables clear the gallery, and as Hugh, Sally, and I leave the courtroom amid the chattering spectators, I look over my shoulder at my father in the dock. The expression on his face is pure panic.

Mr. Owusu joins my companions and me in the hall. "Sir William is speaking with the judge, trying to learn the nature of this new evidence. I'm afraid it cannot be good for Mr. Bain."

CHAPTER 11

It's noon, and Hugh takes Sally and me to lunch. Over our steak and kidney pie, we speculate about the new evidence and agree that it can't be a physical object. What object associated with Ellen Casey's murder could suddenly turn up twenty-four years later? It must be a witness, but who could it be, and what might he or she say? Sally and I talk until we're in a worse state of confusion and anxiety than when Mr. Ingleby dropped his bombshell. Hugh orders wine, and after two glasses apiece, we're calmer if not cheerful about the situation.

When we leave the restaurant, Sally says, "I'm going to the *Daily World* offices to see if the other reporters have heard anything about the new evidence." She heads toward Fleet Street.

"At least we have the afternoon free to investigate the murder of the lady Pinkerton detective," Hugh says.

Although I welcome his company, he looks frail and tired. "Are you sure?"

"Quite."

The underground trains are running again, the wreckage from the accident cleared from the track, but I'm not ready to get back on them, so I'm glad that the demand for cabs has lessened. I hail one, and while we ride, Hugh reaches in his pocket, brings out a bottle of his pain medicine, and takes a swig. After ten minutes, he's asleep. He doesn't rouse until an hour and a half later when we stop at Cremorne Gardens.

"Sorry, I must have dozed off." Climbing out of the cab, Hugh winces.

The youth at the pay box says, "Mr. Flynn said to tell you he'll be at the museum."

Hugh does a double take at the youth's wooden hand as we walk along the avenue. "This ought to be interesting."

The museum is in a long, two-story building that I remember as the banquet hall. Behind the upper and lower terraces are a series of doors that once stood open to let in the summer breeze and give diners a view of the bandstand and dancers. They're closed now, keeping out the cold, foggy drizzle. Hugh and I find Clarence Flynn by the entrance, laughing with a group of ladies.

Flynn smiles at me. "Good afternoon, Mrs. Barrett. Ready for your tour?"

"Yes, if it's convenient." I'm embarrassed to feel that tug of attraction again.

"I've an hour before my show."

When I introduce Hugh as my fellow reporter, the ladies smile at him; his good looks haven't escaped their notice. As he and Flynn shake hands, the two are a dramatic contrast—Hugh tall and blond, Flynn dark and stunted, each handsome in his own fashion.

"I'll see you at the theater," Flynn says to the ladies.

They look envious as he departs with Hugh and me. It's silly for me to feel like Cinderella waltzing away with not just one prince, but two.

"First I'll show you our newest attraction." Flynn leads us to the northeast corner of the grounds. Surrounded by trees, a large mound of rocks cemented together and overgrown with vines forms an artificial cave. Smoke rises from a chimney pipe. "This is the Gypsy Cave."

I remember that when my father brought me, a gypsy woman sat inside the cave, telling fortunes, but we didn't go in because the line was too long. Flynn gestures for Hugh and me to enter. "We hired a fortune-teller this morning."

Ragged tapestries and bead curtains line the hollowed-out space. Candles flicker in metal holders on the wall by the coal stove. Behind a table set with a crystal ball, deck of cards, and human skull, a small, slim, brown-skinned woman sits in an ornately carved chair. She has long black hair and wears a frayed red shawl embroidered with gold thread. A thin, lanky man perches on a stool beside her. He wears a battered black top hat and a tailcoat over mismatched jacket, vest, shirt, and striped trousers. My jaw drops, and Hugh coughs to disguise an exclamation of surprise.

"This is Countess Zelda and Prince Roman, her assistant," Flynn says.

It's Anjali and Mick. Showing no sign that we're acquainted, they bow solemnly.

"I can tell you your past, present, and future." Anjali speaks with an Indian accent instead of in her normal educated, upper-class voice. She extends her hand to me.

"Cross her palm with silver," Mick says.

To my further astonishment, he's dyed his red hair black. Soot smeared on his face masks his freckles. I'm so outraged, I can't speak.

"We won't charge Mrs. Barrett and Mr. Staunton," Flynn tells the "gypsies." "They're reporters from the *Daily World*, here to write a story about us." He says to Hugh and me, "I'll wait outside while you have your fortunes told."

After Flynn is gone, Hugh doubles over with laughter. "Oh God. Countess Zelda and Prince Roman. What a splendid prank!"

Mick and Anjali smile proudly. I'm glad to see Hugh laugh for the first time in ages, but I say, "It's not funny," and turn on the pair. "What are you doing here?"

"We're investigatin' the murder," Mick says. "Undercover, you know?"

So that's what they were whispering about last night.

"Mick had the bright idea to apply for jobs." Anjali beams at Mick.

Preening, he says, "We got ourselves up as gypsies, made up names, and came over."

"I told the boy at the pay box how he lost his hand," Anjali says. "He used to work at a butcher shop, and he had an accident with a knife."

"He sent us to Mr. Flynn," Mick says. "Anjali auditioned for him and some other folks, and she impressed the hell out of 'em."

"Well done!" Hugh says.

I can't help admiring Mick's cleverness, but I sputter with anger. "Why didn't you ask me first?"

"Because I knew you would say 'no.'"

"I told you and Anjali not to come here! It's dangerous."

"Aw, there's lots of people around. Nothin's gonna happen."

"I want to use my gift to do good," Anjali pipes up. "To help you and Detective Barrett catch whoever killed that poor woman."

I think of Kate Oliver lying dead with the ligature mark on her neck. "Not everyone likes having their private business exposed. Saying the wrong thing to the wrong person could get you in trouble. And if the killer is at Cremorne, and he finds out that you and Mick are spying—"

"We'll be careful," Mick says.

I give him a look meant to remind him of how reckless he's been during other investigations. "It's not safe for Anjali."

"I can protect her." Mick pats his vest. "I got my gun."

"Now I have to worry about you shooting somebody."

"Sarah, they could be a big help," Hugh says. "They can mingle with the denizens, eavesdrop on conversations. Why, Anjali might divine who the killer is and save us hours of sleuthing."

I glare at Hugh. "Don't you take their side." I say to Anjali, "You should be in school, not playing gypsy in a murder investigation."

"It doesn't matter if I miss school. I'm so far ahead of my class, I could skip the rest of the year and still pass the examinations."

"I'm going to tell your father."

"Please don't!" Anjali cries. "He won't let me see Mick anymore."

"That might be for the best."

"If you and Barrett don't solve the case, you'll be in trouble," Mick says.

He seems genuinely concerned about us, not just reluctant to quit a game he and Anjali are enjoying. The problem with having such loyal friends is that they too often suffer bad consequences as a result of what they do for you.

"If you flub an assignment from the commissioner, it could be the end of Barrett's police career," Hugh says, "and you'll lose points with Sir Gerald."

He's right, but I say, "Barrett and I can solve the case without help from two fake gypsies."

"Are you sure?" Mick's expression turns cunning. "We found out who the lady in the photo of Cremorne Gardens is. I'll tell you if you let us stay."

"That's not fair!"

Hugh laughs. "They've got you over a barrel. Why not let them stay for a few days? They should be safe enough, and they may turn up other clues."

Glowering, I say, "All right. Who is she?"

Mick grins triumphantly. "Ursula Richter. The proprietress of Cremorne Gardens."

"I could have found that out on my own," I say, disgusted by his trick and my falling for it. "Mr. Flynn is bound to introduce me to her for my newspaper article."

"At least you won't be caught by surprise when he does," Hugh says.

"Miss Richter interviewed Mick and me," Anjali says. "I pretended to read her palm, and I told her that when she was little, she flew through the air like a bird, fell to the ground, and broke her left ankle. She got a strange look on her face, then said we were hired."

"Good job," Hugh says. "A bargain's a bargain, Sarah."

I don't like to break my word to Mick, and I succumb to the temptation to see what other clues Anjali's gift and Mick's covert spying might produce. "Stay away from Ursula Richter and Clarence Flynn as best you can. They're murder suspects. The same goes for Prince Eddy if he shows up."

"Gotcha," Mick says with a grin.

When Hugh and I leave the Gypsy Cave, Clarence Flynn is waiting by the fountain. "What did you learn from Countess Zelda?" Flynn asks.

"That I made a decision I'll probably regret," I say.

"I hope it wasn't a very serious decision. Are you ready for your tour of the museum?"

In the long hall, the tables and chairs have been removed to make space for the exhibits and the crowd milling around them. More people are on the upper galleries that extend the full length of the room. Gas chandeliers illuminate display cases along the walls. The crowd blocks my view of exhibits placed at intervals down the center of the floor.

"You've quite a good turnout." I'm surprised that so many customers have flocked to an attraction I'd never heard of, and on a cold, rainy November day.

"People are always looking for new entertainment," Flynn says, "and I hired boys to blanket the city with handbills."

Hugh gapes at a skeleton, mounted on a stand, that appears human but grotesquely deformed, with an oversized, lopsided head, crooked spine, one arm shorter than the other, and fungus-like accretions of bone. The sign reads "Tibetan Monster." The glass cases nearest me contain enormous beetles and taxidermy specimens that resemble miniature dragons.

"Where did you get all this?" I ask Flynn.

"It was an inheritance from a wealthy private collector. Not all our exhibits are preserved relics." Flynn beckons to someone down the hall.

Towering over the crowd, a man at least eight feet tall lumbers over to us. He wears a turban, white tunic, white trousers, and enormous, pointy-toed shoes.

"This is Omar, the Giant of Arabia," Flynn says, and introduces Hugh and me.

Omar slowly, silently bows. I have to tilt my head all the way back to look at his big, smiling brown face. When I say, "How do you do?" he doesn't reply.

"Omar is mute." Flynn, standing beside the giant, looks shorter than ever.

As we watch the giant stroll away through the crowd, provoking stares and exclamations, Hugh says, "Doesn't he mind being on display?"

"We freaks are on display wherever we go," Flynn says. "Here, at least people pay to stare at us."

"Uh." Hugh reddens, mortified by his blunder. "I'm sorry."

Flynn smiles cheerfully. "No offense taken."

Our progress down the hall is slow because women stop Flynn to beg for his autograph. While he obliges and flirts with them, Hugh and I study a case that contains tableaus of stuffed rodents.

In one scene, mice are dressed like children, seated at miniature desks in a miniature schoolroom; in another, baby rabbits in spring frocks are ladies at a tea party.

"Sorry for the interruption," Flynn says. "Let me show you another of our live exhibits."

In a huge glass aquarium, submerged vertically in the water, floats a green woman covered with scales from her breasts to the end of her fishtail. Her fair hair streams around her as she makes swimming motions with her arms.

"Good lord, a mermaid!" Hugh says.

"This is Lorelei," Flynn says. "Pirates caught her off the coast of Tahiti."

I see the clear glass tube in her mouth that extends above the surface of the water and allows her to breathe. She's a human in mermaid costume, painted green. The effect is nonetheless startling. She smiles and waves at Flynn, Hugh, and me. Her eyes are bright, clear blue. Flynn tells a tall tale about an epic battle between the pirates who captured her and the mermen who fought to save her. I'm more interested in why a woman would want to spend her days underwater, pretending to be a mermaid.

"I'd like to interview her," I say. "Can she speak?"

"Only in her own language." Flynn winks to say we both know she's fake. Lively piano music tinkles from the far end of the hall, and he says, "A show's about to begin." He leads Hugh and me to a stage framed with black curtains.

There, a man plays the piano for a woman who sings the "Habanera" from the opera *Carmen*. She's small and curvaceous, her black hair coiled around her head, her features smooth and pretty. She wears a strapless white frock spangled with sequins, and I'm shocked to see that she has no arms.

"That's Venus de Milo, our Italian diva," Flynn says.

Hugh stares, equally shocked. "She's quite talented."

The song ends; the spectators applaud enthusiastically. Venus curtseys and says in a foreign-accented voice, "Thank you. You are so kind."

Again I think of Commissioner Bradford. A one-armed, titled military man can excel in a conventional profession, but a woman apparently born with no arms has fewer options.

Venus begins another song. Flynn says to Hugh and me, "We keep our special collection on the upper gallery."

Hugh eyes the steep staircase. "You can go, Sarah. I'll watch the rest of the show."

I glance over my shoulder at Hugh as Flynn leads me up the stairs. Concerned for Hugh's health, I decide that after I see the special collection, we'll go home.

Flynn pauses at the top. "This isn't for the faint of heart. Are you faint of heart, Mrs. Barrett?"

His teasing look lends a sexual innuendo to his question. I blush as I say, "Not particularly."

The items on display would tax the fortitude of a woman who's seen fewer gory sights than I. One glass case contains shelves of specimens in jars—stomachs, hearts, and brains; a two-headed baby pig; and a human infant without limbs. The audience here is mostly male. Another case displays wax models of faces and bodies with grotesque tumors and other defects.

"The waxworks came from a medical museum in Bologna," Flynn says.

I'm fascinated as well as repelled by the specimens, and ashamed of my fascination. "May I bring my camera and take photographs next time?"

"Certainly. The publicity will bring in customers." At the next exhibit, Flynn says, "This is our most valuable treasure."

Inside a coffin with a glass lid lies a sculpture of a young woman with long auburn hair, wearing a translucent white nightgown. It's so lifelike that she seems asleep rather than modeled from inanimate wax. Her cheeks are rosy, her lips parted. Men hover over her, transfixed. As I admire the artistry that created her, her bosom slowly rises and falls. I gasp.

"She's breathing! How?"

Flynn replies somberly with just a hint of mischief. "I'll never tell."

There must be some mechanism inside the waxwork. I feel like a voyeur watching the sleeping woman, but I'm enjoying my tour with Flynn, the undercurrent of attraction that seems to flow both ways, and the allure of the forbidden. Barrett is right: I like Flynn, and I don't want him to be the murderer.

A voice blares through a megaphone. Flynn says, "The next act is starting."

We go downstairs and join Hugh by the stage, where the crowd has grown. A gaunt, dark-haired man onstage, dressed in a stovepipe hat and black suit, bears a striking resemblance to the former American president Abraham Lincoln. He speaks into a megaphone, his voice deep and resonant.

"I present Hercules, the illustrated strongman!"

The man who takes center stage is tall, muscular, and handsome with a Grecian nose—a classical statue made flesh. A wreath of leaves crowns his dark hair, which falls in waves to his shoulders, and muscles bulge under his loose white robe. In his late twenties, he exudes vitality and pride, and his smile reveals strong white teeth. The "Abraham Lincoln" announcer narrates the part of the Greek myth in which Hercules accidentally killed a man in a fit of temper because he didn't know his own strength. The strongman pantomimes the action.

"The gods sentenced Hercules to perform twelve labors," the announcer says. "He has a tattoo for each one. That's why he's called the illustrated strongman."

Hercules drops his robes. Underneath, he wears a short, yellowish fur tunic that leaves his muscular arms and legs bare. His visible skin, except on his face, neck, hands, and feet, is covered with tattoos, a pattern of swirling blue and black ink accented with bright color. Women squeal. As he strikes poses, the announcer points to tattoos and describes the stories they illustrate, of battles won and monsters slain by Hercules.

Flynn whispers to me, "Of course he's not the mythical Hercules, but he's impressive, isn't he?"

I have to nod. I've never seen so many tattoos on one person.

"Now Hercules will reveal his most spectacular feats," the announcer says. Hercules peels the top of his tunic down to his waist. The announcer points to the largest of the tattoos that cover Hercules's hairless torso. The image is of a muscular naked man gripping a snarling lion. "In the land of Nemea dwelt a lion who killed and devoured people. Its hide was so tough that no weapon could pierce it. Hercules chased down the lion, seized it in his bare hands, and squeezed it to death. Then he skinned it with its own claws and used the hide to make the garment he's wearing now."

As the crowd applauds, Hugh says, "Bravo!" He seems to be enjoying the show, distracted from his pain and fatigue.

Hercules pulls his tunic up over the tattoos, turns, pounds his chest, and grins. The announcer says, "Who would like to test his strength against the mighty Hercules?"

Hercules points at men in the crowd one by one as the announcer says, "How about you?" The men laugh, shaking their heads. Hercules's finger aims at Hugh. "You, sir!"

Hugh's smile freezes.

"What's wrong? Do you think Hercules will make mincemeat of you?" the announcer mocks Hugh. "Are you a coward?"

It's the same insult that Hugh accused Dr. Lewes of making. The crowd boos, Hercules beckons Hugh, and anger tightens Hugh's mouth. I glance at Flynn. He's frowning and waving at Hercules, who ignores him. The announcer calls, "Step right up. Be a man."

Before his injury, Hugh was an expert fighter, but now . . . I touch his arm and say, "We should go home."

"Not on your life." Hugh strips off his coat, tosses it and his hat to me, and clambers up the steps to the stage.

CHAPTER 12

The crowd cheers as Hugh faces off against Hercules. As the two circle each other, fists raised, I picture Hugh's scarred arm and shoulder and wasted muscles. I clasp my hands under my chin; I can't intervene and make Hugh a laughingstock rescued by a woman. I can only pray he won't be hurt. Hercules swings at Hugh's face. As Hugh dodges, he stumbles. Hercules lunges and in an instant has Hugh pinned to the floor, his wounded arm twisted behind his back. Hugh's screams of agony echo through the hall, drowning the audience's cheers. Horrified, I rush onto the stage, but Flynn gets there first.

"Let him go!" Flynn grabs Hercules by his fur tunic and yanks him off Hugh.

I reach Hugh as the curtains close. On the other side, the announcer says, "Ladies and gentlemen, there will be a brief intermission before the next show."

"Are you all right?" I ask Hugh.

He groans as he struggles to stand up. Pain contorts his face; tears stream from his eyes. Even worse to behold than his suffering are his public humiliation and his naked fear that he'll never be his normal, strong self again. When I try to help him, he pushes me away.

Flynn hauls the tattooed man to his feet and says in a loud, angry whisper, "You're not supposed to hurt anybody."

In his stunned dismay, Hercules seems just a performer in outlandish costume rather than a mythical hero. "I didn't mean to. I didn't think he would take it so bad." His voice sounds Irish, not Greek.

"That's the trouble with you—you don't think." Anger transforms Flynn from my charming host to a dangerous man.

"So I made a mistake," Hercules says resentfully. "It's not as if you never did."

The two men glare at each other. I think their antagonism started long before today and its cause is far bigger than an honest mistake during a show.

Hercules turns to Hugh. "I'm sorry, sir."

Hugh stumbles off the stage. I hurry after him, and the crowd parts to let us through, as if his humiliation is contagious. Outside the museum, he staggers along the avenue, his left hand cradling his wounded right arm.

"I shouldn't have brought you here." Guilt overwhelms me.

"It's not your fault." Hugh wheezes. "I wanted to come."

"We'll go home now." I should have known he wasn't ready.

"You have to investigate the murder." He snatches his hat and coat from me and puts them on, struggling to fit his wounded arm into its sleeve.

"I'm not staying if you go."

"If you need help, get Mick and Anjali out of the gypsy cave."

"I'm not worried about myself."

At the gate, the youth at the pay box is taking fees from customers. Hugh goes out to the street, hails a cab, climbs inside, and slams the door. I run after the cab for some distance, then give up and traipse back to Cremorne Gardens. In the museum, Flynn is nowhere in sight, but I spot Hercules at the center of a group of people who are gawking at his tattoos.

"May I speak with you?" I say.

Hercules grimaces as he recognizes me. "Sure." We walk to a vacant corner of the hall, and he says, "I'm sorry about your friend."

"He'll be all right," I say with more hope than certainty. "I'm a reporter from the *Daily World*, and I'd like to interview you for my story about Cremorne Gardens."

"All right." Hercules's enthusiasm is underwhelming. His eyes shift nervously.

"Your tattoos are beautiful." Up close I see they're miniature works of art. "Where did you get them?"

"In Greece, after I performed each of my labors," Hercules recites as if from habit.

They all look to be in the same style by one artist, and they have the effect of a mask even though his face is unmarked. Because my attention keeps wandering from his face to the tattoos, I can't get a clear sense of him. I don't ask what his real name is; I suppose he needs to keep up his act, and what I really want is answers to questions I couldn't ask Flynn.

"How did you wind up at Cremorne Gardens?" I say.

"I used to work for Rosenfeld's Circus. I made some friends there, and we wanted to run our own show, so we came to England and set up here."

It's the same thing Flynn told me. "So that's how you met Clarence Flynn?"

"Yeah. We're partners." Hercules's manner turns sullen.

It doesn't seem an equal partnership. Flynn clearly has the upper hand. "Do you know him well?"

"So you're interested in Flynn. A lot of women are."

I'm embarrassed that he's misinterpreted my motive, perhaps not entirely. "Mr. Flynn told me that he spent Wednesday afternoon in his office. Is that true?"

Hercules's gaze is suddenly wary. "Why do you want to know?"

I giggle like a schoolgirl, unnatural for me. "I'm hoping he'll be there next Wednesday, so I can talk to him without so many people around."

"Sorry, I don't keep watch on Flynn."

So much for confirming or breaking Flynn's alibi for the murder. Now Flynn himself joins us and says, "I'm glad you came back, Mrs. Barrett." His smile is rueful. "Please convey my apologies to Mr. Staunton."

"I will." I can't help being glad to see him, even though I wanted more time to press Hercules for information.

"Hadn't you better mingle with our guests?" Flynn asks Hercules.

I think Flynn is worried about what Hercules will say to me. The antagonism crackles between the men. Hercules says, "I was just going," and stalks off.

"I'm due at my show, but we can talk more on the way." Escorting me outside, Flynn says, "I'm sorry Mr. Staunton had such a terrible experience at Cremorne Gardens. I noticed he didn't look well. May I ask what ails him?"

"He was hurt in an accident. What's the trouble between you and Hercules?"

"Well, it's not easy running a business with partners. There are bound to be disagreements."

We're near the theater, and I'm about to lose Flynn's company. "Are there other partners besides you and Hercules?"

"One. Her name is Ursula Richter."

Flynn's voice quiets when he says the name, and his faint accent grows stronger. Now I recognize it as German. My heart beats faster even though I expected to hear the name Mick and Anjali mentioned.

"Can you introduce me to her?"

★   ★   ★

Inside the grand, neoclassical main theater, the auditorium is dim, the upper gallery lost in shadow. A smell of dampness and mold shrouds empty seats upholstered with worn red plush. Flynn and I walk up the aisle to the brightly lit stage, where girls and young women hang and swing on trapezes suspended from the high ceiling.

"They're rehearsing for the circus we're starting next summer," Flynn says.

They wear colorful one-piece costumes with low necklines, short sleeves, and short puffed bloomers that expose a shocking amount of bare leg above soft leather boots laced up to their ankles. But of course long skirts would be awkward and dangerous on a trapeze. Their hair is pulled into a tight, sleek knot at the nape of the neck.

"Ursula," Flynn calls, preceding me up the steps to the stage.

The woman who turns is dressed like the others but in black, her slender arms, shoulders, and legs sinewy and muscular. She's only about five feet tall, but her strong physique and upright posture make her seem bigger. Now I recognize her long, rectangular face, and arched brows from her photograph. She's apparently giving a lesson to three girls who look to be about twelve years old. Her hands hover over one girl who balances flat on her back on a low trapeze, arms and legs spread like the points of a star, while the others stand watching.

"This is Mrs. Barrett, the reporter I told you about," Flynn says. "She'd like to interview you, if you have a moment." His manner is diffident, without the authority that subdued Hercules or the flirtatiousness he displays toward his fans.

Ursula Richter studies me, the expression in her deep-set dark eyes alert but unfathomable. She tells the girls, "Keep practicing," then walks with Flynn and me to the wings of the stage.

"Do you want me to stay?" Flynn's face glows with eager hope, as if he's asking Ursula something more important than whether she wants company during my interview.

"Isn't it time for your show?" Ursula's voice is cool, her German accent more pronounced than Flynn's; she sounds like a native of Germany, whereas he must have spent enough time there to learn the language but had been born in England.

"I can be a little late." In Ursula's presence, Flynn looks smaller than his actual, stunted size.

"That's not necessary." Ursula sounds as if she's refusing more than a trivial favor.

"Well, I'll be going then." Flynn hides disappointment behind the smile he gives me. "When you're finished, come to the Little Theater and watch the show if you'd like, and we can finish your tour afterward."

He leaps off the stage and strides down the aisle, but despite his nonchalant poise, he has the air of a dog with its tail between its legs. Ursula waits for me to speak. Her stillness is disconcerting, and I fumble for questions to ask.

"Do you perform on the trapeze as well as teach?"

"Not anymore." Ursula is clearly among those reticent people who don't offer unsolicited elaborations. She seems to be in her late twenties, maybe past the age for trapeze artists.

A stocky blonde woman is coaching two girls who stand on high platforms at opposite sides of the stage. The girls grab trapezes, swing toward each other, and flip around to hang by their knees.

"It looks risky. Were you ever injured?" I'm thinking of the broken ankle Anjali mentioned. I glance down at Ursula's left ankle, which is tightly wrapped with a bandage.

"Broken bones, muscle sprains, and dislocated joints are common for acrobats."

One acrobat lets go of her trapeze and flies through the air, hands outstretched. Her fingers graze those of the other girl, who tries to catch her. She plummets into the net below.

"Weren't you afraid?" I ask.

Ursula shrugs. "One grows used to fear and risk."

I know it's true, even though I've never swung by my knees twenty feet in the air. Ursula is an intriguing person as well as a potential murder suspect. "Did you enjoy the fear and risk?"

"If you don't enjoy it, then you don't keep going back for more," Ursula says.

Our eyes meet, and I think we recognize each other as kindred spirits of a sort. "How did you become an acrobat?"

Ursula's gaze roves to the pupils in her class. One performs splits and contortions on the motionless trapeze. "My family owned a small circus in Germany. My mother taught me. I spent my childhood traveling and performing."

I can hardly imagine. "So your mother was an acrobat too? Wasn't it hard for her to train her child for such a dangerous job?"

"Other jobs are dangerous also." Ursula's attention returns to me. "What did *your* mother do?"

I'm flustered because it's almost as if Ursula somehow knows about my mother, Lucas Zehnpfennig, and Ellen Casey. "She was a housewife. There's little danger in that." I laugh to cover my discomfort.

"There is more than one kind of danger." The heightened interest in her eyes says Ursula realizes she's struck a nerve.

I shy away from the thought that Ursula followed her mother into acrobatics while I followed mine into murder. Seeking to steer the conversation toward the crime I'm trying to solve, I say, "What brought you to Cremorne Gardens?"

"When my family's circus closed, I went to work at Rosenfeld's Circus. That is where I met my partners. Eventually, we decided to start our own business. We came to England·and found Cremorne Gardens available."

She and Flynn and Hercules all tell the same story, but I begin to think it can't be that simple. "Wasn't it expensive to hire people and set up exhibits and shows?" When Ursula merely looks at me, her face impassive, I say bluntly, "Where did you get the money?"

"From an inheritance." Ursula's attention strays to the acrobats.

"An inheritance from whom?" I press.

"A relative of mine." Ursula's tone is a closed door.

"So you own the business? Not you, Hercules, and Clarence Flynn together?"

She nods matter-of-factly.

"Neither of the men mentioned it," I say.

A hint of a sly smile curves Ursula's full, sensuous mouth. "Men like to be in charge or to think they are. Is it not so with your employer at the newspaper?"

It's her second attempt to turn the questions back on me. "Well, Sir Gerald owns the newspaper, so he is in charge."

"Does he constantly watch you and tell you what to do?"

"No, he's too busy. I rarely see him." Her interest compels me to add, "I work with two partners. One of them is Hugh Staunton. He came here with me, but he left." I almost forget not to mention Mick, ensconced in the Gypsy Cave. I've questioned many murder suspects, but never one so adept at diverting me from herself. I wrench the conversation back to Ursula. "I'm interested in your partners. I sensed that the three of you don't get along. Why not?"

Her gaze rebukes me, as if I've trespassed on forbidden ground. "No one gets along all the time. But when people have faced adversity together, and helped each other through it, they have a bond that can't be broken by disagreements among themselves or attacks from outside. Is it the same with you and your partners?"

"Quite." Unbalanced by her deft verbal parry, I think of the secrets, love, and loyalty that unite Hugh, Mick, and me.

"Then you and I are fortunate women."

I get the message: Ursula isn't going to say or do anything to compromise Flynn or Hercules. Forsaking attempts to divide and conquer, I say, "Can you describe your typical daily activities? This past Wednesday, for example."

"I taught lessons here in the morning. In the afternoon, I went shopping in town for material to make new costumes."

She was at large during the time of Kate Oliver's murder. I glance at her hands, which look as sinewy and strong as the rest of her body, strong enough to pull a ligature tight around a woman's neck. "You've managed to bring quite a few people to Cremorne Gardens. Have you had any prominent visitors, such as actors or politicians? Or royalty?" It's as close as I can get to asking about Prince Eddy.

"Not yet that I know of. But we have hopes for the future. Perhaps you'd like to hear about our plans. We want to bring back the fireworks and balloon rides that used to take place here, and the tightrope walks across the river." Ursula gestures toward the acrobats. "A parade of girls walking the tightrope would be dramatic, don't you think?"

The girls seem to be practicing awkward spills from the flying trapezes. One performs a back flip, falls into the net, and bounces wildly. I don't miss the fact that Ursula has changed the subject.

"Do you get visitors from other countries? America, perhaps?" I don't dare mention Kate Oliver or Pauline Chaffin outright.

"I don't mingle much with the visitors. I work mostly behind the scenes. Please excuse me a moment." Ursula strides over to the net, in which two of the girls sit with dejected expressions on their faces, and says, "Your timing is off. The right time for the catch is when you swing closest to each other. The flyer must release the trapeze when she is not moving horizontally. You also cannot be moving horizontally when you dismount. You must land directly under the point where you let go, or you will lose control. Gretchen and I will show you."

Ursula and the stocky blonde woman dust their hands with chalk from a bowl, then climb ladders to the platforms. They shout commands to each other as they grasp the trapezes, swing toward each other, and flip around to hang by their knees. At the height of their next swing, they seem to pause motionless in the air. Ursula lets go of her trapeze. She drops with her hands caught tight in

Gretchen's. The women swing together, then Gretchen releases Ursula, who does a backflip in midair and lands neatly, safely in the net. I've seen as much at the circus, but it's thrilling to watch up close. The girls applaud, and I join in.

Ursula walks back to me, not even winded from the exercise, but her face is flushed, her eyes brighter, her posture looser.

"You're very good." I think she loves the thrill of acrobatics. "Why don't you perform anymore?"

Ursula brushes chalk off her hands. The dust clouds the air around us, and I cough. She says, "Those days are past. Is there anything else you would like to ask me?"

I feel as if my interview technique is as faulty as the young acrobats' trapeze skill, and I'm repeatedly flying at Ursula only to fall when my fingers miss hers. "I've no more questions at the moment."

CHAPTER 13

Instead of watching Clarence Flynn's show and continuing my tour of Cremorne Gardens, I decide to head home. I'm supposed to meet Barrett there at five o'clock. It's three now, and it may take a long time to get across town. Crossing the grounds, I think about Ursula Richter. Perhaps her evasiveness is a clue in itself. People who have nothing to hide, hide nothing. What is Ursula hiding, and might it bear upon Kate Oliver's murder or Pauline Chaffin's disappearance?

Outside the Gypsy Cave, a few people are waiting to have their fortunes told. While I stand at the end of the line, a man comes out of the cave. Dressed in a black coat and derby, he's in his late forties, his rugged face marked by stern lines. His narrow, puffy eyes look briefly at each person in line before he turns back to the cave and beckons to someone. A slender, elegantly tailored younger man emerges and sets his top hat on his head with a gesture that seems affected, vain. He smiles at everyone as if bestowing a favor. My breath catches because I recognize his wispy mustache, heavy-lidded eyes, and pouting mouth.

He's Prince Eddy. My heart stops, then begins to race.

The other man puts his hand on Eddy's arm and steers him toward the river end of the grounds. I have but a second to make a decision.

I hurry after the men despite having promised Commissioner Bradford that I'll stay away from Prince Eddy. Now that I've seen Eddy here at Cremorne Gardens, I don't think his photo in Kate

Oliver's camera was taken randomly in some other, unrelated locale. I've all the more reason to believe he's connected to the case she was investigating, and now that his path has crossed with Mick and Anjali's, I have a personal stake in learning what he's up to and whether he's a murder suspect.

Catching up with him and his companion near the fireworks temple, I call, "Excuse me."

They stop. Prince Eddy smiles and tips his hat. "Well, hello." A flirtatious, belligerent note tinges his aristocratic voice. I think he's the type of man who wants to be attractive to women and resents them because he isn't.

"What do you want?" The other man steps between Eddy and me as if he's a bodyguard and I'm a cutpurse.

"I'm a reporter from the *Daily World*, writing a story about Cremorne Gardens. I'm interviewing visitors."

"Sorry, we're busy."

"Wait." Eddy looms over me and grins into my face. His complexion is like wet wax, and his breath smells of violet pastilles and sour milk. "What would you like to know, Miss . . .?"

"It's Mrs. Barrett." I step backward, and he advances on me. I reach in my satchel, pull out my notebook and pencil, and hold them between us like a shield. "May I have your name?"

"Charles Evans," Eddy says, "at your service."

"And yours?" I ask his companion.

"William Stewart." The man says to Eddy, "Let's go." It sounds like both an order and a warning.

"Not yet." Eddy says to me, "I think Cremorne Gardens is a marvelous addition to the city's entertainment scene. Why don't you come to the museum with me? I'll show you my favorite attractions."

"Thank you, that's very kind of you." For the chance to learn what he's up to, I'll tolerate his repulsive company.

His friend grasps Eddy by the arm and drags him away.

"Maybe another time," Eddy calls over his shoulder.

I'm tempted to follow, but his companion shoots me a menacing look. It's probably best to obey Commissioner Bradford's order now. Why is Eddy using a false name? I think Ursula Richter isn't the only person here with something to hide.

★   ★   ★

It's a quarter of five, dark as midnight, by the time I reach my house. I stand under the streetlamp to search my pocketbook for my keys, but then I discover the door is unlocked. When I go inside, I hear moans and rustling noises in the studio and see two shadowy figures merged on the divan. Somehow Mick and Anjali have beaten me home. Eager to make love, they forgot to lock the door, and they're making so much noise that they didn't hear me come in. I sigh with resignation, for now is the time for my lecture.

I clear my throat.

The two on the divan separate amid a flurry of alarmed exclamations, thrashing limbs, and flapping skirts. When I see their faces, I choke on a gasp. It's not Mick and Anjali. It's Barrett and Jane Lambert.

Barrett wipes his mouth as he beholds me in horror. Jane smiles triumphantly, her long golden hair loose around her shoulders, her cheeks flushed. Her dress is peeled down to her waist, her corset and chemise open to reveal her bare breasts.

I'm filled with such rage and hurt that I can't breathe, let alone speak. All my suspicions were justified; my worst fear is reality. Barrett and Jane are lovers. The man who promised to be faithful to me for as long as we both shall live is just another man who cheats on his wife.

"It's not what you think," Barrett says.

Incredulous, I stare at him, wounded all the more. The husband whose loyalty I trusted has been lying to me, and he's lying now. "Your trousers are undone."

He fumbles with the buttons.

"How long as this been going on?" I demand.

"Nothing's going on, I swear!"

"Don't bother denying what I can see with my own eyes." I turn on Jane, pointing at the door. "Get out!" My voice is harsh with pain and menace.

Her smile fades. She must see in my expression that I could kill her right now, and she's scared, although the smugness in her eyes sends me the message that she and Barrett are a long-standing couple, a fact that my marriage to him hasn't changed. As she starts to fasten her chemise, I seize her arm, pull her up from the divan, and drag her to the door.

"Out! Now!"

"My coat and hat and pocketbook—"

"Sarah," Barrett protests, jumping to his feet.

That he dares object to my throwing Jane into the street half-naked! I grab her things off the floor, open the door, shove her outside, and hurl them after her. I slam the door and face Barrett. "Do you really expect me to believe you weren't having relations with her?"

"I didn't start it. She came over and said she wanted to talk. When I let her in, she threw herself at me. I was trying to fend her off."

"A likely story!"

"It's true. She let down her hair, opened her clothes, and climbed on top of me, and she undid my trousers. I told her I didn't want to, but she didn't listen."

I touch his crotch, feel his arousal. "You didn't want to?"

He looks away from me. I say sarcastically, "I'm sorry I interrupted you and Jane before you could finish."

"I'm glad you came in and stopped her," Barrett says.

"Don't insult my intelligence." The hot acid of jealousy corrodes my love for him. At this moment I hate him more than I've ever hated anyone, even more than I hate Jane Lambert. Tears sting my eyes. He's dishonored our marriage, made a fool of me, and hurt me to the core.

Barrett reaches for me. "You're the only woman I love, the only one I want." His voice is urgent, sincere.

I swat his hand away even as I feel a bolt of desire so strong that my knees wobble. I want to make love to him and take the pleasure that I deprived Jane of when I interrupted her and Barrett. I want to show him that in terms of pleasing him physically, Jane can't hold a candle to me, but I won't give him the satisfaction.

I head for the stairs.

He grabs my arm. "Where are you going?"

"To pack your things. You're not living here anymore."

Barrett clutches my shoulders; his face, tense with panic, is close to mine. "Let's discuss this later," he says. "There's no time now."

I writhe in his grasp. "Get your hands off me!" If he doesn't, I'm going to push him onto the divan and jump on him; my need is so urgent.

The same desire flares in his eyes. I'm a second from mating with him like an animal—or killing him. Then he pulls me toward the door. "We have that meeting with Commissioner Bradford. We'll be late if we don't leave now."

I burst into ragged, sardonic laughter. "Isn't that convenient!"

★   ★   ★

The noise from carriages in the street, the rumble of distant trains, and machinery in factories fills the ominous silence between Barrett and me as we ride across town in a cab. When Barrett asks me how the trial went today, I don't answer. Regarding my trip to Cremorne Gardens, he'll find out soon enough.

At Scotland Yard, when we meet Commissioner Bradford in his office, I try not to stare at his empty sleeve. I wonder if he thinks himself a freak or cares that other people might. The memory of Venus de Milo singing in her sparkly dress is fresh in my mind.

"Please sit down." The commissioner's shrewd gaze lingers on Barrett and me, as though he notices the tension between us, but all he says is, "What have you discovered?"

Barrett reports about Timothy Parnell, the Pinkerton detective. "He told us that Kate Oliver came to England to look for a missing American heiress named Pauline Chaffin. He thinks Kate traced Pauline to Cremorne Gardens."

"What else?" The commissioner seems eager to dismiss Pauline as irrelevant to Kate's murder, and I wonder why.

"Yesterday we visited Cremorne Gardens and identified the other man from the Kodak photos," Barrett says. "He's Clarence

Flynn, the manager. A dwarf, by the way. He formerly worked at Rosenfeld's Circus."

I'll be damned if I'll let Barrett do all the talking. "I went back to Cremorne Gardens today and identified the woman from the photos—Ursula Richter, the proprietress."

"Good work." Commissioner Bradford writes down the names. "I'll have the Foreign Office run background checks on Richter and Flynn."

Barrett regards me with surprise colored by irritation because I didn't tell him earlier. By blindsiding him, I've made things worse between us, but I don't care.

"Mr. Flynn doesn't have a solid alibi for the murder. Neither does Miss Richter." I aim a smug glance at Barrett; he frowns. There's a new sense of competition between us, and I've won this round.

"So one of them could be the killer." Commissioner Bradford sounds relieved.

I brace myself and say, "I met Prince Eddy at Cremorne Gardens today."

"What do you mean, 'met him'?" Barrett says. "You spoke to him?"

I address the commissioner. "I introduced myself as a newspaper reporter writing a story about Cremorne Gardens and interviewed him about his impressions."

"You shouldn't have done that," Barrett says, clearly angry because I'm giving him the cold shoulder as well as because I disobeyed orders. "Commissioner Bradford told us to stay away from Prince Eddy."

I narrow my eyes at him, displeased that he's scolding me in front of the commissioner.

"Mrs. Barrett, what were you thinking?" the commissioner demands.

I don't want to explain to him about Mick and Anjali's job at the Gypsy Cave. He surely wouldn't approve, and he would be angry because I didn't tell him earlier that Anjali knows about the investigation. "I thought that giving a wide berth to a potential suspect is hardly the best way to go about solving a murder."

The commissioner leans backward, surprised by my outspokenness. "Well, what did you find out?" His tone is leery, as if he doesn't really want to know.

"Prince Eddy introduced himself as 'Charles Evans,'" I say. "Why use a false name if his business at Cremorne Gardens was aboveboard? The man with him called himself 'William Stewart.' I suspect that's an alias too."

Apprehension draws the commissioner's eyebrows together. "What did this other man look like?" When I furnish a description, he says in a hushed voice, "Jonas Murray."

"Who is Jonas Murray?" Barrett asks.

Instead of replying at once, Commissioner Bradford stares out the window. Darkness obscures the view, and from the river comes the sound of boat horns, warning signals in the fog. "Murray was Prince Eddy's valet." The commissioner adds quietly, as if to himself, "I thought I'd heard the last of him."

I sense forbidden territory, but Barrett steps into it, asking, "How do you know Jonas Murray?"

The commissioner refocuses his attention sharply on us. "Remember that everything you hear in this room is not to be repeated elsewhere to anyone."

"Yes, sir," Barrett and I both say. I'm excited because at last we're going to receive the information the commissioner has been withholding, and it could help us solve the murder.

"Prince Eddy has been a problem for the Crown for some time." The commissioner speaks as if he's about to make a shameful personal confession. "He consorts with people of ill repute."

I found Eddy repulsive, and other women probably do too. Maybe he uses prostitutes because nobody else will have him, even though he's royalty. It's a sordid business, but hardly uncommon, and a far cry from killing a Pinkerton detective. I can't see why it matters to Commissioner Bradford.

"Last year, the vice squadron raided a house of assignation. The boys who worked there named Prince Eddy as a regular customer."

"I've heard nothing of that." Barrett sounds surprised that it hasn't been all over the police grapevine.

"The story was hushed up in Britain, but the colonial and American newspapers had a field day with it. The *New York Times* dubbed Eddy a stupid perverse boy who should never be allowed to ascend the throne. On the Continent, Eddy can't show his face in the street without being hissed by the public."

I think of Hugh, disowned by his family and ostracized by society after he was caught in a vice squadron raid; that story hadn't been suppressed. Royal blood has its privileges. I wonder uneasily where Hugh is and whether he's safe.

"Prince Eddy also enjoys the services of persons who operate outside the houses of ill repute. Jonas Murray was his procurer."

I thought the man unpleasant, but other valets surely must perform similar services for their masters. Why should Commissioner Bradford care about the private arrangement between Eddy and his valet? Barrett and I wait eagerly for an explanation.

"Rumors about Eddy began filtering through London society. To avoid a scandal, he went on a seven-month tour of India. Jonas Murray accompanied him. That's where I met them. I was still serving in the British Indian Army, and I conducted the tour."

That he's personally acquainted with Prince Eddy goes some way toward explaining his special stake in the murder case, but not the whole distance.

"In India, Eddy kept up his habits. Murray arranged meetings for him with local women. As long as they were discreet, I looked the other way. Then on New Year's Eve in Calcutta . . ." The commissioner pauses, as if disturbed by the memory. "I woke to a knock at my door in the villa where we were quartered. It was Murray. He said Eddy was in trouble. He took me to a room in town—a squalid, filthy place. Eddy was curled up sobbing on the floor, covered with blood. In the bed was a naked Indian woman. She'd been stabbed to death. Murray said her jealous husband had caught her with Eddy and killed her." The commissioner inhales and exhales deeply before he says, "I had Eddy and his retinue on the road out of town by daybreak."

I see a large gap in the story. My imagination fills it with a vision of the commissioner bundling Eddy into a carriage and speeding him back to their villa while Murray removed all traces of Eddy from the room.

"I believed Murray," the commissioner says, "and why not?" Defensiveness steals into his voice. "I thought Eddy was foolish but not evil. I blamed Murray for pandering to Eddy's vices and risking his safety. I paid the man a large sum of money to quit his post, go back to England, and keep his mouth shut. For the rest of the tour, I put Eddy under strict guard. He was meek and grateful. I thought he'd learned the error of his ways. But now . . ."

Now Eddy is connected with Cremorne Gardens, which in turn is connected with the murder of one woman and the disappearance of another.

"What if they were lying? What if Eddy killed that woman?" The commissioner obviously fears he's made a mistake that's come back not only to bite him but to cost other people their lives. I think of the Ripper's victims, and I pity Commissioner Bradford because I know that such mistakes can weigh sorely on one's conscience forever. "I never told anyone about that night. I figured the fewer people who knew, the less chance of a scandal. I was doing my duty to protect the Crown."

Barrett and I look at each other, hiding our alarm behind blank expressions. Now we know why the commissioner is afraid Eddy is guilty. It's a development that has disturbing implications.

"Sir, why are you telling us now?" Barrett asks. "Why not before?"

"Because with Jonas Murray and Eddy back together again, the picture has changed." The new picture is incriminating evidence against Eddy.

"What are you going to do if we find out that Eddy committed this murder?" I ask. "Protect him again?"

Commissioner Bradford strokes his chin and ponders, hamstrung between his loyalty to the Crown and his duty to uphold the law.

"What would you expect Sarah and me to do?" Anger harshens Barrett's tone. "Help you pin the crime on someone else? Well, we won't."

Although I'm furious at him, I'm proud of him for standing up for our principles. It's not that our professional and personal integrity is so impeccable that we're in a position to criticize the commissioner's; covering up murder counts among our own various sins. But shifting the blame for a crime to an innocent person is a line I hope never to cross. I think of my father. When his trial resumes tomorrow, the prosecution's new evidence may condemn him even if he isn't responsible for the crimes of which he's charged. I couldn't wish that on anyone.

Commissioner Bradford speaks slowly, as if measuring each word, looking us each in the eye in turn. "I expect you to investigate the case to the best of your ability. That means no stone unturned; no suspect, witness, or evidence overlooked." Before Barrett can question him further, he stands. "Report to me tomorrow, same time."

His dismissal brooks no further questions. After Barrett and I leave Scotland Yard, while we walk down the street in search of a cab, I ask, "What do you think?"

Barrett watches the fog that rolls in from the river. "I'm no longer sure the commissioner is a right kind of guy."

My own trust in police hasn't been this low since the Clerkenwell constables threatened and beat my father twenty-four years ago. Now Inspector Reid's grudge against me has set in motion the trial that could end with my father's death sentence, and Barrett has cheated on me with Jane Lambert. Why should I put my faith in Commissioner Bradford or any policeman?

"If Eddy is guilty, and the commissioner covers for him, I won't stand for it," Barrett says.

"Nor will I." We're in accord on that, at least.

"It could mean trouble for us. On top of the usual." Barrett's words allude to the fact that the wrong side of the law is familiar territory.

If Hugh were present—if he were his normal, humorous self— he would make light of the situation to cheer us up. I say, "A little more trouble for us would be icing on the poisoned cake."

Delivered in my bitter, unhappy voice, the quip falls flat. Barrett says, "Joke all you want, but I'm afraid we're being set up.

If we find out that Prince Eddy is guilty, and we accuse him of the murder, Commissioner Bradford can deny that he had anything to do with it. 'Top secret,' you know? The consequences will be all ours."

He's right. Accusing Eddy of murder could be construed as an attack on the Crown—treason, a capital crime. If not for my anger at Barrett, I would admit that I'm afraid too, and we could comfort each other. Instead, I snap, "You're always warning me not to leap to conclusions. Prince Eddy is only one of the suspects, and you should have noticed that we have a new one. Jonas Murray was mixed up in the Indian woman's murder, and he was with Eddy at Cremorne Gardens today."

"He's as likely a culprit as Eddy," Barrett admits.

"So let's explore all the avenues before we throw up our hands and resign ourselves to meeting the hangman."

CHAPTER 14

Back in Whitechapel, Barrett and I hesitate outside our door. The matter of Jane Lambert is like a foul, invisible presence in the fog, insinuating itself between us.

"Can I stay?" Barrett says cautiously.

I chew my lower lip, still hurt and furious, but if I send him away, he'll probably run straight to Jane. "Oh, all right."

In the house, we find Mick and Anjali seated on the divan in the parlor, still wearing their gypsy costumes.

"I was just about to take Anjali home," Mick says, in an obvious attempt to ward off a reprimand. "We thought you'd want to hear what happened at Cremorne Gardens."

"Is it about Prince Eddy?" I say.

"How did you know?" Anjali says.

"I saw him coming out of the Gypsy Cave."

"What's the Gypsy Cave?" Barrett stares at Mick. "Why did you dye your hair black?"

After I explain, Barrett glowers at me. "Well, well. Something else you neglected to tell me." But he can't help laughing at Mick's disguise. "Very clever. But the commissioner said *you* could help with the investigation, not Anjali. He also said to stay away from Prince Eddy."

"But Eddy and that other gent walked right into the cave," Mick says.

"I had to read his palm," Anjali says.

Barrett and I don't mention that I too disobeyed the commissioner's order. It would only encourage the youngsters. We perch on the chaise longue, and I say, "Tell us everything."

"So Prince Eddy says to Anjali, 'Well, hello.'" Mick does a wicked imitation of Eddy's aristocratic accent and belligerently flirtatious manner. "'You're the prettiest gypsy I've ever seen.'"

I'm disturbed but not surprised that Eddy behaved the same toward Anjali as toward me. Anjali says, "His friend scared me. I think he's a bad man."

Jonas Murray, the procurer who'd helped cover up Eddy's role in a murder in India. Whether or not Anjali has psychic powers, her instincts are right on the mark.

"Eddy gave her three crowns instead of three pence,'" Mick says.

I hate to think that Eddy's extravagant tip was intended as an advance payment for other services besides fortune-telling.

"When she held his hand, he did like this." Mick puts his hand palm up in Anjali's and strokes her thumb with his. "The slimy bastard."

"He felt as hot as fire," Anjali says. "When I looked up at him, I saw a vision of him screaming with flames and smoke all around him." She shudders.

"Fire and brimstone," Mick says. "Ain't that a bad sign?"

I'm skeptical about supernatural phenomena, but Anjali's visions have come true in the past, and this one troubles me, for it suggests that Eddy is a murderer destined to burn in hell.

"But I kept up the act." Anjali smiles, proud of her own poise. "I told Prince Eddy that I saw a beautiful woman, lots of money, and great happiness in his future."

"He had the gall to ask her to a party," Mick says, "but the other guy dragged him away."

"We have something to tell you," I say. Barrett and I relate the commissioner's story about Prince Eddy and Jonas Murray, edited for Anjali's innocent ears.

Mick whistles. "What a couple o' blackguards."

"That's one reason why you and Anjali shouldn't go back to Cremorne Gardens," I say.

"But we just started spying," Mick says. "By the way, Hugh didn't come home. Fitzmorris is out lookin' for him."

"Oh no." I realize Mick changed the subject as a ploy to distract me, but I'm afraid Hugh is wandering around town, drinking too much and picking up strange men, his dangerous habit when he's troubled.

"I'll take Anjali home now." Mick hurries her down the stairs, neatly avoiding further discussion of their job at Cremorne Gardens or their relationship.

Barrett and I sit in uncomfortable silence. "What's for dinner?" he says.

"I don't know." The nerve of the man, expecting me to cook for him!

He grimaces, recognizing his misstep. "I'll cook. I learned at the police barracks."

Soon we're at the kitchen table, eating a meal of fried eggs, bread, and sausage. It's good and I'm hungry, but he can't appease me with food. His is too major a transgression to be atoned for so cheaply. We eat in silence. When we're done, he washes the dishes, the first time ever, then says, "Shall we go upstairs?"

My body floods with heat at the thought of bed, but I won't let him seduce his way back into my good graces. "We need to find out what's behind the scenes at Cremorne Gardens."

"You mean now? It's almost nine o'clock, and they close at six."

"If they're hiding something, we won't find it in broad daylight when they're open to the public." I rise from my seat and fix him with a challenging stare.

Barrett shakes his head and chuckles as he gets my message: The nighttime expedition I'm proposing is a hoop he must jump through before I'll forgive him. His face takes on the expression of a man accepting a dare he knows he shouldn't.

"All right, if that's what you want."

★   ★   ★

When we climb out of the cab that brought us to Cremorne Gardens, I regret coming. A cold wind stirs the fog that hangs heavy over King's Road. Lights shine in the windows of tenements and public houses, but beyond the padlocked gate to the gardens, all is darkness. Barrett tells the cab driver to wait two hours. As he and I stroll alongside the iron fence, foghorns blare from the river, whose fetid breath fills my lungs.

"We don't have to stay," Barrett says.

I shiver and think longingly of home. "Yes, we do."

He stops and points through bars of the fence. A light moves through the darkness; footsteps rustle on damp leaves. It's someone carrying a bull's-eye lantern. As the beam slices through the fog, coming toward us, we duck behind a tree that stands on our side of the fence. The unseen person approaches. We wait motionless as the fence's iron bars shine in the moving beam. The light fades into the darkness, and the footsteps recede.

"They have guards patrolling," Barrett says. "They don't want uninvited visitors."

"All the more reason to think they're hiding something."

We turn left at the corner and walk along the western perimeter of the gardens. The street is narrower and darker than King's Road. The area of Cremorne Gardens that we're passing is heavily wooded, and through the trees we glimpse other patrolling guards with lanterns.

"I don't think we'll get a good look around, even if we find a gate they forgot to lock," Barrett says.

"The fence isn't that high."

"Are you serious?" Disbelief raises Barrett's voice.

I don't really want to climb the fence, and it's foolhardy to trespass in a dark place patrolled by guards and inhabited by potential murder suspects. But to give up and go home seems tantamount to admitting that my husband has the right to consort with other women and I've no choice but to swallow my pride. Irrational as that may be, I jam my handbag inside my coat, grasp the iron bars of the fence, and step up onto its brick base.

"Hey, wait!" Barrett says.

I swing one leg, then the other over the fence. My skirts catch on the pointed finials atop the bars, but I shake them loose, then jump down to the other side. As I start walking into Cremorne Gardens, Barrett curses while scrambling over the fence. When he catches up to me, he says, "Are you doing this because you're mad at me?"

I'm too ashamed to admit that's one reason. Forcing him to follow me into a risky situation is a way to make him prove he cares about me, but I also want to know what's going on in here. "If the guards catch us, show them your police badge and tell them you're chasing a criminal."

We slog through high grass, around vine-covered structures— the ruins of swings, game booths, and refreshment stalls. Soon we're beyond the light from the streetlamps, and Barrett whispers, "It's pitch-dark in here. How do you expect to see anything?"

I point to a faint glow that brightens as we draw nearer. We emerge from the woods into the deserted space around the band-stand. The light is a gas globe burning over the entrance to the Cremorne Hotel. The door of the hotel opens, and a man and a woman emerge. She's small and slim, he broader and abnormally shorter.

Ursula Richter and Clarence Flynn.

Hiding behind the bandstand, Barrett and I listen as Flynn says, "At least think about it."

"I've thought enough," Ursula says. "I've already told you—I can't go along with it." The fog obscures their faces so I can't see their expressions, but his tone is urgent, hers distraught.

Ursula moves away from Flynn, but he grabs her hand, stop-ping her. "We haven't a choice. It's the only solution."

She utters a mournful laugh. "That's what you said last time."

"This time will be different."

"And the next time?"

"This will be the end," Flynn declares.

"Don't you see? If we do it, there will be a next time, and a next, and eventually—" She sighs. "We can't go on like this."

"I'll handle everything," Flynn says. "You needn't be involved."

"Is that all you think matters to me? Keeping my hands clean?" Ursula's sharp tone softens. "I care about you." She tugs their joined hands. "I can't bear for you to sink yourself deeper in sin."

"For you I'll do anything." Flynn's voice is quiet, tender. He lifts his other hand and gently cups Ursula's face.

I saw Flynn romance a woman onstage as they played Romeo and Juliet. His acting had been superb, convincing, but now I'm certain his emotion is genuine. Flynn, admired by so many women, is in love with Ursula Richter.

She turns her face from his touch. She obviously doesn't return his feelings. "It's late. We have to go."

Flynn drops his hand and releases Ursula. "Yes, it's late. And if we don't act soon, it'll be *too* late." His voice is raw with the pain of rejection, dark with implications that I can't fathom.

They walk down the path that leads to the fireworks temple and the main gate, a dwarf shrunken smaller by his unrequited love for the woman at his side.

"Late for what?" Barrett whispers to me.

"Let's find out."

There's no time to speculate about the nature of Flynn and Ursula's problem or how their conversation and relationship might bear upon Kate Oliver's murder. We trail them at a distance, the way lit by lanterns placed on the ground along the path. The Little Theater comes into view, the pendant lamps at its entrance illuminated, the white building like an ivory figurine in a gray velvet jewel box. We watch Flynn and Ursula hurry up the steps. A man opens the door for them, then closes it and stands outside it like a sentry.

"There must be another way in," I say.

Barrett groans but follows me around the theater. The back door in the vine-covered wall is made of old, weathered wood, but the lock is shiny and new. I remove my picklocks from my handbag.

"If I go in there with you, will you believe that it was Jane who went after me and not the other way around?" Barrett says.

"I'll think about it." I fiddle with the lock, the tumblers click, and I open the door.

A smell of dust and dampness issues from a dim, empty hall. Light shines from a door through which I hear voices murmuring. I tiptoe through the door, Barrett behind me. We find ourselves backstage amid jumbled furniture, scaffolds with ladders, and racks of clothing. Beyond the backdrop, the stage is unfurnished, the tattered green velvet curtains closed. The murmuring comes from the audience on the other side of the curtains. At center stage stands Flynn, conferring with three men dressed in black, who look to be stagehands. Flynn, in street clothes rather than

Shakespearean costume, turns and walks straight toward us. We're concealed behind the clutter, but the stagehands come with Flynn and start moving things around. Flynn leans against the wall by the door, looking at his pocket watch. If we leave, he'll spot us; if we don't, the stagehands will. I rue my curiosity, for I intuit that something sinister is afoot, and the cost of being discovered will be dear.

Barrett points to a scaffold, and we hurry up the ladder mounted on it to the wooden upper platform, some twenty feet high. Standing in the shadows above the backdrop, we can see down at the stage, into the wings. It's the perfect place to observe whatever happens.

Flynn's theatrical voice sounds from somewhere below us. "Welcome, ladies and gentlemen. Tonight we have a special show for your pleasure."

The murmurs rise to a crescendo of anticipation, then fall quiet as the curtains open. The stage lights dimly illuminate the auditorium's first two rows of seats, occupied by men and a few women, all of whose faces I can't see. The rest of the audience is mere black silhouettes. Across the room, in the center of the balcony, a bright spot of light aimed at the stage casts a beam that shimmers with dust motes. It's from a magic lantern. Beside it stands Ursula Richter. Peering over the edge of the backdrop, I see that it now shows a projected image, a town of white houses on mountainside, a blue ocean below it, a blue sky above.

"In ancient Greece, there once was a sculptor named Pygmalion," Flynn narrates.

A man strides onto the stage. It's Hercules costumed in a short white toga, the tattoos on his arms and legs garish in the lights.

"So great was his talent that he became rich and famous," Flynn says. "He was the toast of the town, and he could have any woman he desired."

The next image is of a Grecian town square with a fountain and tavern. A flock of young women prance onto the stage. They wear white drapery that wraps around their bodies and leaves their breasts naked. The audience stirs, and Barrett inhales sharply. This is our first hint of why the show is held late at night with guards outside. The women fawn over Hercules, stroke his face, press themselves against him, and play tug-of-war with him as the rope.

"But Pygmalion grew disgusted by their lewd antics. He decided that women were vile creatures and swore never to waste another moment on them." Hercules pushes the women away. "He dedicated himself to his art."

The women slink offstage, and the picture of the town square is replaced by a sculptor's studio with unfinished statues on platforms and sketches hung on the walls. A stagehand pushes a tall white block of a substance that looks to be marble on a large, wheeled plinth onto the stage. Hercules pantomimes carving the stone with hammer and chisel.

"He created a statue named Galatea, who was purer and more beautiful than any woman who had ever lived," Flynn says.

The lights go out, and I hear movements on stage. When the stage lights and the magic lantern slide of the studio come back on, Hercules is still beside the plinth, but the marble block is gone, replaced by a statue of a nude, armless woman, her weight balanced on one foot, the other knee crooked, and white drapery around her hips. Her flesh has a pink tinge, and her eyes and coiled hair are dark. I gasp along with the audience. She's Venus de Milo, the woman who sang yesterday, not merely a replica of the famous statue. Barrett exclaims under his breath. Because I didn't tell him about her, she's even more of a surprise to him than to me.

"Galatea was so beautiful that Pygmalion fell in love with her," Flynn says. Hercules drops to his knees before Venus, his hands clasped in a worshipful attitude. "How ironic that he who had scorned women should fall in love with the one who could never love him in return." Hercules bends over, his face in his hands. He shudders with fake sobs. Venus stands immobile, indifferent. "But Aphrodite, the goddess of love, took pity on Pygmalion. She worked her magic."

Venus stretches, breathes deeply, and glances around, her expression filled with wonder. She steps down from the plinth and gently kisses Hercules's shoulder. Hercules startles, looks up at the smiling Venus, and raises his hands in feigned shock.

"He couldn't believe that his creation had come to life!" Flynn says.

Hercules stands, and Venus falls into the embrace of his tattooed arms. He caresses her shoulders, and his hands move down to fondle her breasts. Her lips part, and her back arches. I stare in shocked disbelief.

They're going to make love on stage, in front of the audience!

Cremorne Gardens is a veritable garden of sins.

Embarrassment flushes my cheeks, but I can't look away. I've seen photographs of men and women engaging in carnal relations, but never live, and I'm fascinated. Venus's lack of arms adds extra titillation.

Hercules lowers his face to Venus's bosom and suckles at her nipples, provoking from her a moan that echoes through the theater. Barrett touches my arm and gestures toward the ladder—he wants to leave so that I needn't see this lurid performance. But Flynn and the stagehands are somewhere below us; we mustn't risk being noticed. Venus leans toward Hercules, catches the cloth of his toga between her teeth, and pulls. The garment falls away. His manhood, erect amid a tangle of dark pubic hair, is plain, unmarked flesh, an erotic contrast with his tattooed body. Venus presses herself against Hercules, slides down him, and kneels at his feet, then takes his manhood in her mouth.

From my high vantage point, I can see everything—the motion of her lips and tongue, the wet shine of her saliva on him, his hands buried in her hair. I hear gasps from him and the audience, and their arousal is contagious. I feel the swelling in my breasts, the heaviness and warmth down below. Ashamed of my excitement, I can't look at Barrett. Nothing like this has ever happened to us, and to see each other aroused would be embarrassing. Now Hercules withdraws from Venus's mouth, clasps his hands around her waist, and lifts her. They move as gracefully as ballet dancers; they've done this before. He sits her on the plinth, and she lifts and spreads her legs. Kneeling, he puts his head between them and pleasures her. Groans erupt from the audience. My heart is throbbing, and I'm wet between my legs. Hercules rises, draws Venus's legs around his waist, and enters her. They moan in time to his quickening thrusts. His tattoos writhe with the clenches of his muscles. Then she screams, a high, ululating wail. He pulls out of her, yells, and spurts into the air.

Loud applause ensues. A thought spins through my shock and arousal—shows of this sort must be what Kate Oliver had discovered at Cremorne Gardens. They're surely illegal, and possibly something that Clarence Flynn, Ursula Richter, and their gang would have killed her to keep secret.

Backstage, Flynn's quiet, authoritative voice speaks: "Close the curtains. Get everyone out of here."

The curtains swing shut. The audience boos. Venus sits up on the plinth; Hercules stands naked, still erect and panting. When Flynn walks onto the stage, they behold him with confusion.

"We have trespassers." Flynn picks up Venus's drapery, throws it over her shoulders, and says, "Go to the hotel and stay there." She hurries off. Flynn says to Hercules, "Don't just stand there like an idiot; get dressed and go help track them down."

My fever of arousal turns to sheer, cold panic. Barrett and I look at each other, horrified because *we* must be the trespassers; the guards must have spotted and reported us. Hercules pulls on his tunic, and he and Flynn depart. We're the quarry of the people who may have killed Kate Oliver, perhaps because she had spied on a show just as we did.

From the other side of the curtain comes the bustle of people rising from their seats. I'm thinking that Barrett and I can wait until everyone is gone, then make our escape, when the stage lights go out. Complete, black darkness immerses the theater. Suddenly blind, I cling to the scaffold, as if in danger of falling.

"Now what?" Barrett whispers.

As a photographer, I've spent what must be years of my life in darkrooms; I've learned to operate via touch and memory rather than sight. I close my eyes against the darkness, and in my mind there appears a dim, hazy picture of my surroundings. I find Barrett's hand.

"This way." With my eyes still closed, the picture as ephemeral as a reflection on water, I carefully pace three steps along the scaffold and reach below it with my foot. "Here's the ladder. I'll go first."

I sit on the edge and awkwardly maneuver myself onto the ladder. My hands grip the sides while my feet fumble for each rung on my way down. Touching solid floor, I say, "Your turn. There are eighteen rungs."

I wait anxiously while he clambers down the ladder to me, then I take his hand and guide him through my mental image of the space backstage. I bang against something, stub my toe on something else. Objects fall and crash. My memory is faulty, or the stagehands moved the props. I open my eyes, my mental image disappears, and I inch forward, the blind leading the blind. When light filtering through the windows appears, I gasp with relief. The door is locked, but the deadbolt easily turns, and then we're outside in the cold, foggy, blessed night air.

Lantern lights move in the distance, many more than before. Twigs break and leaves rustle under footfalls. We run, hand in hand, across lawns and cracked pavement, through woods and flowerbeds, veering to avoid the searchers. At last we see the iron fence illuminated by a streetlamp. As we climb the fence, my petticoat snags and tears. Then we're on the other side, running free.

★   ★   ★

Back in Whitechapel, as soon as we're safely inside the studio in our house, the door locked, Barrett takes me in his arms.

"Let me go!" Furious because he dares to touch me after I caught him with Jane Lambert, I struggle in his embrace.

His mouth claims mine, and the arousal I experienced during the show flares up in me, hot and urgent. He must have been just as aroused as I. His tongue in my mouth, the taste of him, enflames my desire. So does our narrow escape from Cremorne Gardens. We tear off each other's coats as we stumble across the studio. I rip his shirt open, and buttons clatter on the floor. He peels my dress down around my waist, yanks open my chemise and corset, and fondles my breasts. My anger about Jane Lambert only excites me more. I think of Venus using her teeth to undress Hercules, and I lean over and bite Barrett on his shoulder. He yells, then lowers his face and sucks my nipples. He, too, is reenacting the show. Brazen with illicit excitement, I slide down Barrett, kneel before him, rip open his trousers, and do something I've never done before. Him in my mouth, his hands in my hair, and his moans—it's so dirty, so thrilling.

He pulls away from me and lifts me by my waist. We're not as graceful as Hercules and Venus, and as he carries me, he staggers, and I clutch him for fear that he'll drop me. He throws me onto the table, flings back my skirts and petticoats, and pulls off my knickers. I don't want to reward him for his infidelity, but I spread my legs; I can't help myself. The touch of his lips and tongue in the place where they've never been before is so intense, with my excitement already so high, that when my pleasure reaches its crest, I shout, and I don't care who hears. Barrett thrusts himself into me and almost immediately withdraws. As he yells and the warmth of his satisfaction wets my thighs, applause from the audience at the theater echoes in my memory.

CHAPTER 15

In the morning, Hugh hasn't returned, and his absence casts a pall of foreboding over the breakfast table where Barrett and I sit. Mick isn't up yet, and Fitzmorris has gone out on another probably fruitless search for Hugh. The house feels colder and less cozy than usual.

"Sarah, could you please pass the butter?" Barrett says.

I oblige without looking at him. When we went to bed last night, he'd apparently thought we'd made up, and he tried to hold me. I pushed him away, ashamed because I'd been aroused by the show at Cremorne Gardens. It was lewd and sinful, and therefore so was my behavior. I'm angry at myself because I gave in to desire, because I let Barrett have me after cheating on me with Jane. I as good as told him that he can have his cake and eat it too! Far from bringing us together, last night widened the distance between us.

"Did you and Jane ever do those things?" As soon as I blurt the words, I want to snatch them back.

"What things?"

Barrett's voice is cautious, and when I glance at him, his shoulders are hunched up to his ears. He knows exactly what I mean, but I spell it out for him. "The things we did last night when we got home."

His cheeks flush, he chews his lip, and he looks everywhere but at me. "I don't think we should talk about this."

I don't really want to know what he and Jane did together, but an irresistible compulsion makes me say, "Answer me."

He shakes his head and exhales; he's damned if he does, damned if he doesn't. "Jane and I never went all the way. Because we didn't want her to get pregnant. All right?" His jaw is set; he's not going to supply details. His gaze begs me not to press him for any.

I avert my eyes, ashamed of my curiosity and my jealousy and more miserable than ever. Does he not want to hurt me, or is he protecting Jane? I picture him and Jane doing the same things to pleasure themselves that he and I did before we married.

Barrett finishes breakfast, stands, and bends to kiss me. "See you tonight?"

I turn my face, and his mouth grazes my cheek instead of my lips. "Yes, we have a meeting with Commissioner Bradford." My implication is that's all we'll have together tonight.

Barrett hesitates. "I'm off, then."

Soon after he leaves, Mick comes downstairs in his gypsy costume and grabs a piece of toast on his way out.

"Not so fast," I say.

"I got to pick up Anjali and go to work."

"I have to tell you something. Sit down." When Mick reluctantly obeys, I say, "Barrett and I broke into Cremorne Gardens last night."

"Really?" Mick's reaction blends surprise, admiration, and disappointment. "I wish you'd taken me. What happened?"

"There was a private show." I blush at the memory and search for words that will get the message across without embarrassing me. "A man and woman . . . unclothed . . . had physical relations. In front of the audience."

Mick's eyes pop. "Gorblimey!"

"You mustn't take Anjali back to Cremorne Gardens. It's dangerous enough for her to be around murder suspects. Now we know those people are doing things that a young girl shouldn't go near."

"Yeah . . ." Mick frowns, disturbed by the thought of corrupting the innocent Anjali. "But one o' them's gotta be the killer, right? I mean, if the lady Pinkerton got wise to the shows, that was a reason to bump her off. We can't stop spyin' just when we're gettin' close."

"Too close. Listen to what Barrett and I learned from Commissioner Bradford." I tell Mick about Prince Eddy, Jonas Murray, and the murdered Indian woman. "We don't want Anjali around Prince Eddy. This is the end of Countess Zelda and Prince Roman."

"Aww!"

"You know I'm right. You don't want Anjali to get hurt."

"I can protect her. I'm bringing this." Mick reaches in his pocket and pulls out his pistol.

"Don't be ridiculous! If you start shooting, you might hit Anjali. And remember what happened to Hugh."

Stubbornness tightens Mick's jaw. "I'm a good shot."

I take a deep breath. There's no time like the present for a difficult conversation that's been delayed too long already. As gently as possible, I say, "You two shouldn't see each other for a while."

"What do you mean, 'a while?'"

The discomfort of talking about the show at Cremorne Gardens is nothing compared to this. "Until you're old enough to marry if you get her with child."

Mick flushes bright red. "People our age get married."

I sit back, surprised to learn that he's serious enough about Anjali to think of marrying her. "You know her father wouldn't approve." I think Dr. Lodge never would want Mick for a son-in-law at any age.

"I won't get her in trouble. I'm careful," Mick mutters.

I remember how careless Barrett and I were before our wedding, and we weren't fourteen and fifteen. "For Anjali's good, call it off."

"But we're—I never felt like this about any girl before—she's the only one—" After a pause, Mick says in a quiet, awed voice. "The only one who ever loved me."

"I understand how you feel." I remember his background, and I myself never loved anyone as much as I love Barrett, the only man who's ever loved me. The realization that he cares so little for me that he would carry on with his former girlfriend is devastating.

"No, you don't understand." Mick jumps up from his chair. "If you did, you wouldn't tell me to call it quits with Anjali."

I feel sorry for him, but I say firmly, "You aren't taking her to Cremorne Gardens."

"You can't tell me what to do. You ain't my mother." Mick stomps out of the kitchen and down the stairs.

My marriage is in shambles, Hugh is missing, and I should have known what would come of trying to restrain Mick. If only Anjali won't come to grief and I haven't lost his friendship. I prop my elbows on the table and hold my head, which is starting to ache. The strain of a secret investigation, marital torment, and domestic problems is taking its toll on me, but I can't rest for long. My father's trial resumes in an hour.

★ ★ ★

The courtroom buzzes with excited speculation. From our front seats in the gallery, Sally and I confer with Mr. Owusu and Sir William.

"We haven't been able to determine what the prosecution's new evidence is," Mr. Owusu says.

"Neither have I," Sally says. "I asked all around the courthouse. Nobody's heard anything. I went to Mr. Ingleby's office and tried to question the clerks, but they threw me out. The other reporters at the *Daily World* are in the dark too."

My little sister has come a long way from the shy, timid girl she was when we first met. I admire her initiative, and I feel bad because I spent my time on the Kate Oliver murder case. I glance at my father in the dock. He looks ill, as if he expects to see proof of his guilt revealed, while the jurymen eye him with unfriendly judgment.

Sir William fixes his supercilious gaze on Sally and me. "Is there anything about the case that you haven't told Mr. Owusu?"

"No, sir," we say. The secrets we've kept from the barrister weigh heavily on me.

"All rise," the clerk orders.

The judge seats himself on the bench and says to the prosecutor, "Call your first witness."

Sally's hand grips mine. I feel our pulses racing together. Mr. Ingleby stands and says, "I call Mrs. Genevieve Albert."

Shock jolts me forward in my seat, and Sally gasps with horror. Behind us, the audience stirs as Mrs. Albert, dressed in a somber black coat and hat, walks to the witness box. Her eyes glint with nervous bravado.

"Mother?" Sally cries.

"Genevieve!" My father grips the wooden barrier at the front of the dock and leans toward Mrs. Albert.

The audience clamors, and the judge pounds his gavel. "Order!"

Mrs. Albert accepts the Bible from the clerk, and when asked if she swears by Almighty God to tell the truth, the whole truth, and nothing but the truth, she says, "I do," in a firm, loud voice. She takes the witness box and gives my father a look of pure, venomous hatred.

"She's going to testify against Father!" Sally's voice resounds with the same disbelief that I feel. I never thought Mrs. Albert would go to such lengths. Sally shouts, "Mother, no!"

"Quiet, or you'll be removed from the courtroom," the judge says.

Sally subsides into incoherent whispers, beating her fists against her lap. I press my hand down on hers to calm her and say, "She doesn't know anything. The worst she can do is speak ill of Father's character." Again I suspect she knows more about him than she's told Sally or me.

"Mrs. Albert, can you please tell the court your relationship with the defendant?" Mr. Ingleby says.

"I'm his wife. We're separated but still legally married."

"Yesterday you came to my office and informed my clerk that you had a piece of evidence that you wanted to bring to my attention." Mr. Ingleby's voice is taut with excitement. "Is that correct?"

"Yes, sir."

"What can it be?" Sally asks me.

The judge glances at us, and I put my finger to my lips. Mr. Ingleby says, "And you think it's proof that your husband raped and murdered Ellen Casey?"

"Yes, sir."

My heart plummets—my suspicions were justified. Sally groans under her breath while our father drags his hands down his cheeks.

"Please tell the court where and when you found it," Mr. Ingleby says.

"I found it in 1879, a few days after *he* disappeared and abandoned me and our daughter." Mrs. Albert aims a bitter glance at the dock. "It was hidden in the lining of an old trunk he'd left behind."

Mr. Ingleby holds up a brown envelope that looks to be about eight by ten inches. "Is this the evidence?"

"Yes."

"Your Lordship, may I show the evidence to the jury?" Mr. Ingleby says.

Sir William rises. "Your Lordship, I request that the defense be allowed to examine the evidence first."

"Request granted." The judge doesn't seem surprised by the new developments; the prosecution must have informed him in advance.

Mr. Ingleby walks over to the defense table. He's grinning, his lips wet with saliva, as if he's about to eat his adversary's dinner. He hands the envelope to Sir William. Sally and I lean forward to watch Sir William open the envelope and remove a colored picture. It's an enlarged, tinted photograph of a naked girl, her arms crooked above her head, her face upturned, her pink-skinned body twisted as though in agony. Her wavy red hair hangs down to her waist, and a wisp of drapery at her loins hides nothing. Her wrists are bound. She's Ellen Casey in a photograph apparently taken by my father. I feel sick to my stomach because it's a hundred times worse than the other I saw, which I was glad Meg hadn't brought to light.

Sally wails into her hands. Her mother's testimony is a betrayal of her as well as our father, who looks as horrified as we are. Although he can't see the photograph, he must have an inkling of what it is. Mr. Owusu and Sir William shake their heads; this evidence is damning for the defense.

Puffed up with anticipation and triumph, Mr. Ingleby takes the photograph to the jury. "Gentlemen, brace yourself for a disturbing sight." As he holds it in front of them, their eyebrows rise, and their jaws drop.

Whispers sweep through the audience and the gallery. "What is that? What's going on?" Reporters in the press box call, "Show it to us!"

The judge pounds his gavel. Mr. Ingleby says, "The evidence is a photograph that's unfit for public viewing. It depicts Ellen Casey unclothed, in a seductive pose."

An uproar ensues, loudest from the Casey family. I turn to see Meg stand and shout at Mr. Ingleby, "You're dirtying Ellen's reputation!"

"Sit down and be quiet," the judge orders.

As Meg crumples into her seat, Mr. Ingleby says, "My apologies to Ellen's family, but I must introduce the photograph as evidence because it will greatly strengthen the prosecution's case against the defendant." He asks Mrs. Albert, "Who took the photograph?"

"My husband." Mrs. Albert smiles nastily at him, as if twisting a knife in his heart.

"Your Lordship, I object," Sir William says. "The prosecution has produced no evidence that the photograph is indeed the work of the defendant."

"The witness has stated that she found it in his trunk," Mr. Ingleby says. "Let the gentlemen of the jury draw their own conclusion about its origin." At a nod from the judge, he resumes questioning Mrs. Albert. "How did you feel when you found the photograph?"

"Horrified. Revolted. But not surprised. My husband had never talked about his past. So I knew he must have dirty secrets."

"What did you think the photograph meant?"

"That he'd done other things to that girl besides take her picture."

"'Other things,'" Mr. Ingleby repeats with heavy emphasis.

Anyone who saw the photograph would think the same, and I can tell from their disapproving expressions that the jurymen do. Indeed, it's fueled my own doubts about my father's innocence. Amid mutters from the Casey family, I hear Meg sob. The reporters are scribbling so fast, their pencils seem to fly. Sally, her hands over her face, whispers, "Father, what have you done?"

Her belief in his innocence is wavering at last, which gives me no satisfaction; I long to believe the opposite of what I'm seeing and hearing.

"Mrs. Albert, when you learned that your husband was wanted for the rape and murder of Ellen Casey, what did you think?" Mr. Ingleby says.

"I thought he must have killed her so she couldn't tell anyone what he'd done to her."

"Objection," Sir William says. "The witness is stating opinions, not facts." But it's a futile protest that the judge dismisses with a wave of his hand.

"You kept the photograph hidden until yesterday, when you brought it to me," Mr. Ingleby says. "Why?"

"Because I didn't want my daughter to know about it." Tears glitter in Mrs. Albert's eyes as she glances at Sally.

Sally looks wounded, like a child awakened by a slap on her face.

"Why did you show it to me?"

"Because my husband is a criminal." Mrs. Albert's voice shakes with rage and anguish. "I don't want him going free to hurt other girls."

She means Sally most of all, I'm sure. Mr. Ingleby says, "Thank you for your testimony, Mrs. Albert. I know it caused you considerable distress, but it was in the service of justice." He announces, "The prosecution rests," and turns to smile at Sir William like a fencer who's dealt his opponent the fatal jab.

While Sir William cross-examines Mrs. Albert, I can't listen. I suppose he's doing his best to discredit her and her testimony, but the damage is done; I smell it in the air, as though it's dust from a collapsed building. After she leaves the stand, he addresses the judge. "Your Lordship, in view of this unexpected development, I request a private consultation with my client now, and a recess before I begin his defense."

"Granted. Court is adjourned until Monday at ten o'clock AM."

During the mass exodus from the courtroom, the Casey family shouts at my father, "Murderer! You'll burn in hell!"

Mrs. Albert steps down from the witness box. My father's sorrowful, broken voice calls to her, "Genevieve, how could you?"

"It's no more than you deserve," she retorts.

Reporters surround Mr. Ingleby, shouting questions. I follow Sally as she rushes to Mrs. Albert and calls, "Well, Mother, are you proud of yourself?"

Mrs. Albert declares, "It was for your own good."

"Don't lie to me! You did it because you hate Father."

Mrs. Albert thrusts her face close to Sally's. "I did it to pull your head out of the sand. I've been telling you he's evil. Now you know why I think so."

Incredulous, Sally says, "You should have explained before."

"I didn't want to hurt you. I thought he was dead and so it didn't matter."

"Well, you've hurt me." The pain on Sally's face suits her words. "And it does matter."

I pity both of them—Mrs. Albert, who'd hidden her ugly suspicions about the husband she once loved, and Sally, her trust in her father shattered—but my loyalty belongs to Sally. We're both daughters whose mothers deceived us, and I can't condone Mrs. Albert's testifying against my father and validating my own suspicion that he's guilty.

"Oh, Sally." Anguish replaces Mrs. Albert's self-righteous ire.

Mr. Owusu says, "Excuse me, Mrs. Barrett, Miss Albert, would you like to join Sir William's and my meeting with your father?"

"I certainly would," I say.

Sally glares with contempt and hatred at Mrs. Albert and says, "I never want to see you again." She stalks out of the courtroom with the lawyers and me, leaving her mother alone to face the reporters who swoop down on her like ravens ready to peck her to pieces.

We gather in a small conference room in Old Bailey. A constable stands guard outside the door. My father sits at the table, his head in his hands. Mr. Owusu pulls out chairs for Sally and me and seats himself. The table's wooden surface is scratched and worn from generations of people who have conferred across it. My feet rest in dents in the stone floor where countless other feet must have tapped nervously. Sally breathes hard, struggling not to cry. My mind is a jumble of so many questions for my father; I can't think which to ask first.

Sir William stands over my father, glaring down his long, haughty nose. This extraordinary occasion apparently merits breaking the custom of barristers keeping a distance from their clients. "That was incredibly stupid, leaving that photograph for your wife to find."

My father peers up at Sir William, his face gray, his eyes red. "It's not how it looks."

Sir William takes the chair across from him, next to me. "Then by all means explain." Cold anger frosts his voice.

I feel sorry for my father; I wouldn't want the barrister's wrath directed at me. But I'm angry too, and the fact that my father carelessly left a compromising photograph in the possession of the wife he'd abandoned isn't my only reason.

"I was doing a series of photographs based on paintings," my father says. "That one was from *Andromeda* by Peter Paul Rubens. Do you know the Greek myth?" He launches into the story of Andromeda, the daughter of a king who sacrificed her to save his kingdom from a sea monster. The king chained Andromeda to a cliff, but just as the monster came to devour her, the hero Perseus slew the monster and rescued her. "I used Ellen as my model for Andromeda. That's all. I didn't kill her. I swear!"

"And I'll sell you London Bridge for two pence," Sir William says.

Indeed, my father's excuse sounds like rubbish that no intelligent person would buy.

Mr. Owusu frowns and Sally shakes her head sadly, but I sit stunned by an unexpected memory. "I know that painting of Andromeda. It was in a book we had when I was a child. Engravings of paintings by old masters. Father and I used to look at the pictures together."

"So Father really was just recreating the painting," Sally exclaims. "The photograph doesn't mean anything else."

He gives her a fond, thankful look. "Yes, that's right."

Sir William regards my sister and father as though he's never seen two such naive, foolish people. My anger at my father resurges, and I demand, "How could you take such photographs? Didn't you think about how they would look?"

"I thought of them as art," he says, chagrined.

But I never saw him photograph Ellen; he did it when I wasn't home. He must not have wanted me to see, which meant he was aware of how wrong it was to take nude, seductive pictures of a young girl. And what else might he have been up to besides taking the pictures?

"You should have thought twice," Sir William says.

"He made a mistake," Sally says earnestly. "He doesn't have it in him to do what Mr. Ingleby and my mother say he did to Ellen."

This turn of events has further entrenched her belief in our father's innocence while my own doubts have only grown. Sir William and Mr. Owusu exchange skeptical glances. Maybe my father really had raped Ellen; maybe he had killed her to prevent her from telling. I've never wanted so much to believe him, never had so much cause for suspicion.

Sir William regards my father with disgust. "I've never had another client shoot himself in the foot as badly as you have." Mr. Owusu nods in regretful agreement. My father hangs his head. "Well, the milk is spilled. Now we must clean it up as best we can."

"I'll testify," my father says eagerly. "I'll explain the photograph to the jury."

"That would be unwise," Mr. Owusu says.

"That's an understatement. Mr. Ingleby will crucify you." Sir William stands. "On Monday, I'll put your daughters in the witness box. They'll testify to your *good character*." His sarcastic tone implies that my father doesn't have one. A hard, warning gaze accompanies his advice to Sally and me. "Be prepared to speak for your father as if his life depends on you. It does."

The barrister strides out of the room. The constable takes my father back to Newgate Prison, and Mr. Owusu escorts Sally and me to the street outside Old Bailey and bids us farewell.

"When you testify, what are you going to say?" Sally asks me. We're back where we started—at odds regarding our father's innocence—and now that we're to be witnesses whose task is to convince the jury that our father isn't a rapist or murderer, our feelings matter much more than when they were just between us.

"I'll answer Sir William's questions."

Sally must sense my uncertainty, for she says, "Sarah, Father is counting on you. You can't let him down!"

"I know." I remember my love for my father and the loyalty required of me as his daughter. I picture Ellen Casey posing in the Andromeda photograph and her body found at a road construction site instead of the burned house where my father says he left her. I have only his word that she was my mother's and Lucas's victim, not his own, and I balk at giving him a glowing character reference.

"Sarah, please!" Sally cries.

I don't want to think about Monday, when I'll have to decide whether to withhold information that could condemn him or lie after I swear to tell the truth. I don't want to let my sister down and ruin our relationship for good. Seeking distraction, I look down the street instead of at Sally.

Newsboys are hawking papers, shouting, "Murder in Whitechapel! Jack the Ripper strikes again!"

CHAPTER 16

Riding toward Whitechapel in an omnibus, Sally and I skim a newspaper, a one-page, hastily printed extra edition headlined "The Ripper's Latest?"

"Body of an unidentified woman found dead under a wagon in Castle Alley early this morning," Sally says. "Multiple knife wounds."

Below the article are portrait sketches of the Ripper's previous victims. I don't need to read the captions to put names to Martha Tabram, Polly Nichols, Annie Chapman, Liz Stride, Kate Eddowes, and Mary Jane Kelly. I remember Kate aiming bare buttocks at my camera; Polly posing in corset, garters, and black stockings; Liz spreading her legs; Mary Jane nude on the divan. Their images, lit by white explosions from the flash lamp, blur together and dissolve into a dark maelstrom of shame, horror, and guilt. If I'd never taken those photographs, the women might still be alive.

"This is what everyone hoped would never happen," Sally laments. "After two years, the Ripper is back."

I don't want Sally to labor under a false assumption, but I can't tell her that the new murder isn't the work of the Ripper. "Maybe this is an unrelated crime.

"Murder is common in Whitechapel. We shouldn't jump to conclusions." I hate lying to Sally, but I can't trust anyone with a secret that, if made public, would send not only myself but also everybody else involved to the gallows. And if I did tell her, she surely would see me in a new, terrible light when our relationship is already troubled.

"You're right," Sally says, chastened. "We're reporters, and we need to be objective."

My guilt increases because she trusts me and because I can't ignore the fact that the Ripper murders had a silver lining for me. Those photographs of Martha, Polly, Annie, Liz, Kate, and Mary Jane led me into my first murder investigation, if not for which I wouldn't have become fast friends with Mick and Hugh, married Barrett, or become a crime scene photographer. One could say I owe my life and career to the Ripper. But now it looks as though the Ripper has inspired another murderer to perpetuate his reign of terror, and that could reopen the police's dormant investigation, which could have dangerous ramifications for everyone who's in on the secret.

The omnibus inches along in slow traffic where Aldgate High Street joins Whitechapel High Street. Sally and I squeeze our way out and run two blocks. We turn left through a narrow, covered archway that leads to Castle Alley. The alley, about eighteen feet wide and a hundred long, lies within the quarter-mile radius of the Ripper murders. On the west side are warehouses and the back of the workhouses and public baths. On the east side, a wall hides the ruins of demolished lodging houses. Sally and I hurry past the wagons, tradesmen's carts, and costermongers' barrows lined up along both sides. I remember the horror of Polly Nichols lying dead in a pool of blood with her throat cut, and I steel myself for a similar atrocity.

A few people loiter, but all seems ordinary. I'm both disappointed and glad that we're too late to view the intact crime scene. "Where's the body?" Sally asks the loiterers.

"Police surgeon took it to the morgue at Old Montague Street."

"Sarah, let's go," Sally says.

"You don't want to see." Neither do I, really, but I'm hurrying toward Old Montague Street.

Sally runs beside me. "I have to get the news."

The morgue is attached to the Whitechapel Workhouse, where the homeless and destitute perform menial labor in exchange for bed and board. Steam from its boilers cloaks the upper stories of the huge brick building. Outside a green-painted gate at the rear,

Sally and I find Barrett conversing with two constables. I'm surprised to see him, not ready to face him again. He doesn't look surprised to see me.

"So you heard." His expression is carefully neutral.

"Was it the Ripper?" Sally pulls notebook and pencil out of her handbag. "Who is the victim?"

"It's early in the investigation, and no determinations have been made." As Barrett recites the official police statement, he catches my eye, and we experience one of those moments that many married couples probably share, when each can tell what the other is thinking. We're both hoping that the person responsible for this new murder is not the Ripper miraculously returned or an imitator just beginning a murder spree.

"May we see the body?" Sally says.

"There's no need," Barrett says, as if loath to test Sally's stomach. My heart sinks. The victim's injuries must be as dire as those of the Ripper's victims. "Other reporters from the *Daily World* have already been here."

"I'm not going to faint or be sick," Sally says.

After I've caused Sally so much pain, I hate to deny her anything. "Just a peek?" I say to Barrett.

He hesitates, then nods to the constables, who've apparently been ordered to guard the corpse against trespassers. They open the gate, and Barrett leads Sally and me into a yard. I've been here once before, at night, and now I see what was invisible then. There's a carpenter's workshop with benches and tools visible through the dirty windows, and a shed containing dustbins. The mortuary is a small brick building with an arched window and a metal roof. Outside the open door stands a three-wheeled cart with a leather cover, for transporting bodies. My stomach churns as my vision darkens with the memory of the last time I was here. Maybe Sally isn't the only one at risk of losing her intestinal fortitude. Inside the morgue, which reeks of spoiled meat, bodies covered in sheets lie on racks along one wall. Gas lamps cast meager yellow light on the sink, the worktops, the glass-fronted cabinets, and the middle-aged man who stands at the table at the center of the room.

"Sarah, do you remember Dr. George Phillips?" Barrett says.

"Yes, of course." I met him when he performed the autopsy on a victim from our last murder case.

"A pleasure to see you again, Mrs. Barrett." Muttonchop whiskers, a high-collared white shirt and black stock tie under a gray smock, and his gallant manners lend Dr. Phillips the air of an eighteenth-century gentleman.

I focus my attention on him instead of the figure on the table. Last time I was here, it was Polly's corpse after the autopsy, her stomach cut open and her innards removed. My breaths come faster, shallow and uneven. Barrett introduces Sally as my sister, also a reporter from the *Daily World*. Sally is pale, her lips compressed. When Barrett says that she and I want to see the body, Dr. Phillips draws back the sheet from the corpse, revealing long, tangled blonde hair, then the face of the woman. Her eyes are closed, her skin grayish white.

"She was young, in her twenties, I estimate." Dr. Phillips gradually pulls the sheet lower.

A deep, ugly, red gash crosses her neck. Smaller, shallower cuts surround the gash. I inhale sharply. Sally puts her hand over her mouth. The woman's clothes have been removed, and stab wounds pierce her full, pink-tipped breasts, the flesh between her curved hips, and her slender thighs. My stomach lurches. It's terrible, albeit not the worst I've seen.

"Oh God," Sally whispers.

"The results of my examination weren't what I expected when I heard the Ripper had struck again." Dr. Phillips covers the woman, mercifully hiding all of her except her head and neck. "There was very little blood on her clothes." He gestures toward a mauve and black printed frock and pale undergarments on the worktop. "And less at the crime scene. The knife wounds were inflicted after death."

"So it wasn't the Ripper." Sally sounds disappointed as well as relieved.

An inside track on solving the crime of the century would have done great things for her newspaper career. Barrett and I exchange glances, sharing our relief that the Ripper investigation won't be revived. The police won't reexamine the past crime scenes, evidence, and witnesses and uncover a trail that will lead to us. Our secret is safe for the moment.

"Remember, the Ripper found and attacked his victims in the same places as where he left them," Dr. Phillips says. "But this woman was killed elsewhere, and her body moved to Castle Alley."

"The murder was staged to look like the work of the Ripper," I say.

"Why would the killer go to all that trouble?" Sally says.

"Perhaps to cover up the real story behind the crime," Barrett says.

"What was the cause of death?" I ask.

"Observe the bruising under the cuts." Dr. Phillips points to the woman's neck. "She was strangled." He lifts her eyelids with his fingertip. The whites of her blue eyes are laced with tiny red lines. "Strangulation ruptures the small blood vessels in the eyes."

"Sarah, do you know her?" Sally asks.

"No. I don't think she's from Whitechapel." I take a closer look at her face. Her nose is a trifle wide, her lips too thick for beauty, but she would have been pretty enough when alive. She has three tiny moles on her right cheek near her mouth, a triangle of black dots. I feel a sudden, disconcerting sense of familiarity.

"Here's something strange." Dr. Phillips turns her head to the side, lifts her hair, and runs his finger along her hairline. "Specks of green paint."

Green paint. Where . . .? I feel my eyes and mouth open wide as my brain makes the unforeseen connection. My breath catches as I remember where I saw the triangle of dots.

Sally regards me with concern. "Is something wrong?"

I put one hand to my forehead and say, "I feel ill."

As Barrett puts his arm around my waist and hurries me out the door, I call to Sally, "You stay and interview Dr. Phillips. I just need fresh air." I drag Barrett through the yard and gate to the street.

"Sarah, this isn't like you." Barrett is all alarm and confusion. "Shall I take you home?"

"I'm fine. I know who the woman is. I couldn't tell you in front of Sally and Dr. Phillips. She's Pauline Chaffin!"

Surprised, Barrett asks, "Why do you think so? She doesn't look like the girl in the photograph we found in Kate Oliver's hotel room."

"The moles on her cheek. They're in the photograph."

"I didn't see any moles."

"They barely showed. She must have covered them with makeup. I thought they were defects in the photograph."

Barrett shakes his head in amazement. "This adds a new twist to the case. Pauline Chaffin disappears and ends up dead in Whitechapel, staged to look like a Ripper victim."

"That's not all. I know where the green paint came from. Yesterday, when I went to Cremorne Gardens, Mr. Flynn showed me the museum. It had a mermaid swimming in an aquarium filled with water."

"A *mermaid*?"

"Not a real one, a woman painted green and wearing a costume."

Barrett flings up his palms as if I'm charging full tilt at him and he wants to prevent a collision. "Wait. You're telling me Pauline Chaffin was posing as a mermaid in the freak show?"

"Yes! She was wild and adventurous. She must have done it for a lark. She was hiding in plain sight. But I think Kate Oliver recognized her. Maybe that's what Kate meant to tell Mr. Parnell. The private shows weren't the only secret at Cremorne Gardens."

We're stunned speechless as three cases that seemed unrelated— the Ripper, the missing heiress, and Kate Oliver's murder— suddenly join with a force as shocking as the train crash.

Barrett clasps his head between his hands and contemplates the fog-shrouded distance as if searching for the answer to a riddle. "You saw Pauline at Cremorne Gardens yesterday afternoon. Dr. Phillips thinks she died sometime late last night."

Thinking of our clandestine expedition, the sex show, and our narrow escape, I say, "My God. What happened after we left Cremorne Gardens?"

"Pauline could have been killed there and her body moved to cover up her connection with the place."

A new theory about the murder is no consolation in view of the terrible fact that Pauline died violently, too young, and far from home. I'm about to wonder aloud why someone there wanted her dead, when the gate to the morgue opens, and Sally comes out. Just then, a carriage stops by us and disgorges Inspector Reid and two constables. My heart plummets, but my temper heats up. Reid's grim expression turns stormy as he beholds me.

"Interfering with the Ripper investigation again, I see."

"This wasn't the Ripper," Barrett says. "The victim was strangled, not stabbed to death, and she was dumped in Whitechapel, not killed here."

Disdain twists Reid's mouth. "Why should I believe you? You're not even on the case."

"Ask Dr. Phillips. He'll tell you."

Unfazed by the news that the evidence says the murder isn't the Ripper's work, Reid says, "So the Ripper changed his pattern. Makes no difference. I'm going to get him this time." His cold eyes gleam with determination.

"Inspector Reid, why do you think the Ripper would change his pattern?" Sally prepares to write his answer in her notebook.

I shush her. Heaven help her if she aggravates Reid! I should keep quiet too, but I unexpectedly feel sorry for him. According to what Barrett once told me, Reid was a thorough investigator with high professional standards until the Ripper case. He became obsessed with the case, corrupted by his obsession; he's lost his way, and he needs to be set straight.

"Ignoring the evidence and assuming this murder is the work of the Ripper will send you down the wrong track." I wish I could tell him the truth. But Pauline Chaffin's murder is part of our top-secret investigation for Commissioner Bradford. No matter that our withholding information will hinder the official investigation, we must keep the police away from Cremorne Gardens and especially from Prince Eddy.

Reid clenches his fists as if to hit me. Barrett steps between us. Then Reid smiles, his smile as ugly and threatful as his anger. "Mr. and Mrs. Barrett, you're under arrest."

My first reaction is horror; my second is *Here we go again*. Sally cries, "No!"

"Why?" Barrett demands.

"For obstructing justice in the Ripper investigation." Reid nods to the constables.

One grabs Barrett while the other yanks my hands behind my back. Handcuffs jingle, and cold steel locks around my wrists. Reid says, "Unless you each want the other to get hurt, you'll both come quietly."

It's the one condition that can prevent us from fighting back with all our might. That holds true no matter the state of our marriage. Passersby gawk as the constables push Barrett and me toward the carriage and Reid follows. Sally runs after us, crying, "Let Sarah go!"

She tugs Reid's arm. Reid pauses, turns toward her. The last thing I want is my sister arrested too. I call, "No, Sally! Go to the *Daily World* and tell Sir Gerald what's happened."

CHAPTER 17

In the police station jail in Whitechapel, I pace the six steps across the dirty stone floor of my cell, turn, and pace six steps back. I check my watch for the hundredth time. I've been imprisoned three hours, and I'm cold even though I haven't taken off my coat. The window behind the iron bars is open, deliberately I'm sure, and it's too high for me to reach and close. Wind damp with fog wafts in on me. I tried to avoid using the bucket under the wooden bench, but I couldn't wait, and the air is foul.

This is a rare occasion when fear doesn't make me feel more alive and danger holds no attraction. Terror is a leaden malaise that started in the pit of my stomach, gradually spread outward to my whole body, and worsens with each second that passes.

I don't know what's become of Barrett. Inspector Reid stopped the carriage at the police station and let me out with the constable who'd handcuffed me. When I asked where Reid was taking Barrett, he slammed the door in my face, and the carriage rattled away. I think I could endure anything if only I knew my husband were safe. No matter how he's treated me, my love for him is stubborn.

Worn out from pacing and worrying, I sit on the bench and listen to the distant sounds of traffic outside and the footsteps and voices of policemen in the station. No one has come near me. No doubt Reid has ordered me deprived of human contact, the better to break me.

I mustn't let him break me. Other lives besides my own depend on my silence.

Another hour passes before the key rattles in the lock. I remind myself that I've clashed with Reid before and lived to tell. My anger at him fortifies me.

Reid enters the cell, wrinkling his nose at the smell from the bucket. "Sorry to keep you waiting." His cheery expression says he's anything but sorry. Indeed, his face looks plump with self-satisfaction, a bad sign.

Standing up, I demand, "Where is Barrett?"

"Don't worry—he's in good hands."

I picture constables holding Barrett immobile while others punch and kick him, his face bruised and bleeding. "I want to see him."

"Not yet." Reid closes the door and leans against it.

"Then I'm not saying anything more." I clamp my mouth shut, cross my arms, and stare at the wall.

"That's all right," Reid says. "You can listen while I tell you a story."

No interrogation? His new approach makes me all the more uneasy.

"Tuesday, August seventh, 1888. At four forty-five AM, a tenant at George Yard buildings discovered the body of a woman lying in a pool of blood on the landing."

The woman was Martha Tabram, the Ripper's first victim. I suppose I'm about to find out why Reid is rehashing an event with which he must know I'm familiar.

"The tenant fetched a policeman," Reid says. "It was PC Thomas Barrett."

My stomach turns queasy. Reid also surely knows that I know Barrett was the first policeman at the murder scene. Where is this story heading?

"PC Barrett later claimed that at about two AM he'd seen a soldier loitering in George Yard. The incident seemed unimportant at the time, but after the murder, the soldier became a suspect."

Barrett had told me all this. Why is Reid telling me now?

"PC Barrett described the soldier as a private in the Grenadier Guards. That same day, I staged two identity parades at the Tower of London. At the first one, Barrett failed to identify the soldier he'd seen. At the second, he identified a private who turned out to have an alibi for the time of the murder."

The episode had caused Barrett's first clash with Reid, who'd been furious about the false lead and banned Barrett from the Ripper investigation. I know Barrett still thinks his mistake wasted precious time and cost the police their chance to catch the Ripper, who went on to kill five more women. Maybe Reid is rubbing my nose in my husband's disgrace just to torment me, but I'm afraid he has other, more diabolical reasons.

"Now we skip ahead to Friday, August thirty-first," Reid says. "At 3:40 AM, the body of Polly Nichols was found in Buck's Row."

That morning I'd gone out early to photograph the dawn over the river and happened onto the crime scene. That was the day I first met Barrett.

"Then, on Saturday, September eighth, at a little after six AM," Reid says, "the mutilated corpse of Annie Chapman was discovered behind a lodging house in Hanbury Street."

I'd taken a tour of the crime scene, conducted by the landlady's grandson. A vision of blood thickly spattered on the ground flashes before my eyes.

"All these events have one thing in common besides the Ripper. PC Barrett was on patrol duty during each of those nights. *Alone*."

Ice water trickles through my chest as I begin to perceive Reid's intentions.

"Is it a coincidence that PC Barrett was out roaming Whitechapel the nights of the three murders?" In case I've missed his point, Reid says. "He hasn't an alibi." I can't resist the impulse to turn and look at Reid. He grins, pleased that he's gotten to me. "Did Barrett lie about seeing a soldier in George Yard? When he botched the identity parade, was it an honest mistake or ploy to divert the investigation away from himself?"

His insinuation is so absurd that I laugh in spite of my dismay. "You can't be serious."

"Why not? I figure the reason you won't tell me what you know about the Ripper is that you're protecting someone. Barrett is the likeliest candidate."

"Barrett isn't the Ripper!"

"I've wondered if the Ripper could be one of us," Reid says. "A job as a constable on the night beat in Whitechapel would be a perfect cover. He could stalk and kill women, and any witness who saw him near the scene would think he had a legitimate reason to be there."

Incredulous, I stare at Reid. "You don't really believe it's Barrett." Yet maybe his obsession with the Ripper and his grudge against Barrett and me have driven him insane.

"I can make a case for Barrett being the Ripper. Just as I made the case that your father is a murderer." Reid's eyes shine with gloating. "Mark my words—this new murder will settle the Ripper question once and for all."

This cruel new twist in Reid's plot against me brings a full onslaught of horror. First my father was accused of heinous crimes, now my husband. And while I have doubts about my father's innocence, I have none whatsoever about Barrett's.

"Barrett must not have been on duty during the other Ripper murders, or you would have mentioned them," I say. "He must have alibis."

"Three is enough to get the ball rolling against him."

"Barrett has an alibi for this new murder. He was with me."

Reid tilts his head, skeptical. "Oh yeah? Where were the two of you? What were you doing?"

I hesitate because I can't reveal that we were spying at Cremorne Gardens.

He waggles his finger at me. "You're lying to protect him."

"Your case is nothing but circumstance and speculation!"

"The top brass is eager to close the case, and the public is so eager to see Jack the Ripper hanged that if Barrett stood trial, the jury would be likely to convict."

My mind tells me Reid is bluffing. My imagination puts me in the gallery at Old Bailey with Barrett in the dock instead of my father. "Your selfishness and greed are disgraceful. You weren't satisfied with arresting my father, so you're after my husband, just to hurt me!"

"Aww, I'm not that bad." Reid feigns sheepishness.

The troubling fact is, he's right about himself. The "new Ripper murder" is his worst nightmare come true, a glaring reminder of his failure to solve a famous crime and protect the public. It's not just vengefulness against me that drives him; it's his desire to do whatever is necessary to catch the Ripper and prevent more deaths. A desire that I share, and upon which I acted.

"I could be satisfied with your father. It's up to you." Reid's manner turns as blunt as a police truncheon. "All you have to do is confess what you know about the Ripper, and I'll leave Barrett alone."

It's as if I'm standing at a window inside a building that's on fire, and there's no way out except the fifty-foot drop to the ground below.

Reid smiles at my distress. "Think what will happen once Barrett becomes the prime suspect in the Ripper murders. He'll be thrown off the police force."

That would be the least of his troubles. While my heart lunges like an animal trying to escape my ribcage, my mind careens between two impossible alternatives. Confessing wouldn't protect Barrett; it would only imperil everyone else who's in on the secret.

"His name and face will be on the front page of every newspaper." Reid pantomimes holding up a paper and reads an imaginary headline: "'Detective Sergeant Thomas Barrett Is Jack the Ripper!' Everyone will believe it, and remember what happens to men when the public believes they're the Ripper?"

I remember innocent men chased through the streets and beaten by angry mobs. I picture them with Barrett's face.

"If he goes to trial, he's sure to be convicted. The jurors would jump at a chance to send the Ripper to the gallows."

For the first time I entertain the possibility of unburdening myself of the secret, of having it roll off my back like a boulder dislodged by an earthquake. What an exhilarating freedom from fear and guilt!

"I'll give you two minutes to decide." Reid pulls out his pocket watch. "If Barrett isn't the Ripper, then who is?"

I've never seen a hungry wolf, but I imagine its expression would resemble Reid's. Maybe I could satisfy him with the part of the secret that doesn't involve the night at the slaughterhouse. But every detail is connected to every other detail.

"I can hold a press conference today and announce that Barrett is the new prime suspect in the Ripper case," Reid says. "The news will be all over the city by tomorrow."

I'm like a sailor adrift on the ocean, ravaged by thirst and tempted to drink the saltwater that would kill me. One sip, and I wouldn't be able to stop drinking; one chapter of the story leaked, and the rest will come out.

"Time's up." Reid puts away his watch, and when I remain silent, his frustration is like corrosive steam emanating from him. He stretches his mouth in a poor imitation of a friendly smile. "Tell you what—if you talk, I'll retract the testimony I gave at your father's trial. I'll have the defense put me back in the witness box, and I'll say that a new prime suspect in the Ellen Casey murder has turned up."

Even as I tell myself this is just his new ploy to coerce me, I blurt, "Who is it?" I can't help hoping that somehow Reid really has found an alternative suspect.

"A criminal who was executed for the murder of another girl in Clerkenwell a few years after Ellen Casey's death," Reid says. "I can't guarantee an acquittal, but I can poke a big hole in the prosecution's case."

He's proposing to pin the crime on a dead man, and what would it hurt? I'm sorely tempted to leap at his offer. My father deserves a break because he's as likely innocent as guilty, and here is my chance to save both my father and my husband.

I choose my next words with extreme care. They might be the most crucial I've ever spoken. "Suppose I did know something. I'm not saying it's so, but if I were to tell you, would you promise to keep it to yourself?"

Reid's eyes light, saliva glistens at the corners of his grin, and I can smell his anticipation, sweet and rank. "I would."

I don't trust him, but this is probably the best deal I'm ever going to get. I must protect both of the men I love, even if I doubt my father's innocence and my husband's fidelity. I succumb to the impulse to stave off the immediate danger and worry about the consequences later; I'll jump from the burning building and hope a miracle will save us all before I hit the ground.

As I open my mouth, my heart pounds in my throat, a wave of nausea washes over me, and I taste sour bile. I'm afraid that when I speak, I'll vomit.

Reid's eyes fill with astonishment; he can't believe he's finally gotten the best of me.

A knock at the door startles us. A male voice outside calls, "Guv."

"Not now!" Reid barks.

"Guv, you have to send Mrs. Barrett to Scotland Yard right now. Commissioner Bradford's orders."

★ ★ ★

A constable accompanies me on the carriage ride to Scotland Yard. When I ask him why the commissioner sent for me, he says he doesn't know, and I believe him. My emotions swing wildly between relief that I didn't have to confess and my distrust of the miracle that saved me just in time.

When I arrive at Scotland Yard, Barrett is in the office with Commissioner Bradford.

"Sarah!" Barrett bolts up from his chair, overjoyed to see me.

I'm so happy to see him, I want to fling myself into his arms. The presence of the commissioner, standing behind his desk, inhibits me. So does the knowledge of what I almost did to Barrett and our friends. I must have been insane to think of accepting Reid's deal! Reid would never keep our secret to himself, and he would never help my father off the hook.

"Where have you been?" I ask Barrett. "What happened?"

He looks tired but unhurt. "After Inspector Reid let you out of the carriage at the police station in Whitechapel, I was driven around the block, then brought inside and locked in an office. I sat there by myself until Commissioner Bradford sent for me." His anxious gaze searches my face. "What did Reid do to you?"

I can't say it in front of the commissioner and risk the possibility that he'll buy Reid's theory that Barrett is the Ripper. "He let me cool my heels for three hours. As soon as he came to talk to me, I was whisked off to Scotland Yard."

Barrett expels his breath. "I'm glad you're all right."

My relief at seeing him alive and well gives way to irritation because he'd been left in peace while I was threatened. I think of Jane, and my face throbs with angry blood. That I almost sacrificed everything, and everyone else, to save him! He's an adulterer and I'm a fool.

We take our seats, and the commissioner says, "Sir Gerald sent me a telegram saying you'd been arrested."

Thank God for Sally. She must have rushed straight to the *Daily World* headquarters, fortunately found Sir Gerald there, and informed him of our plight.

"Inspector Reid believes you two know something about the Ripper murders. I don't think so." The commissioner seems sincere, but my guard goes up. Officials in high places know part of the secret about the Ripper. Is he among them? The secret is like a tangled ball of yarn, and anyone holding one end might unwind it to the bloodstained clump at the center. "I'll have a word with Reid. You needn't worry about him."

I would be happier if I could believe that Barrett and I are safe from Reid for more than the moment. "Has Detective Sergeant Barrett briefed you on our investigation?"

"No, he arrived only a few minutes before you. Proceed."

"Last night we went to Cremorne Gardens to see what goes on after hours, behind the scenes," Barrett says.

"It was my idea." He thinks he can treat me however he likes, but I won't let him claim credit where credit isn't due.

"There were guards patrolling," Barrett says. "We observed activity at the theater. We managed to gain access."

"I picked the lock on the door."

Neither man acknowledges me, which is infuriating. Now that the immediate danger is past, I have the capacity for petty emotions. Barrett says, "There was a private show. It had a tattooed man and a woman without arms. They had sexual relations on stage in front of an audience whose faces we couldn't see."

Thinking of what happened at home afterward, I look at the floor and hope Commissioner Bradford doesn't see me blush.

"Well, that is an interesting development." The commissioner sounds both shocked and gratified to hear of it. "If the Pinkerton detective witnessed a show of that nature, it could be a motive for her murder."

"There's more." Barrett describes the new murder in Whitechapel. "We—" He glances at me. "Sarah identified the victim as Pauline Chaffin, the missing American heiress."

To protect him, I almost put myself, Hugh, Mick, and others in Reid's power, and after Barrett cheated on me, he tried to take credit for my accomplishments. I'm even madder at him because he's letting me score a point in our unspoken competition, trying to get on my good side. I tell Commissioner Bradford about the green paint and say, "Pauline was posing as a mermaid at Cremorne Gardens. I think she was killed there last night."

The commissioner nods as he absorbs the news. "That's evidence against the dwarf, the proprietress, and their colleagues. Very good."

I don't disagree, but my contrary mood makes me say, "Prince Eddy is still a suspect."

"Was he at the show last night?"

"We didn't see him," Barrett says.

"He could have been in the audience," I say.

"Or not," Commissioner Bradford says. "And so far, you can't place him in Whitechapel, where Pauline Chaffin's body turned up."

I can guess what he's thinking: It was bad enough to have Prince Eddy linked to one murder, but this second one makes matters far worse because the victim came from a prominent American family.

"Have you revealed her identity to anyone?" Commissioner Bradford says.

"Not yet," Barrett says.

"Don't. News of her murder could cause an international incident."

"We'll have to tell Timothy Parnell so he can notify her family," I point out.

"Keep quiet for now."

Because of my own experience with a missing relative, I can't condone keeping Pauline's family in the dark. "It's cruel to let them think Pauline is still alive."

"Perhaps it's kind to delay the bad news." The commissioner speaks with finality and authority.

Never has the secrecy of this investigation disturbed me so much. I start to say it's wrong of him to deceive Pauline's family and wrong to bend over backward to protect Prince Eddy, but Barrett quickly speaks up. "I'll make inquiries in Whitechapel. Maybe I can find witnesses who can place someone from Cremorne Gardens near the alley where Pauline's body was found."

"We've good reason to focus the investigation on Cremorne Gardens." Commissioner Bradford lifts a paper from his desk. It's a telegram. "My contact in the Berlin police department made inquiries about Ursula Richter and Clarence Flynn. Rosenfeld's Circus has no record of either individual."

★   ★   ★

On the way home in a cab, Barrett says, "I don't appreciate you outdoing me in front of the commissioner."

"I don't appreciate you cutting me off when I was about to give him a piece of my mind."

"I was only trying to keep you out of trouble."

I'm glad he did, but I retort, "Thanks to my troublemaking, we know what's going on at Cremorne Gardens."

"Thanks to Commissioner Bradford, we know that your friend Clarence Flynn lied about his background. What else did he and Ursula lie about? Who are they really?"

I'm stung by his pointed reminder that he perceived my attraction to Clarence Flynn, hurt because Flynn deceived me. "I suppose you think it's all right for you to make love to your friend Jane Lambert because she's not a murder suspect."

"Oh for Christ's sake!" Barrett yells.

My temper explodes like a gas flame turned too high, shattering a lamp. "Would you like to hear what I was almost forced to do to keep *you* out of trouble?" I tell him about Reid's deal.

The look on Barrett's face is darker than I've ever seen, ferocious in its intensity. He huffs while his fists clench and his body jerks violently, as if his anger at Reid—and at me—is a demon he's fighting to contain. "How could you even think of trusting Reid? Are you crazy?"

For the first time I think my husband is capable of putting his hands on me in anger, but I'm beyond caution. "You should be thankful I wanted to protect you in spite of everything!"

"Oh, was it me you wanted to protect?" Barrett retorts. "Are you sure it wasn't your father?"

"It was both of you," I protest.

"Hah! You'd have thrown me, Hugh, and Mick to the wolves for Benjamin Bain's sake. You chose him over us."

"I didn't." My denial collides with the uneasy inkling that he's not wrong.

"You choose not to believe me about Jane, but you choose to believe he's innocent. You take him at his word, but you won't take me at mine." Barrett's voice and expression are fierce with rage. "Your father could be guilty. You would have sacrificed us to save a murderer!"

I'm so gobsmacked I can't answer. It seems that all the while Barrett stood by me and sympathized with me through my father's legal troubles, he's been harboring his own doubts about my father, about my judgment. I've kept him and my father apart, and not let them get to know each other, for fear that Barrett would sense guilt in my father. But now it seems Barrett suspects him of the murder, even though they've never met. My eyes sting as if Barrett had slapped my face. This new instance of his disloyalty is so painful.

Barrett's anger gives way to dismay as he realizes he's gone too far. "Sarah, I'm sorry." But he doesn't take back what he said.

The cab stops at a traffic jam on Whitechapel High Street. I jump out and run, hear Barrett curse as he chases after me.

Outside my house, a police constable interrupts my headlong rush. "Mrs. Barrett, I was just coming to tell you, I have bad news about your friend Hugh. He collapsed on the street. He was taken to London Hospital."

★ ★ ★

At London Hospital, I hurry into the men's accident ward, a long room with beds positioned against the walls and separated by curtains. Barrett had wanted to come with me, but because I couldn't stand to be near him, I jumped in a cab and left him standing in the street. I don't know where he is, and right now I don't care. All my concern is for Hugh.

The beds are all occupied because of the traffic collisions that abound during the fog and the usual pub brawls and factory and railway accidents. Families huddle around men who lie bleeding from wounds on their heads, faces, and limbs, amid the reek of illness and disinfectant. Groans of pain emanate from behind the curtains as doctors work on patients. Nurses rush back and forth, ministering to the afflicted. I find Hugh lying on a bed, fully dressed except for his shoes and hat, with a distraught Fitzmorris seated in a chair by his side.

Breathless from exertion and anxiety, I cry, "What happened?"

Hugh doesn't answer. His eyes are closed, the bones sharp in his blanched face. His coat, trousers, and hair are caked with mud. Only the rise and fall of his chest shows that he's alive.

"He fell in the Whitechapel High Street," Fitzmorris says. "An omnibus was coming. Someone pulled him out of the way just in time."

Fitzmorris's voice breaks, and I think we both suspect that Hugh's latest brush with death wasn't an accident. "Oh, Hugh." I'm beyond scolding and pleading, at a loss for words. Guilt tortures me as I think of how I almost betrayed him to Inspector Reid. Where do my loyalties ultimately lie—with my husband and friends or my father? My love for Barrett, Mick, and Hugh is of two years' duration; my love for my father spans my whole life. My dilemma feels impossible to resolve.

Hugh's eyes crack open. They're bloodshot, the lids crusted, A bitter smile twists his colorless lips. "This has become vexatiously redundant. I think I'm headed for the other side, then someone drags me back to the land of the living." Forlorn laughter heaves his chest, and he grimaces in pain. "Fate is conspiring against me."

I take his cold, thin, muddy hand. His fingers cling weakly to mine, and he whispers, "I can't die, but I can't go on like this."

CHAPTER 18

Church bells awaken me early the next morning. Drowsiness gives me the brief illusion that it's an ordinary Sunday, I don't have to work unless there's an especially important crime scene to photograph, and if Barrett has the day off, we can lie abed late. But when I reach for him, he's not there, and I remember that after our quarrel, he didn't come home. Last night was the first we've spent apart during our marriage. I groan, wishing I could go back to sleep and forget everything that's happened, but I'm wide awake now, and I have much to do.

I force myself to get up, wash, dress, and go downstairs. On the way I check Mick's room—it's empty; he's gone back to Cremorne Gardens. He was out late last night, and I didn't have a chance to tell him about Inspector Reid. Fitzmorris is at the hospital with Hugh, who's been transferred from the accident ward to the general ward. I eat a solitary breakfast of coffee and toast in a house that feels newly fragile. That it's stood for a hundred years doesn't mean it will stand for much longer.

The doorbell jangles. I go downstairs to find Dr. Lewes.

"Good morning, Mrs. Barrett. I'm here to see Hugh."

"I'm sorry, he's not home."

After I explain, Dr. Lewes says, "Oh dear. Well, I'll visit him in the hospital."

"I don't think that's a good idea. You pushed him too hard last time. Now look what's happened."

"His actions are his own choice," Dr. Lewes says mildly. "As are the consequences."

I can't argue, but I say, "Please at least wait awhile before you see him again."

"I understand your concern, but Hugh is my patient, and I have to do what I think is best for him." Sympathetic but firm, Dr. Lewes tips his hat. "Good day."

I've no time to indulge my temper, because someone calls my name, and I turn to see Barrett's mother coming up the street.

"Hello, Sarah." Small and pretty, dressed in her Sunday coat and feather-trimmed hat, she smiles. "I'm glad I caught you before you ran off somewhere."

"How nice to see you, Mildred." When we first met, my mother-in-law and I got off on the wrong foot because she didn't approve of my job, my style of living, or my independent attitude, and I didn't care for her attempts to mold me into a conventional wife for her son. After some heated quarrels, we called a truce. Now I muster my nicest behavior. It's like putting on a frock made of scratchy wool, but I'm getting used to it. "Won't you come in for a cup of tea?"

Upstairs, while I put on the kettle, Mildred says, "How are you?"

"I'm fine."

Getting along with her requires avoiding sensitive topics such as the trial. She thinks my father is guilty and a disgrace to her family. We drink tea and chat about the weather, and then I say, "Thomas isn't here." The only time I call him by his first name is when I speak of him to his family. "He'll be sorry he missed you."

"I saw him this morning. He slept at my house last night."

"Oh." I'm relieved that he didn't go to Jane Lambert, but embarrassed because my mother-in-law knows we've quarreled.

"A month since the wedding, and he's already running home to Mum. That's not good." Her reproachful look says she blames me.

I hurry to make excuses. "Things are in a bit of an upheaval. Thomas is on a special case, and Hugh is in the hospital."

Mildred gasps in dismay. "What's wrong?" She once hated Hugh because she disapproves of homosexuals, but then Hugh saved Barrett's life, and she now cherishes him as a member of her family.

"He's still weak from his injury, and he fell." The whole truth, which involves my job, is off limits. "The doctors are keeping him under observation."

"I'll bring him some of my special chicken soup, to build up his strength." Then Mildred says, "Thomas didn't tell me what the problem is, but I can guess. Jane Lambert came to see me yesterday. That's why I want to talk to you."

I feel a resurgence of anger and jealousy, tinged with apprehension. Once, in the heat of a quarrel, Mildred told me she wished her son had married Jane instead of me. Since our truce, Jane has been another taboo topic.

"Jane is a wonderful girl, so sweet and kind. She's like the daughter I never had."

The praise rankles. Is Mildred reverting to her old ways, joining forces with Jane to oust me from her family?

"She told me that she's very concerned about you and Thomas."

"How nice of her." She's so concerned about us that she's trying to ruin our marriage. I paste a smile on my face.

"She's afraid that if you have children, they'll inherit bad blood from your father."

Meaning, I'll hand down the bad blood of my father the rapist and murderer to my offspring, who will grow up to be criminals. Such beliefs about inheritance are widespread, and I don't want to listen to them now. "There's no bad blood. My father is innocent." I only wish my heart could convince my mind.

Mildred fidgets with her spoon, uneasy because she's skating on the thin ice of our relationship. "I'm just telling you what Jane said."

I breathe deeply, trying to tamp down an outburst, but I fail. "Of all the nerve! My marriage is none of her business, and she has no right to insult my family."

"That's what I told Jane, although not in the same words." As I stare in surprise that she would take my side against her "daughter," Mildred says, "She means well, but she shouldn't meddle between a husband and a wife."

"*Meddling* is a polite term for it." My rage bursts through the boundaries that my mother-in-law and I have so carefully established. "She's trying to break up our marriage!" And Barrett has given her license to do so.

"I wouldn't have thought her capable of such a thing. I'm afraid she's upset because Thomas didn't marry her, and she's determined to get him back. That's why I came—to warn you. You're Thomas's wife, he loves you, and you're one of us."

Devastated by the proof of how little he loves me, I'm grateful for Mildred's support. She knows where her loyalty lies. Then she says, "There's never been a divorce in our family, and there never will be if I can help it."

So she's as eager to avoid the stigma of divorce as she is loyal to me. Still, I respect and envy her for the certainty of her convictions. "Thank you for the warning."

"You're very welcome." Mildred sets down her empty cup and rises to leave. "Jane has become a desperate, ruthless woman. I'm afraid she'll stop at nothing to take your place as Thomas's wife."

★ ★ ★

The day is wintry, with a stiff breeze that whips the fog and clears patches of blue sky over Cremorne Gardens. Intermittent sunlight restores the dilapidated park to something of its former glory. Larger crowds than usual flock to the museum and theater; children run laughing down the paths, around the fountains. I note the long line outside the Gypsy Cave. When I'm ready to leave, I'll drag Mick and Anjali home and tell them, in no uncertain terms, that Countess Zelda and Prince Roman are finished. In the meantime, I must find out who killed Pauline Chaffin. No matter how Barrett treats me, he doesn't deserve the blame for a crime I know he didn't commit. There's nothing I can do about the fact that he lacks alibis for some of the Ripper murders, but I'll be damned if I'll let Reid get him on this one. I vowed to protect him as long as I live, and I'll do so even though he's broken his promise to forsake all others for me.

I head for the Cremorne House Hotel. As Ursula and Clarence Flynn are suspects, I want to know their true identities, and a search of their rooms seems a good starting point. In the full light of day, I observe that the hotel's stone facade, once white, is stained gray and coated with moss and vines. Large, many-paned windows once sparkled with reflected lights from the dance pavilion at night; now, some are boarded up. Broken, headless statues decorate the roofline and a frieze over the main door. I steal down the passage that separates the hotel from the theater, find a side door, and pick the lock.

Inside the hotel, I find a deserted corridor, its floor covered with shreds of carpet. I try the doors along either side; they're unlabeled except for room numbers, their dark green paint peeling, all locked. I proceed to a lobby stripped of furnishings except the counter and the board where keys once hung on hooks. My shoes clatter on broken black-and-white floor tiles. Cheap, dark cotton curtains hang over the windows, for privacy rather than decor. The best rooms would be on the upper level, with a view over the bandstand, dance pavilions, and supper rooms. I ascend a curved staircase made of cracked marble, to another vacant corridor with more unlabeled green doors. I listen at each and hear nothing until I reach the third. A woman's muffled voice issues from the room. I recognize Ursula's German accent, but I can't discern what she's saying. The next door is unlocked. I cautiously open it and peek inside.

The room is unoccupied, furnished with a mismatched bed, dresser, and chair that look like they came from junk shops. Slipping in, I see Hercules's lion-skin tunic on the chair. The air is cold and smells of male sweat. Ursula's voice is louder, coming from an open door near the window. I tiptoe through the door, into a bathroom with white tile walls, old porcelain fixtures, and rusty pipes. Shaving implements lie scattered around a discolored basin. A door on the other side stands ajar. Peering through the crack, I see Hercules sitting naked on the side of a brass bed, holding his head in his hands. Ursula lies in the bed, propped on white pillows, the white duvet covering her lower body, her breasts bare. A decanter and wineglasses sit on a table, and a fire crackles in the hearth.

So Hercules and Ursula are lovers. Just as I suspected, the relations between the Cremorne Gardens partners aren't strictly business.

"It's all right," Ursula says softly.

"No, it's not," Hercules mumbles. His flaccid penis tells the story. He drops his hands and says with a bitter laugh, "How can I make love to you when I'm performing like a stud bull every night for a pack of rich voyeurs?"

I didn't realize he minded; he'd seemed to enjoy sex with Venus. Ursula flings off the bedcovers, kneels behind him, and puts her thin, muscled arms around him. Now I see what the puffed bloomers of her acrobat costume had covered—a growth that extends from the bottom of her spine. It's about an inch wide at the base and five inches long, tapering to a narrow tip.

Ursula has a tail!

Covering my mouth to stifle a gasp, I study her with a mixture of fascination and revulsion. Her tail is covered with smooth skin, studded with bony bumps along the top. It looks as flexible as a cat's, dangling between her buttocks. I'm so distracted that I miss Hercules's next words.

Ursula sighs as if he's suggested something impossible. "Where would we go?"

"Someplace that's warm and sunny all year round. Tahiti is beautiful."

"How would we get there?" Ursula's tone seems intended to nip a fantasy in the bud rather than encourage false hope.

"I've a little money saved up. I could work on the ship to pay the rest of our fare."

"What would we do in Tahiti?"

"It costs almost nothing to live there. I could fish. We could build a hut on the beach. You wouldn't need to work."

Ursula rests her cheek against Hercules's hair. "We could swim in the ocean and collect shells." She sounds half ready to be persuaded.

"And never come back," Hercules says.

"And never come back," Ursula echoes in a quiet, dreamy voice.

Hercules turns to her. "Let's go now!"

She stiffens and withdraws her arms from him. "It's not that simple. We can't outrun the past."

"They'll never find us. We can start fresh."

"We can't leave Flynn."

"Bloody Flynn!" Hercules pounds his fist on the bed. "It always comes down to him, the little bastard."

"Don't talk about him like that," Ursula says sharply.

"Why not? Everything is his fault."

Just as I'd thought, there's bad blood between Flynn and Hercules.

"Flynn saved us!" Ursula says. "If not for him, we would be—"

"And where are we now?" Hercules demands. "Right back in the same prison, only with different jailers."

I listen eagerly, willing them to hint at where they'd been, what prison, and who their jailers are now.

"Flynn didn't know what would happen," Ursula says. "Neither did we. It was our choice to go along with his scheme."

Resentment darkens Hercules's expression. "You always take his side."

"When we were children, he took care of me and protected me."

"Yeah, and he suffered because of you. You told me. But you're not a child anymore. You've a right to do what's best for yourself."

"I won't abandon Flynn." Ursula's tone is regretful but firm.

Hercules turns a challenging stare on her. "You have to choose. Is it going to be me or him?"

She flings up her hands. "I can't. You're my love, but he's my best friend."

The sound of footsteps in the hall alarms me. Flynn calls, "Hercules, are you in there?"

"Dammit," Hercules mutters, then calls, "I'm coming." He stands, pulls on his trousers, and stalks toward the bathroom— toward me.

Caught between him and Flynn, I back into his room.

He comes in, sees me, and scowls. "Hey, what are you doing here?"

Flynn opens the door and says, "What's going on?" Both men glare at me, suspicious and angry. Flynn is no longer my genial host, and the tattooed strongman is more intimidating than entertaining.

"I was looking for you," I lie to Flynn as my heart hammers a cadence of fear. "I wanted to ask some more questions for my article. The door was open, so I came in. I'm sorry."

They look askance at me. Flynn says, "I'll see you out, Mrs. Barrett." He glances toward Ursula's room, then at the half-naked Hercules. The resignation in his eyes says he already knew that Hercules and Ursula are lovers, and the pain says he minds terribly. "You're late for your show," he tells Hercules.

Then he takes me by the arm and propels me out of the room, down the hall and stairs. His grip is strong, adding to the illusion that he's larger than his actual size, and I think of the bruises around Kate Oliver's and Pauline Chaffin's throats. Flynn marches me out the main door of the hotel and tucks my arm around his. Some women gathered near the bandstand call to him. He smiles and waves. They gaze enviously at me, but I feel like Cinderella about to be thrown back in the ash heap.

Instead of escorting me to the main gate, Flynn leads me into the narrow passage between the hotel and the theater. "I'm disappointed in you, Mrs. Barrett." His tone combines flirtation and reproach. "I thought we could be friends."

Anxious to get back in his good graces, I say, "Friends can make mistakes. I found the door to the hotel open and assumed it was all right to go in. Won't you please excuse me?"

"For you, I could excuse almost anything except a blatant lie." Flynn's smile is both fond and sardonic. "The door wasn't open. You forced your way in."

Had he been watching me? "You're very concerned with security, Mr. Flynn." I mimic his flirtatious tone. "I wonder if you have something to hide."

"Everyone has something to hide. What are you hiding, Mrs. Barrett?"

I suppose he's guessed that I'm not here to write a story. If I can make him think I'm coming clean, perhaps he'll trust me. "Actually, I did tell you a little fib. The *Daily World* didn't assign me to write about Cremorne Gardens. I'm sick of photographing crime scenes, and I thought that if I wrote a feature story, and the editor liked it, I could switch jobs." Flynn chuckles as if to say we both know I'm still fibbing, but I stubbornly persist. "You could help me by letting me finish my interview with you. May I ask you a few more questions?"

Mischief dances in Flynn's eyes. "You have until we reach the gate."

"Fair enough. You said you once worked for Rosenfeld's Circus. Can you tell me about your most interesting experiences?"

"That would take too long."

"Who were some of the other performers?"

"If you're such a good reporter, you can find out for yourself."

I think we both know he lied about Rosenfeld's and I'm trying to find out who he and Ursula Richter really are. "May I stop at the Gypsy Cave before I go? I'd like my fortune told again."

"I'm sorry." Flynn releases my arm. We're at the gate, and he unlocks and opens it. "Goodbye, Mrs. Barrett." His manner is half apologetic, half threatening.

My attraction to him persists, but the quality of it has changed. Now it's less a feminine interest in a handsome, charming man and more akin to my affinity for danger. "Where were you the night before last night?"

Flynn doesn't ask why I want to know. "If you're as smart as you think you are, you won't come back."

I suddenly remember the newspaper photograph of myself with Sally at Newgate Prison. My expression was fierce as I raised my hand to hit the photographer who frightened my sister. Flynn's expression is the same—he's protecting his people just as I do mine.

"You're not welcome here anymore, and neither are your husband and your friend Hugh Staunton," Flynn says. "We'll be on the lookout for both of you."

CHAPTER 19

Outside the gate, I pace the road that separates Cremorne Gardens from a row of warehouses. I once again remember the day with my father, disembarking from the ferry at the pier and strolling a crowded promenade along the Thames, but now workers are loading goods onto wagons, and the only sign of the river is the dense, foul-smelling mist that obscures the rooftops. I can only hope Mick and Anjali will be safe until I convince them to quit their fortune-telling jobs. I'm at loose ends, while Inspector Reid is hellbent on persecuting Barrett for Pauline Chaffin's murder and the Ripper's crimes because I didn't accept his deal.

The gate creaks open, and two women come out. The shorter one, who wears a plain gray coat and hat, is Gretchen, the blonde acrobat I saw perform with Ursula Richter. The other, glamorous in a black cape and broad-brimmed hat trimmed with fake cherries, is Venus de Milo. They take no notice of me. I wait until they pass, then follow them at a distance. Across the road from the warehouses are tenements, shops, and businesses. Venus and Gretchen enter a pub named the Cremorne Tap. Once it must have catered to people coming to visit or on their way home from the pleasure gardens. The building, which has a balcony where customers can enjoy a river view in summer, is dingy, its ornate gas lamps broken. Inside I notice framed, faded posters from Cremorne Gardens' heyday: a balloon ascent, men walking a tightrope across the river, a medieval tournament. The customers look to be laborers from the docks. They surround Venus and Gretchen, who are seated at a table with glasses of ale. Gretchen is a prim, unsmiling chaperone.

Venus kicks the black leather slipper off one foot, bends over, and uses her teeth to pull up her skirt and remove her stocking while the men ogle, nudge one another, and grin. She swings up her leg, lifts her glass with her toes, and drains it, showing pink petticoats.

I approach the table. "Hello—may I join you?"

A man pulls up a chair for me. As I sit, Venus narrows her luminous black eyes, as if she thinks I want to steal her admirers.

"I'm Mrs. Sarah Barrett, a reporter from the *Daily World*, doing a story about Cremorne Gardens," I say. "I heard you sing, and I was impressed with your talent. May I interview you?"

She smiles and says in a lilting foreign accent, "But of course."

I pull my notebook and pencil out of my satchel. "First of all, where are you from?"

"Italia."

"I assume that 'Venus de Milo' is your stage name?"

"Yes. I cannot tell my real name. I am a princess from an important family. They would not like it known that I ran away to sing for the public."

The men wander over to the bar; they must have heard this story, which I suspect is just as fake as the one about Flynn and Ursula working for Rosenfeld's Circus. Gretchen sits like a sentry, guarding Venus.

"Why did you run away?" I ask.

"My father put me in a convent, to hide me from the world. He is ashamed to have a child born without arms. Everyone says it was because he or my mother committed some terrible sin." Tears glisten in Venus's eyes.

The story of her family's shame could be true. In England, children with deformities are often cast out by their kin and sent to orphanages.

"My only happiness was singing in choir," Venus says. "But I was not happy to become a nun. I wanted to perform on stage for many, many people. One night I sneaked out of the convent and went to Roma. I sang on streets, then in taverns. I met an Englishman who fell in love with me. He said he was rich, and he would take me to London and put me in the opera. But when we got here, I found out it was all lies. He was not rich, and he had—how do you say—no connections." Venus makes a moue of disgust. "So I left him, and I worked singing in pubs. Then I heard about Cremorne Gardens. I came and sang for Mr. Flynn. He hired me." She dimples. "It is not opera, but I have a bigger audience every day."

I scribble notes. "My readers will be inspired by how you overcame your difficulties. I think they would especially like to hear about the show I saw you in last night."

Venus's smile freezes. "Last night?"

"There is no night show," Gretchen says in a German-accented voice. "Cremorne Gardens closes at six."

"Gretchen, will you let us speak privately?" Venus says.

Gretchen, apparently not in on the secrets of Cremorne Gardens, goes to the bar. I hear Venus tapping her feet. Lacking hands, she must feel the urge to move other parts of her body to release nervous tension.

"You were there?" she says in a low voice.

I nod, letting her think I was seated among the audience.

"I beg you not to write about it. You will get me in trouble."

"I won't, if you'll answer my questions."

Venus shrinks inside her cape as if caught between a steamroller on one side and a wall of flames on the other. "All right."

"Why do Clarence Flynn and Ursula Richter put on those shows? If the police should find out, everyone involved could go to prison."

"To earn money. Much, much more than from the other attractions."

That must be how Cremorne Gardens stays afloat despite charging only three shillings for admission. "How does the audience know about the shows?" They couldn't be advertised on handbills.

"I don't know."

"Why do you do it?" I'm interested in Venus's motives as well as the possible connection between the shows and the murders.

Venus shrugs. "Singing doesn't pay enough."

"Can't you ask your family for help? Wouldn't the convent be better than . . .?"

"I have no family. I was never in a convent. That is just a fairy tale people like to hear." Venus's expression scorns me as gullible for believing it. "I was born in the whorehouse where my mother worked. She died of the French disease. I was put to work when I was eight. Some men liked me because I was a freak. One of them brought me to England."

I pity this woman who'd begun life at an extreme disadvantage and been forced into sexual servitude. She says matter-of-factly, "I don't mind the shows. Hercules is clean and healthy and does not harm me. Flynn does not make me do anything I don't want. And the men in the audience give me big tips."

"Do you know who they are?"

"Rich, important people." Venus sits up straighter, as if proud of moving up in the world after leaving the Italian brothel. "But I will not say more."

"Is Prince Eddy one of them?"

Venus's eyes flare with alarm. "I—I don't know."

"Was he there last night?"

"I don't know who was there. The show ended early because of trespassers." Venus's feet tap a staccato rhythm. "People sometimes sneak into Cremorne Gardens after it closes. Flynn sent the audience away."

Her reaction tells me she's acquainted with Prince Eddy, and I'm almost certain, to my dismay, that he was at Cremorne Gardens the night Pauline Chaffin died.

"I don't know if the audience came back later for—" Venus gulps, swallowing the words.

I feel a tingle of dreadful anticipation; I sense that I'm on the brink of a discovery that will do more harm than good. "Came back for what?"

"Nothing."

"I could publish a story about the show and everything you've told me so far."

Venus's eyes glint with hatred, but she capitulates. "There are parties after the shows, for special guests."

"What happens at the parties?"

"I don't know. I'm never invited." Venus calls, "Gretchen! I want to go home."

As Gretchen comes over and puts Venus's stocking and shoe back on, I say, "Do you know what happened to the woman who pretends to be a mermaid?"

"Flynn said she quit." On that note, Venus hurries out the door with Gretchen.

★   ★   ★

Along the Whitechapel High Street, the crowds are thicker than usual for a cold, damp Sunday. I squeeze past people gossiping on the sidewalks. Lurid excitement animates their conversations. A man in a top hat and gaudy plaid coat speaks through a megaphone to a group at the archway that leads to Castle Alley.

"And here we have the scene of the Ripper's new murder!"

The folks who've made a business of the Ripper have lost no time capitalizing on his supposed latest crime. Outside the Red Lion pub, a gang of toughs surrounds three bearded Jewish men. "Which of you's the Ripper?"

A widespread theory, based on flimsy evidence, says the Ripper is a Jew. Innocent men were attacked, and a Jewish friend of mine wrongly arrested. I'm horrified to see the persecution starting again, and angry at these ignorant hooligans.

"This murder wasn't the Ripper," I tell them.

The biggest, ugliest tough glares at me. "Mind your own business, lady." He and his friends grab, punch, and mock the Jews. A crowd gathers to watch, and other men join in.

Police constables wade into the melee, shouting, "Break it up!" They separate the attackers and victims, scatter the crowd.

I see Barrett across the street, and the cauldron of anger and hurt inside me begins to simmer. As I hurry toward home, he falls into step beside me, and we glance at each other as if we're strangers who've suddenly found ourselves in close, accidental, uncomfortable proximity.

"Your mother came to see me this morning," I say.

Barrett speaks at the same moment. "Witnesses saw a carriage going round the streets near Castle Alley last night. It could have been the killer looking for someplace to dump the body. But they didn't get a look at the driver."

"That's too bad." I'm glad I lost the chance to tell him what Mildred said; I'd have sounded as jealous, angry, and insecure as I am. Better to let him think I don't care that he didn't come home last night or where he was.

"Where've you been?" Concern tinges Barrett's accusing tone.

"At Cremorne Gardens."

"By yourself?"

"Who would I have gone with?" A sharp edge to my breezy manner reminds him that his company was scarce this morning.

"What happened?"

I deliver the good news first. "I spied on Ursula Richter and Hercules. They're lovers. And Ursula has a tail."

Barrett emits a sound that crosses a laugh with a snort. *"What?"* After I describe Ursula's tail, he says, "Well. It might help identify her. There can't be many female acrobats with tails."

"That did occur to me." My voice is chilly.

Barrett puffs out his breath, venting frustration. "What else?"

"Hercules and Flynn are rivals for Ursula's favor. The three of them are bound together by something from their past." I summarize the conversation I overheard.

"But what is it, and what might it have to do with the murders?"

"I don't know," I snap. "Did you expect me to solve the whole case *by myself?*"

"I'm sorry. I was just wondering out loud." He sounds annoyed as well as apologetic. "Let's go back to Cremorne Gardens and see if we can solve it together, shall we?"

Now for the bad news. "Flynn caught me spying. He escorted me off the premises and said you and I are no longer welcome there."

Barrett hurries ahead of me, plants himself in my path, and forces me to stop walking. "You got us banned from Cremorne Gardens?" His face darkens with anger. "How could you?"

I'm furious because he's blaming me for my bad luck, furious at myself because I deserve his scolding. "I didn't do it on purpose."

"The result is the same as if you did." His voice rises. "You've lost us our access to the suspects, not to mention the probable scene of Pauline Chaffin's murder."

That I know how badly I erred makes me bristle at his rebuke even more. "It's not the end of the world."

"It could be the end of the investigation. And my job. And yours. I guess you don't care about any of that, but it'll be my neck in the noose if Inspector Reid charges me with Pauline's murder."

We're standing on the sidewalk, shouting at each other. Pass-ersby turn to stare. I'm embarrassed that we've turned our private quarrel into a public spectacle, and I feel sick because Barrett is right—I've put not only justice for Kate Oliver and Pauline Chaffin at risk, but his life. And part of the reason I went to Cremorne Gardens alone was my jealousy, my hurt feelings, and my reckless need to act independently of Barrett. His betrayal of me is ruining everything. I'm about to cry and make my disgrace complete. All I want is to get away.

When I push past Barrett and run for home, a newsboy waves a paper in my face and yells, "The Queen's grandson is a suspect in the murder on the train!"

Shock stops me cold. Then Barrett is beside me, snatching the paper. It's the *Chronicle*, chief rival of the *Daily World*. The article is below the lead story about the murder in Castle Alley, accom-panied by a small illustration of a woman lying dead inside a train.

Barrett reads aloud, "'A reliable source says that Prince Albert Victor is under investigation. The source shall remain nameless, but we will state that she is employed by a major newspaper, and along with her tip, she provided certain favors, whose description is unprintable.'" Barrett stares at me, confusion and shock written on his face. *"Sarah?"*

CHAPTER 20

"It wasn't me," I say.

Barrett and I are at the *Daily World* headquarters, in Sir Gerald's office. Sir Gerald sits behind his desk while we stand on the other side like insubordinate soldiers facing the general.

"Then explain this." Sir Gerald taps his finger against the copy of the *Chronicle*, which lies open on the desk.

"I'm not the source. I don't know who is." These are the same words I repeated over and over to Barrett during our rush from Whitechapel to Fleet Street. Although the article didn't name me, it's as if the thousands of copies, distributed all around town, are fingers pointing at me. Stories about my father's trial have inured me to bad publicity, but this feels as shockingly intrusive as a lantern shined in my window while I was naked in the bathtub.

"You're a female reporter employed by a major newspaper," Sir Gerald points out. Of course he won't accept my denial at face value. He didn't get where he is by trusting people just because they've been trustworthy in the past.

"There are other female reporters at other major newspapers besides the *Daily World.*"

"You're the only one who knew about the connection between Prince Eddy and the murder on the train."

I look to Barrett, who gazes stonily out the window at the fog that veils the rooftops. "I didn't tell anyone."

Sir Gerald taps the byline on the article. "Then where did Leonard Dawes get this tip?"

"There are other places it could have come from besides me." I cut my eyes at Barrett. "The police, for example."

"I didn't talk," Barrett says with quick, defensive anger. "And even if I wanted to tell a reporter about a top-secret case, I wouldn't frame my wife."

"After everything else you've done to me, why not frame me?"

Barrett sidesteps away from me, disconcerted because I brought up our marital quarrel in front of Sir Gerald. I'm immediately embarrassed because I couldn't hold my angry tongue.

A shrewd glance from Sir Gerald says he knows there's something amiss between Barrett and me, but he doesn't comment. He crumples the paper, throws it in the waste bin, and says, "This is bad enough, but the other papers will pick up the story and turn it into a full-blown scandal. The Crown must be looking for the troublemaker as we speak. And who will they find?" He jabs his finger at me.

Braced by my anger at the injustice, I point out facts that are getting lost in the shuffle. "Part of the story is true. Prince Eddy *is* a murder suspect, and he *is* under investigation."

Barrett says nothing. Sir Gerald shakes his head. "Doesn't matter what's true. Also doesn't matter whether I believe you're the source. Which, by the way, I don't believe. You're not that stupid." It's a backhanded concession, all I'm likely to get from him. "The Crown will want someone punished. You'll be the scapegoat, along with the *Daily World*. You'll never work for the press again. You'll be lucky if you aren't hanged for treason."

Despite my heart-sickening dread, I try to use logic as a shovel to dig my way out of trouble. "I think Pauline Chaffin was killed at Cremorne Gardens. I just found out that Prince Eddy was there that night. He looks to be a good suspect in her murder as well as Kate Oliver's."

Although a spark of interest animates Barrett's stony expression, Sir Gerald acts as though I hadn't spoken. "I'll be lucky if this isn't the end of my newspaper business."

Furious as I am, with as much as I have to lose, I can spare a little pity for him. I know how much his business means to him, a man who's lost his family—one son kidnapped and murdered, another estranged, and a daughter also deceased. I've heard that his marriage crumbled under the strain of failed attempts to have more children, and he and Lady Alexandra are separated. Sir Gerald, one of the richest men in England, must also be one of the loneliest.

"I'm sorry this happened," I say.

"Sorry isn't enough. The damage is done," he says.

"You can fire me," I say. "That should mend your fences with the Crown." He usually fires me when I'm a liability, only to hire me back later, and by suggesting it myself, I can lessen my humiliation, although not my misery. I love my profession despite the gory murder scenes and dangerous investigations; but better to get out than fight to stay where I'm unwanted.

I'm about to beg Sir Gerald to keep Mick and Hugh employed, when he says, "No, you'll stay at the paper until I decide you're through, and you're going to find out who the source is."

"Of course I am." I hide my relief, which would only lower Sir Gerald's opinion of me. "I want to clear my name."

"Good."

I'm grateful that he's giving me a chance, resigned to the fact that despite his generosity in paying Hugh's hospital bills and my father's legal fees, he's my employer, not my friend. Business is business, and if I don't succeed, he will fire me.

"Watch your back," Sir Gerald says. "The source is someone who wants you ruined. They may attack you again."

I have a good idea who "they," or rather *he*, could be. "I'll get to work right away."

"First things first. I'm not the only one you need to answer to about this," Sir Gerald says. "I sent a telegram to Commissioner Bradford, warning him about the article in case he hadn't seen it. He wants you at Scotland Yard immediately."

★　★　★

Outside, walking down Fleet Street, I say sarcastically to Barrett, "Thank you for speaking up for me to Sir Gerald."

"I thought that since he's your boss, you would want to do the talking," Barrett says.

"You were quick enough to speak up for yourself."

"What should I have done?" Barrett demands. "Let you throw me under the train?"

I'm appalled that we've sunk to this level of nastiness. "I only pointed out that the tip could have come from the police. Not necessarily you. Quite a few other men on the force must have heard something of the case when Commissioner Bradford sent down orders to hush it up. I'm betting that Inspector Reid is the source of the tip."

Barrett reacts with dismayed surprise. "Not Reid."

"You're defending him?" I'm outraged, especially since he'd neglected to defend me.

"No! I just can't picture him revealing sensitive information about a top-secret case that involves a member of the royal family."

I think Reid is ruthless and obsessed enough. A horrible suspicion dawns. "You think I'm the source."

"No!" Barrett says too quickly.

The idea is so distressing that I walk faster, as if I could run away from it. "But you aren't sure."

He hurries to stay in step with me. "I know you wouldn't . . . do the other thing the article mentioned."

"Really? Don't you think that because you cheated on me with Jane, I got back at you by cheating with a reporter and having him put it in the newspaper? God, I almost wish I had!"

I see a cab coming, wave it down, and climb in. When Barrett follows before I can slam the door, I say, "Where do you think you're going?"

"To Commissioner Bradford's office."

"Why? He didn't summon you. You could spare yourself an unpleasant scene."

"I'm not letting you face him alone. What kind of husband do you think I am?"

My ferocious stare is my answer.

Barrett looks stricken, crestfallen. He takes my hand and says, "Sarah, we're in this together."

I laugh bitterly. "Oh yes, because of the investigation. But for how long afterward?" I pull my hand free, turn away from him, and glare through the tears that I don't want him to see.

★ ★ ★

Foghorns moan along the river, and mist cloaks the turrets of Scotland Yard headquarters. Late on this Sunday afternoon, only a few windows are illuminated. The constable on duty leads Barrett and me through the empty building, in which cold, dank drafts whisper through the dim passages. The light from the open door of Commissioner Bradford's office is more like a warning beacon than a promise of hospitality. When we enter, he rises from behind his desk, on which I see a copy of the *Chronicle*. The usual twinkle in his eyes hardens to a glint as sharp as a cut diamond.

When I deny that I'm the source of the tip, he raises his hand to silence me and says, "You not only break your oath of secrecy, but you do it in the most flagrantly vulgar way possible, by telling the press and serving yourself to the reporter like a dish of pudding!" He's changed from the genial, popular superior of Barrett's description to the tough, blunt military commander he must have been in India before he lost his arm to a tiger.

Shame heats my cheeks, although I know I've done nothing wrong. Barrett scowls, affronted by the insult to his wife, even though he's mad at me himself. "Sarah didn't do it." He's forced to stand up for me despite his own suspicions.

"I've been fielding messages and visits from representatives of the Crown, who are demanding to know what's going on and why Prince Eddy's role in the case wasn't handled discreetly," the commissioner says. "Mrs. Barrett, you've put me in a bad position."

His rush to judgment provokes my impulse to fight back rather than meekly take his tongue-lashing. "Have you any proof that it really was I who tipped off the *Chronicle*? No, you don't, because *I am not the source!*"

Commissioner Bradford looks surprised at my rejoinder. Barrett says, "Sarah." His tone warns me to curb my temper.

At this moment I don't care that Bradford is the powerful top official in the police department. "Did you bother to investigate the tip before you decided I'm to blame?" The commissioner's abashed look tells me he didn't. "Who did *you* tell about Prince Eddy? Someone from your office could have talked to a reporter, and the reporter covered for him by hinting that it was me."

"I've confronted many a criminal in my time, and I've learned that attempting to deflect the blame onto someone else is a mark of guilt," Commissioner Bradford blusters.

"Well, you also should have learned that jumping to conclusions is no way to get to the truth."

"Sarah!" Barrett says.

I'm on a roll, and not even God can stop me. "You'd have done better to inform the Crown at the start. But no—you chose to handle the case on the sly, and now that it's blown up in your face, you're looking to blame *me* for your own mistake."

"Control your wife, Detective Sergeant Barrett," the commissioner says between clenched teeth.

"I'm sorry, sir." Barrett seizes my arm. "Sarah, let's go home."

"Don't apologize for me! I'm the one who deserves an apology." Infuriated at both him and the commissioner, I twist out of his grasp.

"She's off the case," the commissioner says to Barrett. "You'll conduct the investigation on your own. And if you let her near it or tell her anything about it, you're off the case—and off the police force."

★ ★ ★

The cab is too crowded, filled with our mutual antagonism. Barrett says, "You should have kept quiet. You only made things worse."

"You didn't even try to make them better," I retort.

"How could I? You didn't let me get a word in edgewise." Barrett rubs his face. "God! I'm lucky the commissioner didn't throw me off the force then and there."

I can't help realizing he's right. No matter that my anger was justified and my remarks spot-on, I say, "I'm sorry."

"Sorry isn't enough," Barrett echoes Sir Gerald's words.

With a mighty effort, I tamp down a fresh spate of temper and resist the urge to bring up Jane Lambert. This isn't about our marital troubles; our livelihoods are at stake. So is justice for two dead women. So is Barrett's neck. "I'll make things right. I'll find out who the source is. I'll help you solve the murders and get back in good standing with the commissioner."

"Didn't you hear him? You're off the case."

"That doesn't mean I should sit back and leave you in the lurch. There must be something I can do. The commissioner doesn't need to know."

"You want to do a secret investigation behind his back?" Incredulity raises Barrett's eyebrows.

"A secret investigation is how Hugh, Mick, and I identified the Ripper."

Barrett is momentarily silenced; he can't deny that my friends and I ended the Ripper's reign of terror by digging up clues in places where only we knew where to look, keeping the police in the dark. "Taking the hunt for the Ripper into your own hands is why we're in trouble now."

"If we hadn't, there would have been more murders. And there may be more murders to come if this killer isn't caught. The commissioner shouldn't make you work by yourself."

Barrett gives me a long, somber look. "Maybe it's best that I work by myself."

My earlier suspicion comes back with a vengeance. "Oh God. You really do think I am the source!"

Barrett's eyes search my face as if for hidden guilt. "I don't want to think so. But—"

"But what?"

He turns away. "This wouldn't be the first time you went behind my back."

Now our old issue rears its ugly head. He can't forget that I've kept secrets from him; he hasn't quite forgiven me and still doesn't entirely trust me. My spirits wilt like a flower chopped off the plant. "I didn't this time."

"I'm not bringing you in on the investigation behind the commissioner's back. It's too much of a risk."

"Well, it's a risk you can't afford to refuse. Even if Reid can't pin the Ripper murders on you, there's still Pauline Chaffin's. Both you and Prince Eddy were at Cremorne Gardens the night Pauline died. If it comes down to a choice between him and you for prime suspect, whom do you think Reid will choose?"

"Don't you think I realize that?"

"Then for God's sake, let me help you solve the case!" I'm faintly aware that I'm not just asking to do a little investigation on the sly; I'm asking him to let me make it up to him for my past sins.

His expression turns resentful. "Are you implying I can't do it without your help?"

"No." I curse myself for saying the wrong thing. "I just think the more hands on deck, the better." I'm angry because I'm the wronged party, but trying to placate him. "Do you really believe I gave myself to that reporter?"

"Once I wouldn't have believed any such thing. But now—"

"Now, what?" I'm aghast that he thinks me so faithless when I've barely looked at other men since I met him. My attraction to Clarence Flynn was fleeting, trivial.

"You said it yourself. Why wouldn't you do it, to get back at me because you think I'm involved with Jane?"

"I would never—"

"*I* would never cheat on *you*." Barrett's indignation equals mine. "You won't believe me, so why should I believe you?"

Now the shoe is on the other foot. Distrust is like a cancer, spreading and growing, destroying loyalty, sabotaging love. We ride in a silent, angry stalemate until the cab stops at our house. Barrett jumps out and helps me descend. The touch of his hand on mine is as impersonal as though he were a hired liveryman. Instead of paying our fare, he tells the driver to wait. As soon as I've unlocked the door, he climbs back in the cab and calls his parents' address to the driver.

He's gone without saying goodbye.

I go inside the house, lock the door, and collapse on the divan in my cold, dark studio. Everything that happens widens the rift between Barrett and me. I can't believe that after we've been through so much, we've foundered into such a bad place. Tears flood my eyes as I remember how happy we were at our wedding. I want to rush to Barrett and beg him to come back. But

I shan't have him back if the price is letting him do whatever he wants with whomever he chooses from now on. I'd rather be alone for the rest of my life. I wipe my eyes, compose myself, and go upstairs.

Mick is alone in the kitchen, wearing his gypsy costume, eating lamb stew. "Want some? Fitzmorris made it when he came back from the hospital. He's there now. He told me about Hugh." His face, under the charcoal smudges, is pensive, worried. "It's bad, ain't it?"

I nod, ladle stew in a bowl, and drop into a chair. My stomach feels like an empty burlap sack sticking to the inside of my ribcage, but I can't eat. My marriage is all but over, my friend seemingly at death's door. I'm thankful for Mick's company.

"Where's Anjali?" I say.

"At home. We quit our jobs at Cremorne Gardens. She didn't want to, but I decided you were right—it's too dangerous for her."

"Good." At least that's one positive development.

"Anything happen?"

I tell him about spying on Ursula and Hercules, getting caught by Clarence Flynn and banned from Cremorne Gardens.

"Now we got nobody inside there. Maybe Anjali and me should go back."

"No, you shouldn't." I tell him that Venus placed Prince Eddy at Cremorne the night of Pauline Chaffin's murder. "We don't want Anjali near that place or that man. And there's another reason she should stay home." I tell Mick about Inspector Reid's threat. "He's going after Barrett. If he knows Anjali is associated with me, she could be next." My bad blood with Reid could spill over onto the innocent girl.

"Bugger Reid," Mick says. "He's lost every round with us so far. He ain't gonna get anywhere now."

I want to believe Mick, and his confidence cheers me up, but he's a fifteen-year-old who thinks playing gypsies among murder suspects is a good idea. "There's more bad news." I tell him about the article in the *Chronicle* and its consequences.

"Of course it weren't you that tipped off that reporter! The commissioner is crazy."

"Thank you." Tears sting my eyes; I'm so glad somebody believes me, so grateful for Mick's loyalty.

"So we're done investigatin'?" Mick's face falls. "Just like that?"

"I'm afraid so." But I feel an obstinate wish to solve the case, prove my worth to Barrett and the commissioner, and make them regret their distrust.

"Where's Barrett?" Mick asks.

My tears spill. I shake my head, unable to speak. Mick looks almost as upset as I feel. He can tell that Barrett and I have quarreled badly and shaken the foundations of our whole family. He pours me a cup of tea and says in a gruff voice, "He'll come back, Sarah. Everything'll be all right. Just wait and see."

On top of everything else, my father's trial recommences tomorrow, and I have to testify.

CHAPTER 21

At ten minutes to ten, Sally and I are sitting in the courtroom gallery, shoulder to shoulder, chins up, braced for battle. The audience buzzes with anticipation to hear the defense's case. At the defense table, Sir William reviews his notes. When I look at the dock, my father briefly meets my gaze, and I see pleading in his eyes before he bows his head. We both know how much he's counting on Sally and me, and how much his fate may hinge on us.

"After the opening speech, you'll be the first witness," Mr. Owusu tells Sally. He's already briefed us on the questions we'll be asked. "Are you ready?"

"Yes." Sally sounds anxious but tries to look brave.

The clerk says, "All rise." The judge takes the bench, and Sir William stands for his opening speech.

"This case is like a book that has a beginning and an end but no middle." He holds up a leatherbound notebook. "In the beginning, Ellen Casey went to Benjamin Bain's house on the afternoon of April twenty-second, 1866. At the end, she was found dead in the neighborhood the next morning. But what happened between those hours?" Sir William opens the notebook and displays pristine white pages. "The middle of the book is blank. The events of that time period are unknown, but our esteemed prosecutor has written his own story onto the blank pages. It says Benjamin Bain raped and strangled Ellen Casey, and it offers not one shred of proof. Instead, it presents a policeman whose sole motive in investigating the crime is to satisfy a personal grudge and who never bothered to look for any other suspects."

Inspector Reid must be here, but I avoid looking for him. I don't want to know if he'll be watching me testify.

"The prosecutor has presented a sister who says Ellen was a good girl, and a neighbor who saw Ellen go into Benjamin Bain's house and didn't see her come out. That doesn't fill in the blank pages. And so what if Benjamin Bain was a troublemaking labor organizer? It might be pertinent if he were charged with instigating a protest march, but he isn't. And although his photograph of Ellen Casey is shocking, it doesn't show him raping or strangling her. It's as if the esteemed prosecutor is a hack writer scribbling lurid romances for the penny magazines."

Prosecutor Ingleby shifts in his chair. Behind me, the Casey family stirs with the same uneasiness. Sally nods, and I commend Sir William for framing the case in such a way that the jury can't help but see the weaknesses of the prosecution's evidence.

"In the absence of physical evidence and eye-witness testimony, the case comes down to a matter of character," Sir William says. "Benjamin Bain has been slandered by the prosecution. I will present testimony that gives a true picture of him. It will show that the prosecutor is asking you, gentlemen of the jury, to send an innocent man to the gallows based on totally fictitious claptrap." Sir William slams the notebook down on the table.

For the first time, I see hope on my father's face. The same hope rises in me, then turns to apprehension as I realize that Sir William could get him acquitted even if he's guilty.

Sir William calls Sally to the witness box. She takes a deep breath, rises, and crosses the courtroom. When the clerk gives her the Bible to hold, it shakes in her unsteady grasp. When he asks if she swears to tell the truth, she says in a timid voice, "I do."

Seated in the witness box, she looks small and vulnerable. I long to stand between her and the reporters, lawyers, and jury, who regard her like vultures waiting for her to be killed.

"What is your relationship to the defendant?" Sir William asks.

"I'm his daughter." Pride amplifies Sally's voice.

"Can you tell us about his character?"

"He's a good, kind, gentle man."

The Casey family mutters, but Sally maintains her composure. Sir William says, "How do you know he's good?"

"He's always been kind to me." Sally smiles at our father. He smiles back fondly, his careworn face transformed by affection. "He's never struck me or hurt me in any way."

"Has he ever touched you?"

"He's kissed me and hugged me as any loving father would."

"He never molested or violated you physically?"

"No." Sally's voice rings with certainty. On this point I can agree with Sally—our father treated me with the same loving kindness.

"Did you ever see him molest, violate, or harm any other girl?"

"No, I did not." Sally boldly addresses the jury: "My father wasn't capable of such things. He didn't kill Ellen Casey. He's innocent."

The Casey family hisses. I only wish I were as sure as Sally. Sir William says, "Thank you, Miss Albert. No further questions."

Mr. Ingleby rises. Sally leans back as if he's raised a fist to strike her. I lean forward, trying to lend her my strength. Mr. Ingleby says, "How long have you known your father?"

Caught off guard by the seemingly innocuous question, Sally stammers. Mr. Ingleby says, "Let me refresh your memory. Your father abandoned you when you were ten. So you knew him for ten years."

"Yes, but—"

"And during that time, you never saw him molest, violate, or harm anyone?"

"Never!" Sally is adamant but rattled by the prosecutor's hostile manner.

"Did you go to school?"

She frowns in confusion. "Yes?"

"Did you go out to play with other children?"

"Yes . . ."

"Did you go to bed at night before your father did?"

Sally flushes pink with anger because he seems to be toying with her. "Yes, but what does that have to do with anything?"

Mr. Ingleby pats the air as if soothing a lapdog. "Is it true that your father could have been up to no good during all those hours while he was out of your sight?"

"Yes. I mean, no." Sally is clearly flustered, her cheeks bright red now.

"Your Lordship," Sir William says, "the prosecution is asking the witness to speculate."

"I'm merely pointing out that Benjamin Bain could have violated or killed girls while his own daughter was none the wiser," Mr. Ingleby says.

"You're writing more claptrap on blank pages," Sir William says with disgust.

"Objection noted," the judge says. "Watch your step, Mr. Ingleby."

"I know my father!" Sally bursts out. "He didn't do anything wrong!"

"Your loyalty is touching. Suppose I grant you that he lived a blameless life when you were young. But then he left. How do you know what he was up to during the eleven years afterward? How do you know he didn't change?"

"When he came back, he was the same as when he left!" Sally cries.

"In your opinion." Mr. Ingleby holds up a stack of notebooks and tells the jury, "What this naive, foolish young woman doesn't know about her father could fill a hundred blank books. No further questions."

Tears rolling down her cheeks, Sally stumbles back to her seat in the gallery amid laughter and jeers from the Casey family, under our father's mournful gaze. Burning with fury at the public humiliation of my sister, I pat her hand and murmur, "It's all right."

Sally shakes her head, wiping her eyes. "No, it's not. I let Father down."

Sir William is stoic; he must have known this was a risk, and he's taking his best shots like a soldier who knows his ammunition is faulty. "I call Mrs. Thomas Barrett."

I hesitate, immobilized by sudden, awful indecision.

"Don't keep us waiting, Mrs. Barrett," the judge says.

I can't repeat what Sally said. I don't think the jurors believed her; why should they believe me? And if I say I think my father is innocent, will the jury sense my doubt? Panic sets my heart racing and my knees quaking as I rise and start toward the witness box. I don't have to tell the story that Sir William expects me to tell. There's another story with which I could fill in the blank pages of the book. But should I?

The clerk puts the Bible in my hands. It feels as heavy as a lead brick. After I'm sworn in and seated in the witness box, I see the courtroom from a new, disorienting perspective. The space and the crowd seem expanded to vast proportions while I've shrunken to the size of an ant. All eyes are on me, stares focused like hot sunbeams through magnifying glasses.

I have seconds to decide whether to follow the script or take matters into my own hands.

"Mrs. Barrett, please state your relationship to the defendant," Sir William says.

My heart beats so hard I can hear it, and I clench my hands to still their trembling. Fear of speaking in public adds to my discomposure. I inhale deeply as if before diving off a cliff into the ocean, then I say, "He's my father. And I know that he didn't kill Ellen Casey because I know who did."

Sir William's face elongates as his mouth drops and his eyebrows fly skyward. It may be the first time that surprise has robbed him of clever remarks. I'm suspended between the impulse to laugh and the terror before I plunge into treacherous waters.

"This is absurd!" Mr. Ingleby says. "One daughter vouched for the defendant's innocence based on blind faith, and the second is making wild claims in an attempt to confuse the jury."

I look at my father. He leans with his hands extended toward me and panic in his eyes. His lips form the word *no*.

Sir William recovers his poise. "Your Lordship, I ask for a recess to confer with my witness."

"You've had adequate time to confer. Recess denied."

"Very well." Sir William addresses me, his eyes blazing with fury in his rigid face. He must hate asking questions to which he doesn't know the answers, and he's warning me that my response had better be good. "Who killed Ellen Casey?"

"It was my mother. Mary Bain."

The words are out; I can't take them back. My father drops his face into his hands. A glance around the courtroom shows Mr. Owusu shaking his head, Sally with her hands over her mouth, and reporters scribbling frantically. The audience in the gallery is a noisy, turbulent mass. Mr. Ingleby sits slumped in his chair as if he's been shot in the back and he's wondering if the wound is fatal.

I raise my voice over the noise. "Lucas Zehnpfennig was the man who raped Ellen."

Cautiously, as if following me into a dark tunnel, Sir William says, "Who is Lucas Zehnpfennig?"

"My mother's illegitimate son. She had him before she married my father." I feel bad for blindsiding Sir William and worse for breaking my promise to my father, but I'm doing what I think necessary. "I didn't know of Lucas's existence until last year."

Sir William hesitates, then asks, "How did you learn of his existence?" Unprepared for this line of questioning, he's improvising while relying on me to lead us safely out of the tunnel.

"I was looking for my father, and I investigated my family's background." My speech comes with unexpected fluency; a part of my mind must have expected this day to come. "I went to my mother's hometown. Someone there told me about Lucas."

Sir William glances at the jurors, who are leaning toward me, listening avidly. "What led you to believe that Lucas raped Ellen Casey?"

"He raped at least three other girls. And he was in Clerkenwell at the time of the murder. He came to my family's home when I was ten. He held me on his lap and fondled me."

There's a moment of shocked silence; the only sound in the courtroom is pens scratching. Then comes a muted uproar like gas igniting in a furnace.

"So one crime can be laid at Lucas Zehnpfennig's door." Sir William sounds both hopeful for and surprised by the sudden, unexpected possibility of victory. "Why did your mother commit the murder?"

"To stop Ellen's screaming."

"Gentlemen of the jury, we now have two alternative suspects in the crimes for which the defendant is charged. No further questions." Sir William's parting glance at me says he's played the hand I dealt him as best he could, and God help me from now on.

Mr. Ingleby jumps to his feet. From my position trapped in the witness box, he seems bigger than his actual size and closer than the few yards of distance between us. He scrutinizes me as if I'm a fly he's about to swat. After standing up to murderers, I shouldn't be scared of Mr. Ingleby, but I am.

"Were you present when Ellen Casey was raped and murdered?" he asks.

I interlace my cold, damp hands in my lap. "No, sir."

"So you didn't see the crimes with your own eyes?"

"No, sir." I'm afraid I know exactly where this is going.

"Then how do you know that this Lucas Zehnpfennig"—Mr. Ingleby stumbles over the name, but it seems less a difficulty with pronouncing a foreign word than an insinuation that it's nonsense I made up—"that he raped Ellen Casey, and your mother strangled her?"

My heart skitters, and I stall for as long as possible. "I was told by a witness who was present."

Impatience flickers across the prosecutor's face. "Who was this alleged witness?"

There's no sidestepping the issue now. "My father."

"Ah. *Your father.*" Swelling with elation, Mr. Ingleby gestures toward the dock, where my father cowers with his hands over his head, as if the rumble from the audience is the sound of the sky falling. "Benjamin Bain, the defendant on trial for the crimes, told you a cock-and-bull story that puts the blame on other people."

"It's true." My insistence is vehement even as my doubts gain strength. Telling the story in public, to a hostile interrogator, makes it seem all the flimsier.

Mr. Ingleby sneers. "Let's suppose, just for the sake of argument, that your father's story is true. Why didn't he tell the police in 1866, when he fell under suspicion for the crimes? Why did he run away instead?"

Those incriminating circumstances sound even worse now. My stomach churns as I muster the conviction to defend my father. "He wanted to protect my mother. He sacrificed himself."

"How noble of him." Mr. Ingleby's voice drips sarcasm. "But now that he's been captured, he has you serving her up on a platter to save his own skin."

"He didn't want me to! It was my decision."

Mr. Ingleby dismisses my words with a flick of his hand. "Where is your mother?" He exudes confidence; I think he knows the answer.

"She's dead."

"Where is her illegitimate son?" He speaks with the brazenness of a gambler betting his all on a throw of the dice.

"Lucas Zehnpfennig is dead too." The first trickle of despair chills me.

"How convenient." Mr. Ingleby smiles, delighted. "Gentlemen of the jury, the witness is accusing two people who aren't here to speak for themselves, and one her own mother. That's a shameless, deplorable ploy to trick you into acquitting her father. Don't be fooled." He addresses me with pitying contempt. "You swallowed your father's lies hook, line, and sinker. And now you've written your own claptrap into Sir William's blank book. No further questions." He sits down, the triumphant gambler raking in his winnings.

I totter out of the witness box on legs that feel made of wood. My clothes, damp with sweat, cling to my skin. Hot with humiliation, I trudge across the courtroom, which seems miles long, through a forest of stares and whispers. When I reach the gallery, the people in the upper tiers are a blur. All I see is the empty seat once occupied by Meg Logan. Why didn't my best-friend-turned-enemy stay to gloat over my downfall? Sally takes my hand and pulls me into my seat, murmuring words of comfort that don't penetrate my misery. I didn't know until now how much I wanted to believe my father's story. How foolish I was to divulge it! I could have been the ten-year-old girl who blindly loved her father, instead of a grown woman who knew better. I'm rabid with anger and revulsion toward myself. Whether he's guilty or innocent, I haven't swayed the jury in his favor; more likely, I've sealed his condemnation.

Sir William stands and says, "Your Lordship, I request a conference with my client and a recess to prepare witnesses who can confirm Mrs. Barrett's story."

"Both granted. Court is adjourned until Wednesday at ten AM."

Alas, I've wrought more havoc than I can fix during a two-day hiatus. The jury might as well convict my father now.

Sally guides me from the courtroom, past the reporters shouting questions and the photographers with their cameras. Then we're with Mr. Owusu, Sir William, and our father in the room where we had our previous conference.

"Father, I'm sorry." My voice is raw with remorse.

"It's all right, Sarah. I know you were only trying to help." He turns away as if he can't bear to look at me.

I wish he had struck me instead. I deserve it for breaking my promise to him and smearing my mother's memory.

"No, Mr. Bain, it isn't all right," Sir William says, then unleashes his fury on me. "That bombshell you dropped made us both look like idiots. And you made your father look like a bastard who slandered his wife to save his own guilty neck." It's hard to tell which he's angrier about—his losing face in court or the possibility of his client losing his life. "I should walk away from this case. But thanks to Sir Gerald Mariner, I'm stuck with you." His resentful gaze encompasses Sally, my father, and me.

Mr. Owusu regards us with a mixture of disapproval and sympathy. "We should discuss how to move forward with the defense."

"There's no need for discussion." Sir William points at me. "You find witnesses and evidence to prove that your mother killed Ellen Casey, or your father will hang."

He strides out of the room, Mr. Owusu follows, and the constable escorts my father back to Newgate. Sally and I walk arm in arm out of Old Bailey, leaning on each other like wounded refugees from a war. I'm realizing that I can't be a hundred percent loyal to everyone at the same time, but now I've betrayed both my parents, probably for naught. I try to plot my next step, but my thoughts are a dark jumble, and time is speeding toward

Wednesday. Reporters and photographers accost us with shouted questions and white explosions. They part to let a man approach us. Amid the dark afterimages that blotch my vision, I recognize Inspector Reid.

"Your father is going down." Reid licks the corners of his wolfish smile. "Your husband is next. Or are you ready to talk?"

Anger revives my spirits like a whip lashed against a horse that's worn out after a long gallop. "Yes, let's talk. You can admit that you're the source who told the *Chronicle* that Prince Eddy is a suspect in the murder on the train."

Reid's eyebrows fly up as if in surprise. "Hey, it wasn't me." He sounds honestly puzzled, but it must be an act.

"You're lying. You did it to get me in trouble and ruin my marriage and my reputation!"

"You must have plenty of other folks out to get you," Reid says. "One of them did me a favor."

"I'm going to prove it was you. And then you'll be sorry because it'll be *you* in trouble!"

"Don't waste your time." Disdain twists Reid's mouth. "You'd do better to think hard about taking my deal if you want me back on the witness stand when your father's trial resumes."

CHAPTER 22

The foggy, rainy cityscape outside the window of the omnibus suits my desolate mood. I've probably ruined my father's chances of acquittal, and despite my doubts, I love him and can't bear for him to die. Barrett is working alone on the case we were supposed to solve together, and I don't know whether he'll come back to me. My old fear of losing every man I love is a barbed-wire cage around my heart. I disembark at London Hospital and buy hothouse roses from a flower seller. With Hugh ill, there's a big empty hole in my life where I once had a friend and confidant, and if I can see that he's better, perhaps I can concentrate on the job of finding witnesses and clues to prove Lucas raped and my mother strangled Ellen Casey.

In the hall on my way to the ward, I encounter Dr. Lewes, who tells me that he just had a session with Hugh.

"How is he?" I ask.

"Physically better."

I exhale with relief. "Good. What are you doing to help him?"

"I'm sorry, I can't discuss his therapy with you."

Taken aback, I say, "But I'm his closest friend—his family, really."

Regret tinges Dr. Lewes's smile. "His therapy is private and confidential."

"Oh. Well, then, I'll just ask him."

"He's not receiving visitors."

Now I'm getting angry. "Is that by your orders?"

"No, it's his own wish. He doesn't want to see anyone."

The news is hurtful, bewildering. "Surely he'll make an exception for me."

"Sometimes patients need time apart from their family and friends, so they can concentrate on working on themselves," Dr. Lewes explains gently.

"Did you put that idea in his mind?" It seems to me that Dr. Lewes is turning Hugh against the people who love and care about him the most.

"I'm sorry, I can't tell you—"

"Look what's happened to him since you came into the picture! How can you be sure that more of your therapy won't make him worse?"

Dr. Lewes replies with his same gentle, infuriating calm. "Sometimes psychological therapy can succeed when there are no other remedies; sometimes not. There are no guarantees. Sometimes we just have to trust in the means we have at hand."

★   ★   ★

After leaving Hugh's flowers with a nurse, I burst out of London Hospital, fuming at Dr. Lewes. How dare he spout such condescending mumbo-jumbo? Maybe Hugh was right to say that the psychologist is a quack. Being denied access to Hugh seems the last straw on this bad day. The drizzle turns to hard rain, and I duck into a tearoom. When I smell the food, I'm suddenly starving; I was too nervous for breakfast before court. I order tea, toast, and poached eggs, and after I've eaten, I feel calmer if not happier. It's nice to sit among strangers, temporarily without conflicts or plans. My thoughts wander back to Dr. Lewes's words: "Sometimes we have to trust in the means we have at hand."

On second thought, maybe it's not mumbo-jumbo. It's what my friends and I do in detective work—rely on clues, circumstances, and picklocks to lead us to the killer. But there's another, less tangible means, an ingredient that is to detection what grease is to machinery: instincts. Whether my mother killed Ellen Casey, or my father's story about her and Lucas Zehnpfennig is a lie, if I use my instincts, maybe they'll lead me to the truth.

I pay my bill, go outside, and hail a cab. I don't know where I'm going until I tell the driver, "Clerkenwell."

Half an hour later, I'm standing on Gough Street, where Ellen Casey's body was found twenty-four years ago. The road construction site is now covered with buildings, streets, and railway tracks. People hurry past me, oblivious, as though they've forgotten the murder or never knew about it. I think of Kate Oliver, the traces of her murder cleaned up along with the wreckage from the train crash. I begin walking, and my footsteps take me to Greville Street. I picture my father and Lucas carrying the heavy trunk that contains Ellen's body into the ruins of a burned house. The ruins are gone, the whole terrace replaced by a three-story brick tenement. My instincts have led me to the old conundrum, the discrepancy between my father's story and the police report. Someone must be mistaken or lying, because the body had to be found at the same place where it was left. Both accounts can't be true.

Or can they?

My mind whirs like rusty gears set in motion by a drop of oil as I walk back toward Gough Street. An idea chimes within me: *Maybe someone moved Ellen's body.* It's a heart-jolting thought. But who would move a body, and why? I picture the night Ellen was left for dead and see a red-haired girl walking through fog, darkness, and gaslight. What if Ellen was *alive* when my father and Lucas left her? What if my mother's strangling hadn't killed her? I picture her lain amid ashes and charred wood in the burned house, then awakening after hours spent unconscious. Am I grasping at straws because I don't want either of my parents to be guilty of murder? Instinct tightens my grip on the fragile straw. Suppose Ellen was alive and did regain consciousness: Where would she go?

I turn down the street that her family and mine once called home. Maybe she met her killer along the way. I study the faces of men I pass. Maybe he's here, hiding in plain sight, but how would I recognize him? I shut out deliberate thought, make my mind a blank stage on which intuition leaps and twirls like a ballerina. I see an empty seat in the crowded gallery in the courtroom. My feet move of their own accord, to Clerkenwell Close, where I enter a tenement and climb the stairs. On the second floor, I remember which door to knock on.

Meg Logan answers, wearing a clean white apron over a dark blue housedress, and a frilled white cap on her red hair. Alarmed to see me, she tries to slam the door, but I hold it open.

"Why did you leave the courtroom?" I ask.

Meg pushes against me for a moment, then wilts and sighs. "You'd better come in."

The flat is small, warm, and very full of things. I recall that Meg and her husband have three children, but her family seems to be elsewhere now. Furniture takes up most of the space; children's drawings cover the walls; and shelves are crammed with flowered dishware, china dolls, toy trains, books, and other possessions. But all looks spotless; green calico curtains decorate the windows, and the air smells of freshly baked bread. The effect is cheerful, similar to Meg's parents' home, where I loved to visit when I was a child, a pleasant respite from the austere rooms my mother kept. We sit at the kitchen table, and Meg serves tea and chocolate biscuits. I feel nostalgic for the cozy times we once had playing house. Drinking and nibbling fills the awkward silence. Instinct brought me here, but it hasn't told me what to say. Meg frowns as she avoids my gaze. I sense she wants to tell me something important, so I wait.

"All these years, I was so sure your father was guilty," she says. "Then I heard what you said today in court."

"You believed it?" I'm surprised; I'd thought nobody did.

"I don't know." Meg looks into her cup as if the tea is a deep pool she's about to dive into. "When I testified that Ellen was a good, decent girl, I didn't exactly lie. She *was* good, and kind and generous. She took care of me when we were kids. When I fell down, she would pick me up, wipe my tears, and say funny things to make me laugh. She let me play with her toys, and she didn't scold me for breaking them. If I did something bad and Ma wanted to punish me, she said it was her fault and took the spanking herself." Meg smiles through tears of grief for the sister she'd lost.

I feel guilty because, no matter what happens to my father, at least Sally and I managed to reunite with him, but Meg will never see Ellen again. Meg keeps silent for many minutes, and I understand her strong loyalty toward Ellen, her reluctance to speak ill of the beloved dead.

"But I didn't exactly tell the truth either. Ellen liked boys, and they liked her. When she was only twelve, they started walking her home from school. Not just the boys in her class, but older ones. She would tell Ma she was taking me to the park, and when we got there, some boy would show up, and she would go off with him and leave me alone."

So Sir William's speculation had been on the mark. Ellen had, according to proper society's standards, been a "bad" girl. Maybe she was as wild as Pauline Chaffin, who'd played mermaid at Cremorne Gardens. Had she thought it a lark to pose as Androm- eda for my father?

"I never told Ma or Pa," Meg says. "I promised Ellen I wouldn't. But I should have known something bad would happen to her."

"You were too young to know better," I say in a futile attempt to soothe Meg.

Meg wipes her eyes. "I recognized his name."

Disconcerted by the abrupt change in subject, I say, "Whose name?"

"Lucas Zehnpfennig."

"You knew him?" It's a startling development I hadn't imagined.

"Not me." Meg explains, "Ellen used to make lists in her school copybook. Lists of boys she liked, in order of how much she liked them. On the last list she made, Lucas Zehnpfennig was at the top. I remember because his last name was so odd and because he was the only boy I didn't know. The others were all from school."

Ellen knew Lucas. He was twelve years her senior, but she'd liked him, and maybe they'd been more than casual acquaintances.

"When you testified about Lucas, I realized there could be things I didn't know about Ellen," Meg says. "I realized I might be wrong about your father, and I was so upset, I had to leave the courtroom."

I'd thought Lucas had come to my family home to visit my mother, found Ellen there by chance, and attacked her. The idea of a relationship between Ellen and Lucas changes my whole concep- tion of the crime.

"After your father disappeared, my family turned everyone against you and your mother. I said bad things about you at school. I've always felt guilty about it." Regret saddens Meg's expression. "I'm sorry now. If I was wrong, I want to make things right."

I'd thought the whole neighborhood was responsible for the ostracization and never blamed anyone in particular. It hurts to know that my best friend had played an active part in it. "You can make things right by helping me get to the bottom of them."

"All right." Her eager cooperation moves me a considerable distance toward forgiveness.

"Ellen never mentioned Lucas to you?"

"No. Maybe nothing ever happened between them." Meg seems anxious to preserve a vestige of Ellen's honor.

"But you don't know for a fact."

Meg sadly shakes her head. "If Pa found out she was seeing a man, he'd have whipped her. She wouldn't have trusted me with a secret that big."

"Who might she have trusted?"

"She was best friends with Patsy Fallon. Murphy, now."

I have a sudden memory of Ellen and a pretty dark-haired girl, whispering and giggling together. "Where can I find Patsy?"

"She lives right upstairs. Flat number 302."

★　★　★

The door to flat number 302 has a splintered hole near the bottom, as if someone had kicked it hard. Screams blare from within. When I knock, a boy who's perhaps eight years old answers.

"Yeah?"

"Is your mother home?" I ask.

Another boy tackles him from behind. As they wrestle and yell, a woman shouts, "Timmy! Joey! Stop it, or I'll smack you!" She comes to the door, wearing a dressing gown, nightcap, and slippers, as if she just got out of bed. She must be in her late thirties but looks a decade older, her figure pudgy, her dark hair thin, and her round pink face sagging into jowls. She brandishes a spatula at the boys, who run into the flat.

"Who are you?" Her unfriendly glance rakes me up and down.

"Hello, Patsy. I'm Sarah Bain. Do you remember me?"

Patsy drops the spatula, clutches her throat, and stares. "Oh God."

She backs away, and I follow her into the room. The flat is a mess, with clothes piled on the furniture and toys strewn across the floor. A smell of hot grease wafts from the kitchen, where I glimpse stacks of dirty dishes, pots, and pans.

"I want to talk to you about Ellen Casey," I say.

Patsy's dark eyes glitter with fright. "I don't know nothin'."

"You were her best friend."

"That was a long time ago." In the bedroom, the boys yell; thumps shake the floor. Patsy shouts, "Jenny!" From an armchair whose back is piled so high with clothes that I didn't see her, a slender, dark-haired teenage girl rises. "You're supposed to be watching your brothers."

"Yeah, Ma." Jenny shuffles to the bedroom.

Smoke and a burning smell drift from the kitchen. "Shit!" Patsy runs in and lifts a frying pan off the stove. I follow her. The teakettle whistles, and Jenny's shrill voice, scolding Timmy and Joey, adds to the din.

"Did Ellen talk to you about boys?" I say.

Patsy dumps burned sausages onto a plate. "What does it matter? She's dead."

Her queasy expression tells me I've struck a nerve. "You must have heard that my father is on trial for her murder. I'm trying to find out what really happened to her."

Scorn pulls Patsy's mouth sideways. "Your pa killed her. Everybody knows."

I picture Ellen stumbling out of the burned, dark house, instinctively running toward home. A man emerges from the fog into the light from a streetlamp. The theory that she died by neither my father's nor my mother's hand is so new, so astonishing, that I've yet to imagine possible scenarios or suspects.

"I think that before Ellen died, she was seeing someone," I say. "A boy, or man, from the lists she used to make."

Patsy gasps. "How did you know about the lists?"

"Meg Logan told me."

Patsy wrinkles her nose. "The little brat was always spying on Ellen."

"She remembered the name that was at the top of the last list Ellen made," I say. "Lucas Zehnpfennig."

Shock turns Patsy's complexion as pasty gray as the leftover oatmeal in the dirty pot in the sink. Her gaze oozes away from me like grease from the sausages. "Never heard of him."

I'm getting somewhere, even if I don't know what I ultimately expect to learn. "Was Ellen seeing Lucas? Did she tell you?"

"It had nothing to do with what happened to her!" Patsy cries.

Her slip-up illuminates yet another dark corner of my half-brother's life. "Lucas and Ellen must have met at my house. She didn't go there just to model for photographs. She went because Lucas would be there." I imagine my father in his darkroom, my mother out doing errands, and Ellen and Lucas left alone together. "Were they having relations?"

"It wasn't wrong. They were in love." Patsy sounds like a young girl romanticizing an illicit affair.

My view of the rape changes. Ellen could have been a willing participant and the blood between her legs from her period rather than injury, but it still seems wrong. "She was fourteen. He was twenty-six."

"So what? Lots of girls that age marry older men."

The implication of her words stuns me. *"They were planning to marry?"*

"Yeah." Patsy smiles as if proud to defend her friend's honor. "To elope."

I think Lucas had led Ellen on with no intention of marrying her. "None of this was in the police report about Ellen's murder. You didn't tell anyone."

"Why should I have? It just would've upset her family and ruined her reputation."

Sudden fury boils up in me. "Because Lucas was a possible suspect in her murder. If he did it, you let him get away with it!" And let my father become the defendant in a trial that's heading toward his conviction.

"Lucas wouldn't have," Patsy says. "He was a nice fellow." Of course she doesn't know about Lucas's history of preying on girls. Her manner turns spiteful. "But if your pa didn't do it, I can guess who did. Your ma."

Sir William ordered me to produce evidence to support my claim that my mother killed Ellen, and as much as I want the murderer to be neither of my parents, perhaps here is evidence that will exonerate my father. Since I can't be a hundred percent loyal to both parents, I'll settle for choosing him. "Why do you think it was my mother?"

"She hated Ellen."

My father's story said that my mother had killed Ellen only to protect Lucas, but Patsy's words trigger a sudden memory. *I'm in the living room, helping my father set up his photography equipment. Ellen is there, pretty in a yellow frock and white straw hat. My mother stands in the doorway. The look she gives Ellen could curdle milk. Ellen responds with a pert, smug smile.*

"She was jealous," Patsy says, "because she wanted Lucas for herself."

Neither Patsy nor Ellen knew Lucas was my mother's son; nobody did, because my mother had kept it a secret. The scene, which I hadn't understood then, makes sense now. I'm appalled because Patsy's claim supports a story that someone else once told me about my mother—that she and Lucas had been lovers. I didn't want to believe it then, and I resist even now. The idea that Lucas committed rape and my mother, murder is terrible; that they also committed incest is disgusting.

"Ellen told me that whenever she went to your house and Lucas was there, your ma tried to get rid of her. Once they got in a fight, and your ma scratched Ellen up something awful. Ellen said that if Lucas hadn't pulled them apart, your ma would've killed her."

I don't reply at once because it's as if a walled-off corner of my mind has been broken open, and out comes another memory— Ellen at church with bandages on her face. I'd had no idea of the goings-on at my house. "Where was I?"

Patsy regards me with scornful pity. "Probably playing at Meg's house. The two of you were thick as thieves. Ellen told me what happened, but she told everybody else she'd gotten scratched by a cat."

"Why didn't you tell the police?"

"Ellen's uncle was a copper. He said your father did it."

My doubts about my father's innocence fade, and I'm so thankful, I can forgive Patsy for not speaking up twenty-four years ago. She'd been little more than a child, believing what her elders said. But things are different now. "Patsy, you have to come to court and testify."

"Me?" She recoils in dismay. "Why?"

"Because you just gave me evidence that my mother killed Ellen." And supplied my mother with an age-old motive—eliminating a rival. "Your testimony could save my father's life."

"You want me to speak in front of all those people?"

My own ordeal is fresh in my mind, but I say, "Yes."

Patsy's hands flutter. "I couldn't. What would everyone think? The Caseys would be so angry."

Stifling my impatience, I say, "It doesn't matter what they think. This is about justice for Ellen. You don't want the wrong person to hang for her murder, do you?"

"No, but . . ." A true best friend, Patsy had kept Ellen's secrets for twenty-four years, and if I hadn't come along, she probably would have taken them to her own grave.

A man walks into the kitchen on heavy-booted feet. He's tall and dark, with slim hips and broad shoulders, dressed in rough, dirty clothes. Patsy gasps. "Sean. You're home early."

I remember Sean Murphy. He was a handsome older boy, leader of a gang at school. Girls used to hang around him, vying for his attention. He's still handsome, but his eyes are puffy and red, his hairline receding, and he smells of liquor.

"I got sacked," he says.

"Oh, Sean, not again," Patsy wails.

He notices me, frowns with displeasure at finding a stranger in his house, and asks Patsy, "Who's she?"

Patsy hesitates as if afraid to tell him yet afraid to refuse. "This is Sarah Bain."

A glint in his eyes says Sean recognizes my name if not my face. "What d'you want?"

"She was just leaving." Patsy makes frantic, shooing motions at me.

Sean stands in front of me, hands on his hips, feet planted wide. "Cat got your tongue?"

I'm wary of irate, aggressive drunks, but I'm not going yet. "I need Patsy to be a witness at my father's trial."

"My wife's not getting mixed up in that dirty business." Sean grabs my arm and drags me to the door, slings me out of it, and slams it.

As I leave the tenement, I hardly mind Sean's rough treatment of me. I feel light enough to fly because I've finally gotten to the truth about Ellen's murder. All that anchors me to earth is the fact that my father's life depends on Patsy Murphy testifying. I'll have to come back and pressure her when Sean isn't around. Still, I have an exhilarating sense of freedom that reminds me of my solitary life before I knew Hugh, Mick, and Barrett, when I was lonely but self-reliant.

There's nobody to offer ideas or moral support, or share my triumph, but also nobody to restrain me from the course of action I'm about to set off on now.

CHAPTER 23

Ye Olde Cheshire Cheese is one of many pubs along Fleet Street where reporters congregate while waiting for stories, writing stories, or relaxing after turning in their stories. I walk down a narrow alley to the entrance under the sign shaped like a wheel of cheese. Beside the door, a notice board lists the monarchs who have reigned since the pub was rebuilt after the Great Fire of 1666. In the small bar and dining room with sawdust on the floor, a gray parrot squawks in its cage. A worn stone staircase takes me to a subterranean labyrinth of twisted, dimly lit passages where crooked doorways lead to wood-paneled bars and rooms smoky from cigars, pipes, and open fireplaces.

When I inquired at the *Chronicle* office, I was told that Leonard Dawes is usually at Ye Olde Cheshire Cheese this time of day and is wearing a red tartan bow tie. I search the rooms and locate him in a scene from a Franz Hals painting. Amid a crowd of men laughing and drinking with bawdy women, Leonard Dawes sits at a table, a blonde tart on his lap, the red tartan bow tie hanging loose. He has a pink, round-cheeked face, a red mouth, and curly auburn hair. One hand holds a pint of ale; his other hand, around the tart's waist, creeps up toward her breast as he banters with her. Under ordinary circumstances, I would be too timid to approach a company like this, but Dawes is the man whose article smeared my reputation and landed me in hot water with Sir Gerald and Commissioner Bradford.

I say to the tart, "I need a word with your friend. Go away." I've been told I'm formidable when I'm angry, and it must be true, for she hastily decamps.

"Why'd you do that?" Dawes looks irate, then grins, says, "Wanna take her place?" and pats his knee.

I sit in the chair opposite him. "Do you know who I am?"

He squints through the haze of smoke. "Don't believe we've met."

"I'm Sarah Barrett."

"*What?*" Dawes gapes in disbelief and confusion.

His playing dumb makes me angry enough to spit nails. "So you don't know me? That's funny. Wasn't Sarah Barrett your source for a story that said the Queen's grandson is a suspect in the murder on the train?"

"Yeah," he blurts, as if startled into a confession.

"Well, I wasn't your source! I've never spoken to you before now. You're a fraud."

"Madam, I can assure you that I adhere to the highest standards of journalism."

"Oh, spare me. You made false allegations that got me in trouble with the police, my employer, and the Crown!"

"But it wasn't you. I mean, you're not her."

Oddly, against my will, I begin to think he's telling the truth. Somebody gave him the tip and the sexual favors and used my name. I reach in my pocketbook, pull out a card that identifies me as Sarah Barrett, photographer and reporter for the *Daily World*, and slap it on the table. As Dawes stares at it, I say, "Did your source show you any identification?"

"No, but . . ."

He may be honest, but he's a sorry excuse for a reporter. "So you accept tips from anyone off the street without bothering to check on whether they're who they say they are?"

Dawes huffs. "Of course not. But in this case, I didn't think checking was necessary. I've seen photos of Sarah Barrett in the newspapers. When she came to me with the tip, I recognized her." He takes a second, closer look at me, and his indignation deflates. "Or I thought I did. She looks very like you."

★ ★ ★

In Whitechapel, I walk the streets around Castle Alley until I find Barrett by a lodging house, interviewing the people who loiter outside, searching for witnesses related to Pauline Chaffin's murder.

"Come with me," I tell him.

Barrett frowns, puzzled. "Where? Why?"

"You'll understand when we get there."

I hail a cab and instruct the driver in a low voice that Barrett can't hear. Barrett, obviously annoyed by what he thinks is some wild goose chase, climbs in the cab with me. My glowering silence wards off further questions until the cab lets us off on St. Peter Street in Bethnal Green. Barrett beholds the Romanesque church, built of flint, stone, and brick, with a square tower. It's the scene of our wedding and our previous murder investigation.

"What are we doing here?" he asks.

I walk past the church and turn down a narrow lane. He follows me to a schoolyard enclosed on two sides by brick buildings with gables, mullioned Gothic windows, and many chimneys. One is the vicarage. I head to the larger, three-story section, the school. My heart thrums with apprehension. If I'm on the right track, the truth will out, but if I'm wrong, everything will be a hundredfold worse.

Barrett grabs my arm to stop me. "This is where Jane teaches."

"I know."

A bell rings. Children rush, babbling and shrieking, out of the arched main door. I weave through the mob, pulling Barrett along.

"You aren't going to make a scene, are you?" he says anxiously.

"That depends on her." We enter the passage that smells of coal smoke, chalk dust, and lye soap. "Which classroom is Jane's?"

"What are you going to do?" Barrett demands.

"Which one?"

He exhales, shakes his head, and points. From the doorway, we see Jane erasing the blackboard. She's pretty in her blue-and-gray-striped frock, her blonde hair in a coronet of braids—just like mine. Someone who'd seen me only in newspaper photos could mistake her for me. I shove Barrett. Caught off guard, he stumbles into the room.

Jane turns, sees him, and her face lights up. "Tommy!" When I follow close behind him, her smile fades. "Sarah."

I don't give her a chance to regain her composure or Barrett to speak. I say, "Leonard Dawes."

Jane freezes and stares at me, eyes wide and unblinking. Tendons in her neck stand out like iron cords. "Who is Leonard Dawes?" Her voice and smile have an artificial gaiety.

"A reporter from the *Chronicle*," Barrett says, then to me: "What the hell?"

"You gave him the tip about the murder on the train," I say to Jane. Her reaction was a dead giveaway that confirmed my suspicion. I'm so relieved that I was right.

She clutches the blackboard eraser to her chest. "I—I don't know what you're talking about."

Her denial infuriates me. "I just spoke with Mr. Dawes. He certainly was surprised to meet me. When you brought him the tip, you introduced yourself as Sarah Barrett."

Jane turns to Barrett. "Tommy?"

"Sarah, this is ridiculous," he says.

That he's defending her makes me even angrier and more jealous. "If it weren't bad enough that you impersonated me, you tried to ruin my reputation. How far did you go with Mr. Dawes? A little kissing and fondling or all the way?"

She laughs, a tinkly, brittle sound. "Sarah, you have quite an imagination."

"That's right," Barrett says. At this moment, his old loyalty to Jane is stronger than his newer bond with me. I might as well have pushed him into her arms. "Why else would you accuse Jane? How would she even know anything about the case?"

Whether I'm on the right course or running off the rails like the train that crashed, I must finish what I started. "Your father is on the police force. He must have heard something from the commissioner's office, and he told you. Then you told Mr. Dawes."

The eraser falls from her hands, and her nostrils flare as if she's smelled her own excrement. Barrett turns a searching gaze on her. "Jane?"

"You know I would never do such a thing," she says, breathless with her need to convince.

"Oh no." Barrett looks appalled; even he can tell she's lying. I smile with grim satisfaction.

Jane says, "This is all a misunderstanding—"

Barrett shouts, "Stop!"

"Tommy?" Her voice is small; she resembles a child who teased a dog she thought was tame, and it has bitten her.

Barrett stares at her with dismayed astonishment. *"Why?"*

Jane's face shifts rapidly from a smile to a frown, to a grimace, and her fingers claw her folded arms, as if her control over her emotions and body is breaking down. She speaks in a rush, jerks her chin in my direction. "I had to get you away from *her*."

"So you impersonated Sarah with that reporter so I would think she cheated on me and I would divorce her." Barrett has the dazed look of man who'd fallen asleep in one room and awakened, inexplicably, in a different one.

"She's not worthy of you." Jane's eyes blaze with passion. "She won't do right by you. Eventually she would have hurt you."

"And you think that what *you* did hasn't hurt me?"

"It was for your own good!"

I'm amazed that she really seems to believe her excuse. I'm afraid Barrett will too, but anger dawns on his face, and he says, "Hurting my wife hurts me. Your giving confidential police information to the press put my job in danger and hurt me. Being deceived by someone I thought was my friend hurts me." He clenches his fists and turns away from her as if to prevent himself from striking her. "God damn it!"

I'm glad of his rage, glad my name is cleared, glad that at last he sees his goody-goody childhood sweetheart for what she is. She presses herself against him, crying, "Tommy, I didn't mean to hurt you. I love you. And I know you love me."

The stare he turns on her is so menacing that she recoils. "I don't love you. I love Sarah."

That's exactly what I wanted to hear, spoken with utter conviction. But Jane cries, "She dazzled you. She made you forget that we're meant for each other." She speaks as if I'm not present, snakes her arm through Barrett's, and smiles. "But it's all right. You can divorce her and come back to me."

Her persistence is astounding. Barrett says in a cold, hard voice, "I'm never coming back to you. It's over."

Desperate now, Jane pleads, "We can get married, just like we've always planned."

Barrett shakes his head. "Sarah and I are for keeps. From now on, stay away from us."

Jane's face sags, as if the bones have shattered beneath the skin. Her eyes are glassy with tears, and her slender frame begins to heave; her throat contracts as she swallows sobs. If Barrett repudiated me, I think my reaction would be similar. Even in my moment of vindication, I can pity Jane. I suppose it's always easy for the winner to pity the loser.

She makes a clumsy motion to flee. Barrett says, "Not so fast," in his police voice, as if to a criminal he's caught red-handed. "I want you to tell Sarah what was going on that night she caught us together. Tell her you jumped on me and I tried to make you stop."

Jane turns to me. If the hatred and humiliation in her eyes were acid, her tears would burn black rivets down her cheeks. "I tried to make love to him," she whispers. "He didn't want to." She runs out the door, and her sobs echo down the hall.

Barrett turns to me. He looks tired, disillusioned, and abashed. "Can we go home now?"

★ ★ ★

That night, Barrett and I prepare for bed in our room. By tacit mutual agreement, we've not talked about Jane. We ate dinner with Mick and Fitzmorris, who obviously sensed that something had happened between us and kindly asked no questions.

"I'm sorry," Barrett says now.

"I'm sorry too."

I'm apologizing because I didn't trust him when he said Jane had forced herself on him. I think he's apologizing because he didn't trust me when I said I wasn't the source of the tip, but then he says, "I never really believed you talked to Leonard Dawes or slept with him. I only let you think I did because I was mad at you for misjudging me."

Oh. I can't decide whether to be annoyed or relieved, so I just nod and let matters lie. The air is clear now, but discomfort lingers. He removes his jacket by himself instead of letting me take it off him. I use a button hook instead of having him undo the buttons at the back of my frock. The absence of our customary little intimate gestures points up the fact that Jane shook the foundation of our marriage, which will take time to rebuild.

In bed, we lie side by side in the dark. The bed is so narrow that we can't avoid touching. I remember our intoxicating, shameful experience after the show at Cremorne Gardens, and my body swells with desire. His restless movements tell me that Barrett feels it too. But our old, spontaneous ease with sex is gone. Now that the initial glow of my triumph over Jane has subsided, I understand that the past few days have been difficult for him as well as me. We're in unfamiliar territory, and Heaven knows when—or if—we'll ever find our way home.

The clock ticks, I can't sleep, and when I cautiously turn my head toward Barrett, his eyes gleam in the faint light from the streetlamp outside the window. To fill the uncomfortable silence, I say, "How is the investigation going?"

"You know I can't talk about it." Reproach inflects Barrett's tone.

Alas, I opened my mouth and put my foot in. "You don't have to tell me any details. Just if it's going well."

A sigh of frustration is his answer. I want to help him, but I'm off the case, and if I push myself into it, I'll get him in more trouble. But if he doesn't solve the case, he could lose his job and his life, and whoever killed Kate Oliver and Pauline Chaffin will go free. I sway on the fence, then jump off on what I'm afraid is the wrong side.

"I have a lead that might be worth following."

A moment passes before Barrett says, "What is it?"

"We need to find out who Ursula Richter and Clarence Flynn really are. I know people to ask."

"What people?" Barrett says in the reluctant tone of a man who knows he shouldn't take the bait.

"A few years ago, I was hired by a circus owner, to take photographs for publicity. I met everyone who works for him. Circus folk must know others in the business."

From the quality of his silence, I can tell that Barrett is intrigued in spite of himself. He says, "Even though I can't tell you anything, I suppose it's all right for you to offer clues. Tell me his name, and I'll question him."

I balk at handing over the clue and staying on the sidelines of the investigation. "I'll go with you."

"No," Barrett says, adamant.

"The circus people know me. They'll be more willing to talk to me than to you."

"Don't you think I know how to get information from reluctant witnesses?" An edge sharpens his voice.

I wince because I've unintentionally impugned his police skills. "Of course you do."

"I've been doing it for a lot longer than you have. At any rate, you're off the case."

"That's because the commissioner thinks I'm the source of the tip. But it was Jane."

"I'll tell him tomorrow. If he wants to put you back on the case, then—"

"After you tell him, he's liable to take *you* off. It was your former fiancée who tipped the reporter. He might think you have other skeletons in your closet who'll cause problems."

Barrett groans and rubs his eyes. "You're right. He's liable to fire me on the spot."

"So before you tell him, let's solve the case. Together. What better way to get us back in his good graces and save your job— not to mention your life?"

CHAPTER 24

"Cross your fingers," Barrett says as we walk along the Strand on Tuesday afternoon.

This morning we visited the circus owner, who didn't know of a dwarf actor who fits Clarence Flynn's description or a female acrobat with a tail. He directed us to some performers, but those we managed to find couldn't identify Flynn or Ursula Richter. Others were abroad, working at circuses in warmer climates. I'm carrying my camera and satchel, and Barrett, my tripod and flash lamp, because we're investigating on the sly and we need a cover story. So far all we have to show for our efforts are photographs of an equestrienne, a tightrope walker, and several acrobats. Now we're on our last chance, and more is riding on it besides solving the murders. Barrett and I are being careful with each other, tiptoeing on eggshells. Our marriage might not survive another quarrel, and we need to stick together to save him from Inspector Reid.

We pass the Law Courts, a huge grey stone edifice built in Gothic style, with turrets, arches, and spires, that opened eight years ago, but looks transported from the Middle Ages. We turn down a lane into genuinely ancient surroundings. Clare Market is one of London's few areas that weren't destroyed by the Great Fire in 1666. Narrow, cobbled streets wind through a decrepit slum. People crowd the butcher shops, greengrocers, and market stalls, and the smells of decayed meat and blood, rotten fish and vegetables, permeate the fog. On St. Clement's Lane, tall buildings lean over dirty pavement, their projecting upper stories blocking the light from the sky. Children playing ball in the courtyard ignore the vagrant who lies asleep beside trash bins. Rancid cooking odors and quarrelling voices emanate from broken windows. We enter a building, climb the rickety stairs to the attic, and knock on the door.

The man who pokes his head out is in his fifties, with gray whisker stubble on a long face. Gray hair sticks up in tufts on the sides of his bald, shiny scalp, and purplish bags of flesh sag under his eyes.

"Are you Mr. Fred Rice?" I ask.

"Yes?" His expression is cautious but not unfriendly.

I introduce myself as a photographer and Barrett as a reporter from the *Daily World*, then explain that the circus owner sent us. "We're doing a story about circus performers. May we interview you?"

Mr. Rice's face relaxes into a broad smile. "I'd be delighted. Come in, come in."

His small flat has a slanted ceiling and a dormer window. It's so full that he and Barrett and I stand squeezed together on the scant area of floor not covered by boxes and trunks, piled newspapers and books. The walls are hidden behind pictures, shelves crammed with miscellany, and a veritable museum of items hung from hooks. I notice musical instruments, hats, wigs, a saddle, and a bicycle.

"That's me." Mr. Rice gestures toward a framed picture, a crude chalk portrait of a clown in pantaloons and puff-sleeved shirt decorated with multicolored dots. He also wears striped hose and tasseled slippers, and a conical hat sits on tufts of red hair. His face is a white mask with thick black eyebrows, curved red triangles on the cheeks, and a wide red grin.

I suppress a shiver. I've always thought clowns more sinister than funny. Anyone could be hiding behind that costume and makeup—even the Ripper—and anyone who saw him turning somersaults at the circus would think him just an amusing entertainer. But Mr. Rice, in his baggy trousers, frayed jumper, and bedroom slippers, seems a harmless sort.

"I worked for Hengler's Circus, among others." He points to a poster that shows horses galloping around a ring, with clowns and female riders standing on their backs.

I once went to Hengler's at the London Palladium and watched such a spectacle amid a cheering crowd of thousands. Now I detect a faint, circus-like odor in the flat, perhaps from the leather saddle hung on the wall.

"Tea?" Mr. Rice offers.

Barrett and I accept, although I don't see where we'll sit. The only furniture visible is an old armchair where Mr. Rice must spend most of his time. He shifts piles until he's cleared two wooden chairs and part of a table. Then he limps to the kitchen, an alcove that's surprisingly clean and uncluttered.

"You don't do horseback stunts without falling off, and you don't fall off a hundred times without breaking bones," he says as he puts on the kettle. "I broke just about every bone in my body and finally had to retire. What a great life, though."

We sip the tea from china cups on which clown faces are painted and eat biscuits from a tin decorated with a picture of a lion and tamer. Mr. Rice regales us with tales of traveling and performing with circuses all over the kingdom and abroad. He obviously misses the old days and loves an audience, so we let him talk while Barrett takes notes.

When we're finished with our repast, I set up my camera, and Barrett says, "Another performer we met told us about an acrobat named Ursula Richter. Do you know her?"

Seated in his armchair, Mr. Rice watches me duck under the black drape attached to my camera. "The name doesn't ring a bell. She could be new since my time."

I sorely regret that Barrett and I spent our time running all over town only to hit another dead end. If we can't find any dirt on Ursula or Flynn, then Prince Eddy is the prime suspect, and I'm afraid the commissioner would rather let Inspector Reid charge Barrett with Pauline Chaffin's murder than accuse the prince. And what good would Barrett's alibi from me do against Reid, the commissioner, and the Crown?

I focus Mr. Rice's image, hold up my flash lamp, and open the shutter. The explosion lights up the room. As I change the negative plate, Barrett says, "Ursula Richter has a tail."

"A tail?" Mr. Rice's startled face fills the viewfinder. "Wait a minute . . ." He holds up his finger. "There was a girl acrobat, but her name wasn't Ursula." He limps to a bookshelf, rummages through large rolled-up sheets of heavy paper and selects one that he unfurls. "Here."

I hurry from my camera to look at a circus poster titled, "Zirkus Lange," with illustrations of women swinging from trapezes above elephants, lions, clowns, and other human and animal performers. Printed in full color, it's not the usual cheap advertisement, and the detailed illustrations are lifelike.

"That circus was owned by a German named Karl Lange." Mr. Rice points to the largest-drawn acrobat, a girl with short, curly blonde hair. "Look."

A flesh-colored tail protrudes from a hole at the back of her brief red costume. It's longer than Ursula's, perhaps an artistic exaggeration. Beneath a headdress that resembles two furry, pointed black ears, her long face, deep-set dark eyes, and full lips are instantly recognizable despite the black whiskers painted under her humped nose. She's a younger Ursula, her hair bleached blonde.

Barrett and I exchange triumphant grins, resist the urge to hug each other. Mr. Rice reads the smaller print at the bottom of the poster. "'Irmgard Blutchen, das Katzenmädchen.' The Cat Girl."

"She changed her name," I say.

"That's common in the business," Mr. Rice says. "A new name can get you a fresh start at a new, better job."

I think I know why she doesn't perform any more: She's afraid she'll be recognized. Recalling Ursula and Hercules's conversation about the past, I think she also had other reasons for hiding her true identity. "Did you know her?"

"Not personally."

Barrett points to two male performers. "What about them?" He widens his eyes at me.

One is a youth in a fur loincloth, his skin covered in tattoos; the other is dwarf in a military uniform with a bicorne hat, his hand raised in a salute. He's a handsome, boyish Clarence Flynn. I search the small print and find "Illustrierte Mann" and "General Nat Bonaparte."

"I only know them from stories I've heard," Mr. Rice says. "The tattooed man is Frank O'Connell, an Irish sailor. He got in some kind of trouble on his ship and was kicked off. He was stranded in Germany and went to work for Zirkus Lange. At the time he had only a few tattoos. Lange hired a Japanese tattoo artist to cover his whole body."

"Ouch. That must have hurt," Barrett says.

The true story of the man portraying Hercules at Cremorne Gardens is sadly far less romantic than the myth of the Greek hero.

"The dwarf is Nathaniel Chester. He's English," Mr. Rice says. "Karl Lange bought him from his parents when he was a child. The same with Irmgard."

"That's awful!" I exclaim. Ursula's story about growing up in a circus clan and Flynn's about running away from home to be an actor are as false as their story about working for Rosenfeld's Circus.

Mr. Rice shrugs. "It's common. Families want to get rid of their freaks, and the circuses snap them up."

I picture money changing hands by a circus tent, and outcast children crying as their parents turn their backs on them and leave.

"Word in the business was, don't work for Lange unless you're desperate," Mr. Rice says. "His people were like slaves. He docked their room and board from their pay and kept them in debt. He whipped them for the slightest little things they did wrong, and he had guards to keep them from running away. But he got his comeuppance. There was an accident . . ."

Mr. Rice pulls a scrapbook off a shelf and shows Barrett and me a newspaper clipping mounted inside. The clipping is from the *Chronicle*, August 22, 1885, and the headline reads "German Circus Fire." The brief article says Karl Lange, owner of Zirkus Lange, burned to death in the town of Schwabach when his caravan caught fire. A small, blurry photograph shows people standing by the blackened ruins of an enclosed wooden wagon.

"The fire put Zirkus Lange out of business," Mr. Rice says.

"What became of Cat Girl, General Nat Bonaparte, and the Illustrated Man?" Barrett asks, as if we didn't know.

"Some of Lange's people ended up at other circuses, but I never heard of those three again. I wouldn't be surprised if Cat Girl is retired and living off her inheritance."

"What inheritance?" Barrett says.

"She was married to Lange. When he died, she got all his money and everything he owned."

Barrett and I glance at each other, realizing that after Irmgard Blutchen and her two partners changed their names and came to England, they'd used her money—the inheritance she'd mentioned during my interview with her—to reestablish themselves.

"I just remembered something else about Zirkus Lange," Mr. Rice says. "Whenever it came to a town, girls went missing."

★   ★   ★

Outside, Barrett and I skip through Clare Market, past sides of meat hanging in butchers' storefronts. We cheer, clap our hands, and jump up and down, and we don't care about the curious looks from passersby.

"Girls went missing in Germany. Ursula Richter, Clarence Flynn, and Hercules came to London, and Pauline Chaffin went missing," I say.

"It sounds as if whatever Lange's was up to in Germany, they restarted it here," Barrett says.

"One of them could have killed Kate Oliver because she'd caught on to them." My exhilaration fades because I hate to believe that poor children sold to the cruel circus owner had turned to murder.

"Prince Eddy is still a suspect," Barrett says, "but Commissioner Bradford will like this new evidence against the Cremorne Gardens folks. Maybe it'll be enough to get us back in his good graces after I tell him about Jane. Maybe not." Apprehension clouds his eyes.

We slow our pace, no longer dancing in the clouds. It's a long way from connecting Ursula and Flynn with an unconfirmed story about missing girls in Europe to proving them guilty of present-day crimes.

"Are you coming with me to Scotland Yard?" Barrett says.

"I wish I could, but I have to go to Clerkenwell and talk a witness into testifying at my father's trial." I'm knackered from shuttling back and forth between our investigation and my work on behalf of my father. If only there were two of me so that I could manage both at the same time and not give one short shrift. I promised to forsake all others for my husband, but the truth about Ellen's murder has been buried too long, and the trial resumes the day after tomorrow. "I haven't much time left."

CHAPTER 25

The afternoon fog in Clerkenwell is black with soot and weeps chemical tears onto the tenement where Patsy Murphy lives. Climbing the stairs inside, I hear screams from the third floor. I find neighbors standing in the hall, gazing at Patsy's flat. The screams, accompanied by a man's voice, ranting, blare through the closed door.

"Sean's beatin' Patsy again," someone says.

This is far worse than a disruption of my plan to coax Patsy to testify. She could be in serious danger. I move toward the door, but someone grabs my arm. It's Meg Logan.

"Sarah, you can't go in there."

Everyone else is standing around like spectators at a boxing match. "Someone has to." I pull away from Meg and say, "Fetch the police." However, I know that people in this neighborhood distrust the law and hesitate to turn in someone who lives under their roof. I knock on the door and call, "Patsy!"

I hear a fist socking flesh, a loud shriek, and a child's wail. I open the door, peer inside. The three children are huddled together on the floor, Jenny in the middle with an arm around each boy as they watch their parents. Sean stands over Patsy, who's sprawled atop the clothes piled on the divan. His right fist is raised; his left hand clutches a whiskey bottle.

"Sean, please," Patsy whimpers. Blood oozes from her nose; one eye is red and swelling.

"Shut up, bitch!" Sean punches her chin, lets loose a stream of obscenities. She and the children scream.

Stepping into the flat, I speak in as authoritative a voice as I can muster. "Leave her alone, Sean."

He turns. His face is livid and engorged with anger, and he gives off such strong fumes of liquor, I think that if I lit a match, he would go up in flames.

"This's between me and my wife. Get out." He shakes the bottle at me.

He's not the Ripper or any other murderer I've confronted, but I wish I had the gun I told Mick not to carry. "Jenny," I say without moving my gaze from Sean, "take the boys outside."

Jenny gapes mutely at me. Panic-stricken, she doesn't budge.

"I'll teach you to interfere with my family!" Sean hurls the bottle at me.

I duck, and it shatters against the wall. Liquor splashes.

"Damn you, that's all I had left." Sean lurches toward me.

"I'll buy you more." I quickly reach inside my pocketbook, pull out some coins, and say, "Jenny, you and the boys go to the store and get a new bottle for your father."

Sean hesitates, wanting the whiskey but wanting to punish me. Then he says to the children, "What are you waiting for?"

They jump to their feet. Jenny snatches the coins from me, and she and the boys scurry out the door. I've no time to feel relieved that they're out of immediate danger, for now Sean has a knife in his hand—a long, sharp butcher knife.

"I told you to get out," he says. "Didn't you understand? Are you stupid?"

I should run rather than oppose a violent drunk, but if I leave, Sean could kill Patsy, and I've a selfish reason to protect her. If she's injured badly or dead, she can't testify in court.

"Why don't you put the knife down, and we'll talk?" I say with false calmness.

"I don't have to talk to you." Sean raises the knife at me.

I flinch hard. "You seem upset. I want to help you if I can."

"Mind your own business."

"This is your fault, Sarah," Patsy whines. "You came here asking about Ellen Casey. Now he's taking it out on me."

"Shut up!" Sean slaps her across the face.

Patsy wails. I see a broom I could use as a weapon, but Sean is too big and strong for me to win a fight with him. "Why don't you like talking about Ellen?" I ask.

"He doesn't like raking up the past," Patsy says.

"Don't put words in my mouth. I can speak for myself." Sean draws back his hand to hit her again.

Without a chance to mull over what to say, I can only follow my instincts. "Then why don't you tell me, Sean?"

Breathing hard, he glances from left to right, as if unsure which direction to go. Even as he scowls at my attempt to manipulate him, he blurts, "Everybody talks like she was nothing but a girl who got herself raped and killed a long time ago. They didn't care about her. They just like to gossip."

A new, intriguing scenario takes hazy shape in my mind. "Did *you* care about Ellen?"

"They were sweethearts in school," Patsy hastens to say. "It didn't mean anything."

Sean utters a scornful laugh. "Yeah, that's what you tell yourself."

Sean was in love with Ellen. I'm excited for reasons I dare not let him or Patsy catch onto.

"She's been gone twenty-four years, Sean." Tears mix with the blood on Patsy's face. "Why can't you just forget her?"

"The damned trial's in every newspaper. It's all I hear about everywhere I go."

"It'll be finished soon," Patsy says.

"*She'll* never be finished with *me*." Sean grinds out his words between clenched teeth. "She's on my mind every day. The only time I'm not thinking of her is when I'm too drunk." He's remained faithful to Ellen all these years, just as my father has remained faithful to my mother. The fact that they'd both married other women didn't release them from their first loves, and neither did Ellen's murder.

Sean glances at the door. "Where's those damn kids with my whiskey?"

I wish the police would come, but I sense that I'm nearing one of those moments in life upon which fate hinges, and an interruption or wrong word could ruin it. I say cautiously, "What do you think of when you're thinking about Ellen?"

A reminiscent smile drains some of the anger from Sean's face. "I remember how beautiful she was. That red hair and that smile that made me go all soft inside. I couldn't believe she picked me when she could've had any boy in town. We were gonna get married someday."

There's much more to his story; I can almost see it rising up in him like hot lava from a volcanic eruption. The trial was the pressure that breached his buried reservoir of thoughts and feelings about Ellen. I hide my excitement. "What else, Sean?"

His expression turns woeful. "Then she called it quits. She said she wasn't in love with me anymore. Later, I found out why."

Patsy gasps and cries, "No!"

I shush her. Sean says, "It was the night she went missing. Everybody was out looking for her. I'd been walking around, searching everyplace I could think of, worrying about the bad things that might've happened to her. I was half out of my mind."

I fit together his account of that night with my father's, as if they're pieces of the same puzzle, supposing for the moment they're both true. Sean's story begins perhaps twelve hours after my mother strangled Ellen. During those hours, my father and Lucas put Ellen's body in the trunk in the cellar, then waited until long after dark to dispose of the body. Somehow they managed to evade Sean and the other the searchers.

"Then I'm on Greville Street, and I see Ellen coming toward me." Sean sighs with the relief he must have felt.

"Sean, that's enough," Patsy says.

It's enough to prove some of my new theory correct. Ellen *was* alive when my father and Lucas left her in the burned house. The knowledge brings a flood of relief and dismay, bewilderment and elation. The crime still isn't solved; I think I now know *who*, but not *how*, and I rue my previous ignorance.

"I was so happy to see her." Recollected joy makes the years drop away from Sean; I can see the handsome, vital boy he was in 1866. "But when I put my arms around her, she pulled away." Sean's arms form an empty circle. "She said, 'Oh. It's you.' I said, 'Who did you think it was?' She started crying. I said, 'Where've you been? Everybody's worried sick about you.' She started running. I caught up with her and said, 'What's the matter?' She said, 'He told me to be quiet and wait for him. He promised he would come back. But he didn't.' I said, 'Who're you talking about?' She said, 'Lucas.'" Sean's mouth turns down. "That's when I realized why she'd dumped me. She had another guy."

I picture a handwritten list of names with "Lucas Zehnpfennig" at the top and "Sean Murphy" crossed out. I picture Lucas whispering to Ellen when my father was out of earshot, while she lay in the burned house pretending to be dead.

"Ellen and Lucas were in love," Patsy says. "They were gonna elope. She told me."

Sean scowls at Patsy. "Yeah, you knew all along, and you didn't bother telling me."

"I wish I had told you. Maybe it wouldn't have happened."

A feeling of expectancy grips me; the atmosphere in the room is as tense as the moment between dropping a glass and the crash when it shatters on the floor. "What wouldn't have happened?"

Sean's broad shoulders sag as the internal wall that guarded his secrets crumbles. "I told Ellen she should've had the decency to tell me there was someone else instead of letting me wonder what I did wrong.' But she didn't listen, she didn't care. She said, 'I have to find Lucas.'"

Patsy jumps up and embraces him, heedless of the knife. "It's water under the bridge. There's nothing you can do about it now. We should just live our lives and be happy."

"*Happy?*" Sean shoves her, and she falls back on the divan. "With you?" A bitter laugh tears from his throat. "I only married you because I didn't have a choice."

"Darling, that's not so! We were in love." Patsy sounds desperate to believe it.

"You mean, *you* were in love. I remember the way you used to look at me when I was going with Ellen—like you were a hungry dog and I was a bone. Just like you're looking at me now." Contempt twists Sean's features. "I was never in love with you.

I only married you because I told you about that night. And you pretended it was you I wanted all along."

With the yearning devotion in her wide, tearful eyes, Patsy does resemble a dog. She falls on her knees, throws her arms around Sean's legs. "No!"

Sean kicks savagely until she lets go of him. "I couldn't keep my damn mouth shut. So I had to marry you so you wouldn't snitch on me."

Patsy shakes her head violently; tears and blood droplets fly from her face as she tries to deny the humiliating reality of her marriage. "You're just saying that because you're upset." She tells me, "He doesn't mean it."

"Don't contradict me!" Sean raises the knife at Patsy.

I'm afraid that if I don't intervene, he'll kill Patsy, but if I say the wrong thing, he'll kill both her and me. Would that my instincts don't lead me astray! "Sean, you loved Ellen. You owe it to her to tell the truth."

He stares at me, swaying on his feet, his eyes bloodshot, the knife trembling in his hand. "I chased her to Gough Street, where they were putting in the new railroad tracks." He's as drunk and garrulous as he must have been when he first confessed to Patsy. "I caught her and begged her to come back to me. But she said, 'I did it with Lucas yesterday. I belong to him.'" Sean gnashes his teeth on his jealousy. "She would never do it with me. She said she wanted to save herself until she was married."

Ellen had lost her virginity to Lucas. That explains the blood found on her corpse.

I fill in other pieces of the puzzle that apparently Sean doesn't have because Ellen didn't tell him the whole story. I think my mother caught Lucas and Ellen engaged in sex. In a fit of jealousy, she attacked Ellen, and when the girl screamed, my mother strangled her in order to punish her as well as silence her. Then my mother let my father think Lucas had raped Ellen, probably because she didn't want him to know that her love for her son was incestuous and Ellen was her rival. Luckily for her, my father was more intent on protecting her than on determining what had actually happened and why.

If he'd known the truth, would it have destroyed his loyalty to her? Maybe he would have reported my mother to the police, and everything would have been different.

"Ellen fought me and said she never wanted to see me again. And then . . ." Sean's body heaves as if with the urge to vomit.

Patsy moans. "Sean, for the sake of the children!"

But he can't stop the gush of confession that's been pent up for twenty-four years. "My hands were around her neck. I was choking her. She fell on the ground." His voice catches; his eyes well. "I shook her. She didn't move. I called her name, but she didn't answer. She was dead."

My father didn't kill Ellen, and neither did my mother! They have other sins to their names, but not this one. Dear God, the real killer was Sean Murphy, who'd never even been a suspect. It's as if I'd been photographing the crime, and I missed the most important feature because my head was under the black drape on my camera. Anger at Sean burns in me. How different things would have been if he hadn't crossed paths with Ellen that night, hadn't taken out his jealousy on her! I also stagger under an avalanche of horrified self-recrimination. I doubted my father, and he's innocent of everything except trying to cover up the murder, just as he said. I wanted to incriminate my mother, who strangled Ellen but not fatally. And now, to learn that Sean Murphy—someone I'd barely known—was responsible for not only Ellen's death but the breakup of my family and my father's twenty-four years on the run from the law. My lungs are pumping hard from the shock; I can't catch my breath. My speeding heart feels ready to explode. I clasp my chest, lean against the wall for support.

I sense a movement behind me and turn to see Meg Logan. She must have been eavesdropping outside the door, and her face is white with shock. She points at Sean and cries, "*You* killed my sister!"

"I didn't mean to." Sean looks stricken by genuine remorse.

Meg's anger is pure, unadulterated by the guilt and shame that beset me. "Don't you lie to me, Sean Murphy!"

"It was an accident," he protests.

"Accident, my arse!" Meg the respectable matron is gone, replaced by a vengeful fury. "You killed Ellen because she threw you over for someone else and you were jealous." She advances on Sean despite the knife he still holds.

I manage to regain my composure, put aside my own emotions. "Meg, don't." I grab her arm.

"I'm sorry," Sean says.

Wrenching free of my grasp, Meg eyes Sean with contempt. "And then you had the nerve to come to Ellen's funeral and cry as if your heart was broken."

"It was!" Sean is weeping now, tears streaming down his face.

"Everybody felt sorry for you. And all those years after, whenever you happened to see me and my family, you said hello as if butter wouldn't melt in your mouth. You bastard!"

"Don't talk to him like that," Patsy says.

Meg turns her contempt on Patsy. "You're almost as bad as he is. You knew all along, and you kept mum. You let Sarah's father take the blame, just to protect a rotter who everybody knows never cared a tuppence for you."

Patsy stands up and thrusts herself between Meg and Sean. "He does love me!"

"Get out of my way." With a savage motion of her arm, Meg sweeps Patsy aside. She lunges at Sean, pummels his face and chest with her fists. "Bastard! Murderer!" She tears at his shirt as if it's skin she wants to rip from his body. "I'm telling the police what you said. They'll throw your miserable arse in jail."

Blubbering like a spanked child, Sean cowers. "I'm sorry. I'm sorry." The knife dangles in his hand.

As I move to pull Meg off Sean, Patsy shrieks, "Leave him alone!" She hurls herself on Meg. Their frenzy of screaming and flailing engulfs Sean.

"I'll see you hanged!" Meg screams.

Sean drops the knife, and when I bend to snatch it, Patsy kicks my jaw. As I fall on my side, Meg yells, "Sarah, look out!"

I see Patsy swoop down at me like a crazed bird, ferocious with a loyalty that knows no bounds. "I won't let you take him away from me!" She clutches the knife in her fist.

Meg screams.

The blade comes slashing toward my face.

Instinct spurs me to action. I roll.

With a hissing sound, the blade slices my hat.

Meg has the broom in her hands, and she screams as she whacks Patsy and Sean, knocks them down. Male voices shout amid the sound of heavy footsteps. Clambering to my feet, I see a constable grappling with Patsy, wresting the knife from her as she sobs wildly. Another constable has Sean pinned against the wall.

Breathless and distraught, Meg points at Sean. "It was him that killed Ellen!"

"What are you talking about, Auntie Meg?" demands the young, red-haired constable who's holding Sean.

"He confessed. I heard it with my own ears. Billy Casey, you arrest him right now!"

Anger hardens the constable's face. He handcuffs Sean's wrists and shoves him toward the door. "I ought to beat the shit out of you for what you did to my family."

"Go ahead." Sean is a miserable, shambling wreck. "I don't care."

"Rot in hell, bastard." Meg spits in Sean's face.

Her saliva mixes with his tears. Sobbing, he says to Meg, "I'm sorry. I should have been hanged a long time ago for what I did to Ellen. I don't mind dying. I only wish it could bring her back."

CHAPTER 26

I come home to find Sally at dinner with Barrett and Fitzmorris. When I tell them about Sean and Patsy Murphy, Sally exclaims, "Oh, Sarah, you did it! You proved Father is innocent!" She bursts into tears of joy, jumps up, and hugs me.

All our differences are erased, and my internal tug-of-war between the murder investigation and my father is over. That alone is worth my brush with death.

"Whew." Barrett pretends to wipe sweat off his forehead. "Just in the nick of time."

"Now Father will be set free." Sally claps her hands and beams.

Perhaps I'm numb from shock, but my own elation is muted, and I think rejoicing too soon is tempting fate. "We still have to get through the rest of the trial."

"Once Sean Murphy's confession is introduced as evidence, the judge will surely dismiss the charges against your father," Barrett says.

"It's fortunate that Meg and the other neighbors overheard Sean and Patsy," I say. "They can't deny what they said. It won't be my word against theirs." When the police had walked them out of the flat, an angry mob of neighbors had attacked Sean. I'd warned Constable Billy Casey—Meg's nephew—to make sure no harm comes to Sean in jail. We need Sean alive. His trial and conviction for Ellen's murder will remove the shadow of suspicion from Benjamin Bain once and for all.

"This calls for a celebration," Fitzmorris says. "I'll open the wine."

He and Sally go to the kitchen. Barrett speaks in a low voice covered by the sound of glasses rattling and a cork popping. "Commissioner Bradford wasn't happy to hear about Jane. He said that if I have any other talkative former girlfriends, I should put a gag on them." Barrett grins sheepishly. "But he apologized to you, and he likes that you discovered Clarence Flynn's and Ursula Richter's true identities. You're back on the case."

I sigh with relief. We clasp hands, and I'm hopeful that solving the case together will repair the wound that distrust dealt our marriage. Whatever the future holds, this is the best night I've had in a long time.

Fitzmorris and Sally return. Wine is poured, and as Sally raises her glass to make a toast, the doorbell jangles. "That must be Mick," I say. "Let's wait for him."

Instead of Mick, it's Hugh who walks into the kitchen, accompanied by Dr. Lewes. "Look who's back," Barrett says.

I jump up from my chair. "Hugh!" I'm so delighted that I want to embrace him, and only the psychologist's presence inhibits me.

Hugh is thinner, but with some sparkle returned to his eyes and some color to his cheeks, he looks alive again. Glancing at the wine, he says, "Am I interrupting a party?"

"Not at all." Fitzmorris wipes his eyes. "Welcome home, my lord."

It's on the tip of my tongue to ask Hugh what brought about his recovery, but Dr. Lewes catches my eye, smiles, and shakes his head. I stifle my resentment toward the doctor as he and Hugh join the rest of us at the table. When Fitzmorris offers them wine, Hugh says, "Actually, I'm not drinking. Tea is fine."

Well, if Dr. Lewes effected Hugh's new sobriety, I won't quibble with his withholding information about his patient.

"What's happened while I've been out of the picture?" Hugh sounds genuinely interested.

"We're celebrating because Sarah has proved that our father is innocent," Sally says.

After we fill Hugh in on the details, he says, "I'm so happy for both of you. In no time at all, your father will be here with us." He does look happy, but beneath his usual optimism, there's a fragility that reminds me of a glass Christmas angel. I want to wrap him in cotton wool and tuck him in a box.

"Goodness, it's late," Sally says. "I'd better tell Mr. Owusu about Sean Murphy's confession." She gets up to kiss my cheek, then Hugh's; she bids farewell to Barrett and Fitzmorris.

After she's gone and Fitzmorris is washing dishes in the kitchen, Hugh says, "What's happening with the new murder investigation?"

"Dead end," Barrett says. "Plenty of circumstantial evidence, no proof."

"Is this the murder at the train crash where you and Mrs. Barrett discovered the body?" Dr. Lewes says.

Hugh must have told him about the crime. I hope he left out the Prince Eddy angle. "Yes," I say.

"Aren't there any witnesses?" Hugh says.

"None that I can find," Barrett says.

"I see two witnesses right here." Dr. Lewes points to Barrett and me.

"By the time we discovered the body, the killer was gone," I say.

"You might have seen him and forgotten."

"I don't think so," Barrett says.

"Immediately after you were in a train crash, you walked into a murder scene," Dr. Lewes says. "That sort of trauma can bury memories."

"No matter what we saw, if we can't remember, then we're useless as witnesses," Barrett points out.

"Maybe not," Dr. Lewes says.

"We really shouldn't be discussing the case with you." I feel a pang of satisfaction, getting back at him after he refused to talk about Hugh's therapy.

"You needn't tell me any details," Dr. Lewes says. "You can just let me help you remember."

"How?" Barrett leans forward, intrigued.

"With hypnotism."

The idea immediately puts me off, and Barrett laughs. "That old carnival trick?" He pulls out his pocket watch, swings it by its chain, and intones, "You are getting sleepy."

Dr. Lewes smiles, unoffended. "Hypnotism has been used as entertainment, but also for therapeutic purposes. It can relieve pain, and during the American Civil War, it was successfully used as anesthesia for surgical operations. That was before the advent of ether and chloroform. The French neurologist Jean-Martin Charcot used hypnosis to treat mental patients at the Salpêtrière asylum and to recover lost memories."

"How does it accomplish all that?" Barrett says, still skeptical.

"Early practitioners like Franz Mesmer believed hypnosis triggered animal magnetism, a natural force within the human body. Modern scientists like myself think it harnesses the power of the mind, which isn't yet fully understood."

"Well, if it might solve this case, I'm game," Barrett says. "How about you, Sarah?"

I once saw a music hall show at which a hypnotist put a volunteer from the audience in a trance and made him bark like a dog. I thought it was faked, but what if it wasn't? I strongly dislike the idea of someone taking control of my mind and body. Still, I need to solve the case, and I don't want to seem a coward.

"Very well." If I have further qualms about the experiment, I'll call it off.

We all go into the parlor. Dr. Lewes instructs Barrett and me to sit on the divan, leaning back with our heads resting on cushions and our feet up on the ottoman. Barrett offers the doctor his watch. "Do you need this?"

"No, the movement interferes with inducing a hypnotic trance." Dr. Lewes tells Barrett and me, "Just close your eyes."

Obeying, I feel blind, vulnerable, and nervous.

"Now breathe slowly and deeply."

The doctor's calm, quiet command penetrates the darkness behind my eyelids. I dislike him telling me what to do, and I remind myself that it's for a worthy cause.

"Concentrate on your breathing. In, out. In, out. Good."

I'm surprised that it feels good. How often do I allow myself to do nothing but breathe? Probably never.

"Focus your attention on your face. Feel the tension and let it go. Let your jaw relax. Now move your attention to your neck. Let the tension go."

I'm amazed at how much tension I store in my facial muscles, keeping control over my expression and emotions. What bliss, the release.

Dr. Lewes directs us to relax our backs, stomachs, legs, and feet. By this time, I'm limp and comfortable, on the verge of sleep but calmly alert. If this is a trance, it's unexpectedly pleasant and nonthreatening.

"Visualize a blue sky on a summer day."

As my mind's eye fills with serene blueness, I can feel the warm sun on my face.

"Watch the white, puffy clouds drifting."

I'm getting impatient. How can this help retrieve memories that probably don't exist?

"If any thoughts come into your mind, let them float away with the clouds."

There go my thoughts about the murders, Clarence Flynn, Ursula Richter, Prince Eddy, and my father's trial, floating out of sight, out of mind.

"Now imagine a clock with its hands turning backward."

My clock has a round white face and curly black numbers. I never knew I was so suggestible. I feel a spinning sensation as Dr. Lewes says, "You're riding in the train, just before the crash." And there I am in the carriage with Barrett. The racket of the iron wheels reverberates through me.

"When I touch your arm, tell me what you see and what's happening."

Barrett speaks, his voice drowsy and placid. "Sarah and I are reading the newspaper."

The headline, "Benjamin Bain Murder Trial Begins Tomorrow," flashes in my mind. I feel a light tap on my arm, and I speak as though I'm a puppet and Dr. Lewes has pulled the string connected to my mouth. "There's a family across the aisle— wife and baby, the husband with the boys. In front of them, a gray-haired woman with spectacles." I hadn't remembered her until now.

"Now the train crashes," Dr. Lewes says. "Describe it for me."

"There was a loud noise," Barrett says. "The train went off the tracks, and the carriage we were in tipped over and was smashed between the ones in front and back of us."

I feel the collision, see the sparks outside the window, and hear the screams, but it doesn't disturb me. The hypnotic trance is a buffer between past and present.

"Everything went dark," Barrett says. "People were crying. There was fire outside. I got the door open, and Sarah and I helped people out of the train."

I feel the warm, solid weight of the squalling baby that I hand to the father, who's outside the tilted carriage. As Barrett describes our next moments, we're crawling from the wreckage, searching the train for passengers to rescue. In the carriage where we found Kate Oliver, I step on blood-spattered broken glass. Barrett's words show me her body lying on the floor, her bulging eyes and swollen face, the ligature bruise around her neck.

Dr. Lewes taps my arm. I say, "There's a gold cross on a chain over the bruise." Another detail I'd forgotten. I describe our argument with the constable who tried to evacuate us from the scene, and our discovery of the Kodak camera. Through all this, my voice is calm, dreamy. Then it's Barrett's turn again.

"The station was like a war zone," he says. "People crying and bleeding. The family with the four children. The police rushing in. I kissed Sarah before she left to meet her father."

We're frozen in that moment, arms around each other; I feel his lips warm on mine. Dr. Lewes says, "I'm going to bring you out of the hypnotic trance. At the count of three, you'll open your eyes. You'll feel completely refreshed and content. You'll no longer be susceptible to suggestions from me, but you'll remember everything you said and experienced during the trance. One . . . two . . . three."

My eyes open. Barrett and I stretch, yawn, and smile. I feel as rejuvenated as from a good night's sleep. Dr. Lewes and Hugh are intently watching us from their seats in the armchairs by the hearth.

"That was astonishing," Barrett says.

"My work here is done." Dr. Lewes stands up and turns to Hugh. "See you tomorrow?"

"Right," Hugh says.

I still wonder what happened between them, but I can't quibble with the results. "Thank you," I say to Dr. Lewes.

"It was my pleasure." Dr. Lewes smiles, acknowledging that I'm grateful for more than just the hypnotism session.

"I'll see you out." Hugh goes downstairs with Dr. Lewes.

"I remembered more than I thought I did, but none of it seems related to the murder," Barrett says.

"The same here." My sense of well-being fades into disappointment. Still, it's astonishing that I recall everything from the trance with complete clarity. Now the new details merge with my previous memory of the train crash and the murder. Sudden uneasiness stirs in me. "There's something that doesn't fit." I raise my hand to prevent questions from Barrett while I strain to identify what's bothering me. *The family with the four children.* Light dawns. "You said there were four children. There were only three."

"I'm sure there were four," Barrett says.

"No, I remember. The mother was holding the baby. The father was sitting between the two boys, who were fighting with each other across him."

Barrett's gaze turns inward, studying the image in his memory. "I saw too. But when we were in the station, I saw them again. And there were three boys."

"The third boy must have been somebody else's."

"But he was standing with the family."

I followed my instincts to Clerkenwell and the truth about Ellen Casey's murder, and I follow them now. "Describe the boys."

"Two of them were nine or ten years old, blond-haired, almost like twins."

Thanks to the hypnotism, I see them clear as day. "And the other?"

"His back was turned to me, so I didn't see his face, but he was older, I think. Stocky, with auburn hair. His head seemed too large for his body and his legs too short."

Revelation shocks us both at the same moment. As we stare at each other, Barrett says, "Oh God," and I exclaim, "You saw Clarence Flynn!"

A dwarf, not a child.

"He was on the train. He must have killed Kate Oliver!" Of course I didn't know Flynn then, and while I was surrounded by so many alarming sights, it was natural that one person would have escaped my notice. I'm stunned that Flynn had been right there in Barrett's unconscious memory all along. I'm horrified that a man I'd liked and sympathized with, to whom I'd been attracted, is the murderer we're seeking.

"He must have followed the family to the station, so that anyone who saw him would think he was one of the children and wouldn't suspect him of the murder," Barrett says.

"He escaped by hiding in plain sight." How clever of Flynn or, rather, Nathaniel Chester.

Barrett's gaze reminds me of shattered glass. "Oh no. How could I forget?"

"Forget what?"

"He was winding a yo-yo. I saw him put it in his pocket. He must have used the string to strangle Kate Oliver. It was the murder weapon." Barrett pounds his fists on his thighs. "If only I'd remembered sooner, I could've solved the case long before now."

I don't mention that if he had remembered, Pauline Chaffin might still be alive; I don't want to make him feel worse. "In all the confusion after the crash, anyone would forget seeing what they thought was a child with a toy."

"Tomorrow, I'm going to take a squadron of constables over to Cremorne Gardens and arrest Clarence Flynn," Barrett declares.

Hugh returns and hands me a scrap of paper. "Sarah, here's a note from Mick. He probably left it just inside the door where you would see it, but the wind must have blown it farther into the studio."

The note reads:

Dear Sarah

Anjali and I went to Cremorne Gardens. Mr. Flynn asked us to put on a speshul fortuntelling show tonite. We thought it would be a good chance to do some detectin and find out whatsup overthere. We wanted you to know where we are just in case.

Mick

P.S. I didn't egzakly lie when I said we quit our jobs. After this one more time we're dun. I didn't tell you about this show because we knew you would say no.

CHAPTER 27

I kneel on the pavement by the front gate of Cremorne Gardens. Barrett, Hugh, and five police constables shine bull's-eye lanterns on the ornate, old-fashioned lock so I can see while I maneuver my picklocks inside the hole.

Mick's note plus the fact that we now know Flynn is the killer means we can't wait until tomorrow for Barrett to arrest Flynn. Our virtual certainty that Pauline Chaffin was murdered after one of Flynn's private, late-night shows, plus Mr. Rice's story about Zirkus Lange and missing girls, convinced us that Anjali is the next intended victim. Hugh insisted on joining us to rescue her, and the constables are Barrett's best, trusted friends from the police force. Commissioner Bradford wouldn't approve of bringing outsiders, but we may need help, and we shan't risk Anjali's life for the sake of secrecy. All the constables know is that we're going to arrest the dangerous criminal who murdered the woman on the train. We didn't tell them about the connection between Cremorne Gardens and Prince Eddy.

The fog obscures everything beyond ten paces from us. It's as though we inhabit our own capsule of vapor that glows in the lantern light and contains only the gate, the ground immediately under us, a segment of iron fence, and the low branches of the trees on the other side. My fingers are slippery from the moist air, numb from the cold; I can hardly feel the slim metal shafts. The lock's mechanism is a stiff, complex, hidden puzzle, and I have perhaps seconds until the patrolling guards come back. We have to go in through the gate because Hugh, with his wounded arm, can't climb the fence. I employ all the picks before the tumblers shift and the gate creaks open.

"Thanks," Hugh whispers.

He, Barrett, and I draw our pistols. Mine feels like an iron scorpion in my hand, dormant but lethal. Barrett goes in first, Hugh and I next; the constables, armed with truncheons, form a rear guard. Concealed by the fog, Cremorne Gardens seems more a mirage than a solid physical reality. The yellow beams from our lanterns glance off the pay box, stone arches, and fountains, which disappear into the murk as we move past them. Glass lamps dangle overhead, as if suspended in thin air. We're under the row of iron arches, invisible in the fog, along the avenue where I first saw Ursula Richter in the Kodak photograph. The lamps are unlit. The fog plays tricks on my ears. I can't tell whether sounds I hear are our footsteps or someone else's, voices or my nerves chattering, near or distant. The avenue leads us toward the far end of Cremorne Gardens and the theater, the place we presume Mick and Anjali went for their special show.

Barrett freezes in his tracks and raises his hand. We all stop to hear squishing noises—footsteps that grow louder, faster. A faint yellow glow in the fog at our left brightens and divides into five round moving lights. Mist swarms in the beams they emanate.

"Who goes there?" a man's voice calls.

"Damn," Hugh whispers. "It's the welcoming committee."

Any moment, the guards will become visible to us and us to them. We can't let them prevent our reaching Mick and Anjali. Barrett tells the constables, "Create a diversion."

The constables head toward the lights, vanish into the mist. Soon I hear shouts and running footsteps as they lead the guards on a chase. Hugh, Barrett, and I run onward. The fog is glowing everywhere now, from more lanterns, as if a whole army is pursuing us. The theater comes into view, a ghost palace whose white columns shimmer in the mist. Lamps burning at the head of the staircase reveal a man's shadowy, towering figure—Omar the giant. There are only three of us, and how many adversaries inside? Guns may not be enough to get Mick, Anjali, and ourselves out safely. Near the hazy form of the bandstand, lantern beams crisscross. We flee toward the right side of the theater, into the woods that were once a lawn for picnicking, with trees for shade. Now the lawn is choked with wet leaves and underbrush. We're near the back perimeter of Cremorne, and I can taste the fishy exhalations of the river. The woods hide us from our pursuers, but we're far from rescuing Mick and Anjali. Then we hear, from someplace between us and the river, the sounds of a chase—two pairs of feet pounding the earth, two bodies crashing through foliage, and panting breaths. Barrett's and Hugh's faces show the same surprise I feel: the guards aren't after us. We've stumbled into their pursuit of somebody else.

A loud thud accompanies a yelp of dismay. My heart jumps because I recognize the yelp. "That's Mick!" I whisper.

He's the quarry, and he's been caught. But where is Anjali? Now I hear noises of combat—thrashing; grunts from a man who sounds older and bigger than Mick; and Mick's cries as he struggles to free himself. Hugh, Barrett, and I hurry toward the noises, plow through underbrush, and come up against a high, solid wall of leaves and interwoven branches.

"It's the maze," I say.

Long ago, my father and I had wandered through it to a fountain at the center. Now, Hugh, Barrett, and I search for the entrance. Once an arch carved into the hedge, now it's a jagged gap overhung with vines. We push through them, and our lanterns show a narrow path overgrown with grass between the hedges' protruding branches.

Mick yells, "Lemme go!" His opponent grunts as though kicked in the stomach.

Solving the maze was hard enough in daylight when the hedges were neatly pruned. Dead ends block our way. We turn, forge ahead, and backtrack. At last our lanterns illuminate two figures struggling on the ground by the vine-covered fountain in the center. Mick is pinned under a large fellow clad in black. Barrett grabs the guard by the collar, pulls him off Mick, and hurls him against the hedge. Hugh swings his pistol, clubbing the man's temple. The man crumples and lies unconscious.

Mick scrambles upright, his clothes muddy, his face bruised. When he recognizes Barrett, Hugh, and me, he exclaims, "It's you—thank God! They got Anjali!" He talks fast, his words jumbling. "When we got here, Flynn and Hercules met us at the gate, all friendly like. They brought us inside the theater. Nobody was there. I said, 'Who're we doin' the show for?' Then Flynn grabbed Anjali and held a cloth over her face. It musta been chloroform, 'cause she passed out. I drew my gun, but Hercules grabbed me and took it and tried to strangle me. I gouged his eye, and he let go long enough so's I could run. But all those blokes started chasin' me. I couldn't get back to Anjali." Mick gulps down a sob. "We gotta save her!"

"Don't worry," Hugh says, "we will."

There's no question about it. Anjali is one of us, and she's in danger because she tried to help us solve a crime. We escape the maze's convoluted paths and blind alleys via a gap that some other lost soul must have hacked through the hedge, and we find ourselves by the gate that leads to the riverfront. I would have expected the area to be quiet and deserted at this time of night, but lights are moving up the road outside the fence, footsteps and muted voices approaching. We duck back into the maze to hide and watch a strange procession file in through the gate. In the lead are two men carrying lanterns, their coat collars turned up and their hats pulled low over their eyes. The followers are some thirty men and women in dark coats, surely the audience for the private show. Their two escorts wait for them inside the gate, where the lanterns briefly, dimly illuminate each person. Their faces are black voids. They've arrived by ferryboat, as if Charon has rowed them down the river Styx to hell. Death has robbed them of their features, their mortal identities.

My heart vaults. I hear my companions' breath catch.

A second look shows us that the people are wearing black masks, their eyes glinting through holes. After their escorts secure the gate, they march into Cremorne Gardens. Their masks, their silence, the smoke from the lanterns give the impression of some sinister funeral rite. My companions and I, hidden by the fog, trail them to the theater. The people in the procession seem oblivious or indifferent to the moving lights in the distance and the sounds of running footsteps. We shelter behind the bandstand as they mount the steps to the theater, and the giant lets them in.

When Barrett motions Hugh, Mick, and me to follow him around the theater, Mick hurries ahead of us. The building's ground floor has windows set in ornately carved arches between pilasters, half hidden by ivy. Mick reaches the nearest window and bangs the grip of his pistol against the glass. As the glass loudly shatters, I wince.

Barrett shakes his head. "Great. You just announced that we're here."

"Yeah, well, we just gotta save Anjali before they catch us," Mick says as he knocks the jagged glass out of the frame and kicks in the wooden mullions. Too impatient for caution, he crawls in the window.

"Wait here," Barrett tells Hugh and me as he follows Mick.

We can't let them take on everyone by themselves, and there's no use our being safe while they're not. Hugh says, "Last one in's a rotten egg." Then we're all inside the lower lobby of the building. Our lanterns shine on a cracked marble floor. Twin open staircases with missing balustrades ascend to the upper, main lobby. Voices murmurs from a corridor. We steal along the corridor to a doorway that leads to stairs descending to the cellar. Even as Hugh, Barrett, and I hesitate to enter a dark underground place where peril surely awaits us, Mick is already tiptoeing down the stairs, his gun drawn. The rest of us follow suit.

Cold, dank air smelling of earth and drains envelops us; dim light flickers below. At the bottom of the stairs, the space under the theater is like the crypt of a vast church. Brick pillars on the stone floor support the ceiling, a maze of wooden rafters and exposed pipes draped with cobwebs. Trunks and crates are piled amid theater paraphernalia—racks of costumes, painted backdrops, mechanical equipment. Some twenty feet distant from us, light radiates from a cleared-out space in the center, the source of the voices. We shutter our lanterns so that we won't be seen, then advance toward the central space and hide behind a pillar. Scaffolds surround a low stage on which flaming gas jets mounted on a pipe along the edge serve as footlights. The stage is furnished with a bed covered in white linens and white curtains hung on the scaffolds. A few rows of chairs between us and the stage contain the masked audience. How will this show differ from the one Barrett and I spied on? What darker dramas are acted here in this intimate, makeshift theater under the main theater? What makes the audience willing to sit in a cold, foul basement in the dead of night?

Anjali is nowhere to be seen.

Mick gestures, indicating that we should circle to the back of the stage. We set down our lanterns, to leave our hands freer. As I move cautiously, I'm afraid that in his desperation to find Anjali, Mick will be careless and get us all caught. The stage lights fade to weak, flickering stars, and I can barely see my companions' faces. The audience stirs in anticipation. Piano music booms from somewhere out of sight, melodramatic and ominous. A large square of purple light appears high up on the drapery behind the bed onstage. It's a magic lantern show. The image is a sky at sunset and a castle on a cliff. The piano music quiets, and a woman's voice speaks.

"Come with me to a land between day and night, where the sun is motionless in the heavens and dusk lasts forever."

The solemn, German-accented voice belongs to Ursula Richter. I spot her, a slim figure in a full-skirted dark frock, on a scaffold that faces the stage from behind the audience. The ominous music, light, and atmosphere wrap a chill around me. Mick, undaunted, weaves between pillars and crates, forcing Hugh, Barrett, and me to hurry after him. Cobwebs graze my face, and I flinch.

"This is a land of enchantment, of magical spells and dreams," Ursula says.

"Stop right there." The quiet command, spoken from the shadows ahead of us, coincides with a loud glissando of music from the piano.

The audience seems oblivious to us, their attention on the show. Mick skids to a halt. Barrett, Hugh, and I freeze behind him as the man emerges from the shadows. In the faint light from the stage, I see his rough face and puffy eyes. It's Jonas Murray, Prince Eddy's valet. My attention rivets on the pistol he holds. My chest clenches as if my ribs have suddenly contracted around my lungs.

"Out." Aiming the pistol at us, Murray tilts his head in the direction of the door through which we entered the basement.

My companions aim their guns at him. I aim mine an instant later, delayed by fright. Barrett says to Murray, "Detective Sergeant Barrett, Metropolitan Police. Drop your weapon."

Confronted with so many intruders, one a lawman, all armed, Murry frowns. The silence that befalls us vibrates with the unspoken question: *Who can shoot first?* My wounded shoulder aches while I hold my gun trained on Murray. I'm a good shot, but only in target practice; I've never shot anyone, and I don't know if I could. I suspect that if Jonas Murray shot someone tonight, it wouldn't be the first time. I think of Prince Eddy. *Where is he now?* I'm far from certain that my companions or I could bring Murray down before he kills one of us.

The piano player executes a series of dulcet notes, and Mick demands, "Where's Anjali?"

"In the castle sleeps a young virgin," Ursula says.

It's as I dreaded: Anjali is to be the star of the show. "What're they gonna do to her?" Mick says.

"She dreams of the lover who will awaken her and fulfill her most erotic fantasies," Ursula says.

"I went to a lot of trouble to produce this show," Murray says. "You're not going to interfere with it."

I'm surprised to learn that Murray is in cahoots with Clarence Flynn and Ursula Richter, not just a customer. Those guards outside must be his men, not circus folks. Barrett says, "My officers are raiding Cremorne Gardens as we speak. They'll be here any minute. Unless you want to get hurt, call off the show and tell everyone to cooperate."

Murray scrutinizes us, obviously wondering if Barrett is bluffing. Then his cold, hard gaze fixes on me, and he points the gun at my chest. "Do you want to wager you can shoot me before I kill her?" He's singled out me, the woman, as the most vulnerable person among us, the one the others need to protect.

Barrett steps between Murray and me. He does it so fast that I can't believe I ever doubted his loyalty to me. My quarrel with him over Jane Lambert seems so trivial now! I move beside him and put myself back in Murray's sights. Even while in grave peril, a glance of deep, intimate understanding flashes between us: we know that each of us is willing to die to save the other.

"You can only shoot one person at a time," Barrett tells Murray. "No matter who it is, you'll be the next to die."

As Murray beholds the four guns pointed at him, his jaws clench.

"If you care so much about the show, are you really gonna blow it with a shoot-out?" Mick asks.

Murray utters a tense laugh. "We'll see, won't we?"

"And now comes the moment she's been waiting for all her life," Ursula says.

The stage lights suddenly shrink into tiny gold pinpoints, the image from the magic lantern disappears, and the audience murmurs expectantly while the piano thunders. It's pitch-dark where I am; Murray and my companions are as invisible as if they've disintegrated into the air. Not one of us moves. I hear shallow breaths, mine as well as everyone else's; I sense fingers poised on triggers while my clammy hand squeezes my gun so hard, the metal ridges dig into my flesh. Whoever breaks the stalemate will set off a barrage of gunfire that's bound to kill someone. Then, who will be left to save Anjali?

CHAPTER 28

The music lowers to a bass rumble, and the footlights brighten. Murray and my companions are black statues amid the deep shadows, but I can see that the bed onstage is no longer unoccupied. There lies a slim, motionless girl with long, tumbled black hair, her eyes closed, her lips parted. *Anjali!* Dressed in a transparent white negligee, she's asleep or unconscious, perhaps drugged. The sound from the audience is like the growl of a predatory animal. Mick moans at the sight of his beloved on the bed where, I'm morally certain, Pauline Chaffin had lain the night she was murdered.

"Enter her phantom lover," Ursula says.

Onto the stage walks a slender man clad in a purple satin dressing gown that gleams in the footlights. His hair is short and sleek, his feet bare. A black mask conceals the upper part of his face, but I recognize his wispy mustache.

He's Prince Eddy.

He faces the audience, one foot placed ahead of the other, one hand on his hip, and the other extended, like a fashion mannequin modeling clothes. The audience responds with a smattering of applause. Barrett and I exchange alarmed glances. I think we'd both hoped that Jonas Murray was here on his own and whatever happened tonight needn't involve the royal family, but Prince Eddy is obviously the male lead in this clandestine show. His pouty mouth smiles below his mask, and he makes a self-conscious little bow.

Murray, pointing his gun at me, says to Barrett, Hugh, and Mick, "All of you, stay where you are." The stalemate unbroken, we watch in helpless horror while Prince Eddy sashays toward Anjali.

"In her dream, the virgin senses his presence." Despair inflects Ursula's voice, as if she knows what's going to happen and wishes it wouldn't. The music climbs up the scale, growing louder. "She waits, breathless with desire."

Eddy unties his robe and lets it fall to the floor. His body is all stringy muscles, knobby knees, and jutting shoulder blades. His long, thin erection protrudes from a bush of black hair. Groans sound from the audience, as if they feel the same arousal. With the sash of his robe in his hand, Eddy climbs onto the bed. The same scene must have transpired Friday night, with Pauline Chaffin the prey of this man who takes pleasure from strangling helpless young women.

"Anjali!" Mick, heedless of the danger, runs toward the stage.

"Stop!" Murray orders.

As he starts after Mick, I shove him. He jigs sideways, crashes into a pillar. Mick is at the stage, Barrett, Hugh, and I rushing to join him. Prince Eddy crouches over Anjali, unbuttoning her negligee. Under the rippling music, I hear Murray curse, and the muscles in my back tense, anticipating the bang of a gunshot, the impact, the pain. But I'm more afraid for my friends than myself, and I can't stand idle while Prince Eddy murders Anjali.

A thud precedes an explosion like a flash lamp igniting. On the stage, flames burst amid a spray of white sparks. My companions I recoil from the sparks while the audience laughs. The fireworks must be part of the show, cheap symbolism for the sexual act about to take place. Then come more thuds and explosions. Smoke billows thick and black, engulfing the theater. Mirth gives way to screams. Someone is throwing bombs, and not for entertainment. A man in the audience yells, "Fire!"

Chairs scrape the floor as the audience rises. The smoke blinds me, stings my eyes, fills my lungs as I grope toward the stage. I hear a scream, shrill with terror. The explosions stop as the clatter of the audience's footsteps fades out of the building. The smoke thins to a gray haze, and now there are three figures on the stage. Anjali is still asleep on the bed, two men on the floor near her. One man is Prince Eddy, lying naked beneath the other, who's pinned him to the floor amid charred scraps from the fireworks. It takes me a second to recognize Hercules, dressed in ordinary clothes for the first time I've seen him. He pushes Eddy's head against the floor while holding a knife to Eddy's throat.

"Jonas!" Eddy screams.

Gun in hand, Murray squints through the smoke. "What in the devil . . .?"

Mick leaps onto the stage, rushes to Anjali. Hugh, Barrett, and I are scattered below the stage. Hercules looks aghast to see us. Murray points the gun at one of us after the other, uncertain whom to shoot first.

"Help!" Eddy cringes from the knife blade, scrabbling his fingers on the floor like a mole trying to dig himself underground.

As Murray takes in the scene, anger dawns on his face. He shouts, "Flynn!"

"Surprise." Flynn's deep voice, tinged with amusement, is unnaturally loud and reverberant; he's speaking through a megaphone somewhere above us.

Barrett, Hugh, Murray, and I look up. I don't see Flynn, who must be on the scaffold behind the stage, hidden by the white drapes. Mick bends over Anjali, squeezes her hand, and pats her cheek. "Anjali, wake up." She stirs and groans, her eyes still closed.

"This is our final show," Flynn says.

Murray aims the gun at Hercules and calls to Flynn, "Tell your man to let Prince Eddy go."

"But that would spoil my surprise." Flynn chuckles. "Tonight, our leading actor is going to get a taste of his own medicine."

"No!" Prince Eddy screams, his spindly legs kicking.

"And you, Mr. Murray, shall star in the encore performance," Flynn says.

I was wrong, so wrong—Murray and the Cremorne Gardens folks aren't happy co-conspirators in the shows. Flynn set off the bombs to chase out the audience, and he intends for Hercules to kill Prince Eddy and Jonas Murray. Anjali and my companions and I are caught in the middle of Flynn's trap.

Murray's expression alternates between fear and rage. I can't tell if he cares about Eddy for Eddy's sake. Is he afraid of having the prince die on his watch as well as of losing his own life? He's obviously furious that his partners in crime have turned on him. "Drop the knife and let him go, or I'll shoot," he orders Hercules.

Hercules's eyes dart like fish when a cat dips its paw in their bowl. His blade jerks against Eddy's throat. "Don't come any closer!"

Our plan to arrest Clarence Flynn falls by the wayside for the moment. My comrades and I have to rescue Prince Eddy, the Queen's grandson. Our duty to country and Crown obligates us, even though Eddy is a monster.

Barrett jumps onto the stage and points his gun up at the scaffold. "Flynn. Call off your show. Come down here, or I'm coming after you."

Flynn laughs. "Haven't you heard the saying 'The show must go on?'"

Barrett flings aside a swath of white drapery and begins climbing the metal scaffold. I'm scared for him, but I can't stand idle. Hugh and I edge toward the shadows at opposite ends of the space below the stage, intending to sneak behind Murray while he's pre-occupied and take him down before he can shoot anyone.

"Anjali, we gotta get out of here." Mick pulls the girl into a sitting position.

Eyes cracked open, she mumbles, "What . . .?" She cants backward.

Mick slings her arm over his shoulders, moves her legs over the side of the bed, and raises her to her feet. She crumples, and her head lolls. He half drags, half carries her across the stage.

"I can kill you before you can cut his throat," Murray tells Hercules.

The strongman raises his eyes up toward the scaffold. Sweat glistens on his face. I recall his conversation with Ursula when he'd suggested running away from their problems. He clearly wants to run away now, but he's beholden to Flynn, and he stays, just as Ursula had told him he must.

"Do you really want to gamble with His Highness's life?" Flynn asks Murray.

Sobs heave Prince Eddy's body. "Please! I don't want to die."

I have to buy time for Mick to take Anjali to safety and Barrett to capture Flynn. "Mr. Flynn, why are you doing this?" I call.

"Mrs. Barrett, I told you you're not welcome at Cremorne Gardens." Flynn's tone is at once chastising and flirtatious. "You're abusing my hospitality." The actor in him can't pass up the opportunity for witty banter. "But since you're here, I'll tell you that Mr. Murray has forced us to stage these deplorable shows for Prince Eddy's pleasure." And like other criminals I've met, he can't resist the urge to justify himself.

"Bosh," Murray says. "You and your friends staged these shows when you were with Lange's in Europe. You were perfectly happy to let Eddy be in them and take his money."

So that's where Murray and Eddy met Flynn, Ursula Richter, and Hercules. Prince Eddy must be responsible for at least some of the girls who went missing from the towns where Lange's Circus performed.

"Karl Lange forced us into it." Anger infuses Flynn's voice.

"I'm sorry!" Eddy cries. "I won't do any more shows. Just please don't kill me!" A puddle spreads on the floor under him, and there's a sharp, sour reek of urine.

"We put all that behind us when we came to London," Flynn says. "We ran a legitimate business until we had the bad luck of crossing paths with you again."

"A dinky storefront museum of oddities," Murray scoffs. "You'd have starved if Eddy and I hadn't invested in Cremorne Gardens."

"You call yourself investors? 'Blackmailers' would be more accurate."

Now I understand how and why Flynn and company set themselves up at Cremorne Gardens. The public attractions are just a cover for the secret, illegal, lucrative entertainment. What I don't understand is Murray's motive. Outraged by his pandering, I say, "How can you help Eddy kill women?"

"I've served the royal family all my life. So did my father, and his father. We do what's required of us." Murray speaks with pride.

I think of Fitzmorris, bound to Hugh by the same tradition. I'll never quite understand the loyalty of servant to a master, but I know it's powerful.

"Eddy has compulsions," Murray says. "He needs to relieve them on women who don't matter. I help him so he doesn't get in trouble."

It's a twist on the common, socially acceptable idea that men should satisfy their sexual urges with servants or prostitutes and preserve the chastity of upper-class ladies.

Mick lifts Anjali in his arms like a baby and, staggering under her limp weight, carries her down the steps from the stage. Flynn must be someplace where he can't see them, and Murray, his attention fixed on Hercules and Prince Eddy, doesn't seem to notice them. *Where are Hugh and Barrett?* I need to stall longer.

"Mr. Flynn, why did you and your friends let yourselves be blackmailed? Mr. Murray and Prince Eddy were participants in the shows. They're just as guilty as you are. Isn't it in their interest to keep the secret?"

"You underestimate Mr. Flynn," Murray says, chuckling as he yields to the temptation to malign his adversary. "This little theater isn't his only secret." He calls up to Flynn, "Hey, I've an idea. Let's reenact the end of Lange's Circus."

"This is my show." Hostility edges Flynn's voice. "You don't get to change the plot."

"Oh, but this is good, "Murray says with sardonic relish. "The scene is Schwabach, Germany, the date August 1885. It's after midnight. The tents are closed, the animals asleep in their cages, and the circus folk retired to their caravans." He gestures with his free hand, as if painting the scene in the air. "All the customers have gone home, except one." He points to his chest. "And what do I see? Ursula sneaking out of the caravan she lived in with Karl Lange. And here come Flynn and Hercules to meet her. Only, those weren't their names back then. They were Irmgard the Cat Girl, Nat Chester, and Frank O'Connell. They splash the caravan with water from buckets." Murray pantomimes. "At first, I think they're washing it, a strange thing to do in the middle of the night. Then Ursula and Hercules run past me. They reek of kerosene. It wasn't water in their buckets. Flynn throws something in the window, then runs after them. The caravan explodes into flames."

Shock robs me of speech. The trio had murdered Karl Lange—the man who'd bought Flynn and Ursula when they were children, had Hercules covered with tattoos, and abused them while keeping them in debt and servitude. And Murray had witnessed the murder. That's the hold he has on them, the reason he could blackmail them into staging murders during sex shows. I remember Ursula instructing the girls on the trapeze, showing them how to time their releases and catches so they wouldn't fall and hurt themselves. She and Flynn and Hercules had thought they'd escaped Karl Lange and flown to freedom, but their unfortunate timing had put them in Murray's power. It's as if they'd fallen into the net and bounced into a frying pan.

"You've had us under your thumb long enough. It's over," Flynn says.

"Did Ursula drug Lange before you set the caravan on fire?" Murray is breathing fast, as desperate as I am to keep Flynn talking. "Is that why he couldn't get out and he burned to death? Well, I know one thing for sure: The fire was your idea, Flynn. The others wouldn't have had the nerve without you. You're the ringmaster."

Now I understand more of the conversation I'd overheard between Hercules and Ursula. They couldn't abandon Flynn because he'd freed them from Lange, whose murder is the darkest secret from their dark past, the glue that binds the trio together. Little did they know that their past would follow them, and another cruel man would force them to commit crimes.

"Yes, I'm the ringmaster," Flynn says with impish cheer. "And His Highness is a dead man."

Below the stage, Anjali, half asleep, leans against Mick and stumbles as he walks her through the theater.

"Please, have mercy!" Prince Eddy cries.

Murray jitters, trying to see where Flynn is while keeping an eye on everyone else. "If you want me dead, then come down here and get me, you little coward."

I sense Hugh circling around behind Murray. I have to keep the conversation going. "Mr. Flynn, you won't get away with killing Prince Eddy in front of seven witnesses. Somebody will tell."

"I'm rewriting the script," Flynn says. "Six witnesses."

A loud bang reverberates through the theater. My heart spasms; my ears ring. Eddy screams. Murray reels backward as if punched in the chest, his eyes and mouth open wide. His gun falls from his right hand; he claps his left hand against the front of his coat.

Flynn has a gun. It could be the one Hercules took from Mick. He shot Murray. The realization pierces my mind as Murray topples onto the floor. The smell of sulfur tinges the air. Even as Murray fumbles, searching for his gun, blood foams from his lips. Prince Eddy screams, "Jonas! Don't leave me!"

Hugh, standing near Murray, picks up the fallen gun. Murray writhes and mewls, then his eyes go blank, and he lies still in a spreading puddle of blood.

"Oh God," Eddy wails, bursting into tears.

Hercules looks as frightened as the prince. Mick pauses to gape at the scene, Anjali's head lolling on his shoulder.

"I'm sorry, Mrs. Barrett, I don't want to hurt you and your friends." Flynn sounds truly regretful. "It's too bad you didn't mind your own business."

Another gunshot blares from the scaffolding. I instinctively crouch. The bullet strikes a pillar beside Mick and Anjali, spraying them with brick dust. I yell at them, "Go!"

Despite his need to save Anjali, Mick hesitates, reluctant to abandon his friends.

"We'll hold the fort," Hugh says.

Mick lifts Anjali in his arms and disappears into the shadows. Hugh and I aim our pistols at the spot on the scaffolding from which the gunshots came. Flynn is still hidden behind the white drapery, but he must have a perfect view of us. I can't fire because I might hit Barrett.

"Drop it, Flynn," Barrett shouts.

On the scaffold, high above the stage, two gunshots bang simultaneously. Barrett and Flynn are shooting at each other. Terrified that my husband has been killed, I scream his name. The white drapery parts, and Flynn jumps down onto the stage. Barrett, apparently unhurt, jumps after him. My relief is enormous. Hugh fires at Flynn, but the bullet hits the bed. Flynn runs to Hercules and says, "Go after the boy and girl."

Hercules lets go of Prince Eddy, clambers to his feet, and bounds off the stage. I yell, "Stop!" I don't want to shoot him, but I will for Mick and Anjali. I aim and pull the trigger.

The bang jolts my body. Hercules dives to the floor; the bullet whizzes over him and smacks into something out of my sight. Barrett and Hugh take aim at Flynn, but now he's crouched atop Eddy, pressing the barrel of his gun against Eddy's head. Eddy weeps, his face a red mess of tears, mucus, and saliva.

"Do you want to bet you can kill me before I shoot His Highness?" Flynn grins at Barrett and Hugh.

Hercules is on his feet, running. I hate to abandon Hugh and Barrett, but Mick and Anjali need me more; I can't let them be caught. I run to the lantern I left, grab it, open the shutter that covers its light, and hurry after Hercules. I weave between pillars and crates, his rapid footfalls pounding ahead of me. I follow him up a staircase that's wider than the one Hugh, Barrett, and I came down, and arrive in the lower lobby. It's deserted, the front door open. I run outside.

The quick rhythm of footsteps resounds through the cold fog that swirls in Hercules' wake. Auras of light from lanterns fade in the distance. My heart sinks at the thought that Hercules has recruited guards to chase Mick and Anjali. I fire my gun above the lights. The bang sends them scattering as if they're birds startled by a hunter. I run to the point from which they diverged, and the fireworks temple materializes before me, its striped towers all but lost in mist. I hear gasps and whimpers—Mick and Anjali. The glow from a lantern moves toward their sounds. I run faster despite my pounding heart, the weeds that snag my skirts, and the fear that dogs me. Within the glow, the man carrying the lantern comes into view. It's Hercules.

"Stop, or I'll shoot!" I cry.

He half turns, and when he sees me with my gun trained on him, panic leaps in his eyes. He stumbles and falls to his knees. He drops the lantern, raises his hands. "No. Please!"

In that moment I know I haven't the will to shoot a man in cold blood. This isn't like other times when I was in the throes of fighting for my life. Hercules is a sitting duck, at my mercy.

I'll have to stall him so Mick and Anjali can get out of Cremorne Gardens, but I'm panting from exertion, so rattled I can't think what to say.

The terror fades from Hercules's eyes, and he grins because he sees I'm not going to shoot him. He drops his hands, rises, picks up his lantern, and turns to run after Mick and Anjali.

I shoot. The bang provokes a yell from Hercules. His lantern explodes in burst of flaming oil, flies out of his hand, and lands on the wet grass, where it smolders. He puts his singed fingers in his mouth, like a child burned while playing with fire. His eyes fill with the awful realization that I mean business after all.

"Put your hands up. Walk that way. Slowly." I gesture in the direction of the lawn where hot-air balloons used to land.

Hercules obeys. *What in the world am I going to do with him?* I haven't anything with which to restrain him, and I mustn't take him to the theater, where he could rejoin forces with Flynn. We've advanced some twenty steps when moving lights shimmer through the fog. Hercules yells, "Help, over here!"

The lights speed toward us amid pounding footsteps. Hercules doesn't know about the constables, and I hope it's them coming, but it could be the guards. Hercules runs away from me, calling, "Look out, she's got a gun!"

I fire into the air. The noises halt the lights and footsteps. I fire twice at the ground near Hercules's feet. He yells and hops as the bullets kick up mud that spatters his trousers. I pull the trigger again, and the gun clicks. I'm out of ammunition. Hercules stares, then laughs as if he's received an unexpected gift. I experience a moment of despair laced with resignation. There's only one thing to do. It might save Mick and Anjali, but God help me.

"You can't catch all of us, and I'm right here," I tell Hercules. "Come and get me."

CHAPTER 29

Hercules hesitates, pondering the fact that he can't go in two directions and capture three fugitives at the same time. He lunges at me, the bird in the closer bush.

I turn and run, drawing him farther from Mick and Anjali. He's stronger, faster, my skirts hamper me, and he's close on my heels. His hand grazes my shoulder, but I'm desperate. Even as my heart feels ready to explode and my lungs can't get enough air, I force a burst of speed from my tired legs. I outpace Hercules into the thick, dark fog on the lawn. I still have my lantern; he's running blind. I hear him stumble and curse. I tuck my empty gun in my coat while I improvise a plan. Hercules is a coward who wanted to run away from his problems, so I head toward the main gate, hoping he'll think I would leave Hugh and Barrett and save my own skin. It's what he would do. Then I veer back toward the theater. Its facade wavers in the fog, then gains solid substance as I draw near. The open doorway on the ground floor beckons. As I cross the threshold, footsteps come pounding up behind me. Iron arms encircle my waist.

I thought I'd shaken Hercules off my trail, but now his weight knocks me down, and I scream as I fall into the lower lobby of the theater. My chin, chest, and elbows slam against the marble floor. The bone-rattling thud jolts the lantern out of my hands.

"I've got you, bitch." Hercules's voice is a breathless growl. His arm locks around my neck, his wrist pressed hard against my throat. I'm gasping and choking, kicking and flailing, the blood roaring in my ears. My vision turns red, pulses, and blackens at the edges. My struggles weaken as consciousness fades. I only hope sacrificing my life has saved Mick's and Anjali's. I soar high above ground and see myself lying facedown with Hercules crouched over me, strangling me. My lips form Barrett's name.

Suddenly, Hercules is wrenched off me as if he's a boulder hefted by the Greek god whose name he appropriated. The pressure on my throat eases, and with a violent snapping sensation, I'm back in my body. I suck huge, wheezing gulps of air. My vision brightens; the redness clears. With great effort I raise myself onto my hands and knees. A puddle of oil spilled from my lantern burns on the floor. The flames illuminate two men fighting by the stairs that lead to the basement.

Hercules and Hugh.

Hugh aims a punch at Hercules's jaw. He must have heard me scream and come to my rescue. When Hercules dodges, Hugh kicks his knee. Hercules staggers backward, but quickly regains his balance and charges at Hugh. I'm aghast because after his earlier defeat at the museum, Hugh is taking on Hercules again to save me.

"Shoot him!" I cry.

Hugh must have his gun, but instead of using it, he rams his head into Hercules's stomach. I'm even more aghast to realize that Hugh wants to defeat this man who humiliated him in public, and not by simply pulling a trigger, but in hand-to-hand combat. His masculine pride is at stake.

Hercules punches Hugh's injured arm. Hugh yells, clutches it, and starts to fall. Hercules seizes Hugh around his neck and chokes him. Hugh tries to pull Hercules' hands off him, but he's too weak. I crawl to them and grab Hercules by the ankle. Hercules kicks my head. A black tide swamps my vision as I flip backward onto the floor. Dizzy from the blow, my head throbbing, I see Hugh drop to his knees, gagging and gasping while Hercules squeezes the life out of him. With a reckless, desperate motion, Hugh throws himself down the stairs to the basement, dragging Hercules with him. They roll body over body and land with an awful thud at the bottom.

I exclaim in horror as I crawl down the stairs to the immobile heap in which they lie. With the light from the theater blocked by the pillars and crates, with both men dressed in dark clothes and their faces turned away from me, I can't tell who, if either, is alive.

"Hugh?" I whisper, forcing his name past the terror that rises in my throat. If he's dead, his pride wasn't his only downfall; so was his loyalty to me.

The man on top stirs, then sits up. His hair is blond. I moan, "Thank God," almost fainting with joy.

Hugh grimaces, rubbing his neck, and crawls off Hercules. The man doesn't move. He stares at the ceiling, his mouth agape, while a dark halo of blood grows around his head, from a wound at the back. He must have cracked his skull. I didn't want more carnage, but as I help Hugh to his feet, I gasp out incoherent words of thanks and praise, indebted to him for saving my life, once again, at the risk of his own.

Unsteady and gasping, doubled over with pain, Hugh contemplates Hercules's dead body. "Well, how about that." He sounds amazed that he came out the winner. He straightens his posture, throws back his head, inhales and exhales a deep breath through his mouth. If he were a lion, he would roar.

From the stage drifts Prince Eddy's voice, shrill and vicious. "The Queen will hang you from the highest tree, you little freak!"

Scornful laughter issues from Clarence Flynn. "You, sir, are more a freak than I. You, who can't satisfy your lust except by killing girls in front of an audience."

Flynn must still be holding Eddy captive, and Barrett is alone with them. Dread launches me toward the stage.

"Wait," Hugh calls. I pause to see him bend over and sling Hercules's arm around his shoulders. With a groan and a heroic effort, he drags the inert corpse, his knees buckling as he follows me to the stage.

Flynn calls, "Did you catch them?" He must hear us coming and think it's Hercules bringing the news that Mick, Anjali, and I are dead, silenced forever.

We emerge into the makeshift theater area, at the back row of chairs. Onstage, as if they haven't moved since we left, Eddy lies under Flynn, who presses the gun against his head. Eddy is so terrified, he seems barely human, his eyes like a tortured beast's.

Flynn's face shines with perspiration that belies his calmness. Barrett stands near them, his own gun aimed at Flynn. The tension in his jaw, the steel in his gaze, says he's about to shoot Flynn and gamble that Eddy won't be killed, and he won't be shot himself. It's a stalemate deteriorating fast. The three men look up at Hugh and me.

Hugh drags Hercules's corpse to them and lifts it with his one good arm and a strength I didn't know he had. He throws it onto the stage, like a warrior presenting his battle trophy. "Your chum's dead, Flynn. Mick and Anjali escaped. You might as well surrender."

Flynn stares in shock at the corpse and the red trail that Hercules's wound left on the floor. He blurts, "'Yet who would have thought the man to have so much blood in him?'" At a loss for his own words, he quotes Shakespeare's.

Barrett beholds me, his expression shifting from surprise to relief to a frown whose meaning I know well: *What have you and your friends done now?*

"Thank God, thank God!" Prince Eddy blubbers.

A cry of anguish bursts from the scaffolding behind the chairs. Ursula, who must have been watching by the magic lantern until now, comes rushing toward the stage. She vaults onto it, graceful as the acrobat she is despite her full-skirted violet taffeta frock. She drops beside Hercules, cradles his head in her lap, and strokes it, heedless of the blood that stains her hands.

"My love! My darling!" she wails, covering his still face with kisses. She glares at Flynn through the tears that stream from her eyes. "Look what you've done!"

Flynn looks flabbergasted by the new developments. "What *I've* done?" But he's a seasoned actor, trained to cope with mishaps onstage; he has the presence of mind to hold the gun firm against Eddy's temple. He tilts his head at Hugh. "*He's* the one who killed Hercules."

Ursula's eyes spark with fury. "If not for your schemes, Hercules would be alive."

Flynn's handsome face takes on the look of a tragedy mask—mouth downturned and eyes woeful because his actions hurt the woman he loves. "I'm sorry."

"No, you aren't. You wanted to be rid of him, and you're glad he's gone." Ursula rocks back and forth, weeping as she embraces Hercules.

When the mythical Hercules died, he ascended to Olympus on a cloud, to join the pantheon of immortal gods who welcomed him. For Frank O'Connell, the tattooed sailor, there will be only the grave and this one brokenhearted woman to mourn his passing.

"I was only trying to save you." Now Flynn looks as devastated as Ursula. I think that while Hercules was alive, Flynn thought he had a chance to win her; now, he realizes it's hopeless. "I tried to save all of us."

"I know. And I let you. This is as much my fault as yours." Guilt adds to Ursula's anguish.

That first violent death they'd colluded in had brought Flynn and Ursula to this moment. Loyalty has its dark side, and the corpses of Jonas Murray and Hercules are proof of its destructive power.

"But I did save us from Karl." Flynn seems eager to placate Ursula, to plead his case.

"At the time all I wanted was to be free of that monster. To stop the torture and degradation I suffered at his hands. So I let you talk Hercules and me into killing him."

I remember the conversation I'd overheard. Flynn had said, *"We haven't a choice."*

Self-disgust contorts Ursula's face. "What a fool I was to believe it would be the end. What a fool to let you talk me into your scheme this time."

This time will be different. Barrett, Hugh, and I are a silent, rapt audience to a drama that began long ago.

"And now, my beloved has paid the price for all of us." Ursula's weeping echoes through the theater.

"Please forgive me," Flynn begs. "I'll do anything to make it up to you."

Ursula stares at him, a strange expression in her eyes. "Anything?"

I remember seeing that expression before, when I was at school. A pack of boys used to bully a younger one who meekly endured their shoves, punches, and insults until the day they tortured and killed his cat. He picked up a stick and beat them in such a frenzy of rage that they fled, and no one ever bullied him again.

"Just name whatever you want," Flynn says, breathless with hope.

"Let Prince Eddy go," Ursula says. "End this now."

Now that her passiveness has doomed someone dear to her, she's spurred to action. I dare to think she can bring about what my comrades and I can't—a peaceful conclusion to this standoff.

"Yes! Listen to her!" Eddy babbles.

Flynn shoves the gun so hard against Eddy's temple that if the end were sharp, it would pierce the prince's skull. "But he's evil. Worse than Karl Lange."

"We should have known it's not our place to rid the world of evil people," Ursula says. "And that detective woman you killed on the train wasn't evil."

"She was going to report us to the police," Flynn says. "I had to stop her. I followed her until I saw my chance."

It's the confession Barrett and I had hoped to hear at the police station after Flynn's arrest.

Her expression forlorn, Ursula says, "She thought *we* were the evil people. And she was right. We let Prince Eddy kill Pauline, an innocent girl who trusted us. He wanted to play Jack the Ripper, and we helped him."

That explains the stab wounds on Pauline's body, and perhaps why Flynn or one of his people had dumped it in Whitechapel. I can see Flynn's uncertainty in the shifting of his eyes; he sees the truth of Ursula's words. The quiver of his mouth tells me how much he yearns to give her what she wants.

"But if I let Prince Eddy go, he'll tell everyone I killed Murray," Flynn says.

"That's right, and you'll hang!" Eddy says.

"Good God, man, keep your royal mouth shut," Hugh says.

"We'll tell everyone that we've seen him murder eight women," Ursula says.

Barrett, Hugh, and I look at one another, shocked that the number is so high. Prince Eddy not only wanted to play Jack the

Ripper; he's outdone Jack the Ripper! My revulsion is so strong that I say, "Maybe we should just leave him here." Let Eddy die, and Flynn will have saved the world the trouble of holding him accountable for his sins.

Their expressions tell me that Barrett and Hugh were thinking the same thing, but Barrett says firmly, "That's out of the question."

"It'll be our word against Prince Eddy's," Flynn tells Ursula.

"That's right. Who will believe the likes of you?" Eddy says.

"His Highness must have a death wish," Hugh mutters.

I think Eddy is none too bright as well as insane with panic. Ursula says, "We'll tell the truth and hope for a fair hearing."

Flynn shakes his head, pitying her trust in the authorities, while his gaze brims with helpless love. "Turn around and walk away, Irmgard." His use of her real name tells me how serious he is. "I'll finish what I started."

I'll handle everything. You needn't be involved. He's still trying to save Ursula.

"Walking away sounds like an excellent idea," I say to Barrett.

"No," Barrett says.

"I guess you're right," Hugh says reluctantly. "Duty, honor, and the Crown."

"You won't get away with it!" Eddy screams at Flynn.

Ursula caresses Hercules's face. Her tears drip on his cheeks while she gives his mouth a long, tender kiss. Then she eases his head off her lap and onto the floor; his body is just the shell of the man she loved, a burden she must shed. She stands up, and I'm dismayed to see her yield to Flynn's will again.

"Go." Flynn chokes on the word. Tears shine in his eyes. He doesn't want to lose Ursula, but he must know that if he kills Prince Eddy, Barrett will shoot him, and if Ursula doesn't flee, she'll be arrested as an accomplice. And God help a circus acrobat who'd conspired in the murder of the Queen's grandson. "Hurry."

Ursula walks to the edge of the stage but stops by the flaring gaslights. She extends her arm so that the long ruffle attached to her sleeve hovers just above the flame.

"What are you doing?" Flynn's eyes pop. "Get your sleeve away from that light before you set yourself on fire."

Ursula doesn't move. "Let Prince Eddy go, or I'll do it." Her voice trembles, but her face is like stone.

A primal terror grips my heart as I picture a burning circus caravan. I remember Anjali's fire-and-brimstone vision of Prince Eddy, which had been short on details. Anjali hadn't foreseen that my companions and I would be with Eddy when it came true.

Barrett, Hugh, and I move to stop Ursula. She says, "Stay away from me," and lowers her sleeve. The gauzy cloth flirts with the flame. We halt.

Flynn exclaims in horror and disbelief. "Ursula?"

"Let him go." She's found the one strategy that might make him change his mind and spare the prince's life.

Eddy grins, cocky now. "Do what she says, or she'll burn to a crisp."

"You can't throw away your life to save this piece of shit!" Flynn says.

"Why not? I'm a murderess. I deserve to die." Ursula's air of martyrdom brings to mind Joan of Arc on the stake.

Barrett glances at the drapery on the scaffolds, the bare wooden rafters on the ceiling, and the junk piles on the floor. We're both thinking that the whole place could go up in flames with everyone inside. He points his gun at Ursula. "Move away from the gaslight, Miss Richter."

She gazes into the muzzle, unafraid. Of course a gunshot would kill her more quickly and less painfully than fire would.

"Hercules wouldn't have wanted you to die," Hugh says.

"He wanted you to run," I say, thinking again of their conversation. "So run now."

"Go!" Flynn waggles his hand in a frantic attempt to shoo Ursula out of the theater.

Affection extinguishes the anger in her expression. "He was my love. You're my best friend. I can't live without both of you."

She drops her arm. The ruffle falls over the glass sconce of the gas lamp.

Flynn roars, "No!" The full power of his stage-trained voice blares through the theater.

Her sleeve glows bright purple from the light, then ignites in a column of orange flame. Barrett shouts and recoils from Ursula, who cries out as the flame reaches her hand. Flynn scrambles off Eddy and rushes to Ursula, dropping the gun. Eddy flaps his arms and legs, howling and giggling in relief. Flynn tears off his coat and moves to smother the flames burning Ursula's skirts.

"Water!" Hugh yells.

He and I go running in search of it. I can't find a sink, tap, or barrel anywhere. Ursula, shrieking in pain, pulls Flynn to her and wraps her arms around him. She holds him tight as he yells and tries to struggle free. Barrett pockets his gun, slips out of his coat, runs to the couple, and beats the heavy wool garment against Ursula. Flynn pulls Ursula to the floor and rolls with her, trying to extinguish the fire.

By the door beyond the chairs, Hugh and I find two red buckets filled with sand. We snatch them and run up onto the stage. Ursula's taffeta skirts crackle with flames even as Barrett lashes his coat on them. Flynn's wool trousers protect his legs, but hers are red and raw beneath shreds of burned stockings. She screams but holds tight to Flynn. The bed is on fire, the linens blackening, the lights hazy in the smoke that billows up to the rafters. Hugh and I throw the sand from our buckets at Ursula and Flynn. The sand spatters them, but they're still on fire. Ursula moans, her hair burning, her face a rictus of agony. Tears sizzle on her blistered cheeks, but she makes no effort to save herself. Flynn yells her name, his arms embracing her, his eyes brilliant with desperation and reflected flames.

"It ends now." Burned, swollen lips distort Ursula's words.

I think she really wants to die as punishment for her sins, and Flynn would rather die than live without her. A swath of the white drapery that covers the scaffold goes up in flames. The flames race from swath to swath. In no time, all the drapery is on fire. Now the stage seems literally a theater in hell. The flames surround us, the smoke thicker than the fog outside. I cough and choke; my eyes burn.

Barrett tugs my hand. "Sarah, we have to get out of here."

I resist, even though a few minutes ago, I was ready to walk away and let fate take its course. "Not yet!" Ursula and Flynn are a makeshift family not so different from mine with Barrett, Hugh and Mick. Both families were forged in conspiracies of silence that involved murders. In the terror and chaos of this moment, I feel the need to protect and justify Ursula and Flynn as well as myself and my companions. "We have to save them!"

"It's too late." Hugh is dragging Prince Eddy upright. "Come along, Your Highness."

Barrett urges me off the stage. Hurrying for the door with him and Hugh and Eddy, I turn for one last look.

Through the dense veil of smoke, I see Ursula and Flynn. Their black figures lie amid flames, she on her back, he on top of her, as if in the act of love. His profile hovers over hers, prelude to a kiss. Then he sinks into her, the flames obliterate them, and they're together in death as they never were in life.

CHAPTER 30

"Four casualties. Not the outcome I was hoping for." Commissioner Bradford eyes Barrett and me with disapproval.

We're walking along the embankment outside Scotland Yard. Barrett and I have just told the commissioner about last night. The weather is cold enough for snow, but the flakes drifting through the mist are ashes from chimneys. The narrow strip of river visible along the shore is black and fouled with garbage, like the dirty hem of a streetwalker's skirt.

"Still, things would be far worse if Prince Eddy were among the dead," the commissioner said.

I hold my tongue, remembering the aftermath of our escape from the theater at Cremorne Gardens. When Barrett, Hugh, and I emerged with Eddy, the constables rushed up to us. They said they'd heard gunshots, asked what had happened, and gaped at the naked, shivering prince.

"The theater's on fire. It's a long story," Barrett said. "We have to get out of here."

Hugh took off his coat, put it on Eddy, and buttoned it up. He'd lost his hat during the fight with Hercules, so he grabbed Barrett's, jammed it on Eddy's head, and pulled the brim down over the prince's eyes. We managed to elude the guards and reach the gate. A faint luminescence in the fog heralded dawn, and early traffic was moving in the streets. Barrett told the constables to fetch the fire brigade, then hailed a carriage. He bundled Eddy into the vehicle, and the rest of us crowded in with the prince.

"Where to?" Barrett asked Eddy.

Through chattering teeth, the prince gave an address in Kensington. As we rode, I looked at Eddy, seated beside Hugh, across from Barrett and me. Four people were dead, I didn't know whether Mick and Anjali were safe, and it was our responsibility to see Eddy home.

"You won't tell anyone, will you?" the prince asked anxiously.

"You're welcome," Hugh said, a sardonic edge to his voice.

Barrett's face was rigid with disgust. "Our lips are sealed."

I pulled my skirts close around me so Eddy's legs wouldn't touch them. His sour odor of sweat, urine, and stale cologne made me sick. How I wished we'd let Flynn shoot him!

We could remedy that mistake now.

The idea stirred a dark, vengeful energy in me.

"It's too bad I'm out of bullets," I said.

Barrett and Hugh stared at me, first with confusion, then shock as they understood what I was suggesting. Then Hugh said, "I have some left," and after a long, tense moment, Barrett said, "So do I."

We contemplated Eddy, who'd dozed off with his mouth open. But there are some lines we won't cross, and they include murdering a naked, helpless man in cold blood. We left Eddy at his townhouse, where his servants took him in, no questions asked. As the door closed behind Eddy, I felt as though I'd let Jack the Ripper slip through my fingers. Which is the worse sin—killing in cold blood, or letting a killer go free to a warm bed from which he'll rise to kill again?

"Well, how do you like that, Barrett?" Hugh said. "He didn't even give back my coat or your hat."

Now Barrett runs his hand over his bare head. My hair is falling in loose strands from my coronet of braids, and our clothes still smell of smoke. By the time we dropped Prince Eddy off, it was six in the morning, and instead of going home with Hugh to wash and change clothes, Barrett and I returned to Cremorne Gardens to see what had transpired there. Then we came to Scotland Yard and waited until Commissioner Bradford showed up at seven. He took one look at us and suggested a walk along the river instead of the usual briefing in his office.

"You said the theater was destroyed?" he asks.

"Yes," Barrett says. "By the time the firemen arrived, the whole building was on fire. They pulled it down to keep the fire from spreading to the neighborhood."

"So all the evidence of what happened in the theater was also destroyed?"

"All except the bodies." I try and fail to shut out the memory of the firemen carrying out the blackened corpses.

"Burned beyond recognition, no doubt." Commissioner Bradford asks, "Did you tell anyone who they were?"

"No," Barrett says.

We'd joined the crowd at the scene, pretended to be mere spectators, and identified neither the dead nor ourselves. When we spotted Venus de Milo, the giant, and other Cremorne folks, we left before they saw us.

"Clarence Flynn and Ursula Richter's people are bound to realize they're missing and put two and two together," I point out.

"At least Flynn and Richter and Hercules can't talk," the commissioner says.

I suppose that if the others know about the secret shows, they'll be too afraid to talk, and the audiences will probably also keep quiet.

"Jonas Murray's next of kin should be notified," Barrett says.

Commissioner Bradford frowns. "I think not. Mustn't have anyone connected with Prince Eddy also connected with the fire or Cremorne Gardens."

I don't like direction the conversation is taking. "Then what are you going to do about Murray's death?"

"Report it to the Crown. Let them handle it. Probably, their official story will be that Murray quit his post and went abroad. There'll have to be an inquest, of course. His body will be buried as a John Doe in the potter's field. The fire will be ruled an accident, and Cremorne Gardens will be demolished."

Barrett and I look at each other in growing dismay. I ask, "What's going to happen to Prince Eddy?"

"Oh, he'll be spirited off to a royal residence in the countryside."

It's as unjust as I could have feared. "You mean, he'll get away with murdering Pauline Chaffin and the girls in Europe? And conspiring to kidnap and murder Anjali?"

"Not at all," the commissioner says. "His freedom will be curtailed. He'll have a minder who watches him every minute."

"Oh well, that's all right, then." Barrett speaks with antipathy toward this man he once respected. "Prince Eddy gets house arrest in a plush country villa, while common people hang for lesser offenses."

"He'll never have an opportunity to kill again."

"As long as the minder isn't someone like Jonas Murray," I retort.

Commissioner Bradford's face hardens into lines of controlled impatience. "Detective Sergeant and Mrs. Barrett, I understand why you're upset. But this is a matter of the Crown's reputation and national security. My office will inform the Pinkerton Agency that Katherine Oliver and Pauline Chaffin were murdered by Clarence Flynn, who is now deceased. Pinkerton's can inform their next of kin."

I shake my head at the unfairness, and Barrett says bitterly, "Sure, pin all the blame on the dead dwarf."

"Would you really want the whole truth to come out? Your little friend Anjali's name would be dragged through the mud." The commissioner adds, "By the way, you should have told me about her earlier."

Unable to argue, we glower in silence.

"Just to make things clear—the outcome of the case and how you feel about it doesn't release you from your vow of confidentiality."

After all we've been through laboring to conduct the investigation on his terms, he's as good as accusing us of having so little integrity that we would break our word.

"Sir, I'll tell you the same thing I told Prince Eddy when he begged us not to tell anyone about him," Barrett says. "Our lips are sealed."

We stop in our tracks. The commissioner walks several paces before he realizes we're not with him. He turns, and his face seems somehow broken, like that of a statue damaged by vandalism, his eyes filled with the torment of a guilty conscience. He looked the other way when Eddy killed women in India, and now he has to live with the knowledge of Eddy's other crimes, which he could have prevented.

"If you think I like this any better than you do, think again," he says, then strides away toward Scotland Yard.

★   ★   ★

"It's not our first investigation where someone got away with murder and we helped cover it up," Barrett says as we navigate the morning bustle of the Whitechapel High Street.

"Somehow that doesn't make me feel better." The triumph of solving the case can't diminish my outrage about the fact that Eddy can shelter behind the power of the Crown while Ursula, Flynn, and Hercules, who were victims as well as criminals, died for their sins.

"Kate Oliver's killer has been punished," Barrett reminds me.

"Clarence Flynn killed two people to protect his friends. Prince Eddy killed at least eight women to satisfy his sick lust. And if we hadn't stopped him, Anjali would have been one more."

Barrett shakes his head. "Regardless of their motives and the number of their victims, murder is murder. Flynn was as guilty as Eddy."

The memory of the handsome, spirited Clarence Flynn, romancing women onstage and flirting with me, is nonetheless painful. I picture a dwarf boy and a little girl with a tail playing outside circus tents, outcasts finding comfort in their friendship. I think of Flynn and Ursula burning together as if on a funeral pyre. Again it strikes me what a destructive force loyalty can be. If Flynn, Ursula, and Hercules hadn't joined forces, would they still be alive? I don't think any one of them alone would have been capable of murdering Karl Lange. And if they'd gone their separate ways after his death, Murray might not have tracked them down, and last night wouldn't have happened.

If Barrett, Hugh, Mick, and I had never joined forces, how many other people might not have died? If not for my mother's loyalty to Lucas Zehnpfennig, would Ellen Casey still be alive? If not for my father's loyalty to my mother, would he have escaped the murder charge?

Those are questions I'm loath to contemplate. The price of loyalty may be higher than the price of sin.

As Barrett and I approach our house, I see a woman standing outside. "Good morning," Jane Lambert says.

After I confronted her at her school, how dare she show her face here again? I experience fresh anger and dread. Is she back for another try at stealing my husband? Then I notice a difference in Jane. She's not wearing vivid blue today, and in her drab brown coat, with her blonde hair hidden under a brown hat, she looks like a sepia photograph of herself. Her face is sallow and pinched, and she has a cold sore at the corner of her mouth. I must look a fright, but she's no better.

"What are you doing here, Jane?" Barrett says cautiously.

"I came to apologize." Jane says to me, "I'm sorry, Sarah. There's no excuse for my behavior. You're Thomas's wife, and it was wrong of me to try to take your place. And I shouldn't have tried to get you in trouble. I know that now. I hope you can forgive me."

My grievance is still raw. "I accept your apology." That's the best I can do for now.

"You won't have to see me again." Jane glances wistfully at Barrett. "I'm leaving London."

Delight seems an inappropriate reaction in view of Jane's obvious misery, so I merely say, "Oh."

Her wan smile says she sees through my neutral expression. Barrett regards her with surprise. "Where are you going?"

"To Sheffield," Jane says. "I've an aunt and uncle there."

Sheffield is more than a hundred fifty miles from London. The news gets better and better. "What are you going to do?" Barrett asks.

"I'll find a job teaching in a local school."

Barrett smiles with relief that he'll no longer be caught in an unwanted love triangle. "That sounds great."

Jane's mouth quivers. I can tell she wishes he'd begged her to stay, but she nods as if to acknowledge that she's made the right decision. "It'll be a fresh start for me."

"Good luck, then." Barrett offers Jane his hand. I hope he'll never touch her again.

Jane hesitates before she shakes hands; she must have hoped he would kiss her. With a brave, strained smile, she says, "Who knows, maybe I'll meet someone."

For the first time I clearly see the situation from her point of view. She's lost the man she's loved for twenty years to another woman; she's been spurned and humiliated; and she's leaving the only home she knows for an uncertain future in a faraway city.

I say, "I wish you well," and I mean it.

"Thank you." Humble and meek, Jane blinks away tears. "I should say goodbye now."

Yes, before you change your mind. "Goodbye," I say.

"Goodbye, Jane." Barrett regards her with brotherly affection.

Jane walks away, her back stiffened by pride. Relief rises up in me like bubbles in champagne. Barrett unlocks our door for me, and I suppress the smile that tugs at my mouth. His expression is sad, pensive. It must be hard for him, discovering that someone he once loved, whom he's considered a friend since childhood, isn't the person he thought she was. But my marriage feels more solid now that Barrett and I have faced death together and survived—again—and his loyalty to me has passed the most stringent test.

Before I enter the house, I pause and watch Jane until she vanishes into the fog, making sure she's really gone.

★   ★   ★

Barrett and I find Mick in the parlor, lying on the chaise longue. He's in regular clothes, but traces of soot color the skin around his eyes. I'm so glad to see him safe that my knees sag. Resisting the urge to fuss over him, I drop onto the divan and ask, "Where's Hugh?"

"Dunno. Thought he was with you."

"Where's Anjali?"

"I took her home."

It's another load off my mind. "Is she all right?"

"Yeah." But his expression is glum.

"Then what's wrong?"

"Her father was there waitin'. He were supposed to be out wor-kin' on his experiments all night, but he came back early and found her gone." Mick grimaces, shakes his head, and expels his breath through pursed lips. "When he saw us, he were fit to be tied."

I can imagine the scene—Mick costumed as a gypsy, carrying the sleepy, white-gowned Anjali up to the Lodge's townhouse, and her shocked father at the door.

"He took her in and told me to get lost," Mick says forlornly. "I'll probably never see her again."

I suppose he's right, and I feel sorry for him. After what he's been through, I don't have the heart to point out to him that tak-ing Anjali to Cremorne Gardens was reckless and foolish and this should be a lesson.

"What happened after we left?" Mick says. After Barrett fills him in, he says, "Gorblimey!" then, "Sorry I weren't there to help you." I tell Mick about the meeting with Commissioner Bradford, and he scowls. "So Prince Eddy don't get a date with the hang-man. Well, if I ever hear he's up to his old tricks again, I'll string him up myself."

"My sentiments exactly," I say.

The doorbell rings, and Mick groans. "I hope that ain't a call to a crime scene."

"I'll get it." The last thing I want is to photograph a dead body. I trudge downstairs, open the door, and exclaim in surprise. "Anjali!"

The girl is primly dressed in a gray wool coat with black velvet collar and cuffs, black velvet hat, black shoes. Dark rings underscore her eyes, which are red and swollen from weeping. "Hello, Sarah."

I let her into the studio, glad to see her even though I wonder if she sneaked out of her house again. "How are you feeling?"

"I'm fine." But she looks like a different girl, her radiance dimmed, and the world seems a sadder, darker place. "Is Mick here?"

"Yes. Does your father know where you are?"

Anjali glances over her shoulder. "He's waiting for me in a cab down the street. May I come up and see Mick?"

I lead her up to the parlor. When Mick sees her, he jumps up from the chaise longue, all smiles. "Anjali!"

"Sarah, why don't you and I go upstairs," Barrett says.

I'm debating whether to leave them by themselves, when Anjali says, "No, you should stay. I can't be alone with Mick."

Mick looks disconcerted to realize this isn't the happy reunion he wanted. "Why not? Because of your pa?"

Anjali gives him a look filled with yearning and misery. "It's my decision. We did things we shouldn't have. And then last night . . ." Her voice breaks. "Mick, we could have been *killed*." She seems shocked into awareness of their mortality. Fortunately the price of her lesson wasn't higher.

"Yeah. And I'm sorry." Mick is the picture of contrition. "If I'd known what was gonna happen, I never would've taken you to Cremorne Gardens. I never meant to hurt you. I love you." He turns red as he glances at Barrett and me, embarrassed to declare himself in front of us.

"I know. And I love you too. But . . ." Anjali gathers her breath. "I came to say goodbye."

Mick stares, aghast. "You're givin' me the gate?"

Tears sparkle in Anjali's eyes. "I don't want to, but I have to."

"How can you?" Mick demands. "After everything we said, everything we been to each other?"

She bows her head. "Please don't make this harder than it is."

"I know your pa's mad at me for last night, and he should be, but—"

"He's madder at me than at you. He said you're an incorrigible daredevil, but I should have known better. He's right. I had no business playing detective."

"I know better now too." Mick attempts to play the repentant rogue. "I'm gonna be so cautious and gentleman-like, you won't recognize me."

She gives him a smile filled with pain. "We shouldn't see each other for a while. Not until I grow up."

Mick looks horrified. "Anjali—" He opens his arms and moves toward her.

"It's for your good as well as mine. What if something worse had happened to me? You would feel terrible." Crying now, she steps back from his embrace. She takes his hand, presses his palm to her lips, and whispers, "Goodbye, Mick." She runs out of the room, and her footsteps patter down the stairs.

In the awkward silence, Barrett and I try to pretend we're not there. Mick stands with his shoulders slumped and his fingers closed around Anjali's kiss. He lifts his gaze to the ceiling, his eyes shiny and stretched wide, trying not to cry. The orphan boy has lost his beloved, and his other friends can't make up for his loss.

"Well, that's girls for you. Here today, gone tomorrow." Mick manages a semblance of his cocky grin. "They're like trains. Another one'll be along quick." Feigning a yawn, he says, "I'm knackered. Time for bed." He saunters up the stairs, whistling cheerily.

His heartbreak lingers in the room like a shadow. Barrett and I look sadly at each other. There's naught to do but hope that the resilience of youth will heal Mick.

Downstairs, the front door opens, and soon Hugh comes into the parlor with Dr. Lewes. Hugh's face is bruised from his fight with Hercules, and he gingerly lowers himself onto the chaise longue, but he seems happier than I've seen him in a long time. Dr. Lewes smiles as he exchanges greetings with Barrett and me. I'm glad that when Hugh needed companionship, he could turn to the psychologist.

"What a night, eh?" Hugh says while I busy myself making and serving tea. "I entertained Dr. Lewes with the story."

That doesn't bother me, no matter what Commissioner Bradford might think. His opinion means less to me than it did before, and Dr. Lewes is good at keeping secrets.

"Of course I didn't reveal who was who," Hugh says. "I changed the names to protect the guilty."

Furthermore, after rescuing Hugh and helping solve the case, Dr. Lewes is one of us. I smile at him as I hand him a cup of tea. His look says he understands. Because Barrett and I must exercise a certain amount of discretion, we can't speak openly about what happened with Commissioner Bradford, so I tell Hugh that a certain highly placed official is shielding the highly placed culprit from his just deserts.

Hugh gets the message, nods, and shrugs in resignation. "Well, that's typical. How do you think a certain institution has survived all these centuries?" he says, referring to the monarchy. "Its members have had generations of lackeys covering their posteriors."

When I tell Hugh about Mick and Anjali, he responds with his usual optimism. "They'll get back together." His mood abruptly darkens. "Will you excuse me?" He goes upstairs to his room.

"Last night he killed someone," Dr. Lewes says. "He'll need time to cope with the fact. I don't think the rest of us can truly understand what it's like." He looks at Barrett and me, sees something in our expressions. "Or maybe I'm the only one here who can't understand."

For the first time he seems as uncomfortable with me as I initially was with him, his usual calmness disrupted. Soon afterward, he takes his leave.

"What time does your father's trial reconvene?" Barrett asks.

"Ten o'clock." Only two hours from now. Anxiety gnaws away at my fatigue. "I'd better get ready."

Ready for my family's final reckoning with fate.

CHAPTER 31

"**Y**our Lordship and Gentlemen of the Jury," Sir William Hall-Clarke says, "this is an extraordinary case that you have been sworn to try. There is no question that an atrocious murder was committed, or that justice must be served, but today the case has taken a turn which none of us could have anticipated."

It's Wednesday afternoon, December third, the last day of my father's trial, and Sir William is making his closing speech for the defense. The gallery stirs with whispers, mutters, and restless movements like an agitated beehive. In our usual seats, Sally and I hold each other's hands tight, bracing ourselves for what comes next. Barrett, Mick, and Hugh offered to come with us, but I felt that we should see the trial through on our own. There will be time afterward to share our joy, or our grief.

"Ordinarily, I would summarize the evidence that the prosecution has presented and refute it piece by piece," Sir William says. "However, the evidence is no longer relevant because Benjamin Bain did not kill Ellen. We have just heard the confession of the man who did."

When the trial had recommenced, Sir William called Sean Murphy to the witness box. Dressed in prison uniform, his hands cuffed, Sean had sobbed while Sir William coaxed from him a description of his fatal encounter with Ellen. The Casey family raised an uproar while the judge banged his gavel again and again.

"I opine with utmost confidence that no one of us who has heard Sean Murphy's confession does not believe it to be true," Sir William says.

Prosecutor Ingleby had made a valiant attempt to debunk the confession, questioning Sean's memory and sanity, accusing the defense of coercing Sean. To every attempt, Sean repeated, "I did it. I killed Ellen. I'm sorry." Then he put his head down and wept until Mr. Ingleby gave up. When the guards escorted Sean from the courtroom, the Caseys shouted, "Bastard! Murderer!" They pelted Sean with rotten fruit they'd brought to throw at my father.

Now Sir William says, "Ordinarily, I would remind you, Gentlemen of the Jury, that it is your duty to decide whether the defendant should walk out of this courtroom a free man or should suffer a violent, ignominious death and be dispatched, for all his sins, to meet his maker. Ordinarily, I would exhort you to weigh the evidence, deliberate among yourselves, and render your verdict. But today I must depart from the usual court procedure." He turns to the judge. "Your Lordship, in the light of the confession that incriminates Sean Murphy and exonerates my client, I ask that you dismiss the charges against Benjamin Bain."

My heartbeat quickens with unbearable suspense. Sally's fingers clench mine.

"To call off a trial at this late stage is no small matter," the judge says.

My father leans forward, gripping the edge of the dock. He looks like a sailor stranded at sea, who doesn't know whether the ship he sees in the distance is a rescuer or a foe.

"However, I agree that the circumstances are extraordinary," the judge says. "Has the prosecution any objection to the defense's request?"

"No, Your Lordship." Mr. Ingleby's voice is heavy with resignation. He's lost the case that he hoped would advance his career, but he must give justice its due.

"Benjamin Bain, I dismiss the charges against you," the judge says. "You're a free man. Godspeed, and God bless you. Court is adjourned."

Even as the words ring in my ears, I hardly dare believe them. My father gasps his first breaths of liberty. Sally is hugging me and crying, and my tears of joy mingle with hers. I've achieved what I'd feared was impossible—cleared my father's name and vanquished my doubt about his innocence. His lesser crime of covering up Ellen Casey's murder need never be revealed. But I feel a pang of sorrow for Ellen, who suffered more than any of us. Regardless of her poor choices, she didn't deserve her terrible fate. For her, justice is inadequate compensation.

The reporters shout, "Mr. Bain, how does it feel to be exonerated? What do you have to say to all the people who thought you were a murderer?"

My father stammers in confusion. As the Casey family files silently out of the courtroom, none of them speaks to him, Sally, or me. They seem embarrassed about their mistaken belief in his guilt. The only one to look me in the eye is Meg, whose remorseful smile is probably all the apology we're likely to get. Neither prosecutor nor judge offered words of regret for the wrongful charge, the years my father spent as a fugitive, his imprisonment and trial, the scandal, or the effect on our family. But I'm so happy, I don't care that my father's exoneration came with no official amends.

I don't even care when I see Inspector Reid pause in the doorway and fix his angry stare on me, like the bad fairy at the banquet. When he had me in jail, I virtually admitted I know something about the Ripper, and I'm certain he'll be after me harder than ever, but that's a problem for another day.

Outside Old Bailey, reporters interview Sir William amid a white thunderstorm of flashlamp explosions. "A great injustice was averted today," the barrister declares. "The life of an innocent man was saved, thanks to the vigilant efforts of the defense."

I don't care if he takes public credit for my detective work. I'm glad he's drawn the limelight away from Sally, my father, and me long enough for us to steal around the block with Mr. Owusu. The solicitor smiles and shakes my father's hand.

"Please allow me to offer my congratulations."

We all thank him for his services, and he departs, probably glad to see the last of us. I say to my father, "Come home with me for dinner. I want you to meet my husband and my friends and see my studio." I'm giddy with delight; the celebration I've dreamed of is at hand.

My father's smile is fond but distant. "Perhaps another time. This has all been rather overwhelming. I think I'd like to go back to Brighton today."

How can he just leave, after all that's happened? I'm stunned and grieved. He's still upset with me because I aired my mother's dirty laundry! Sean's confession made it an unnecessary betrayal of both of my parents, and now my father and I are at odds. After I've waited so long for this day when we can be together without fear of the law, there won't be any party at my house. I won't be introducing him to my husband and friends, and we won't begin sharing our lives.

"Father, don't be angry at Sarah," Sally pleads. "She saved your life!"

"Yes, I know. Sarah, thank you." My father hugs me and kisses my cheek, but his lips are cool, his embrace brief. "I just need a little time to adjust to—everything."

I try to put myself in his place, to imagine that Barrett and I have a daughter, and years from now, after Barrett is dead, she destroys his reputation to save me from some terrible fate. Would I forgive her sin because his death canceled my obligations to him? I think I would, and it's extraordinarily painful to realize that my father's loyalty to his dead wife is stronger than his love for me, his living child.

"At least stay in London a few more days," Sally begs our father.

"I'm afraid I would be poor company," he says, apologetic but firm. "I'd better see about the next train to Brighton."

Sally bursts into tears as she realizes that after we both went to such lengths to reunite with him and exonerate him, he's leaving us.

"You both can come visit me someday." My father pats her shoulder and kisses her.

Even as my emotions roil with anger and hurt, I make excuses for him. He's been through so much, and he's not thinking clearly; he's old, set in his ways, and after standing by my mother all this time, he can't change. But I can't expunge the devastation of learning that Benjamin Bain, whom I remember as a loving, devoted father, isn't one now and perhaps never was. After I finally learned the truth about Ellen's murder, I'd thought I knew everything about him, but it seems that in some ways he's still a mystery.

He smiles nervously, aware that he's disappointed Sally and me, but he says, "Well, goodbye, then." He walks rapidly down the street.

Sally weeps, brokenhearted. "Oh, Sarah, we're losing him again!"

I experience a lightheaded sensation, as if the city, the world, and the heavens are moving. His disloyalty has removed my father from the center of my universe. He's no longer the star that exerts powerful influence upon my actions and emotions. It's as painful as if I've been cut from an anchor whose line is made of flesh and blood, but it's also liberating, exhilarating.

I put my arm around Sally. "It's going to be all right."

She nods even as she weeps; I'm her big sister, and she trusts me. Perhaps someday we can have a normal father–daughter relationship with Benjamin Bain that's not based on finding him, saving him, or childishly idolizing him.

In the meantime, I say, "Let's go to my house. Barrett, Hugh, and Mick are waiting for us."

How fortunate we are to have the people whose loyalty and love we can count on now.